DEMONS OF NEW ORLEANS

PETER BOUVIER

DEMONS OF NEW ORLEANS © Peter Bouvier, 2023

Peter Bouvier has asserted his rights under the Copyright Designs and Patents Act 1988 to be identified as the author of this work. This book is sold subject to the condition that it shall not, by way of trade or otherwise, be lent, resold, hired out, or otherwise circulated without the publisher's prior consent in any form of binding or cover other than that in which it is published and without a similar condition, being imposed on the subsequent purchaser. This is a work of fiction and any resemblance of the fictional characters to real persons is purely coincidental and non-intentional.

ISBN: 978-1-7395012-0-4

Cover Design © Graeme Parker at Provoco Publishing
Provoco Logo ©MJC at Provoco Publishing
Edited by Jane Murray

Table of Contents

dedication 4
2006 5
one 11
two 53
three 71
four 98
five 110
six 130
seven 144
eight 159
nine 170
ten 183
eleven 208
twelve 225
thirteen 245
fourteen 259
fifteen 277
sixteen 286
seventeen 300
eighteen 324
nineteen 336
twenty 355
About the Author 362

dedication

To Abigail, Joseph, and Audrey.
Please don't read any further.

2006

A year after the storm, as the city embraced the prayer services and memorials to mark the first anniversary of the devastation, Shay Favreau pedaled slowly along Haynes Boulevard, out towards Bayou Sauvage. The cool air against his face was the only respite from the sweltering summer heat. The Pontchartrain levee was one of the few that hadn't broken on that terrible day, but twelve months later there were still mini-diggers and dumper trucks shoring up the damage caused by the wind and rain.

Shay had spent most of the year living with his cousin in Shreveport, but his parents were committed to the Southern Baptist Church's Grassroots Project and had pledged their support to rebuilding the local community. Since the start of the summer break, he had worked tirelessly as a volunteer, dragging away the wreckage that Katrina had left in her wake: sheets of corrugated metal, smashed weatherboards and sidings, ruined furniture, carpets black with mold, rusting useless electrical appliances. For weeks, each day had been the same, punctuated by an occasional fresh horror: a severe injury for a fellow volunteer; the discovery of a body, long dead and stinking in an attic or sucked into a crawlspace; another suicide in the neighbourhood.

That morning, his mother had taken one look at the dark rings under Shay's eyes and decided he needed some time off.

'Why don't you take your dad's fishing gear up to the lake?' she suggested, 'He won't mind you using it.'

Since the hurricane, his father had lost all interest in the few material possessions which had survived. Besides, there was no longer time for hobbies. Together they had stoically shoveled up thirty years of sodden books and notes, a lifetime of photographs, letters and other personal papers. His father made no comment, hadn't even shed a tear. Instead, he thanked the Lord that unlike many of their neighbors in the Seventh Ward, his family had survived, that they still had a roof over their heads, that he still had a job. 'The insurance companies called it an Act of God, but the real act of God was how the storm brought this community closer together,' he would tell anyone who would listen. Shay must have heard that Hallmark line a dozen times.

He picked up the pace. There used to be a lucky spot on the banks of the Pontchartrain - perfect for catching speckled trout - and he wanted to see if it was still there or if it had been washed away. He would have four, maybe five hours' fishing before he was expected home. At the edge of town, he crossed over the Amtrak lines and continued alongside the tracks until he reached the old jetty where supposedly a stilted moonshine cabin had once stood. The storm had ripped away most of the jetty's decking, but the supports and some of the crossbeams remained. The shoreline was littered with debris.

Leaving his bike and bag of supplies on the bank, Shay gingerly made his way across the slick wooden stumps to set himself up on two planks at the far end of the pontoon. He carried his father's bait-casting rod and reel, a metal tackle box containing hooks, chugging corks and sinkers, a fishing knife and a Tupperware full of live shrimp.

At the end of the jetty, by his feet, he noticed a small

thin bone, no bigger than a finger, embedded in a thick pool of yellow candle wax which had melted and hardened over the edge of the boards. He prised it up with the toe of his sneaker and kicked it into the water.

Shay baited a straight hook with a fat, gray shrimp and paid out some line; then, setting his feet firmly across the decking, cast out into the calm of the lake. It would take a few practice swings until he was happy with his distance, but that was part of the enjoyment. At eleven in the morning, it was already too late in the day to hope for a good haul, but it didn't matter. The rod felt light and responsive in his grip, and he reeled in the line to cast again. These were tough times for the Favreau family and Shay had to make the most of any rare moments of pleasure: the sense of achievement in fixing up a battered house, the first bite of a Brandito burrito in a year, the feel of Donna Jackson's lips on the last day of school back in Shreveport.

Shay sat down on the decking and peered at his reflection below. Two months of hard labor had made a difference: he was only sixteen, but his shoulders were broad as a man's and his arms hard and lean. His thoughts turned again to Donna Jackson and her lip-gloss, her denim cut-offs...

Lost in his reverie, Shay didn't notice the makeshift raft, nor the man upon it, floating towards him.

'Hey sonny, where y'at? Fine day fo' fishing!'

Shay started at the sound of his voice. He had appeared from nowhere, this stranger, tall and thin as a dancer, standing perfectly balanced in the center of the raft, which was nothing more than a single wooden pallet with two large, dirty plastic drums strapped underneath. As he pushed a long pine branch into the lakebed and guided the raft towards the jetty, Shay took in his dark beard, the thick dreadlocks hanging halfway down his back, his bare feet and tattered, faded dungarees.

The stranger extended a hand and without thinking, Shay easily pulled him up onto the decking where there was little space to share. Close up, Shay noticed the bloodstains on his clothes and the smell of decay which hung about him: a smell of fish and woodsmoke and garbage. The pallet was already floating away.

'H... how long have you been out there?' Shay stuttered.

The man fixed his pale eyes on the boy and answered simply, 'A year and a day.'

Shay gave a hollow laugh, 'Yeah right. That'd mean you've been out on the lake... since the storm?' He didn't believe it but still, he'd seen so much destitution since he came home, anything seemed possible now.

'Yeah, sonny. All this time. Oh well, oh well.' His voice had a deep, healthy resonance which belied both his slight frame and his story.

'That's... like... impossible?' Shay said, still unsure of himself.

The stranger didn't bother to reply, but moved his head slowly from side to side, as if weighing up the odds of his own survival.

'You'd be... way dead,' Shay continued, just to have something to say.

'Yeah, well.... I been dead before.'

Shay had no answer for that, and the silence hung between them until the stranger broke it. 'Say sonny, can you spare summin to eat? I gots me a hunger that's jus' 'bout eatin' me up from the inside out!' He licked his lips and rubbed his belly for emphasis, the way a child might.

'Sure man. On the bank. I'll fix you up.'

In truth, Shay was happy to have a reason to step off

the decking, and he hastily made his way back to his bag. The stranger picked up the fishing knife from the tackle box and followed, loping across the wooden stumps with long strides.

'I have soda, chips, pie... what do you...' As Shay turned around, the words died in his throat. The midday sun was reflecting off the lake and at first, he thought the stranger was pulling a plastic bag over his own head. Then Shay realized: it was the long, sagging skin of a pig's face. Folds of smooth pinkish-gray flesh hung down around the snout, and the man adjusted his mask so his blue eyes peered out from its tiny slits.

'How old are you sonny?' came his muffled voice.

'Sixteen.'

'You a virgin?'

Shay nodded dumbly, embarrassed and afraid.

'That's fine, that's fine,' replied the pig. He tested the blade of the fishing knife against his thumb.

'Please don't hurt me, man. Take my bike. Take whatever you want.'

'Take whatever I want,' he chorused, 'I *will* takes whatever I wants!' Moving towards Shay, as the child crouched on the ground. 'See, you don't know it, but you is full of *pouvwa*,' he drawled. 'You sees me as the pig now, because I is lowly, but I is changin'. I is becomin'. I need that *power* o' yours to gather my strength again. See? If I *is* to be reborn, I *needs* you.'

'Don't kill me, please,' Shay whispered, scrabbling backwards into the scrub.

The pig lunged forward with the knife but didn't strike.

'Let's hear you scream then, sonny. Let me hear your *pouvwa*.'

Shay screamed as the pig came for him again, slashing at his hands and face and laughing. There was a blinding, searing pain behind his eyes, as though a white-hot needle was being pushed through his skull. He screamed for anybody to hear him, anybody to help, but he was too far from civilization in a city nobody really cared about anymore.

one

2010

'I been called a *lot* of things in twenty-seven years, but nobody ever called me a *coward*. Jesus Christ, didn't I do my time? – eight years, I walked the beat, – I took a bullet for Chrissakes.'

'Brad, nobody's saying...'

'I made sergeant in '88, lieutenant in '97 and when Elaine got sick, it was *my* decision to work detective. I got busted down a pay grade for that, *fuck you* very much. I *ran* the white-collar division before I started on homicide, did you even know that? Child abuse, narcotics, vice, you name it – I worked in every department. I've seen things I hope you *never* have to see. And I was *still* working homicide when the storm hit...'

'Listen, Brad, I'm not trying to say...'

'Do you know how many officers went AWOL that day? Do you? Two hundred and sixteen. Two hundred and sixteen men unaccounted for on August 29. That's nearly a fifth of the entire force. I wasn't the only one.'

'And nearly a quarter of those officers were cleared of the charges against them. But Brad, you didn't even come to your tribunal. What were they supposed to do?'

'Goddamn bureaucrats. Fucking tribunals. Katrina *made* us choose. 'Neglect of duty?' Bull*shit*. We were scapegoats. The city was a goddamn warzone. I was supposed to leave my wife and kid there?'

'No, you did the right thing.'

'I *know* I did. I *know* I did. I don't *need* a goddamn

handshake and a button on my lapel to tell me I did the right thing.'

There was a long silence at the end of the line and Zamora Delgado let it ride, knowing that, just like a hurricane, Brad Durand had blown himself out.

'Look, I'm sorry,' he said sheepishly. 'I guess I've still got some issues with the way the whole thing was managed.'

'I understand.'

'There's nobody to talk to out here,' he added angrily.

'What about Elaine?'

'Me and Elaine.... Elaine and I... we're a little bit separated at the moment. We're not doing so well. She moved back to Tupelo. Besides, she's got her own problems. She probably had enough of me griping about... departmental politics.'

'Oh, I'm really sorry to hear that, Brad. Don't I feel like an asshole...'

'It's not your fault. You didn't know. We'll work it out. Or maybe we won't. Who knows?' he laughed suddenly. 'I still see Kyle every couple of weeks. I go up there, or he comes down here and we take the boat out on the Gulf.'

'That sounds... good.'

'Hey, you should come down too. It never rains here.' There was a hint of irony in his voice.

'That's part of the reason I'm calling. I would like to visit. I've got a couple of days off, but...'

'But what?'

'It wouldn't be just a social trip.'

'F'true...?'

'Before you say anything else, just hear me out. I might need your help.'

'O...K. I'm listening.'

'We're drawing a blank on a couple of... homicides, I

guess.'

'*'Homicides, you guess*'? Jeez, things really have gone down the toilet since I left.'

'Yeah well, it's complicated. I'm putting something together, possibly related to some cold cases,' Zam replied. 'I've got two separate teams working on the fresh ones and I'm overseeing operations. Forensics say they're all unrelated, but I'm not buying it. I wouldn't go as far as to say there's a pattern emerging but there are... parallels.'

'Like?'

'In all cases, parts of the body have been removed. Tillery thinks it's just a gangland fad.'

Brad shook his head at the mention of Tillery's name but said nothing. 'Maybe he's right. Anything else?'

'Yes, but it would be easier if I came down and showed you the case files. I know you don't owe the NOPD any favors, but this is me asking...'

'I don't know Zam.... I haven't looked at a case file in years. I wouldn't know where to start.'

'You know more than most. You've got a good head for these things, and you see things that most of us don't....'

'Enough flattery,' Brad said, joking.

'And I know you're keeping busy,' Zam continued. 'I have colleagues in Florida too you know...'

'It's just local P.I. stuff. Nothing major. Adulterers and petty theft....'

'You found that missing kid. That made network news.'

'I got lucky,' Brad mumbled modestly, but secretly pleased she had heard the story.

'So won't it be good to get your teeth into something bigger?' Zam pressed, adding hopefully, 'It'll be like old times'.

'Yeah maybe. Ah, what the hell - come down this week. I'll give you the nickel and dime tour. And we'll find time to look at your case files.'

'Thanks Brad. You're an angel. I'll see you Thursday night.'

'Cool. Hey - bring some beignets. The donuts down here aren't worth shit. Call me when you get into town.'

He tossed his cellphone onto the couch as he wandered through the empty house. In the kitchen, he finished the dregs of a stale beer and pushed the bottle into the overflowing trashcan. Since Elaine had left, the place had gone to shit. Everything was covered in a film of dust, there was nothing - literally nothing - to eat and the stack of dirty plates in the sink looked like it might collapse under its own weight. Brad rubbed his hands across his stubble and stared out across the overgrown back lawn, wondering how things had gotten so bad.

When anybody asked, he'd say that he and Elaine were going through a rough patch, but Brad knew it was a lie: his marriage had been over for nearly two years. His mother-in-law had called back in May to tell him that Elaine was seeing a guy who sold cars and drove 'one of those new Chevrolets', and who'd found her and Kyle a place in a nice part of town.

'Elaine's happy now,' she gloated.

And his son Kyle, on the few occasions that he had visited, couldn't wait to leave. Since their first and last disastrous trip out on the Gulf - which culminated in a visit to the local emergency room for a fishing hook through Kyle's hand - the boat had festered on the driveway stinking like low tide, its paintwork fading and cracking in the sun.

Just speaking to Zamora Delgado - his former partner at the New Orleans Police Department - stirred up some bitter memories for Brad. Not just of the hurricane, but the fallout which had driven the Durand family from their home to Elaine's mother's place in Alabama, then Georgia and finally to Florida where the lure of the Gulf Coast was just too strong for Brad. He pretended that it was this constant flux in their lives, this lack of stability which had split his family apart, but deep-down Brad knew that it was his failure to come to terms with his wife's illness which had ruined everything. He blamed her for it all, even the loss of his job, after he was fired from the NOPD for 'neglect of duty,' having failed to show up for work for three weeks following the storm.

Brad had loved his work and had been a fine detective - some said the best - doggedly hunting down the murderers and rapists from Faubourg Marigny to Algiers. Born and bred in New Orleans, nowhere else felt like home, even though in Brad's eyes, the city had betrayed him. Life in Florida had nothing to offer by comparison and the few jobs he picked up from his classified ad in the Panama City News Herald were small fry. Hiding in backyards and alleyways, snapping photos of husbands cheating on their wives, or tracking down stolen dirt bikes or outboard motors, he was just going through the motions, a pale imitation of the man he had been a decade earlier when just the germ of a decent case would grow, metastasize like a cancer and consume him.

But Zam's call and the killings she needed help with stirred something in him, and for the first time in months Brad Durand felt alive.

*

'It's good to see you again,' Brad said stiffly, unsure

whether to kiss Zamora or offer a handshake.

'Come here, you moron,' she said, instantly brushing off any awkwardness between them with a hug.

'You look great,' he said. It was his standard remark when meeting any old friend, although in this case it was true. Granted, six years was a long time, but Zam had really changed. When they had first worked together, she had been a rookie, straight out of the academy, assigned to Brad as part of the fast-track program for cops who showed detective potential. The uniform had never suited her – with her bright youthful eyes and rosy apple cheeks, she looked like a kid at a costume party. The years had treated her well. She had lost weight – probably the stress of the job, Brad thought – and looked polished and professional in her dark suit, her hair cropped in a neat bob. In his faded jeans and Hawaiian shirt, Brad felt scuffed and shabby next to her.

'And you look very... relaxed,' Zam replied, with a wide smile.

'Yeah, yeah. Well, these shirts are standard issue 'round these parts. So, you came straight from work? You made good time.'

'Yeah, I was in at six this morning, tomorrow is my first day off in a month, I figured nobody would mind if I left before *another* call came in.'

'Is it that bad?' Brad asked.

'Ha!' Zam scoffed. 'You don't know half of it. Twelve shootings in July, seven murders; fifteen in August, eight murders. September's shaping up to be a record breaker.'

'Still top of the charts then?'

'Oh yeah. Those east coast, west coast boys have got it easy.'

'And now a serial killer?'

'Maybe. I'm not so sure. There've been some developments since we spoke. Let's not get into it now - I haven't eaten since Mobile. What's good here?'

'It's all good,' Brad said, reaching into his cooler box and pulling out a couple of Budweisers. 'The shrimp chalupas are off the chart. Try the fajitas rancheros. Or the chicken enchiladas.' He twisted off the caps and handed one to Zam.

'I guess this isn't your first time here?' she laughed. 'Cheers.'

They had agreed to meet in Valerio's, a big egg-yolk colored restaurant on West 15th Street - an easy place to find for anyone heading into the city and, according to Brad, the best Mexican in town.

It was nearly midnight by the time Zam swallowed her last mouthful of key lime pie and sat back heavily in her chair. 'Jeez, I haven't had a meal like that since… I don't know when. That was amazing.'

'I know. I feel like one of those snakes on the Discovery Channel, digesting a jungle pig.'

'Real nice analogy, Brad,' Zam quipped.

He smiled sadly.

'What's wrong?' she asked.

'I just can't remember the last time I had such a nice… time,' he replied.

'Things aren't so peachy, eh?'

'No, that's one way to put it,' he nodded, and knocked back the last of his beer. 'I'm sorry I chewed your ass off the other day. I know it's got nothing to do with you.'

'*No pasa nada*. Say, did you really take a bullet? I didn't know that.'

'Well, kinda. Somebody fired a shotgun in my rough direction once. I took a ricochet in my ass. You want to see the scar?'

'I'll pass, thanks,' Zam chuckled.

'You know what kills me most of all? Here I am, pushing fifty, semi-retired cop, living alone. My wife won't talk to me, my kid can't stand me, fat, drunk....'

'You're not that fat,' Zam interjected, unhelpfully.

'.... Seriously, I'm a goddamn cliché! I'm like one of those TV cops!' Brad was joking now, but the humor fell flat: there was an element of truth in what he was saying, and they both felt it.

'Get the fuck outta here!' Zam slurred a little too loudly, drawing glances from the diners at an adjacent table. 'Look at me, I've just turned thirty-three. Single, white, female. Married to my job, and - hey – that's cool, because nobody's offering to take me down the aisle anyways. No prospects for promotion either – can we say, 'glass ceiling'? Same old shitty car, same old shitty apartment. I *wish* I had your life. And by the way, you're *not* going bald.'

'I never said I *was* going bald!'

'No, but I thought you might,' she laughed. 'You were on a roll there.'

Brad brushed his thick mop of graying hair over his forehead. 'How's that, babe?' he said, joining in the laughter.

'You look like one of the Beatles,' she hooted.

'Which one? No, don't tell me. You'll probably say Ringo.'

'I don't know. They all looked the same to me,' Zam shrugged.

'And you call yourself a detective? Speaking of which...'

'We are *not* discussing homicide cases tonight, Brad Durand. We'll start in the morning. Now catch the waiter's eye so the NOPD at least picks up the check.'

*

A few blocks down from the beating heart of New Orleans, a couple of hundred yards from the point where the great Mississippi began its sweeping crescent south around the city, Odeo Boucher savored a Cuban cigar outside his failing strip-club, Cheaters.

At his side was Claudette, the girl Odeo employed to stand on the corner of Bienville Street and persuade any eligible male to swing down Clinton for a free champagne cocktail in the company of his exotic dancers. Claudette looked twenty, maybe twenty-one, but she was only fifteen, so Odeo didn't have to pay her much. She had a tight little body with a rack that defied gravity, good cheekbones and *a toothpaste ad smile*. She was a natural conversationalist too and men would seemingly do anything to please her. If she'd wanted to, Claudette could have filled Cheaters twice over; three times if she'd been dancing herself. Odeo looked up at the street as a gang of bawdy marines swaggered down the main strip, not fifty yards from his club's entrance, hooting and whistling like the Steamboat Natchez.

Odeo pulled on his cigar until his tongue itched while he searched for the right words to express his frustration.

'Claudette,' he began, huffing smoke from his nostrils. 'I have asked you repeatedly to stand on the corner and... and... *induce* gentlemen to come to the club. That is your *job*. *Inducement*. Have I not asked you repeatedly to do that, Claudette?'

'Mr Boucher, I get so lonely on that corner. I just wanted some company,' Claudette replied, in a childlike voice, staring up at him with her big caramel-colored eyes.

Odeo clamped his lips around his cigar and tried not

to imagine those same eyes staring up at him as she sucked on *his* Cohiba.

'Don't look at me like that, Claudette. I *knows* what you's doin'.'

Behind them both, Cheaters' only regular doorman looked on with a pained expression of lust and helplessness. Treyvon Plummer had recently left 'The Farm' - Louisiana State Penitentiary up in Angola - where he had served a six year stretch for the statutory rape of a girl about the same age as Claudette. Odeo employed Treyvon because, like Claudette, he too was cheap.

Business was bad. Odeo had bought the place for a song three years previously, when property prices were so low in the city, he could have bought an entire block if he had wanted. He also purchased the abandoned premises next door - formerly Ely's Gift Emporium - and merged the two buildings into one to create a huge expanse for the club lounge. He had a vision for Cheaters as a club to rival the best strip-joints in the state. But powder-coated, titanium gold, hi-rigidity dance poles don't come cheap. From the outset, Odeo had insisted on the best of everything, from the sound system to the shot glasses. When the grand opening finally rolled around, he was seriously overextended.

For the first few months, there was a steady flow of customers - frat boys from Baton Rouge enjoying their first time in a gentlemen's club; bachelor parties; businessmen from Texas and Alabama - and it looked like Cheaters might actually make it. But aside from a holiday rush at Christmas and a Mardi Gras spike, the winter months were slow, not least because the enormous lounge was a bitch to heat when the temperatures dropped.

But the fatal flaw in Odeo's plan was the location of

the club: Clinton Street was nothing more than a service road for the bars and restaurants on Decatur and St Peters, and a back alley of waitresses and busboys taking cigarette breaks behind packing crates and dumpsters didn't exactly say 'erotic burlesque.' Unless Claudette was doing her thing on the street corner, most people didn't bother to venture down.

With fewer customers every week, the dancers' G-string tips and lapdance commissions dried up and they began to skip shifts, calling in sick and complaining that they had better things to do than stand around in an empty room for six hours a night. Three of his best girls left. Two weeks later, Odeo saw Cherish dancing at *The G Spot* on Rampart Street when he went to check out the local competition. He slipped a guy at the stage lights twenty dollars to shove his finger up her ass the next time she bent over in front of him.

In their places, Odeo employed past-their-prime entertainers and plus-sized girls. Most customers would take one look at Daniva - forty-five-year-old mother of three, hoisting herself up the pole for an inverted split, with her sagging thighs and heavy breasts swinging free - and turn right around. Not even Claudette's promise of a free cocktail could keep them there. Odeo, meanwhile, would have been happy to tap Daniva's ass – soft and doughy as it was – but he was too scared to ask.

Despondently, Odeo tossed the stub of his cigar into the gutter and pointed to the end of the street, without a word. Claudette scampered off, her high heels clacking against the asphalt. He gave Treyvon a look which said, 'Don't be an asshole,' and shambled down the steps into Cheaters.

The music was both an assault on Odeo's ears and an

insult in the city of jazz. There were three dancers gyrating on the stage. Odeo thought he recognized one of them – Lavinia? Laveen? Latreen? – but he couldn't be sure. She was planted heavily on all fours, swinging her head from side to side like a dog wrestling a rubber toy from its owner. In the gloom, he made out a smattering of customers: one was arguing with a lap-dancer, pointing his finger angrily at her crotch; another was sprawled across a table, unconscious. One man - probably recently divorced or widowed - was openly crying while a girl in a pink baby-doll patted him on the back and checked her cell-phone messages.

Odeo retreated through the door marked 'private' at the back of the club, past the boxes of napkins and crates of empty beer bottles and into his office, where he flopped into his swivel chair and closed his eyes. He stayed like that for some time, listening to the thumping bass of the music and trying not to think about money, Claudette, money, the strippers, his mother and money. Odeo checked his watch - midnight - then unlocked his desk drawer and pulled out a wrap of cocaine. He needed something to get him through the night.

*

Pure Floridian morning sunshine streamed through the windows into Brad Durand's condominium. The table-tops and work surfaces gleamed, the carpets had been vacuumed, the piles of newspapers and books tidied away. Zamora woke to the smells of coffee brewing and bacon frying.

'Morning,' Brad said cheerily when she emerged from the spare bedroom. 'How did you sleep?'

'What time is it? Jeez, is it late?'

'It's only about ten. I let you sleep in. It *is* your day off, after all,' Brad replied. 'Ready for breakfast?'

'Woah, I can still taste guacamole. Just give me a glass of Florida's best, would you?'

Brad poured two glasses of freshly squeezed orange juice while Zam wandered through to the lounge. 'This is a nice set-up, Brad. I like the whole... open-plan thing. I couldn't really take it in last night. Something to do with six beers and half a bottle of red wine....'

She bent to examine the shelves of CDs beneath the stereo system, and Brad found himself staring at her long, slim legs. It had been months since there had been a woman in the house, not counting the lady from the Diamond Shine cleaning company, who worked two full days and charged $240 for what she dubbed 'a nuclear fallout' service.

He shook his head to clear his thoughts. 'So, listen, how about we take a shower – I mean *you* take a shower, and then *we* get started on the case files over breakfast. Sound good?'

'Yeah, but we need to lay down some ground rules first.'

'Such as?'

'OK...' Zam searched for the right words. 'We both know what you're like when you get your mind set on something, right? When we worked the Crusol case, my first year out of the academy, you were like a man possessed. I remember thinking 'What have I gotten myself into?' Seriously, you scared the shit out of me.'

'Come on,' Brad laughed uneasily. 'That was a pretty heavy case. Crusol was running a major drug operation. There was a lot of pressure to make an arrest. We had the mayor breathing down our necks for Chrissakes.'

'Yeah, but I saw the reports. You worked an eighty-hour week during the stakeout.'

'I got the job done, didn't I?' Brad tried to hold back his irritation.

Zam took a deep breath and continued, 'Look, all I'm saying is, once we get into this, I need you to remember that – yes – while you are doing me a solid favor here, giving your expert opinion based upon years of professional experience in the field, this is still *my* case. And it's *my* head on the block. If Tillery knew I was even talking to you…'

'That shitweasel,' Brad interjected, '… he should have been a politician.'

'Yeah well – he's still the man, and if he knew I was going off the ranch, he wouldn't be too impressed. I just don't want you to get in too deep. I need you to be a fresh pair of eyes, a voice of reason, whatever. Don't get emotionally involved, you… shitweasel,' Zam giggled, and Brad had to crack a smile.

'Fine. What else?' he replied, dismissing the notion immediately.

'Money. Officially, you're off the books, but I'll put you through as an external specialist. There's a ring-fenced budget for technologists, researchers, private pathologists. All that jazz. How's that sound?'

'You get what you get and you don't pitch a fit.'

Brad hadn't considered that he might actually make some money from this venture. He hated having to chase up payments for his P.I. work: more often than not, once people had their property returned, or saw the evidence of their partner's cheating, they weren't inclined to cough up Brad's fees. He layered maple-syrup bacon on to a piece of toast and congratulated himself on this unexpected turn of events.

'Is that it?' he asked.

'Three,' Zam replied. 'Don't talk with your mouth full.

And four, don't talk to anybody else before you talk to me. Don't go calling up your old pals in the MCU, the press, the victims' parents. *Anybody*.'

After breakfast, Brad cleared the plates while Zam brought in a stack of black folders from the trunk of her car and laid them out on the table.

'I'll talk you through them all. Just so you know, there was no sign of sexual assault, or any theft, *per se*, in any case. The victims differ in age, gender, background….'

'You mentioned a pattern?' Brad asked.

'Maybe. There are similarities across the range of victims, but like I said on the phone, it's more of a… *feeling* I get. The *cause* of death isn't an issue, but a couple of these books are still open on the *manner*. The medical examiner won't sign off on them. He's not sure whether they're homicides, suicides, accidental deaths… whatever.'

'You think murder most foul though?' Brad asked.

'That's what they pay me for,' Zam replied. 'But don't let me influence you. See for yourself….'

She opened the first file.

'OK, let's start with the most recent: Nadia Romero. Twenty-two years of age. Student at the University of New Orleans, first year, art history. Bright, friendly, popular, the usual. No criminal record, no gang affiliations. Her body was found on the 14th – three weeks ago – in the London Avenue Canal, near Filmore Avenue.'

'Who found the body?' Brad asked.

'Couple of kids.'

'Cause of death?'

'Officially, Nadia drowned. She'd been in the water about twenty hours when the call came in. The autopsy says...' Zam fanned through the file, found the page and read aloud, 'Death consistent with wet drowning,' but check this out: the pathologist noted that 'a subdural haematoma prior to immersion in water may have led to drowning.'

'So, somebody cracked her on the head and dropped her in the canal.'

'Nice try, but no signs of *head* trauma.'

'Go on...' Brad said, sensing that Zam had more to say.

'She was missing a hand and some pubic hair.'

'Ah – for a minute there, I wasn't sure this was a homicide.'

'It's not. Yet. We're treating it as a homicide, but we could be looking at just some sort of posthumous mutilation,' Zam said.

'That's some leap, isn't it? Somebody just *happens* across a dead body and decides to help themselves to a hand...'

'Precisely. But Tillery's got a hard-on for the gangs right now. He thinks it might be part of some kind of initiation rite. We brought in a couple of the Latin Kings last year and noticed they were wearing jewelry made from teeth. So Tillery thinks this could be more of the same - only taken to a whole new level.'

'And how is *Commander* Tillery?' Brad asked, struggling to keep his tone even.

Zam just gave him a look that said, 'Do we have to go there?'

Brad's strained relationship with Auden Tillery stretched back to the summer of 'seventy-eight, back when they both joined the force as part of an NOPD recruitment drive. Always clean-shaven, always sporting a close-cropped haircut, Tillery seemed determined to ignore the changing styles of seventies New Orleans – but within months of their enrolment, he was making a name for himself as an ambitious and dedicated recruit.

Brad had never known anybody as driven as he was, so soon found himself drawn into competition with Tillery over who could be the better cop.

Young, 'badge heavy' and full of their own self-importance, with the legal authority and means to take a life, field training forced the new recruits to forget almost everything they'd learned in the academy. They were given menial tasks – traffic duty, crowd control at the Saints' home games or the weekend 'drunk wagon' shift. Brad learned to keep his mouth shut and listen to his supervising officers, but his boots and gun-leather creaked with newness, and he longed to break them in on the streets. Meanwhile, Auden Tillery thrived under the scrutiny of his field training officer, his career trajectory already bending toward authority like a plant bending toward the light. 'Young, gifted and black': he was the kind of police officer the NOPD needed to foster better race relations throughout the city.

Tillery made more arrests in that first year, although Brad's count subsequently led to more convictions. They were both smart, both brave and hardworking, and they soon became fully-fledged police officers, the best of the '78 intake, proud to wear the traditional light-blue shirts of the New Orleans Police Department. After less than a year on the job, Brad received a 'Special Commendation for Valor' for chasing down and tackling a mugger in the middle of Canal Street on a Saturday afternoon. Two months later, Tillery scored his own for single-handedly preventing a gas-station hold-up and arresting the two perpetrators. The media didn't seem to care that they were just teenagers armed with toy pistols.

There was friction too. In the early years, while they still worked in the same station, Tillery made a number of formal complaints about Brad's slovenly appearance, his attitude towards his fellow officers, his foul language and his excessive use of force. In return, Brad called in a favor from one of his buddies in the traffic department and in 1982 alone, Tillery racked up twenty-two parking violations.

There was no grudging respect for one another. Brad hated everything about Tillery - his button-down, white-collar, spit-shine attitude to police work, his obsession with the chain of command, his prissy mustache. For his part, Tillery was repulsed by everything Brad represented - with his grubby fingernails, bloodshot eyes and three-day stubble, as far as Tillery was concerned Brad Durand was only one step away from the criminal underbelly of the Crescent City.

Over the years, as they moved up the ranks, Brad continued to focus on the job, the detective work, proving himself to be more than a gifted investigator. He was somebody who got the job done, while Tillery took the political route, furthering his career at every opportunity with high-profile public work and PR stunts. In the mid-nineties, he was instrumental in establishing the Community Relations Division: the success of the city-wide 'Get Behind The Badge' campaign was all his doing. The day that Brad arrested Governor Donald McLaughlin for murdering an underage prostitute in the Royal Sonesta Hotel, he turned on the TV to see Auden Tillery receiving his official promotion to captain at City Hall. The first black captain in the force's history.

When Katrina hit, Tillery seized his chance to reach for the upper echelons. Chosen as part of the review panel in the tribunals, he set out to cleanse the force, using his rank and reputation to clear out not only those police officers who had abandoned the city on that fateful day, but also anyone who had ever stood in his way or posed a threat to his career. Brad refused to give Tillery the satisfaction of seeing him begging for his job.

'Are you still with me, Brad?' Kit asked, pulling him back to the present.

'Sure,' He sucked his teeth and changed the subject. 'You said there was no sexual assault?'

'That depends on your definition of 'sexual'. She wasn't raped. Forensics found the spot where she entered the water. We've got some heel-prints, but I'm not confident they'll yield anything - and that's it. Seems on the surface that Nadia had a brain hemorrhage right at the side of the canal, then somebody chopped her up, gave her a trim and rolled her into the water.'

Brad felt the hairs on the back of his neck rising. He flicked through the folder, skimming through statements, identification sheets, laboratory toxicology reports and HIV tests, and twisted his head to take in the post-mortem photographs of her wrist and pubis.

'Anything else... unusual?'

'More unusual than that?' Zam scoffed, 'No. Why? What are you thinking?'

Something niggled at the back of his mind, but Brad couldn't say what. Give it time, it will come, he told himself. 'Questions mainly,' he said to Zam, 'but I'll save them until I've read the whole pile.'

'Right, then let's move on. There's *boo-coo* here and I want you to get a broad sense of the killings before we start on the nitty-gritty.' Zam pulled a second folder from the pile.

*

Three hours, a large pot of coffee and a box of six Café Du Monde beignets later, Brad and Zam closed the final file. The label read, 'Shay Favreau - August 29,

2006'.

Brad leaned back in his chair and ran his fingers through his hair. 'So, no ketamine, no rohypnol... maybe they were drugged before they died?'

'Yes, we checked and no, they weren't. None of the usual street drugs showed up on any of the tox reports anyway,' Zam replied.

'You've got an answer for everything,' Brad gave a hollow laugh. 'Well, I can see why you think there's a pattern...'

'There's a 'but' coming, right? You don't agree?' Zam asked, surprised.

'I'm not saying that - yet. There's something strange there certainly, but I'm not sure they're connected. For a start, there's no consistency in cause of death....'

'*That's* the consistency,' Zam interjected.

'Listen to what you're saying. Look at the evidence: apart from this kid who was sliced up,' Brad tapped his finger on Shay Favreau's file, 'you haven't even got an obvious murder weapon for the other four.'

'That's my point!'

'No, Zamora, that's *not* a point. You can't stick a clutch of unsolved murders together based on what they're all lacking. What have you got here? A stabbing, an electrocution, a drowning, a heart attack and - which one am I forgetting?'

'A fatal blood clot. In a 28-year-old *marathon* runner for Chrissakes.'

'So, where's the connection?'

'First, they're all missing body parts....'

'Not conclusive. Could have been animals in at least two of your cases. Rats killed a baby in Westwego last year. Poor thing bled to death. Saw it on the news.'

'Are you suggesting that it's a coincidence? In five out of five unexplained deaths?'

'Well, they're not unexplained. They're strange, I'll give you that, but that's the nature of coincidences, I guess,' Brad shrugged.

Zam paused. 'You're so full of shit, Bradley,' she said, smiling suddenly. 'Don't think I don't see what you're doing. I *know*.'

'What am I doing?' Brad asked, with a twinkle in his eye.

'You *do* think there's a connection here and you're pushing me to... make the case for it.'

Brad rubbed his chin and chose his words carefully, 'OK. I would say that - yes - there is something about these five cases. A common theme. Maybe. I'd be interested in seeing the stats on blood clots in under-thirties. And unexplained electrocutions too. You say the girl was nowhere near *any* electrical equipment?'

'That's right. She was found plum in the middle of City Park, three hours after somebody cut out her eyes. And it was a perfectly bright day - blue skies, ninety degrees, typical for July - but that scar is consistent with the shock from a lightning bolt.'

She pulled out the folder belonging to Erica Huffman - a thirteen year old high-school kid and turned to the photo of a livid pattern of scar tissue blossoming across her back like the branches of a tree. 'Nearest streetlight was five hundred feet away.'

Brad shook his head, 'Weird. What about the librarian? What was her name again?'

'Stephanie Dee West.'

'Right,' Brad added her name to a table of notes he'd been compiling all morning. 'She's something of an anomaly, isn't she?'

'Why do you say that?'

'Well, she was forty-eight, so she totally skews the average age of your victims. Plus, she was black.

Everybody else was white.'

'Nadia was Hispanic.'

'Right,' Brad conceded, 'but it all seems very random, doesn't it? Five victims of different ages, backgrounds, found in different parts of the city. Plus, you've got some big gaps in your timeline....' Brad stopped, mid-sentence 'Unless...'

'What?' Zam asked.

'Here's something: at first glance, and without the benefit of the bigger picture, a couple of these cases could be passed off as nothing more than freak occurrences.'

'I suppose so,' Zam said.

'People have heart attacks, people die of blood clots, nothing *too* out of the ordinary. The thing that strings these events together is the body part angle. But what if that had been missed?'

'But it hasn't been missed!' Zam fired back, confused. 'What do you mean?'

'I mean in *other* cases. Widen the search beyond the homicide database, look at the Coroner's records. Is Walt Forager still in charge down there?'

'He is, but they had to move after the storm. Get this: now the office is based in a burned-out funeral home on Martin Luther King Boulevard. They keep the bodies in three refrigerated trailers in the parking lot. I'm not joking.'

'Jesus. You're going to have your work cut out then. Look at the data for the elderly, the sick and the homeless - they're the easiest to murder because no one's looking for it. Get Walt to run a search on old records with missing body parts. That's the key here. You never know, you might get lucky. It would plug some holes in your theories anyway.'

'I'll get Rubino on it right away,' Zam said, fishing her

cellphone from her handbag. While she relayed the request to a member of her team, Brad flicked through the case file for Adam Beaupre, formerly 'systems analyst for Hisix Logistics'. At twenty-eight years of age, he was six-three and weighed only 142 pounds.

'Fitness freak,' Brad muttered.

The toxicology report showed no sign of drugs or alcohol in his system, which might have otherwise accounted for the pulmonary embolism which killed him. On the twenty third of December 2009, Adam's body had been discovered in the parking lot of the Suburban Baptist Church, just off the Chef Menteur Highway. He'd been at the church helping with the preparations for the Christmas celebrations. Until somebody had cut out his heart.

'How do they know he died of an embolism? And not like...' Brad tried to be diplomatic, '... heartlessness?'

Zam raised a finger to show she was on the phone but leant across the table to point out a single word in the autopsy: 'hypoxia.'

Brad nodded. Adam had died of lack of oxygen to the brain. Although he understood, Brad felt the same chill in his bones as he tried to make sense of the whole report. How could somebody *induce* a blood clot? And then, once their victim was dead, claim their heart like a trophy?

He spread out the other files across the table and stood over them like an army general surveying a battle-plan.

'I don't care how busy they are, Rubino - this takes precedence,' Zam was trying to remain calm.

Five names, five victims, five ways to die - what was the connection?

'That's right, Rubino. We're looking for John Does, Jane Does....'

Brad stared at the photographs of Adam's gaping, mutilated chest, the black horrific depths of Erica Huffman's missing eyes, the raw wound where the killer had sliced off Shay Favreau's penis.

Then something fell into place.

'Zam,' he said, cutting her off abruptly as she gave her orders to her subordinate.

'Hold on Rubino. What is it, Brad?' she asked.

'They're all virgins.'

*

The urban alarm-clock of a reversing garbage truck pulled Odeo Boucher from a dream about ants crawling all over his skin. He woke with smears of black newsprint across his face, the coppery taste of blood in his mouth and a cocaine hangover. He had fallen asleep slumped across the desk in his office again, his head cushioned against an open copy of the Yellow Pages. As he opened his eyes and took in his surroundings, the previous evening's problems broke against the shoreline of his consciousness like an oil slick. He was growing accustomed to this mid-morning depression, but the headaches were new. He wondered if he was doing too much, or if he'd had a mini-stroke, or if the quality of the product from Treyvon's supplier was up to scratch. He knew what they cut drugs with these days – crystal meth at best, rat poison in the worst cases. Odeo picked himself up and blew his bloody nose. The thought of breakfast turned his stomach – it was past midday anyway – but he wandered back into the emptiness of the club to pour himself a bourbon.

There was a sense of peace in Cheaters at that time of day, a feeling that the building itself was resting, and a hope that it might still come alive and fulfill its potential later that night. Odeo wished it were true, but he wouldn't have bet on it. Lately, he'd been feeling that the world was against him, and the failure of his business, the threatening letters from the bank and the electric company, even the headaches were part of some dark conspiracy. He stared at his face, distorted in a silver ice bucket, and interrogated his reflection: what had he done to deserve such punishment? Who were the agents of his downfall? 'Why me?'

'Because you done been *fixed*, Odeo. Dat's why.'

Odeo started at the sound of the old man's voice.

'*Jezi-Kris*! What are y'all *trying* to do to me, Lionel? How long have you been sitting there?

'Long enough to hear your troubles and know the truth about it all.'

Lionel Root, a janitor of sorts, had come with the building. Odeo hadn't the heart to let him go, so Lionel pushed a broom around the club a couple of days every week, whenever he felt like it. He didn't have a key, and Odeo wasn't sure how he ever got in, but it wasn't the first time Lionel had discovered Odeo drinking away the profits in the middle of the day. He was a grizzled old Creole, sinewy and long limbed, with a fuzz of white hair atop the sunken features of his face. 'You been fixed - *hoodooed*. I seen it plenty of times before, Odeo.'

'I ain't been *fixed*, you old coot!' Odeo snapped, but Lionel's words hung in the air like mustard gas.

'Come here, let me show you something. And bring me a knife,' Lionel said, as he took a seat at one of the silver tables. 'When you gonna get some decent furniture in this place anyways?'

Odeo noticed his hand was shaking as he poured himself another drink and one for Lionel. He wiped a sheen of sweat from his forehead and tried to relax, but his insides were in turmoil and his mind skittered from one panicked thought to the next. He picked up the knife from the tray of sliced lemons and immediately the thought of plunging it into his own neck and freeing himself flashed across his subconscious. He walked around the bar and over to the table like a man on his way to the gallows.

'You ever seen one o' these?' Lionel asked, taking an old handkerchief from his pocket, and unwrapping it carefully on the table. Inside was a misshapen ball of dusty red wax, no bigger than a plum. Odeo shuddered involuntarily - he could see the imprints of thumbs and fingernails where it had been molded into shape. Odeo wasn't a New Orleanian by birth, but he knew enough about the spiritual culture of the city to recognize a *hoodoo*: a token conjured up to bring bad luck.

'Where'd you find it?' he whispered.

'In the corner, over there, next to the sofa,' Lionel replied nonchalantly, pointing his thumb over his shoulder. 'Not for the first time neither. I found one two weeks ago as big as a fist. Threw that one out with the garbage. Paid it no mind. Goddamn hoodoo witches! Thought it must be somebody got spurned by one of the ladies, but I seen four now,' he said, holding up four fingers, 'and it's your name on the bills for this place. You is the only person who is always here. Now, hand me that knife.'

Taking care not to touch the ball with his fingers, Lionel pressed the blade into the wax until it split apart, spilling its contents onto the folds of the handkerchief. 'What we got here?' he asked himself, peering down with his good eye. 'What's this? A cat's tooth maybes - that ain't nothing but witchcraft. This is just soot and ash. Some shit burnt for *Li Grand Zombi.*'

'Who?'

'Don't you worry 'bout that. I'll tells you some other time.'

'What's this?' Odeo asked, pointing. 'Rust?'

'That's blood, boy. Flakes of dry blood. Probably yours.'

Odeo's heart hammered in his chest. 'How they going to get *my* blood?' he asked incredulously, trying to quell the fear in his voice.

Lionel touched his own nose and then pointed to Odeo's. 'Somebody knows 'bout your lil' habit, I reckon.'

Odeo sniffed instinctively and anger flared from his horror. 'This is bullshit! Some… practical joke! An April fools… nonsense! I don't know!'

'It's September, Odeo,' Lionel replied, fishing a scrap of paper from the ash and blood with the tip of the blade, and unfolding it using the edges of the handkerchief, 'And besides, this ain't no joke…'

In tiny spidery letters, it read:

Odeo Boucher
Odeo Boucher
Odeo Boucher
Odeo Boucher
Odeo Boucher
Odeo Boucher
Odeo Boucher
Odeo Boucher
Odeo Boucher

*

'What makes you so sure?' Zam asked. 'I'll give you Erica - she was only thirteen. We knew she was a virgin.

But Nadia? And what about the rest?'

'What about Nadia's boyfriend? You questioned him, right?' Brad asked.

'Sure, but he didn't go into details about their sex life…. I don't know. It didn't stand out.'

'I get it. You only see it if you're already looking for it.'

Zam picked up the case file and flicked to the autopsy report. '*Mira*, 'No sign of sexual assault' like I said, but this says her hymen was already broken. I guess it's possible she was still a virgin though,' she added, 'lots of young girls break theirs doing sports - gym, horse-riding, whatever….'

'Look, it's still only a theory,' Brad said. 'I can't be sure. Hell, nobody can know for sure.'

'No, it makes sense. We'll have to do some more background checks. I can believe it of Shay Favreau - he was sixteen when he was killed, but Adam Beaupre was twenty-eight. You just don't expect it, I suppose.'

'In these… *modern times*? No, but it's all here,' Brad said, tapping the file. 'Suburban Baptist Church, health freak, no drink, or drugs. A good, clean-living, God-fearing, Southern Baptist boy. Did he have a partner?'

'Fiancée,' Zam answered sadly. 'They were due to get married this year.'

'He was saving himself,' Brad nodded. 'Listen, it might be something or it might be nothing. Everything's important at this stage; you - *we* - have got to sift through it all and find the gold dust. Right now, it's just a hunch…'

'Sure. It's another piece of the puzzle, I guess,' Zam said optimistically.

*

The door to Walt Forager's small office worked like a

kissing gate, and the old man was forced to sidestep through the gap, hold in his paunch with his back pressed squarely against a tower of box files, and then close the door before he could step into the room.

Unlike the rest of the staff members at the Coroner's Office, Forager wasn't concerned by the cramped spaces and substandard facilities. He knew The Rhodes Good Citizens Funeral Home wasn't perfect - the conditions were generally appalling, especially since an electrical fire had rendered nearly half of the premises useless - but it was good enough. In the neighboring parish of St Tammany, by contrast, where the caseload was much smaller than that of the city, the medical examiner had six fully trained investigators and two board-certified senior pathologists at her disposal, not to mention a state-of-the-art forensic center.

Forager blamed himself for the situation, having never bothered to lobby for more funding, but he had never been a political animal – he didn't know who his legislators were or even the name of his senator. At this late stage in his career, he was beyond caring. 'This isn't 'CSI',' he would answer when anybody questioned the state of the services, 'This is reality TV.'

It was grim, primitive work, but Forager accepted it without complaint. After thirty years, he could no longer differentiate between the smells of industrial bleach, menthol salve and dead bodies which lingered in the humid air of the poorly ventilated operating theaters. He had thirty-eight unexamined bodies in cold storage containers outside and only two pathologists and one psychiatric clerk on his books. Bethany, his wife, had been pushing him to retire since 2003. She desperately wanted to take a cruise around the Norwegian fjords. He had a discolored mole on his neck, which in his own medical opinion was probably cancerous. He planned to have it removed when he had a spare morning.

In spite of it all, the only thing which riled Walt Forager was the frequent and unreasonable requests from the homicide department of the NOPD. Zamora Delgado, Tillery's little bulldog, was the worst of the pack, and she had been yapping since midday. Her team of lackeys had phoned five times asking for updates on their latest mission: a foolhardy quest to dig up data on the bodies of the homeless.

Forager had been around for long enough to know that if a murder wasn't solved within the first forty-eight hours - three days at most - then the results of an autopsy were unlikely to help crack the case. These cops thought medical forensics was a simple procedure, like processing a photograph: that the answers would simply reveal themselves when the image floated to the surface of the blank plate.

It was three o' clock and Walt was hungry. He moved a stack of reports from his desk, opened his lunch pail and unwrapped his sandwiches. No sooner had he taken a bite, than he heard the phone ringing in reception, and sighed deeply through a mouthful of mortadella and provolone.

Daphne transferred the call by banging on the other side of the thin wood paneling and shouting, 'It's Detective Delgado!'

Forager composed himself and picked up the receiver. 'Detective Delgado, how nice of you to call. Again. How can I help you?'

'Please Doctor Forager, call me Zam. I was hoping you might have news for me.'

'Detective Delgado,' Forager began, teasing a piece of bread out from between his teeth with a paperclip. 'Let me try to explain something which I think you might have missed. Cadavers – the cadavers we have here that is – they don't tend to move around a lot. They remain - resting in peace, as it were - wherever we leave them. We get to them when we're ready. It's a blessing in a way. It means they're not queuing up outside, banging on the door, asking to be seen. Unlike you and your colleagues, who continue to interrupt my work until you get an answer.'

'Yes, Doctor. That's *our* job.'

'A little professional courtesy would go a long way, Detective.'

'As would a little professionalism,' Zam answered smartly. 'Officer Rubino has been picking through your computer records all morning. Did you know?'

'I wasn't aware he was here, no.'

'He's not *there*. He accessed the Coroner's Office private network via the Public Information System at the Criminal Justice building. There's no password.'

'Ah,' Forager swallowed hard. 'Computing has never been our strong suit, I'm afraid.'

Zam pressed on. 'According to those records - many of which are incomplete by the way - since 2008, sixty-six corpses with missing organs and or limbs have been processed by your office.'

'That does seem rather high. Many of our records are still on paper, I'll have to check the figures.'

'And *that's* why I'm calling, Doctor. Again. Please do check the figures. I've got a killer removing body parts, post-mortem – it would be nice to have a clear idea of the number of victims I'm dealing with. I'll be at your office, 10 am tomorrow.'

'But tomorrow's Saturday,' Forager answered timidly, 'Hello? Hello? Detective Delgado?'

But she had already hung up.

'Looks like I'm heading back,' Zam said as she

snapped her phone shut.

'You can't go yet,' Brad replied bluntly. 'There's still too much to do.'

'The boat trip. Maybe next time, skipper,' Zam said with a mock salute.

'That's not what I meant. I need more time to look over the case files. There's a mine of information here, just waiting to be… um…'

'Mined? I know Brad. Sorry to cut and run, but I've got to get back and sort out this mess at the Coroner's Office.'

'Let Rubino do it,' Brad said.

'He's a pushover. Forager would just give him some sob-story and send him on his way.'

'Then somebody else. Speak to Tillery,' Brad suggested. He was beginning to whine. 'That'll put a firecracker up his ass.'

'Exactly, and it'll get way too political if I ask Auden to get involved. Just let me handle this, ok?'

Brad said nothing.

'Listen,' Zam began, 'it wasn't my intention to drive down here, show you the goods and then leave before we could get anywhere.'

'Are you still talking about the murders?' Brad asked, perplexed.

'Yes, the murders.'

'OK. Just checking. Keep talking…'

'What can I do? I've got to pursue this virgin angle. I should have known you would find something in no time,' Zam said.

'That's my point!' Brad answered. 'Just give me a few more hours. Think of what else I could find. Leave after dinner, you'll still be back by midnight.'

'No. It doesn't feel right. You know how it is. I want - I *need* to be in the center of things.'

Brad understood. A homicide detective needed to be *there*, nose to the ground, chasing the leads, right in the thick of it. You couldn't run an inquiry from the wrong end of a telephone line.

'How about this?' Brad exclaimed suddenly, 'Leave the books with me.'

'Come on. You know I can't do that.'

'You know you can,' Brad insisted.

'I shouldn't even have let you see them in the first place. All our detective notes, witness interviews, forensic reports on six cases? I'd get canned if anybody found out I'd given a civilian unfettered access...'

'I'm not really a civilian.'

'Yes, you are.'

'Not really,' Brad answered petulantly. 'Besides, who am I going to tell? I don't see anyone from one day to the next. You're the first person I've spoken to in two weeks. Come on, let me keep them. Just for the weekend?' He could see that Zam's resolve was beginning to give and leaned harder. 'You're still on leave until Monday morning. If anybody asks, they're at your place. No sweat.'

'And then what? You expect me to drive back here to pick them up?'

'No way. I'll bring them to you.'

'You? Back in New Orleans? I thought I'd never see the day,' Zam joked.

'Well, maybe it's about time I made my peace with the city. We've still got the place there, you know?'

'Yeah, you said. Would you stay there?'

'I could. It's empty. There's literally nothing there. When the insurance company finally paid up, we took the cash for everything. I saw the photos from the real estate agent. It's just an empty shell now. A nicely painted, empty shell. Anyway, it could be an adventure.

So, what do you say?'

'You'll have them back for me by Monday morning?'

'I'll drive over on Sunday and meet you first thing Monday. Scout's honor. I'll even give you a full report of my findings. Assuming there are any, of course.'

'If I know you, there will be. Ok. Don't let me down. You can meet me at the station at...'

'How about we meet on neutral ground?' Brad interjected. 'I don't want to bump into anybody too soon. I'll take you for breakfast.'

'Deal. 8am. Betsy's Pancake House. You know it, right?'

'How could I forget Betsy's?'

*

After doing his best to allay Odeo's fears with half a bottle of George Stagg bourbon, Lionel Root gave up and abandoned him to his paranoia. He sauntered from Clinton Street towards Congo Square, the birthplace of jazz, where the eighteenth-century slaves used to meet on Sunday afternoons to sing and play music on quillpipes, gourds and banzas, while the white folks gathered to watch. *Plus ca change...* he thought, as he made his way through the crowds of tourists standing around outside the Bourbon Street bars. He watched them, these out-of-towners, grinning at one another and supping from 'go-cups' in the middle of the day, as though they had never enjoyed a beer in the open air before. With a wry smile he passed through a lingering cloud of incense outside the Marie Laveau House of Voodoo where the sightseers picked through the dusty shelves of trinkets. Some of the tribal statues which nobody could afford might have been authentic, but the real value of these stores was in hiding the true black magic.

Lionel had been raised with voodoo; his grandmother had been a *mambo* - a priestess - a position of great responsibility within the city's Haitian slave community. It was Mama Audree's solemn duty to maintain the balance between the voodoo spirits and her people, and to preserve the ancestral African roots of the religion through her songs and rituals. Lionel still remembered seeing her dressed in red handkerchiefs and ribbons strung with tiny bells, calling the numbers at the St John's Eve celebrations after the Second World War.

When she died, Lionel's mother Marjorie assumed the mantle, but the world had changed. Somewhere along the way, the traditions had taken on a new meaning. The emphasis had shifted from the spiritualism of voodoo to the superstition of *hoodoo*, a belief in the power - the *pouvwa* - of spells, dolls and candles, rather than the religion itself. And in the pool halls and pawnshops, the shoeshine stands, bars and restaurants of Rampart Street back in the fifties, hoodoo became so commonplace that it crossed over into the white man's world. There was new money to be made in old magic.

Marjorie Laroute's Apothecary opened on the corner of Gravier in 1952, selling toilet products, beauty aids, Citroid Cold Capsules, Geritol Periodic Pain Relief and Dippity-Do pomade. But Marjorie also did a fine trade in Black Cat Oil, Lucky Lodestones, Devil's Shoestrings and powders and potions for her customers' every conceivable whim and desire. While Lionel worked the counter, the men and women of the neighborhood would visit his mother in the backroom of the drugstore. There she would light essential candles around chipped statuettes of Saint Peter and the Virgin Mary and perform the necessary rites to help them work through their problems. All for a price, naturally.

More often than not, Marjorie's 'spells' worked, not because of any mystical interaction on her part but rather because life had a habit of working itself out: untangling the knots in love affairs, smoothing family disputes and settling business deals. And if her magic didn't achieve the expected results, all the better: Marjorie would convince her clients that they had been *fixed* by some enemy's hoodoo, and all that was needed to break the spell was a small investment in more of her conjuration.

Day after day Lionel saw the faith that people placed in his mother's Creole incantations. They paid top dollars for starch-water or talcum powder mixed with food coloring, birthday cake candles or sugar-pills, but Lionel knew the truth: his mother was a charlatan and her magic a sham. Still, there was always food on the table, wood for the fire and a shirt on his back. His mother's magic paid for it all and for that reason alone, Lionel owed a lot to hoodoo.

He took a left and wandered down Dumaine Street to a house he often visited. It stood alone, surrounded by abandoned real estate plots: one had been plowed and planted with potatoes and cabbages. Thick, woody bushes with large, pink pendulous flowers hanging like bells lined the yard. It was a proud little shotgun, with steps scrubbed clean and a neat line of red brick dust in front of an olive-green door.

Before his disillusionment had set in, before he sold his mother's drugstore and dedicated his days to making moonshine and his nights to drinking it, back when Lionel was still a true hoodoo-man, Georgine Rieux had supplied all the herbs and spices that he needed for his rootwork. Those she couldn't grow in her tiny backyard greenhouse, she managed to acquire through a network of contacts scattered throughout the Southern States, across the border, way down south and cultivated over a lifetime.

Finding his faith again had given Lionel a reason to re-establish their working relationship.

Georgine opened the door before he had the chance to knock.

'Well, well, well,' she said, with a knowing smile. 'if it ain't Lionel Laroute. Twice in the same week.'

'You know you still the only person that still calls me by my full name, Georgie-girl.'

'And you the only man who calls me 'Georgie-girl'.' She leaned back on the door jamb and looked him up and down. 'So, what's it going to be? Business or pleasure.'

'Maybe both,' Lionel replied, with a wink. Their blossoming love-affair was a welcome side-effect.

*

Brad waved from the porch as Zam pulled away in her beat-up Honda. He hadn't really wanted her to leave – it felt good to have company around the place – but as soon as he swung the case files for the weekend, he couldn't wait to get down to work and practically pushed her out of the door.

He fired up the old, graying PC in Kyle's bedroom, muttering 'I know how you feel,' as it wheezed into life, then taped his preliminary case notes over his son's Arena Football poster. Names, ages, dates, causes of death.... if there was any pattern at all, Brad was determined to find it. He dug out magic markers, highlighters, a legal pad and brought in the kitchen whiteboard - 'vodka, bread, meat, cat-food, vodka' was scrawled across it in his own drunken handwriting.

Though it made sense to work through the files chronologically, something about the haphazard nature of the 'killings' told Brad he would learn nothing by trying to impose logic and reason where there was none. Until Zam and Forager produced a complete list of victims, and he could start working with an accurate timeline, the whole business was like a scrambled Rubik's cube: it didn't matter where he started.

The first murder-book on the stack belonged to Stephanie Dee West, who had officially died of a heart attack in July 2007, just outside the Avlar Library where she worked three nights a week. The killer had cut off a hank of her hair - roughly six inches according to the report - and sliced off her ears with a 'moderately sharp, long-bladed knife'. Brad made a note to cross-reference the weapons used in the other cases, although he doubted Zam would have overlooked something so basic.

He turned to the crime scene photos: scanning the overviews of Avlar Street and skipping the close-ups of Stephanie's head and chest. A mid-range photograph caught his eye though - it showed the victim sprawled across the concrete steps at the entrance to the library, her jacket and blouse torn open, and blood pooling on the ground around her head. Nothing he hadn't seen a hundred times before, but it was the wide-eyed expression of pure fear on her face that caught Brad's attention. In the camera's flash, Stephanie Dee West's dark skin took on a grayish hue and she looked like she had turned to stone, frozen in a moment of naked terror.

*

The yellow buses streamed away from Walter Cohen

High School. Some seniors drove their own cars and beeped their horns to one another like it was spring break and not just another weekend. While the rest of the pupils scattered, Claudette Tremblay lingered at the gates and lit a cigarette.

Three weeks into the new term and she was already counting the days until she could leave for good. She placed no stock in her education: try applying Pythagoras to a four-year-old kid brother who hasn't eaten a decent meal in a week, or quoting Shakespeare to an abusive stepfather, shaking with fury because he's too drunk to get it up. Her crack-whore mother claimed to have a degree in social science and look where that had gotten her. At best, school was somewhere to hide from the pressures of life, but still Claudette felt like an adult standing in the middle of a kindergarten. She shunned the immature attention of the boys in her class and avoided the infinite social complexities of the girls' cliques. She kept her head down, aimed for average and bid her time until she could join the real world as a singer, she hoped, or maybe a model if she were lucky. Working at Cheaters suited her fine: the money wasn't much and what little she made, she spent on new clothes and cheap jewelry for her weekend shifts. But, more than anything, Claudette lived for the male attention. She relished the way Mr Boucher, Treyvon and every other man on the corner of Bienville Street looked at her. She caught 'The Pretzel' - Mr Wetzel, Junior Math - and Mr Dykes, Phys Ed, staring open-mouthed when they saw her in her gym shorts earlier that week. One time, a Saturday night back in July, the father of one of her classmates tried to hit on her as they rode the St Charles streetcar at two in the morning.

Men wanted her. There was something about

Claudette Tremblay that brought out the animal in full-grown, red-blooded men. She knew it. The words 'sexual awareness' meant nothing to her, but in the last year, she felt like she had emerged from the mist of her own childhood and could see things - see herself - clearly for the first time in her life. In her bottle-green Walter Cohen polo shirt, she was just another face in the crowd, another fifteen-year-old girl – cute, something of a late bloomer, a little taller than most. But out of class, walking through the French Quarter at night or standing outside the club, she was a woman, bursting into life; a peach ready to fall; a black orchid, heavy with promise. Her microskirts, skinny jeans and tight sweaters left little to the imagination. The thrust of her hips, the coquettish tilt of her head, the way she curled her hair around her finger, chewed gum, applied lip balm – men were fascinated by her every move. Claudette saw her charms reflected in the captivation she evoked, and she reveled in it. This power was hers - it was all she had in the world - and she intended to hold on to it for as long as she could.

*

Late afternoon sunlight filtered through the lace curtains. Lionel Root eased himself up and shrugged on his shirt. His waistcoat and flannel pants were folded neatly on a chair next to the bed and Georgine watched as he struggled to bend his thin, hairless legs and dress himself after their lovemaking.

'Not as supple as I used to be,' he muttered to himself as he reached for his socks and loafers.

'*Mon cher*, you is jus' fine the way you is,' she drawled, stretching like a cat, and running her fingers through her mane of gray curls. Her Michel had died just after the millennium and having Lionel in her life felt like the sun shining on her face after a decade of rain. She was wise enough to know that this was only romance – she had no expectations of her new man – but, she had to admit, it did feel good playing again in the autumn leaves.

'I should have those guinea peppers you want by Tuesday. Will I be seein' you 'gain next week?' she asked.

'You can count on it,' Lionel said, tucking his shirt tails into his trousers.

'You got everything else?'

Lionel opened his leather bowling bag to check, 'Mandrake, sassafras, mesquite, arrowroot... yeah, I think that's all I needs. Did you get the other?'

Georgine looked him dead in the eye and nodded solemnly. In her bedside table drawer, she found a tiny cardboard envelope, bound tightly with tape. She held it very carefully, as though she was holding a deadly scorpion's tail between her thumb and forefinger.

'I could only get you a gram. That's two hundred dollars, right there.'

'*Burundanga*,' Lionel whispered reverently as he took it from her. 'The Devil's Breath. This your own brew?'

'No sir,' Georgine replied curtly. 'This is Colombian. More powerful than anything I could *pro*duce. I'm tellin' you *chile*, don't you go playin' with that there magic. That shit will roll you over.'

'Don't you go worryin' about ol' Lionel, honeybee. I be jus' fine.' He grinned widely and tucked the envelope in the pocket of his jacket.

Georgine shook her head. 'I don't know what you are doin', messin' 'bout with all this hoodoo 'gain, but it sure ain't doin' neither o' us no harm,' she laughed.

'You the fire of my loins, Georgie Girl.' He kissed her

on the cheek and ambled out of the house, feeling like a new man.

Down through the Friday crowds swarming home early from the business quarter, Lionel sauntered towards the Sugarbowl, swinging his bowling bag and whistling an old Johnny Pearl tune. He stopped at the Streetcar café on Carondelet and did some business with the bartender there, another of his customers, while he savored an iced tea.

He crossed the stadium's empty car parks, walked under the shade of a giant billboard proclaiming, 'Arena Football is BACK!', and pushed his way through a hole in the wire fence on Le Rouge. A trackman shouted something at him as he crossed over the railway lines, but Lionel paid him no heed and continued to the Expressway. A couple of hollow-cheeked kids were slumped at the foot of a pillar and though they stared with stoned eyes as he passed, Lionel kept his hand on the switchblade in his pocket.

His thoughts turned to Odeo Boucher and his face when the conjure-ball revealed its contents. Lionel laughed quietly to himself. It's a waiting game, he thought. He hadn't needed to lay it on too thick: that little seed of doubt and fear he had planted would grow, and once Odeo leveled out and started thinking straight, he would turn to Lionel for help. He left a contact number where he could be reached, just in case. It was only a question of time, but he couldn't allow Odeo in his fragile, drug-addled paranoia to suspect that Lionel had played any part. The hoodoo was real enough, the blood was indeed Boucher's, and as far as Lionel was concerned, only one person could lift the curse.

The boy from the bayou.

two

Eve Carmel's ambition was as hard and polished as her purple fingernails. On top of her full-time salary, she pulled down an extra $10K in spurious social security claims and almost the same again in sales of her 'Gothica' erotica novels which she churned out in her spare time and published online. Her job at the Coroner's Office might have provided plenty of pulp for her fiction but it was also killing her slowly: she longed to use her medical degree more fruitfully. She dreamed of escaping to a comfortable mental-health facility or cancer ward and screwing a rich consultant.

'What's the matter, Walt?' she asked, as she pushed her way past the box files and into his office. Forager was tapping at his keyboard and squinting over his spectacles. 'Thank you for coming, Eve, I realize it's late,' he said, without looking up. He didn't like to look directly at his assistant - he felt so intimidated by her tattoos and piercings that he couldn't even admonish her for using his first name instead of his full title. 'We've got a problem,' he continued, 'our computer records need updating. Urgently.'

'So? Talk to that guy – what's his name? - Roger,' Eve answered, barely able to disguise the boredom in her voice, 'He's the IT geek.'

Forager ignored her and continued with his point. 'These figures don't make any sense to me,' he said, gesturing at his computer screen.

'Uh-huh,' Eve replied, making a point of checking her watch. 'Want me to take a look?'

'Be my guest.'

She moved around to stand next to him - close enough so that she could see the melanoma on the side of his neck - and subtly positioned herself so that she could rub her crotch gently against the rounded corner of his desk. Anything to alleviate the tedium. While Forager mumbled on about monthly OVS reports and state-wide averages, she casually shifted her weight from one foot to the other.

'Yeah, so... what am I looking at, Walt?' Eve interrupted.

'It seems that an abnormally high percentage of our corpses are missing limbs and organs.'

'Uh-huh. Can't this wait till Monday?' she asked.

'No, it can't. The police are investigating a series of related murders and they've been poking around in our data.'

Eve said nothing, but he had her attention at last.

'You wouldn't know anything about that, would you?' Forager asked.

She had to think fast. 'I didn't want to tell you,' she began, biting her bottom lip and trying to appear contrite. 'You've been so busy lately.'

'What's happened?' Forager asked, in a paternal tone.

'That guy from the bio-med company has been around a few times.'

'Syngenta? Dale Kastelein?'

'That's the one. He's been taking some... bits and pieces off our hands. Nothing anybody is going to miss.'

'Hell's bells, Eve, why didn't you tell me? What have you given him?'

Eve tried to recall all she had 'removed' over the last few years, while simultaneously plotting her escape route from the conversation. 'Not much. Small bones mainly. Some hearts. Hands and fingers. Ears. A couple of femurs. Yeah, quite a lot, I guess. I kept records anyway. It's all in the files.'

'So how do you explain these figures? The computer's telling me that we received these bodies like this, pre-processing. That can't be right. Look,' he said, pointing at the screen, 'this poor man was missing his genitalia!'

'Oh yeah, penises too. I don't know. I guess Roger must have missed the purchase orders from Syngenta when he did the data entry. Everything's been so... *screwed up* since the move,' she feigned indifference as the lies tripped off her pierced tongue.

'Oh, so we are getting paid for this?'

'Not as such, but...' In her mind, Eve weighed up the pros and cons of trying to produce fake purchase orders versus sleeping with Dale Kastelein for real ones.

'But what?'

'Kastelein wants to include your name on any journal papers they publish.' She could take one for the team with Dale. He wasn't a bad looking guy.

Forager brightened immediately, 'Oh really? Well, that's something. What are they working on over there, do you know?'

'Nope,' she shrugged. 'Do you think they're involved in something criminal? Hence the cops?'

'I doubt it, but Detective Delgado has been chewing my ear all day.' Forager leaned back in his chair and stole a glance at the curvature of Eve's derriere. 'She seems to think we're all guilty of something.'

*

Brad took a long pull on his third bottle and succumbed to a pleasant beer buzz. In spite of working four hours straight on the case files, he had turned up very little; so little in fact, he was beginning to think he had jumped the gun and there was no pattern at all: no connection between the bizarre deaths. Forensics had found some pig-skin cells under Stephanie Dee West's fingernails, and there happened to be a chicken feather pinned beneath Erica Huffman's body, but the cells were consistent 'with any uncooked pork product' and the feather - Brad turned back to the evidential analysis - 'a blue-black tail feather, probably from an Ameraucana, a common variety of chicken in the South'. It could have blown in from any backyard henhouse. He wiped 'Old MacDonald' from his whiteboard.

'Find the motive, find the murderer' Brad told himself: a mantra from his days on the force. It was clear that the missing body parts were the key to the puzzle: Brad cast a glance at his list on the wall - 'Penis, Eyes, Hand and Pubic Hair; Heart, Hair and Ears'. Over the course of the afternoon, he'd written down a number of potential lines of enquiry, theories which supported the details of one death, maybe two, but which collapsed under the weight of the others.

The mutilation of Shay Favreau was reminiscent of a mafia execution, but the Tufaro family business was prostitution, loan-sharking and extortion in the Crescent City, not assassinating high-school kids from good homes. Similarly, Brad remembered Ted McKinnley, 'The 'Mississippi Ripper,' who butchered a dozen people back in the 'nineties and kept his favorite parts of his victims' bodies as souvenirs. Then there was Kelvin Owers, 'The Date-Night Cannibal,' who befriended, killed and ate six women he met through internet dating sites between 2003 and 2004. While there were obvious parallels to be drawn, Brad had a hunch that his cases weren't about plain insanity or sexual gratification. He couldn't quite put his finger on it, but there seemed to be an element of *necessity* here - the killer was filling a need. In all cases, the body parts had been removed carefully, cleanly, almost surgically. He added *'medical background?'* to the whiteboard and drummed the end of his magic-marker between his teeth.

The whole affair smacked of that old urban legend, he thought: a night of too many cocktails and a tumble with an Eastern-European prostitute for the businessman who subsequently wakes to find himself in a bathtub full of ice, or dumped in an alleyway, minus a kidney: the victim of some shady underground-economy organ donation racket.

Ludicrous perhaps, but not a million miles away from Brad's reasoning. Then again, as far as he knew, nobody ever needed a pubic hair transplant. That thought alone shook him from his mental block and made him laugh out loud in the empty house. He drained the last of his beer and decided it was time for a break and a snack. He flicked on the radio - Swinging Sixties on Beach 95.1 - and hummed along to 'Time of The Season.'

Taking his mind off a case wasn't easy with nobody else around. In the early days of his relationship with Elaine, there was always an excuse to stop work, usually in the bedroom, sometimes the lounge, occasionally the kitchen. Even when he became a detective and his career began to take hold, Brad lived for the moments when he could get home to spend time with his new wife and their baby son. The crests and troughs of modern American life continued to provide a multitude of distractions over the years: the stress of moving house, two nightmarish visits to the emergency room, camping trips and holidays in Florida, the death of his father and then his heart-broken mother three months later, ten Christmases, eleven Mardi-Gras and one hurricane.

Elaine's illness had changed everything long before it was eventually diagnosed as fibromyalgia. It seemed to blow the spark out of her life. In the space of a year, she lost interest in everything: Kyle, Brad, her friends, her work, herself. Pain and fatigue dictated her entire existence. By the end of 2004, she was spending days at a time in bed, too tired to even sit up or to eat. By then, she had already lost her college job and though Brad tried his hardest to hold it together and keep the family moving forward, inwardly he mistrusted his wife and her invisible disease. He bullishly dragged her to specialists in Georgia and Texas, local support groups, psychotherapy, physiotherapy, hydrotherapy, butting up against the medical profession, demanding answers and challenging the doctors to prove him wrong and cure her. But they couldn't. Brad stood in the ashes of his life and blamed his wife for starting the fire. After three years of silently fighting one another, the breakdown of their marriage seemed inevitable. Katrina sounded the death knell.

Brad found himself in the kitchen and rummaged through the freezer for something edible. Encased in the permafrost was a packet of José Olé Quesadillas – he threw them in the microwave and stood and watched while they twirled around.

'You're listening to Tammy Nolan on Beach 95.1 and the sounds of the Swinging Sixties. Here's another classic from Jimi Hendrix....'

The organ donation angle of the killings niggled at the back of his mind as he thought about Elaine's illness again. Amongst the treatments spouted by the medical professionals over the years - the hormone therapy, antidepressants and spinal decompression surgery - one quack had suggested a stem cell transplant. Ethically speaking, it was a minefield. The cells would have been harvested from an anonymous embryonic donor, but the procedure was untested and the results unknown. There was also a chance the long-term effects would outweigh the benefits: the doctor had told them. Then there was the money: tens of thousands of dollars. It wouldn't have mattered: Brad would have found a way. He would have donated his own cells to have back the woman he married rather than the phantom she had become. Hell, he would have given his right arm...

His thoughts skipped back to Nadia Romero and her missing hand, chopped off at the time of her death. Had she made a similar sacrifice? What did her hand represent to the person who had taken it? The crime-scene photographs of her bleeding wrist were now filed away in a part of his subconscious which liked to regurgitate such images at inopportune moments like speaking to the parents of a missing child, slicing into the Thanksgiving turkey, during sex. Brad shook his head to clear it.

'Focus!' he told himself gruffly.

Nadia. Her hand. Her *sacrifice*. The answer was close, dancing on the edge of his mind, ready to fall like the jackpot of a one-armed bandit as the reels spun triple seven.

The microwave beeped and the moment was gone. Brad knew from years of experience that it would return - he just needed time to let the pieces fit together. He grabbed a fourth beer and headed back to Kyle's room, flopped into the chair and swung his feet up on to the desk, resting the plate on his stomach while he chowed down on rubbery steak and processed cheese.

Hand and hair, eyes and ears – Brad read the list on the wall again. The physical, biological nature of the missing parts was obvious, but the reasoning, the significance behind them eluded him. Cause versus manner, just like Zam had said of the killings themselves. Good people across the country donated their heart, kidneys, liver, blood and God knows what else to help others, those often in desperate need of a transplant. But a hand? Or a penis? There had to be a deeper meaning. He brushed the quesadilla crumbs off his shirt and turned back to the idling computer.

For another hour he scoured the internet for inspiration, his face close to the screen as he pored over images of Catholic sacred hearts, antique playing cards, and illustrations of the Tin Woodsman of Oz; rubber Halloween hands, diagrams of palmistry and pictures of the Hand of Fatima - a palm-shaped amulet worn to promote good luck and protect against the evil eye. He skimmed passages on the symbolism of the ear in Ancient Egypt and the masonic Eye of Providence, adding a word here and there to his whiteboard, but still struggling to find a common theme.

The sun was setting when he turned his attention back to Shay Favreau. He'd deliberately avoided the finer details of this particular case file all afternoon, since it pained him to think of the murder of a boy the same age as Kyle, slaughtered in the mud on the edge of the Pontchartrain.

Instinctively, Brad cast his eyes around his son's old room, already a dusty diorama in the life of a teenage boy: schoolbooks which Kyle would never pick up again, action figures which hadn't been touched in years, clothes which no longer fitted. By now, even Brad knew the names of some of the bands immortalized in posters on the walls. Gaudy trophies for little league baseball and football lined one shelf, and Brad suddenly wished his son were there, so they could toss the pigskin around the backyard for half an hour and forget about everything else.

Kyle had always been a fan of Arena Football. He and Brad enjoyed a Saints match at the Superdome from time to time, but something about the NFL's little brother appealed to Kyle's nature. No punting, no taking a knee – in AFL, the clock never stopped and maybe it was the speed of the game that he liked so much, or perhaps it was the fans' proximity to the action: Kyle could sit right there at the dasher boards, next to the sideline and watch his heroes. Brad remembered the game when Aaron Bailey, the formidable wide receiver, was knocked right over the wall, and Kyle – a pint-sized eight-year-old at the time - tried to help him up. 'Good times' he whispered to himself.

In the five years since they left Louisiana, Brad had tried to take Kyle to the local games in Alabama and Florida. If anything, it was a reason to give Elaine some time to herself. Or an excuse to spend a couple of hours without her. Sure, he got a buzz out of watching the Jacksonville Sharks or the Alabama Vipers, but Brad loved the fact that Kyle had always been loyal to his home team: the New Orleans Voodoo.

Voodoo.

With a shiver, Brad reached up for the 'Victim List' he had tacked across Kyle's football poster, revealing the team's emblem: a grinning skull resplendent in a silk top hat, with two bones bound together to form a 'V.' Its hollow eye sockets brought to mind Erica Huffman's mutilation.

Brad rolled the idea around in his head, considering it in the light of what he already knew. He tested it against the keywords he had jotted on the whiteboard over the course of the afternoon - *'sacrifice,' 'donor,' 'medical background,' 'fertility', 'spiritualism,' 'amulet,' 'virginity,' 'evil eye,' 'religion,' 'love'* - the same way a mathematician might test the logic of a proof, and though he could find no fault, the idea that black magic was the foundation for these seemingly unrelated deaths was beyond implausible, it was ridiculous: the stuff of 1950s 'B' movies and drugstore horror novels. In Brad's experience, in the real world, people killed each other for money. Plain and simple. Sure, there were gang-related killings, crimes of passion and the odd sex-game gone awry, but nine times out of ten, murder came down to money.

He thought back to his years on the force, riffling through his memories of old homicides, searching for a spark of something he'd seen in his career. He drew a blank. Voodoo was the business of superstitions, a gimmick for the tourists, not a motive for murder. Maybe back in the mid-19th Century, back in the days of Marie Laveau, when the Witch Queen of New Orleans was at the height of her power, before the final slave ship cruised up the Mississippi Delta, and the black community still clung to its roots; Brad could imagine that back then, when they still believed in Voodoo, the religion hid a multitude of sins.

Sobriety had crept over him as he tried to pull apart his own theory, but still he couldn't let it go. Or rather it wouldn't let *him* go. Each case fell neatly into place. He accepted with grudging satisfaction and grim foreboding in equal measure that - yes - he had found the motive. The victims *were* murdered, and their body parts harvested for part of some modern-day voodoo sacrifice and that knowledge left him cold.

*

'I been waiting here for two goddamn hours,' Lionel grumbled as Eve turned the corner into Magnolia Street and found him sitting on an ice box outside Brothers Discount Market.

'What else have you got to do, old man? I couldn't get away, ok?' Eve answered by way of an apology. 'Besides we've got problems.'

Lionel spat on the sidewalk. 'I gots problems, you gots problems. We all gots problems, honey. All I wants to know is, do you gots the goods or not?'

'Here,' Eve replied, pulling a big Tupperware box from her shoulder bag.

Lionel's eyes lit up like a child's in a candy store. 'Mmm. That's it, honey. What do we got?'

'Another hand. Male. Twenty-six. Heroin overdose. And a penis…. also, male.'

'Funny,' Lionel said flatly. 'How'd he die?'

'Stabbed. He was nineteen.'

'Sounds good,' Lionel said as he snatched the box from Eve's hands. She shuddered slightly as his fingers brushed against hers. 'Usual fee?' Lionel asked and produced a wad of dirty twenty-dollar notes from his trouser pocket.

'So, listen, we're not doing this again,' Eve said, trying to sound authoritative. 'The cops have been looking at the records at work. I'll be struck off if I get caught.'

Lionel made a face like he was sucking a lemon. 'Never bothered you before, cher.'

'Well, it does now!' Eve snapped. 'So just give me my freaking money, ok?'

'How 'bout we call it a round five hundred dollars?' Lionel crooned, holding out the cash. '*If* you can remember that policeman's name? How 'bout that?'

'*Her* name is Delgado. Welcome to the twenty first century,' she replied sourly.

Lionel nodded. 'Delgado. OK, then. It was a pleasure doing business with y'all, Miss Carmel. See y'around.'

He turned to leave, but Eve stopped him. 'Wait. I know you're just a middleman, but... tell me who you work for... I... I've got to know.'

'Why you so in'erested all a sudden? Y'all couldn't wait to leave ten seconds ago. You been talking to this policewoman? You tryin' to cover your lilywhite ass?'

'No,' Eve answered. 'She's been rattling my boss's cage. Just tell me. What do you want with the bones? What are you into?'

Lionel took a deep breath and cast his yellow eyes up and down the street in case anybody else might be listening.

'Look here, young lady,' he whispered. 'Me telling you what I does with these old bones and the like ain't gonna help nobody, is it? Trus' me when I says that it's best for everybody – 'specially you – if you *don't* know. Some things are best kept *secret*.' Lionel straightened up and pulled a pair of plastic thrift-shop sunglasses from the pocket of his waistcoat. 'Now you be sure and pass a nice night, y'hear?'

*

Sitting in his truck in the parking lot of Crescent City Steaks, Scott Capshaw nursed a warm beer while he waited for the sun to go down. He checked his cell to see if Sherrie had replied about the party at Chad Minton's place - his parents were away for the weekend and Chad was throwing a kegger. Scott was hoping he might get lucky for a second time. She hadn't replied.

His circle of friends was shrinking: kids he used to hang out with were now knuckling down for finals and making career decisions. Those that still liked to party often assumed he would be busy working or plain forgot to invite him along. And as for the girls, Scott knew that couldn't compete with the war of attrition from the guys in class. A year earlier, Scott had thought he hated college – but in hindsight, he realized that dropping out might not have been the smartest move. Finding a decent job hadn't been easy either. Scott had imagined he would breeze into an undemanding position with WWLTV or the Times-Pic. He'd written stuff as a kid after all and given his love of basketball and football, the idea of being a sports reporter held some appeal. After a month of woeful interviews around the city, however, he knew his options were limited. Scott took a ramp-service position at the airport. Two weeks of night shifts, hauling baggage on to cargo dollies was more than he could take. He called in sick, never went back, and opted instead for a delivery job at Gornall's Poultry Farm out in Chalmette where his cousin Beatrice worked. Six dollars, twenty-five an hour and a two dozen eggs *lagniappe* every Saturday night. Scott turned up the music to drown out the sound of the clucking in the back and crushed his empty can against the dash. The 'fucking shitty' dial was stuck on some 'lame-ass old person' radio station, so Scott had to listen to a random old woman crooning about her loser boyfriend.

His last delivery of the day to another of these fruit-loop urban farmers who thought they could single-handedly beat the global economic crisis by raising a few chickens in a backyard coop. Today's bozo had agreed to pay twenty percent extra to have his birds delivered after sunset. It was already gone seven, an hour past punching-out, and the sun was still winking in Scott's rear view mirror.

'Fuck it,' he said to himself, before starting up the chicken-mobile and pulling out of the parking lot. The address was only a couple of blocks over – Scott had already checked it out so that he could make a quick getaway once the job was done. He parked up on the curb, pulled the peak of his Gornall's Poultry cap down low and wandered 'round to the front door, boarded over and whitewashed. Nobody answered when he hammered on the door but peering through a crack in the chipboard nailed over a bay window, Scott could have sworn he saw somebody moving inside. He leaned in for a closer look...

'Hey sonny. What can I do yo fo'?' came a voice behind Scott.

'Jesus, dude, you scared the shit out of me!' he cried before he remembered himself. 'I mean, hello, sir. Are you the proprietor?'

'That's me,' said the man and grinned widely, revealing a row of perfect teeth, which jarred with the rest of his appearance. He was wearing old leather sandals and a filthy brown rain-slicker over a pair of dungarees. 'You's the chicken boy,' he said, looking Scott up and down with his pale eyes. 'You gots my birds?'

'Yes sir,' Scott replied, recoiling from the intense scrutiny. 'I'll go get them.'

'What's the rush, sonny? Sit awhile,' the man suggested, gesturing to a rusting bench on the porch. 'Have another beer,' he said with a wink.

'I'll get the chickens first, if that's ok,' Scott said. 'Where do you want them?'

'I keep them 'round the back.'

Scott ran to the truck and opened the back doors. The fourteen hens started at the noise, squawking and flapping in their individual metal cages. Scott tentatively popped a latch and reached inside: after only a few months on the job, he still found it difficult to handle the birds without being pecked or scratched. In his first week, a rooster buried one of its spurs deep into the flesh of his wrist. The scar was still white against his suntan.

'Let *me*, boy,' the man said, appearing at the back of the truck and blocking out the last of the daylight. Scott had already met a lot of strange folks on his rounds, mainly men who lived alone in dilapidated farmhouses out in Saint Bernard county; men who spent too little time around others, or too much with their livestock. But something about this guy's manner put Scott's nerves on edge. It seemed he was watching his every move, sizing him up.

'See, when the sun goes down,' he drawled, 'chickens starts thinking 'bout roostin' 'n' all. They gets ready *fais do-do* and you can do jus' 'bout whatever you wants with 'em.'

He pulled a fat Ameraucana from its cage, drowsy and docile, as though she had been tranquilized, and proceeded to do the same with five more, holding them upside down between his fingers, soothing them all in hushed tones as he did so.

'Back in two thousand five, the storm blew down a whole bunch o' fences, all over town,' he said. 'Chickens done got loose from theys coops. Black chickens, white chickens, red chickens, hens, roosters, you names it. Anyways, you can guess what happens next with them chickens, strong young Johnny Cockeroo like you, full o' spunk,' he cooed, his pale eyes twinkling. 'I bet you got a girl who knows some tricks…'

Scott thought of Sherrie: the hot night back in June when, drunk on tequila, she pulled off her clothes, straddled him on Jayden Peter's parents' bed and let him go all the way. Before that night, he had never seen dark blue underwear – he thought it was always white or black or red. White or black or red.

'That's right, sonny,' the man said, his deep voice reverberating inside the truck. 'Soon enough, there was chickens everywheres. White uns, black uns, even red chickens. White, black and red.'

White, black, red. Scott felt his heart beating low in his chest and a heaviness in his arms and legs. *The white of the man's teeth as he spoke.* He tried to focus on the words, but they seemed disconnected – he found himself lost in the silence between them. *The black of his eyes, dark and deep as wells.* Scott's fingers tingled with pins and needles. *The red of the hens' combs and wattles.*

'… and that's the way it was. Course the dogs rule the roost now and you can't jus' scoops up wild chickens off the street no more. I gots to buy 'em, don' I?' the man said with a shrug.

'I guess,' Scott replied, his throat dry and his tongue slack.

The man flicked his dreadlocks away from his face and jumped down from the truck, holding three birds in each hand. With long strides he carried them through a yard of withering corn stalks to the back door of the house and placed them inside.

'Ain't you got a coop?' Scott asked when he returned for six more.

'Don't need one. Them chickens gon' live with me.'

'In your house?' Scott asked.

'Oh, they ain't gon' live too long, sonny,' he said cheerily. 'You good with two?'

Scott carried a pair of hens through the back door and placed them sleeping on the floor with the others. In the fading twilight, he stole a glance into the darkness within the house. A pig's head stared back at him from the corner of the room, where it hung on a silver coat rack. There was graffiti on the walls - elaborate crosses, moons and snakes - and the floor was slick with chicken-shit and entrails. The smell was overwhelming. The man appeared behind him again, silhouetted against the sunset, his hands braced across the door frame, blocking Scott's exit.

'How 'bout that beer?'

'I've gotta run, I'll just get your bill,' Scott replied, thinking on his feet, and squeezing out into the fresh air. The man sloped after him, pulling piles of crumpled dollar notes from the pockets of his dungarees and sucking on his teeth.

'How much do I owe y'all, boy?'

In the front seat of the truck, Scott picked up the delivery notes. 'Twenty bucks delivery for one and nine dollars every extra chicken, so seven Ameraucana and seven Wyandotte…'

'… seven black and seven white…' the man smiled.

'… yeah, plus ten dollars for the late delivery, so that's a hundred and forty-seven dollars. Please,' Scott said, trying to be polite but wanting nothing more than to be driving far, far away.

'That's one hunnerd and fifty right there. No need to count it. This,' he said holding up a dirty ten-dollar bill, 'is for yo' trouble.'

'That's very nice of you, sir,' Scott said, pocketing the

cash. 'Can I get your signature here please?' he pointed to the dotted line with his pen.

'You sure about that beer now, *Scott*?' the man asked as he wrote.

'Like, how d'you know my name, mister?'

He tapped the pen against the badge on Scott's chest and grinned widely again as he handed back the clipboard. 'Jus' a parlor trick, sonny.'

'Right. Have a good evening, sir.' Scott climbed into the cab and started the engine.

'You too Scotty.' The man leaned against the open window of the truck. '*Good luck with Sherrie!*'

Scott shifted into gear and pulled away. The sun had gone down, but there was still light in the sky. In his side mirror, he saw the man standing in the yard, in his rain slicker, one arm raised.

'Jus' a parlor trick son,' he yelled, 'Jus' a parlor trick!'

Scott shuddered involuntarily. 'You are a freak of nature, mister…' he looked down at the clipboard on the passenger seat. The name was scrawled across the entire page in childish handwriting.

ike sugar

three

Dale Kastelein was trying to pretend he wasn't crying, but Eve Carmel had made plenty of married men weep in her time - one way or another - and she wasn't particularly fazed by the spectacle. 'Come on Dale, keep it together,' she said, patting him on the back while she scanned the floor of his office for her bra. Just before he came, she'd managed to persuade him to produce the purchase orders for the body parts she'd sold to Lionel Root. Her plan was to wrap up her rendezvous with Kastelein, who in spite of his tears had proven himself a surprisingly energetic lover, and head back to work to file the papers in the relevant patient records. 'Easy as pie,' Eve said aloud.

'Damn air-conditioning,' Dale sniffed. 'I'll have to have a word with the maintenance guys. It *always* affects me like this. This is *normal*. This happens like, five times a day.'

'Yeah, whatever,' Eve muttered, checking her cellphone. 'Listen, I've got to get back to the office and pull a late one, so how about you print off those orders for me. I've got a list. Dates referenced with body parts,' She pulled the file out of her bag.

'Why am I doing this again?' Dale asked, red-eyed.

'Because an hour ago, you hadn't had a blowjob in - what? - a decade?' She handed him a pen. 'Now get busy and I might make time for another.'

*

It was nearly midnight when she wearily pushed open

the door to her apartment building in the Warehouse District. The Coroner's Office was only a few blocks away, but she'd caught a cab home, and nearly fallen asleep on the ten-minute ride. New Orleans was officially the murder capital of the country and the NOCO was open twenty-four-seven, 365 days of the year. Slipping into the office to 'catch up on some paperwork' was not a problem. The night shift - Doctor Moira and the two Toms - didn't even bat an eyelid.

Although she knew she only had herself to blame, she still hated Walt Forager for catching her out. Finding the appropriate patient files and adding Kastelein's purchase orders to each turned out to be a royal pain in the ass. Some of the records had already been digitally updated, so her precious paper copies were all but useless. Over the last two years, her dirty business with Lionel Root had proven very lucrative, and nobody really cared if some dead crackhead or streetwalker was buried whole or in pieces. Or did they?

She'd become complacent. In the early days, when Root had first approached her – asked around and picked her out as the one pathologist on the team who might be willing to make some money on the side – she had been scrupulous, meticulously keeping her records up to date, terrified that somebody would uncover her secret.

But after the first few months of effective bodysnatching, she realized that nobody in the Coroner's Office was interested, especially not Forager. The guy was a relic of a bygone era, bumbling around the corridors like a Parkinsonian relative, lost in suburbia. He couldn't keep a handle on the hair growing out of his ears, never mind the computer records. He was the reason the staff turnover was so high and there was no money for new lab equipment.

The team needed focused management and direction, but what they got was a pathetic, 'keep-at-it' work ethic reminiscent of the Great Depression and a misguided belief in the good of others, particularly politicians. Her co-workers had too much to do, too busy coping with the daily influx of fresh corpses to worry about anybody else's workload.

Back in January, Eve had sawn off a drug-addict's hands while Ruth Berry - the senior pathologist at the time - did a Sudoku on her cigarette break. Tom Dubas, her tech-assistant during a weekend shift, actually helped her to remove the lips and eyelids from a homeless bum. Tom had talked incessantly about seeing Big Sam's Funky Nation at the Preservation Hall while he labeled up the specimen jars.

Eve's thoughts turned back to Root. 'No questions asked' - that had always been the deal, and Lionel paid her well for her silence. But in two years she never did manage to find out what he was up to, and probably never would. Her theories may have provided the foundation for a couple of her Gothica novels, but for somebody with such an inquisitive mind, the lack of real answers gave her a nasty itch that needed to be scratched.

The package she found tucked in her mailbox between a credit card bill and a bunch of flyers for local fast-food joints was more than a pleasant surprise. Her name was scrawled in red ink on the front - no stamp or sender's address - but she knew immediately it was from him and hoped it might bring her some closure at least, if not a decent storyline for one of her books.

With new-found energy, Eve trotted up the two flights of stairs to her apartment and let herself in. She dumped her bag and jacket and flopped on to the sofa so she could savor the moment of opening the mysterious parcel. The brown paper was torn, but the red wax seal was still intact. It cracked satisfyingly beneath her thumbnail. She carefully tore away the paper and the contents fell onto her lap. It was a bracelet of sorts, the kind a child might make: odds and ends of string and twine, twisted together and hung with tiny black feathers and strips of leather. Eve checked the package again for a note, but there was none – just her name scrawled in red ink several times on the paper, and the bracelet, which she slipped on to her wrist without a thought. It reminded her of something from a new age craft fair, one of those supposedly Native American dreamcatchers, only less gaudy, more sickeningly authentic. In her line of work, she had seen, smelt and touched things which would have turned the average person's stomach, but as she rubbed a diamond of the pinkish leather between her thumb and forefinger, its coarse texture was enough to make her retch. 'Hideous' she said aloud in the empty apartment and tossed it into the bowl with her keys and loose change.

As she peeled off her clothes, Eve caught a whiff of Dale Kastelein's cologne and realized with a hint of self-loathing that she could still taste him. Though she wanted nothing more than to crawl into bed and sleep until Sunday, a shower was in order. She padded naked into the bathroom and while she waited for the hot water to come through, felt the first unmistakable scratch at the back of her throat: the ticklish precursor to a cold.

'Well, that's just fucking *great*,' she said to nobody, opening her mouth as wide as possible and staring at her tonsils in the mirror for any sign of inflammation. Not surprising, she thought, given the stress at work, the late hours and the changing of the season. There was a chill in the air on the way home. She washed down two Tylenol extra with a handful of tap water and jumped in the steaming shower, hoping she could nip the infection in the bud before it ruined her weekend.

The jets felt wonderful as they pummeled her tired shoulders and neck, the water ran down the sleek contours of her body, but as she lifted her hands to wash her hair, Eve felt suddenly dizzy and thought for a moment she might pass out. She crouched in the shower tray and put her head between her legs waiting for the sensation to pass, hearing her pulse thrumming in her ears and trying to keep calm. Eve had no idea how long she remained in that position, slipping in and out of consciousness, and only came to her senses again as the hot water began to run cold. Shivering, she crawled from the cubicle, her joints aching, hastily wrapped herself in two towels, twisted another around her wet hair, and shuffled to her bedroom like a woman three times her age. Her face was burning, her throat constricting and she fell on to the bed and rolled the covers around her still wet body, unable to maintain a cogent line of thought but cursing a chimeric hallucination of Dale Kastelein, Walt Forager and Lionel Root.

*

'Hey!' Zam Delgado said with a wide grin. 'I was kinda having this bet with myself that you wouldn't show.'

'F'true?' Brad said, folding his newspaper and returning the smile. 'So, I guess you lost then?'

'Part of me won,' Zam replied. 'Where y'at? It's good to see you.'

'You too,' Brad stood and kissed her on the cheek, thinking - possibly - that she was hitting on him. Just a little.

'What's with the suit?' she asked him. 'You look like you're going to a funeral.' Her face dropped suddenly, 'Oh shit, you're not, are you?'

'No,' Brad laughed. 'This old thing? Hell, I'm not sure really. I always used to wear a suit for work. It just seems... right, I guess. I basically spend my life in jeans and sweatpants anyways. I thought this might make a change.'

'Well, you're looking sharp. For an old guy. Did you order yet?' Zam asked, as she sat down and rolled her chewing gum into a paper napkin.

'Only coffee, I was waiting for you,' Brad replied. 'I'd forgotten how much I used to love this place.'

'I know. I *totally* love it. I'd come here every day if I could, but I'd be the size of a house in a month.'

A heavyset waitress arrived on cue. 'Ya need a refill, hon?' she yelled at Brad, before taking their orders: three eggs over easy, hot sausage, grits and toast for him; silver dollar pancakes for her.

Betsy's was practically an institution in the Crescent City, one of the last true American diners: the kind of place where the clientele consisted of city officials, high court judges, cops, construction workers and college kids who the 'take it or leave it' servers called by their first names. The food was cheap and plentiful, the coffee pot was bottomless, and the bar was fully stocked, which always appealed to Brad. He remembered hearing through the grapevine that Betsy herself had been beaten to death by burglars in her own home back in 2008. They forced her to open her safe, then fractured her skull, broke her ribs, and left her for dead. There was a large portrait of her hanging on the wall, right next to the restrooms.

'So, is it weird being back?' Zam asked, dragging Brad

back to the moment.

'Yeah, it's real weird being back in the house. Doesn't feel like my place at all. The decorators did a decent job though.'

'Thinking of selling up?'

'Maybe. This would be the perfect opportunity. But, you know, this is my hometown. I don't know if I want to cut ties completely. We've got to sort some shit out,' Brad said.

'We?'

'Me and New Orleans,' Brad replied, though he instantly thought of Elaine. He couldn't help but wonder what she was doing at that very moment.

'Ah yeah. Well, I guess you two go back a ways and breaking up is hard to do, so they say.'

'Neil Sedaka, 1962'

Muh!' Zam groaned, 'You and the sixties music!'

'Got the seven-inch,' Brad said proudly.

'Good for you, hipcat. Now - enough chit-chat - what have you got for me?' Zam asked, leaning forward hopefully.

'I got a few thoughts.' Brad lowered his voice in spite of the din in the café. 'Let's state the obvious first of all: we're looking for a male, probably between twenty and forty, although I'd say the younger end of that scale, wouldn't you?'

Zam nodded and Brad continued.

'Um… not physically strong - he chose these victims because they wouldn't put up much of a fight. But he's fully prepared for the act itself. He used two weapons on Nadia Romero - scissors for the pubic hair and a big, heavy blade for the hand. Same with the librarian - scissors and a knife.' He took a sip of coffee.

'Then there's the mess. You cut off a person's ears -' Brad stopped suddenly as the waitress appeared with their breakfasts. She stared at Brad with a look of disgust.

'Oh... thank you. This looks delicious,' he said effusively as she set down the plates, but she gave him the stink eye and stomped off without a word.

Brad salted his grits. 'What was I saying?'

Zam groaned in ecstasy through her first mouthful of hot, buttered pancakes and mumbled 'cutting off ears...'

'Right. Cut off a person's ears, cut out their eyes, heart, whatever.... my point is, he's not walking away clean. He has to have made provisions for the mess. A change of clothes, a raincoat, I don't know. Likewise, to carry his *keepsakes* away. Sure, maybe he sticks them in with his groceries, but that level of planning and preparation shows intellect - he's not a blunt tool, this one.'

'You *have* to try these,' Zam said, spearing a chunk of pancake. Brad willingly leaned over and allowed Zam to push her proffered forkful into his mouth.

'Jeez. They *are* good,' Brad said as he chewed. 'I might have to go for round two.'

'So, you don't think our guy is just an opportunist? Killing at random? Pass the syrup please.'

'Not entirely. He takes risks, but they're calculated risks. He's ready to rock and roll like *that*,' Brad snapped his fingers. 'He killed the girl - Erica - in broad daylight in the middle of a park. He knows what he's doing.'

'So, what *is* he doing?'

'Ah. That's where it gets tricky,' Brad said, dipping a chunk of toast in a perfect egg yolk while he chose his words.

'Come on,' Zam said, 'don't keep a girl waiting...'

'OK, listen. I'm going to say something. I'm just going

to throw it out there. Don't freak out.'

'OK. Go for it,' Zam said, sipping her coffee.

Brad took a deep breath. 'Voodoo.'

'Voodoo,' Zam replied flatly. 'Is that it? What a peak behind the curtain. Well, I'm not freaking out.'

'Don't be like that. I think.... we have... to start considering some alternative explanations,' Brad shook his spoon to stress his point.

'Like voodoo?'

'Maybe,' Brad shrugged, suddenly unsure of himself. 'You have to admit, there are certain... elements to this case that defy logic. You said that yourself.'

'On day one, I did,' Zam nodded, 'but seriously, what are you suggesting?'

'What do you know about voodoo? Really.'

'I don't know,' Zam said, looking around to make sure nobody was eavesdropping. 'Isn't it all sticking pins in dolls? Zombies? Devil-worship?'

'No. You're talking about *hoodoo*.'

'Voodoo, hoodoo, *tomayto*, *tomahto*. What's the difference?' Zam asked.

Brad took a breath, 'Big difference actually. Voodoo's a religion. Hoodoo is...' he struggled to find the word, 'black magic, I suppose. Same roots, but somewhere along the way, the two got confused.'

'So?'

'Voodoo started in Africa, spread to the Americas with the slave trade, diverged, evolved, mixed with local folk religions, mixed with Catholicism in some places, kept some of its traditions, lost others...'

'Get to the point, Bradley,' Zam said, stifling a yawn.

'I'm getting there. Okay, do the terms '*juju*' or '*muti*' mean anything to you?'

'Juju maybe,' Zam shook her head in exasperation. 'Christ, I don't know, man. Where are you going with all this?'

'Just hear me out,' Brad placated her. '*Muti*, *juju* – I'm talking about traditional African medicine usually performed by witchdoctors. Physical and spiritual healing. Protecting warriors, lifting curses, whatever.'

'That's nice.' Zam had lost interest and gestured to the waitress for more coffee.

Brad pressed on. 'Obviously these witchdoctors back home use whatever's available – plants, roots, minerals, but in some areas of Africa - those where voodoo also originated - sometimes animal or even *human* body parts are used.'

Zam's eyes met Brad's. 'Say that again.'

'They're called *muti* killings. People are murdered for their body parts.'

'Like human sacrifice?' Zam asked.

'No, it's not like that. The killing itself isn't religious. Only the body parts hold any significance. It breaks down like this: let's say you own a business, but profits are down...'

'It's a global crisis,' Zam added.

'... so, you go to see your local witchdoctor, who tells you, for a price, that you need to get hold of a hand - a dead one, that is - and touch all your products with it, or bury it in the ground in front of your store to attract more customers. Whatever. Of course, if you can't do the deed yourself, then the witchdoctor can.'

'For a price,' Zam added.

'You got it,' Brad nodded. 'And certain parts of the body carry a big price tag.'

The pair sat in silence for a few moments, as Zam absorbed the impact of Brad's words.

'This sounds like it might have legs,' Zam said.

'Not the best choice of words, detective.'

'What about the virginity angle?'

'Yes,' Brad nodded, 'children are often targeted for *muti* murders, not just because they're easier to overpower but also because it's *believed*, by those in the know, that kids still have most of their 'lifeforce'.'

Zam raised an eyebrow questioningly.

'Lifeforce. Like health or... energy.'

'*Muti* mojo,' Zam said.

'Right. Anyway, listen to this,' he said, picking up his notes for the first time. '*Children and virgins are thought to have more power than those who are sexually active. Their screams wake the spirits and make the muti more powerful.*'

'Nice. Where did you get that?'

'Some website called.... Wikipedia?' Brad wondered if he was pronouncing it correctly.

'Is it me, or did it just get cold in here?' Zam said, trying unsuccessfully to lighten the mood.

'I know,' Brad replied, 'I've spent most of the weekend poring over this stuff. It doesn't get any better, trust me. I've made some notes, but there's not a lot of information on the web. Not from the source anyway, as you can imagine. But there have been *muti*-style killings outside Africa. Europe mainly.'

'But that doesn't explain *how* he's killing people.'

'What can I tell you?' Brad shrugged, wide-eyed. 'This is not your regular madman with a machete. We're talking about somebody sacrificing virgins to... I don't know... appease his gods?'

'Wait, let me get this straight: do you honestly think we're dealing with the *paranormal*?' Zam whispered.

'I'm leaning towards hypnosis or psychokinesis... More *supernatural* than *paranormal*, I suppose.'

'Oh, that's comforting.'

'Yeah well, run it by Forager. He must have seen some strange things in his time. Maybe he can throw some light on it. How did it go on Saturday by the way?' Brad asked.

'It was... frustrating,' Zam decided. 'He was more interested in covering his ass than helping me out. The computer records are a mess, but I couldn't fault him for his paperwork: all present and correct. He's old school.'

'I sense there's a 'but'...'

'*But*, I got the feeling that somebody's hiding something. The Coroner's Office has this long-standing arrangement with some biological test center over in Elmwood. Forager says this 'Syngenta' regularly purchases - quote - 'unwanted materials' - unquote, for testing.'

'Unwanted materials?' I guess that's any old limbs and organs to you and me?' Brad said and Zam nodded.

'Coincidence?' he asked.

'Could be, but here's something else - I noticed the same name on the bottom of every purchase order: Eve Carmel.'

'Who's she?'

'Some pathologist at the N.O.C.O.,' Zam answered, as she mopped up her syrup with the last of her pancake. 'Doesn't that strike you as odd?'

'Not necessarily. Maybe she just has final sign-off on the Syngenta deals.'

'Nope. She's just a minion, only been working with Walt since 2007.'

'So, lean on her,' Brad said. 'See if she squeals.'

'Tried to. We couldn't get hold of her at the weekend. Not important. We'll find her. In the meantime, Rubino's cross-checking her documents against the full dataset of incomplete corpses. I'm sure there are more out there.'

A man on the next table accidently knocked a

saltcellar to the floor and an eerie silence followed the sound of ceramic shattering.

'So, you think this is what we're dealing with?' Zam asked. Brad nodded slowly, his mind somewhere else.

'OK. I'll get on it. I should get going anyway. This for me?' she said, pointing at Brad's folder.

'Yep, that's yours. I've got a copy of my own,' he said, shuffling together the papers and grainy black and white printouts of masked witchdoctors and dismembered torsos. 'And don't forget these,' he handed over the six case files.

'Thanks. Listen, if there are any more results... well, you're not heading straight back to Florida, are you?' Zam asked.

'I'll probably stick around for a couple days, now I'm here,' Brad replied, trying to sound nonchalant.

'Yeah, yeah, yeah,' Zam said.

'One taste of Betsy's pancakes was all it took,' he laughed, happy to change the subject.

Zam gestured for the check. 'I'll give you a call later today. Don't skip town, okay?'

'Yes ma'am.'

She left a twenty on the table and breezed through the crowded café and out into the morning as though she were heading to the hair salon or the movies, and not to begin the hunt for a killer. Outside, she waved as she passed by the window, and for a moment, Brad felt he had stepped back in time – he was still a detective, she was still a rookie. He accepted that he had been looking forward to seeing her again.

The waitress appeared again at his side, holding the coffee jug, her eyebrows raised.

'Yes please, sweetheart,' he said and opened his copy of the Times Picayune. Traffic closures and mudslides. A two-year-old boy had been shot dead in Central City 'when people in two vehicles traded gunfire' and a man in drag who robbed a Burger King at gunpoint had been sentenced to two-hundred and forty-seven years in prison.

'You couldn't make it up,' Brad muttered to himself. He flicked to the back pages and was picking through the weekend's football results when he had the unmistakable sensation that he was being watched. On the other side of the café, Auden Tillery wiped the corners of his mouth, dropped the napkin on his empty plate and walked over to Brad's table.

'Didn't you used to be Detective Durand?' he smirked.

'Tillery,' Brad replied, folding his paper and sighing deeply.

'It's *Commander* Tillery now,' he said, puffing out his chest slightly.

'Not to me, it isn't. You look like you're about to invade Czechoslovakia. Don't sit down. I'm leaving.'

'So, Bradley,' Tillery began, taking a seat. 'What brings you back to town? The company? Was that Detective Delgado I saw a moment ago?'

'Is this an official interrogation?' Brad asked.

'That depends on whether or not you're interfering with an *official* investigation?'

'No, just catching up with an old friend.'

Auden nodded. 'How's your wife? Still suffering from that *mystery illness*?' he asked, wide-eyed, as though he were referring to Munchausen's syndrome. That one hit home, and Brad struggled to hold it together.

'Seriously though, why are you here, Durand? *'You'll see me in hell, before you see me back in New Orleans'* - that's what you told me. Just before your tribunal. Remember?'

'Don't push me, Tillery,' Brad smiled, but his eyes were stone. 'I'll rip your throat out.'

Auden just smiled back. 'I'd like to see you try. I really would. That's the D.A. sitting with Judge Cooley.' He pointed. 'Do you know him?'

Brad didn't answer.

'No, I guess not. Different circles, these days. Now,' he said, straightening up and adjusting his tie, 'why don't you crawl back to that Alabama shithole you call home?'

'It's Florida, actually,' Brad replied.

'Ah, but still a shithole,' Tillery said with a wide grin and turned on his heel. Brad had to watch while he glad-handed the District Attorney, the two of them laughing at a shared joke. Tillery winked at Brad and walked out.

Brad buried his head in the newspaper again, trying to focus on an article about plans for a new shopping mall, but it was useless. It seemed inevitable that he would run into Tillery at some point, but he wished it could have waited until he was ready for the confrontation. An uncomfortable night's sleep on a fold-up camping cot had done him no favors. The old house was cold and bare, cleaned-out and redecorated, all ready for a new family and a new life. But it only stirred up Brad's memories of bad times, hang-ups about his marriage and the horror of Katrina. It felt like a crime-scene that had been processed and concluded, but the new wooden flooring and pristine magnolia walls couldn't cover up the stains of his memories.

He'd driven over late on Sunday night, five hours non-stop from the Panhandle, across the narrow coastal strips of Lower Alabama and Mississippi, the sun setting all the way, and back to his true home, the city that had broken his heart, with a head full of dead bodies and severed limbs. The house was empty and though he didn't intend to throw any dinner parties, he needed the bare necessities: a fridge for his beer and a chair to sit in while he drank it. Everything else would fall into place.

*

'You did the right thing, Odeo.'

'Yeah well, what do I know about all this mumbo-jumbo? Call in the professionals, I say. Let's exorcize the shit outta this place,' Odeo replied, massaging his temples with his fingertips to hold in the headache. The weekend's takings had been painfully low again, and after their talk on Friday morning, he had convinced himself that Lionel was right: this was more than just a streak of bad luck - he *had* to have been cursed.

'That's it. *Professional*. That's it,' Lionel nodded. 'My man is *indeed* a professional. Now, you listen to ol' Lionel. We don't knows whoever done *fixed* you, maybe we never will, but you bes' be sure that hoodoo curse needs *liftin'*. My man believes that a powerful *gris-gris* will do the trick, easy enough.'

'What's a 'gree-gree'?'

Lionel chuckled to himself. 'How long did y'all live in New Orleans? For a smart man, Odeo, you sure is *stupid* sometimes. A *gris-gris* is nothin' more than a lucky charm which you wears about yoursel'. Put it in your pocket every day or 'round your neck, keep it close - it works better if it's touching your skin. See,' Lionel lifted his shirt and sucking in his pale, hairless belly, reached into his trousers to reveal a small, dirty felt bag tied around one of the belt loops and pressed against his pelvis.

'This here is mine' he exclaimed proudly, undoing the knot and placing it on the silver tabletop. 'Don't you be touchin' it now. You be breakin' *my* hoodoo.'

'Oh, I won't,' Odeo replied, curling one nostril in disgust. 'How long has that thing been... down there?'

'Jeez, I don't know. Years, I s'pose. But I'll tell you this much – this lil' ol' *gris-gris* pulled me back from the edge. The man who made this for me – the man who's gon' make yours - he done restored my faith in voodoo. I was *lost*. I was *shipwrecked*. That man done turned my life 'round.'

Stunned by the depth of Lionel's belief in the little bag of tricks, Odeo didn't know what to say. Did the old man really think this baloney could change the fortunes of his club? 'What's in it?' he asked, just to break the silence.

'Prob'ly best you don't know,' Lionel answered cautiously. 'Herbs and stones. Black salt. But I *consecrates* it every Sunday with a red candle and a little van van oil, jus' to *feed* it an' such, y'know? You'll need to do the same wi' yours. And personally, I likes to give mine a drop of jezebel root oil, 'cause I find that helps with my social agenda, if you catch my meanin'.'

'F'true?' Odeo replied, catching Lionel's meaning perfectly, but wishing he hadn't. 'So your guy is going to give me one of these?'

Lionel nodded.

'To wear?'

'Uh-huh. About yoursel'.'

'O-kay. And when do I get to meet him?'

'Oh, he don't do meeting much,' Lionel tutted.

'So, he won't be coming here? I thought he would be coming to do some voodoo shit around the club.'

'I don't think there's need for no cleansing of the vicinity,' Lionel answered, looking about him, as though he could actually *see* the evidence of bad juju around the strip-poles and sofas.

'So, what are you telling me man? You're just going to give a bag of herbs and salt, and I'm supposed to strap it to my crotch? And that's all there is to it.'

'Sure, that's all there is to it. You pays me, I pays him, you gets your *gris-gris*, lickety-split, no more hoodoo,' Lionel shrugged, like he was sharing a tip for removing a stain or mixing a perfect martini.

'Payment,' Odeo nodded, with a wry smile, 'of course. So, what's the going rate for a *gris-gris* these days anyway?'

'Well now, y'all can take your chances with that twenty-dollar *bull*-shit they peddle down Bourbon Street, but this here is the real…'

'*Combien?*' Odeo interrupted.

'Five hunnerd dollars.'

'Five hundred dollars?!' he spat. 'For a bag of potpourri? Are you out of your goddamn *mind*? Do you know how much I have to spend on liquor every week?'

'No, but I reckon you drinks most of it,' Lionel replied bluntly. 'You carry on like that, you ain't gonna have no customers to worry 'bout, hoodoo or no hoodoo.'

'Well, that's… about what…' Odeo sputtered something inaudible. 'Listen, you can tell your man, if he expects me to part with five hundred bucks, he best get his tail down here and show me he's good for it. I want *results*,' Odeo said, stabbing the table with his finger to emphasize his point. 'Then I pay.'

*

Officer Rubino tapped lightly on the window of Zam's Honda, trying not to spill anything from the two paper cups he was holding. Zam leaned over to open the door and let him in.

'What have you got for me?' she asked.

'Café au lait.'

'I meant updates on the case, but thanks,' Zam smiled. 'Any news?'

'Uh-huh. I cross-checked Carmel's list against Forager's database like you told me to. I only went back as far as the Favreau case. The records were outsourced to a federal data service after Katrina. The money ran out in 2006. That's why they're all so screwed up. Some here, some there...' Rubino spread his hands by way of explanation.

'Yeah, yeah. That's fine. What did you find?'

'Four more,' Rubino answered. 'Just like you said. One in 2007, two in 2008, one last year.'

Zam felt elated to hear that there was more evidence in support of her theory, but sick that she had been right: she was dealing with a serial killer. 'OK, give me the details,' she said, blowing the steam off her coffee.

'Let's see,' Rubino said, checking through his notes, 'OK, working backwards, first up is Ralph Miner, um, seventeen years of age at the time of his death, which was August thirtieth, last year.'

'How'd he die?'

'Some kind of fire at the Six Flags Amusement Park,' Rubino read.

'Witnesses?'

'Nope. Something of a loner, liked to visit abandoned places, you know, weirdo geek stuff. The report said he probably lost his hands – both of them, that is – in some kind of explosion.'

'Kids these days. Sounds plausible,' Zam shrugged.

'No sign of any explosives though: no fireworks, no lighter fuel, nothing. But his body burned hot and it burned fast,' Rubino referred back to his notebook 'Close to the temperature of melting sand.'

'Was Ralph a fat kid? When a person catches fire, the

body is kept alight by their own fats melting. Maybe he was carrying a lot of fuel.'

'That is... just *so* gross,' Rubino replied. 'I don't know, I'll have to check.'

'Fine, who's next?' Zam asked.

'Um... September seven, 2008. Kimberly Kelly, female. A fifteen-year-old runaway. Listed as a missing person in Jackson, Mississippi since January of that year. Found dead near the train station.'

'Cause of death?'

'Hypothermia. In September. Seriously?' Rubino made a face.

'Strange, but not impossible. Go on,' Zam replied.

'She was missing her lips and ears. The pathologist thought they had been eaten by a stray dog. Forensics found canine hairs on the victim's clothes and face – no great surprise if the body had been lying on a city street for any amount of time, you might say, but - get this - according to the report, these showed traces of formaldehyde.'

'Who brings a stuffed dog to a murder?' Zam asked, bemused.

'I know, right?' Rubino laughed and then stifled it.

For the next twenty minutes, as they sat in the car on the corner, Zam drilled Rubino on the details of the other cases, until she had finally heard enough. She ran a hand across her face.

'Nice work, Jon. See if you can dig up the case files for me. I'd like to pick through them myself. Anything else?'

'The chief called. He wants to know how the Batiste case is progressing.'

'Batiste? Remind me,' Zam said, pinching the bridge of her nose.

'Royal Street. Single gunshot wound to the back. Wife

found him when she came home from work?'

'Right, right, right,' Zam said, nodding emphatically.

'It's the case I'm *supposed* to be working on. Remember? You're my supervising officer. The chief wants an update on all your cases soon as you come in.'

'Why do you think we're sitting in the car?' she answered curtly. 'Tremane Batiste was shot by his brother, who was having an affair with the wife.'

Rubino looked stunned. 'How…?'

'No breaking and entering. Nothing was stolen from the apartment. Perp was known to the victim. Single gunshot wound in the back? Sounds like something a sibling might do. Plus, he listed the victim's place as his current address on his statement – so he's planning to move in, if he hasn't already. Phone records – if you can get them - will probably show an unusual number of calls between the cellphones belonging to him and the wife. See if you can find the gun – these idiots will risk serious jail time rather than toss a piece they bought for a hundred dollars on the street. That should do it. There, I solved your case,' Zam said, throwing her coffee dregs out of the car window.

'Any chance you could help me with Francisco Pasamontes? Probably drug-related? Patrol pulled him out of the river a few weeks back,' Rubino asked.

'Sure, give me what you got and we'll figure it out,' Zam muttered, absent-mindedly wiping the dust from the air conditioning vents on the dash.

They sat in silence for a while, watching people passing by. An old woman was struggling to pull her shopping trolley up on to the curb.

'This is the safest corner in the whole city,' Zam said quietly.

Rubino scoffed, 'How'd you figure that?'

'You've got the Sheriff's Department behind us. The

Police Department,' she motioned with her head, 'and the Criminal Court right there. That's the Crimestoppers Center and a couple of bail bondsmen have offices just down the block.'

Rubino nodded but said nothing. She was right - there were never any junkies, gangsters or scumbags loitering 'round these parts.

'You really think this is the same guy?' Rubino asked, picking up his notes and pulling Zam back to the moment.

'Mmm,' she answered, biting her bottom lip. She swiveled in her seat to face him, 'It's the same guy all right. And the thing is Rubino, you can solve a hundred Batistes, but when something like these lands on your desk, you can't let it go. If I make this case, I'm looking at Lieutenant. In the entire history of the force, only two other women have commanded a district, did you know that?'

'I didn't know that.' Rubino let that sink in before asking, 'Is that all this means to you? Promotion?'

'No,' she answered, stung by the implication that her career meant more than anything else. 'No, Detective, I want to catch the bastard.'

*

''Plum Hush', 'Kinda Sexy', 'Lovelorn'…'

The words conjured up images of a life she hadn't yet discovered, but when she whispered them under her breath, a little of their meaning seemed to resonate within her.

''Pink Malibu', 'So Chaud', 'Rebel Spirit'…'

She caught a glimpse of herself in one of the tiny tester mirrors and saw the black eye her father had given her late last night. She had almost forgotten. He had been waiting for her when she came back from the club.

"Deep Attraction', 'Wild Honey', 'Hot Passion'...'

Monday morning, eleven seventeen. She would normally have been sitting at the back of double science, but instead Claudette Tremblay was standing in front of a bank of lipsticks in Ultra Beauty. Skipping school had been easy, but her shoulder bag bulged with her uniform and the rent-a-cops in the empty Elmwood Mall watched her closely to make sure she wasn't shoplifting. Claudette sauntered towards the displays of foundations and concealers to find something to cover up the purple bruising around her eye.

It had been a shitty weekend. Around ten o' clock on Friday, a squallish bout of wind and rain had blown in from the Lake and sent most of downtown's revelers into the usual hotspots or home. There was maybe a dozen crummy characters in Cheaters, so Claudette braved the conditions for another hour, shivering under an umbrella and soaking her faux-silk shoes before she called it a night. Odeo paid her for half a shift.

Saturday was no better, though she spent most of the day dozing in the house and watching cartoons with her little brother. She had planned to devote some serious time to flirting with Treyvon in the evening and dressed in her best in the hope of forcing his hand. He wanted to break the law with her, she knew it: he had a way of just looking at her that made her ache. Claudette wanted to be the release for all those years of his pent-up frustration. *Little shook-up soda pop, baby let me twist your top, drink you down and never stop...*' she sang quietly to herself as she dabbed the testers on the back of her hand, looking for the perfect match to her skin tone.

A skinny security guard sidled up: chinless and pock-marked, he wore a sparse mustache to boost his perceived masculinity. 'Need a hand with anything, doll-face?' he asked in a reedy voice, making no effort to hide the fact that he was staring at Claudette's chest. She just shook her head and said nothing, continuing to read the make-up labels until the silence between the two became uncomfortable. Chinless made a point of brushing up against her as he moved down the aisle.

'Boys,' she huffed under her breath.

Claudette wanted a *real* man for her first time, somebody who knew what they were doing, who would appreciate all she had to offer, but in spite of her best efforts on Saturday, Treyvon had spent most of the evening deep in conversation with two Mexicans under the blue light of Cheaters' neon sign. She had no doubt that they were drug dealers – Treyvon made no secret of the fact that he dabbled from time to time – but these guys were higher up the food chain than the usual jugglers her mother entertained. Sharp-dressed in dark suits and Cuban heels – one of them slipped Claudette a twenty-dollar bill from his silver money-clip and told her to 'fuck off while the grown-ups talk.'

Her stomach rumbled angrily. There was a Five Guys in the food court and Claudette had a yen for a bacon cheese dog and Cajun fries. Overwhelmed by choices, she picked up a mochaccino powder compact and headed to the sales counter. The assistant made an almost comical 'sad clown' face when she saw Claudette's eye.

'This is a good one though,' she cooed, 'this here has photo-*chro*-matic pigments that bend and reflect light to erase every flaw. Did you fall down some stairs or somethin' honey?'

Claudette's bottom-lip wobbled as she fought back

crocodile tears.

'He hit me,' she replied.

'Now, you hush now, sweetie. Here,' said the assistant, handing Claudette a Kleenex and patting her hand reassuringly. 'You ever worked in a store?' she asked as she scanned the compact. 'Well, let me tell you, in *this* store, we get *boo-coo* of what they call 'shrinkage'.'

'What's that?' Claudette sniffed.

'Shrinkage is just a fancy word that bosses use. It means like when stuff gets damaged coming from the warehouse or lost in the stockroom,' she tapped at the keys on her cash register, 'or sometimes, the cashiers in here just make mistakes. Y'all have a nice day now, sweetie,' she winked, bagged the make-up and handed it over.

Claudette dabbed at her eyes with the tissue, thanked the assistant profusely, and waved coquettishly to Chinless as she walked out, with her free light-bending mochaccino powder, and a clutch of stolen lipsticks stuffed in her school bag.

*

The trick to bleeding out a chicken, or any living thing for that matter, is preparation.

For Ike, the procedure had become second nature. Every morning, he scooped up one of the white-feathered birds from the back room, tucked it under his arm, and took it upstairs to his temple room, which had been a library of sorts in years gone by. The walls were lined with shelves, floor to ceiling, and old journals, accounting ledgers and archive records filled the top rows. Ike had been burning his way through the paperwork since he moved in a year earlier. It was good to have a place of his own, but the buildings in

New Orleans were not built for the cold, and the humid air of summer became a freezing cold shower in the middle of winter. He lit nine red candles and placed them on the desk, next to a statuette of Saint Peter holding the keys to the kingdom of heaven and another of the Virgin Mary, her arms outstretched to welcome all.

From a shelf he had commandeered, he took a bottle of red wine, a bowl of fireplace ash and an empty dish, then he closed his eyes, blessed the wine, took a long draft and sprayed the mouthful across the table. At the sound, the chicken under his arm began to kick, but Ike stroked its head, soothing it with whispered prayers until the beating of its tiny heart slowed with his, and he felt it relax, completely entranced. He scattered a handful of ash across the table, took a small knife from his pocket and lifting the chicken up by its feet, cut swiftly once, twice, through the carotid arteries of its neck. The blood wouldn't flow until he willed it, holding it back with the power of his mind, and then when he was ready, it poured over the chicken's eyes and down its beak and dripped into the empty dish, pooling like cherry juice.

There were clear messages in the swirls and spatters, a Rorschach pattern of augurs of the days ahead and Ike turned the dish towards the candlelight so he could see the policewoman Lionel Root had mentioned. Sure enough, she was there, but the image was too indistinct to make out a face. *'Del-ga-do,'* Ike said to himself as he stared long at her and tried to reach her thoughts. In the darkness, he thought he saw a shadow of somebody else lingering behind her. Her father? Her lover? The voodooist shuddered involuntarily at a fleeting premonition of his own death but pushed the thought aside. Perhaps later that night, when he offered up a black hen, he might see more details. There was a sacrifice too - another boy. He preferred the girls - Ike liked their silent screams - but he was a servant of the spirits, and their will was his. He lit a stick of incense and breathed in the smoke as it drifted over his face. Then he lifted the dish to his lips - the blood was already congealing and slipped down his throat in one.

Ike Sugar turned his attention back to the bird, stretching it out like he was preparing it for the pot, and gathered more items from the shelf. He chopped off the tail feathers with a cleaver, dipped the bloody stump in rock salt to preserve it, then did the same with the head. The feet he stuffed into a large mason jar, already full of the springy claws of previous offerings - they made excellent fetishes for Lionel to sell on his rounds. He plucked the feathers, strewing them on the floor, removed the breast meat for his own breakfast and peeled back the cardboard taped across the window, then threw what was left of the carcass down to the dogs waiting in the yard below.

Ike blew out the candles and sat down in the darkness to think about the policewoman. She would choose to seek him out, to stop him, because it was her job, because she followed orders and the law of man. These people would never understand, he thought, shaking his head sadly, for while they eked out their petty lives, face down in the dirt, they could not see the giant walking amongst them.

four

Brad Durand muttered angrily to himself as he flipped through the stacks of vinyl. If he had had the time, he would have done the place a favor: tipped out all the sixties boxes and started afresh. A member of staff – plaid shirt and goatee – wandered past aimlessly and Brad pounced on him.

'Hey kid, you got a minute. Look at this. You can't put The Marketts in with the rest of the surf rock – they only had one *surf* hit – 'Out of Limits' and – see this? – you can't put Peter, Paul and Mary in with The Searchers and Herman's Hermits. That's folk music, this is British beat pop,' he said, waving the records in the boy's face.

'Like, who are you man? Bob Dylan?' The assistant laughed as though he was trying to clear a blockage at the back of his nasal passages.

"There are a lot of places I like, but I like New Orleans better.' That's what Bob Dylan said about this city, so don't take his name in vain. And another thing...' Brad's tirade was interrupted by the familiar ring of his cellphone.

'D'you want the good news or the bad news?' Zam asked from the other end of the line.

'Hang on a sec,' Brad said, dismissing the sales assistant with a curt, 'Now go away.'

'Where are you?' Zam asked.

'Bridge House Thrift Store. I need a couple of things for the old place.'

'Oh beautiful. Pick me up a fur coat.'

'*Har dee har*. So, what's up?' Brad asked, reading the track listings on a Del Shannon album.

'Well, you were right. We've got *at least* four more cases. Same M.O. as the others. Strange causes of death. Incomplete corpses,' Zam replied.

'That makes ten, total. How did Forager miss this?'

'*Long* timeframe and a high turnover of staff at that place. Only a couple of signatures appear on the pathology reports more than once.'

Brad shook his head. 'Jesus. Somebody should have noticed, made the connection, asked questions or something.'

'Forager says they run weekly team-meetings for that very reason, but it's an hour in a non-stop week. They only discuss the weird cases, or the ones that make the news. Plus, the night shift staff can't attend obviously. Things get missed.'

'You've changed your tune. Suddenly the NOCO *aren't* the bunch of incompetent assholes they were last week? What gives?'

'Yeah well, they're not having the easiest time at the moment. Walt's just called me actually. That's the bad news.'

'What now?' Brad asked, his tone solemn.

'Eve Carmel. The pathologist? She's dead. They found her in her apartment.'

'In she in one piece?'

'Yes...' Zam answered.

'But?'

'It's.... bizarre, Brad. She swallowed her tongue.'

Brad took a moment to let the information sink in, forcing his brain to think logically. 'Drink? Drugs?' he asked.

'Nothing showing on the preliminary tests apparently. No history of epilepsy, anaphylaxis, nothing. It's like she just lay down and decided to die.'

Brad sighed down the line, unsure of what to say next.

'Don't get too hung up on this, Zam. It could be... just a coincidence.'

'Do you believe that?' Zam said, her voice faltering slightly.

'I don't want to believe the alternative. Wait, just stop for a second here. You're letting your imagination run away with itself. What do you actually *know* about the death?'

'Not much, if I'm honest,' Zam sighed. 'The cops who found her called the NOCO first and I *happen* to know one of the crime scene gals working the case, so I'm going to get the juice from her this afternoon.'

'So, let's not jump to conclusions just yet...' Brad admonished gently.

'Yeah, whatever.'

'Tell me about the other four...' Brad said, taking a seat at a cracked Formica dining table which was priced up at twenty-three dollars. He pulled out a notepad and pen and started jotting down the details of the murders as Zam relayed them: the victims' names and ages, their missing body parts, the locations where their corpses were found. He would add them to the matrix later.

'Where's this Six Flags place?' Brad asked.

'Oh, it's the old Jazzland Theme Park. Remember? Ninth Ward, off the Interstate. It changed its name, like, I don't know when. Everybody still calls it Jazzland, right? Anyway, it closed down after the storm.'

'Yeah, I know it. That's a stone's throw away from the spot where the first kid was found - Shay Favreau.'

'That's right. I haven't had the chance to look at a map yet, but maybe we're seeing the beginnings of a pattern...' Zam said.

'Maybe. Do you want me to look into this?' Brad asked.

'If you're planning on sticking around, then absolutely,' Zam replied, 'but you gotta know, I ran the whole thing past the chief earlier and he chewed me out real bad. Apparently, there're too many fatal stabbings and shootings already. We don't need no more wild goose chases, quote unquote.'

'I suppose any talk of a serial killer won't be well received either...' Brad said.

'You can say that again. So basically, anything we do has gotta be under the radar, at least for now.'

'Sounds good to me,' Brad said, tracing his finger along the cracks in the tabletop, 'I bumped into our mutual friend at Betsy's this morning, just after you left.'

'Auden? How did that go down?'

'Oh, like a turd in a punchbowl. He gave me the whole 'this town ain't big enough for the both of us' shtick,' Brad replied, still smarting at the memory.

'What a dickhead. So does he really think he can run you out of town?' Zam asked.

'If he finds out what I'm up to...'

'He won't,' Zam interrupted. 'Be smart, Brad. Keep a low profile.'

'I doubt he'll find me in here,' Brad answered, 'I might buy myself some disguises. There's a lovely plaid suit I've got my eye on.'

Zam laughed, 'Go for it. I'll catch up with you later.'

Brad flipped his phone closed and sat for a moment in silence, contemplating the current information, while the customers around him picked through old kitchen appliances, incomplete dinner sets and fruit crates of dog-eared paperbacks. A woman with linebacker shoulders was squeezing herself into a purple pleather jacket. 'This fits me perfect,' she mumbled to nobody.

Ten murders was quite a leap from the original six suspicious deaths, and the strange circumstances surrounding Eve Carmel's death added further weight to Brad's voodoo theory. Now he was back in the city, he had somebody in mind who might be able to answer some of his questions. If she was still alive.

*

'That's what I'm tellin' you, Mr. Boucher. They's definitely interested.'

Odeo's eyes glittered. '*The Mexicans,*' he said, with a sense of awe. He turned his head away from Treyvon and snorted another bump of cocaine off the back of his hand. There was something in the air: a buzz, a palpable lust. He could feel it, see it. Damn, he could taste it.

The two men were standing behind a dumpster on Clinton Street, just outside the club, since Odeo was sure that inside, the place was either bugged by the DEA or hoodooed, or perhaps both. Probably both. Definitely both. In the daylight, the surroundings looked even worse: the sunken sidewalks, washed-out graffiti and rusting balconies, the neon palm tree buzzing angrily above the Aloha Spa on the corner, the creepers clinging to the faded brickwork. But this news was proof that his luck was changing. Maybe it was just his imagination or a shift in his outlook on life, but there was a definite sensation of positivity, that the curse was lifting, like a morning miasma over the swamps burning away in the heat of the sun. Where there had been clouds, now there were blue skies. The cocaine was supreme.

'Tell me 'gain what they said, Treyvon. Tell me exactly. Word for word now.'

'Ok so this one guy - his name is Nuno - he says his family is lookin' for a spot to invest in, that this here is a *growth industry,* and that the business they buy has to be a success, so when the IRS comes knockin', y'all can explain all the cash movin' 'round and such.'

'But Cheaters.... is not a success?' Odeo nearly cried, feeling the rug pulled from under him.

'No, they *make* it a success, Mr Boucher. They *make* it a *success*, you sees?'

Odeo nodded enthusiastically and grinned. 'Yes! Yes!' He didn't see, but it didn't matter. He put his hands on the rim of the dumpster and kicked it furiously. 'So, what happens now? How do we contact them?'

'They said they'll be back. Din't say when. But like I says, they's definitely interested.'

Odeo pumped his fists and kicked the dumpster a couple more times for good measure.

From the tiny open window in the cloakroom overlooking the street, Lionel couldn't quite make out all the words, but he sure got the gist.

*

The September heat still had a sting, especially at midday, and it was a long walk from the club. Lionel Root wiped his brow as he shuffled up the steps to the old house. The neighborhood was quiet: the council's repopulation efforts had proved fruitless in this part of the city, where most of the locals washed out by Katrina had simply never returned. Their houses stood empty: the woodwork rotting, blight choking the rafters and forcing tiles off the roofs. Still, Lionel checked nobody was around before he knocked on the door. The silence was broken by the sound of deadbolts being unlocked - Ike Sugar opened the door four inches and peered out through the gap, his expression one of suspicion and irritation.

'Didn' I tell you *not* to come here in the daylight, you *stupid* son of a bitch? Peoples gon' see. And when peoples sees, peoples starts to talk, y' hear?' he muttered crossly.

'Well, why don't you let me in, so we don't have to stand here discussin' it on the porch?' Lionel snapped.

Ike moved aside and Lionel wandered in, stepping across the line of red brick dust on the threshold. His senses weren't what they used to be, so the smell - a pungent cocktail of wet rot, chicken shit, wood-smoke and blood - didn't affect him the way it might a younger man. Ike shut the door quietly and the two men stood in silence while Lionel's eyes adjusted to the dim light cast through cracks in the boarded windows.

'You got what I want?' the voodooist asked.

'Well, hello, Lionel. Nice to see you, Lionel. Can I get you some tea, Lionel? That's what normal people says to one another. That's *civilized*. Not *'You got what I want?'* Is that the way I raised you?'

'Man, y'all din't *raise* me,' Ike laughed derisively. 'Shit, I was getting by jus' fine when you found me. Now, you got what I wants or is you jus' here to *yon-yon*?'

'Maybes I *is* here to *yon-yon*. I heard the police found the Carmel girl dead in her apartment. You know anything 'bout that?'

'Sure,' he said, hitching up the knees of his dungarees and taking a seat on the staircase, 'I killed her.'

Lionel had hoped to maintain the higher ground, but Ike's blasé confession caught him off guard. Suddenly the cold, impassive expression on his face, the sound of the dogs in the yard and the chickens scrabbling on the floorboards at the back of the house, the fetid air in the dark hall - it all pressed down upon Lionel Root and he had to close his eyes and think of something - anything else before he blacked out.

'Is you in my head, Ike?' he croaked presently.

Sugar snorted, 'Ain't gonna find nuttin' in there, old timer, 'cept maybe some younger man's desires. Why is you so concerned 'bout Carmel anyways? You knew I couldn't let her live. Smart girl like her – she'd come snoopin' 'round soon enough. Can't let that happen,' Ike tutted and shook his head, like he was lamenting the loss of nothing more than a ten-dollar bill.

Lionel nodded sadly. He knew Ike was right: Eve Carmel *was* too inquisitive; she would never have let it lie. But in spite of her prickly nature, Lionel had grown to enjoy their frequent meetings. The knowledge that - almost on a whim - Ike had snuffed out her life, made Lionel worry about his own future.

'Don't burden yourself, Monsieur Laroute,' Ike grinned widely as if reading Lionel's mind. 'Who'm I gonna git to replace y'all? Hmm? Now, won't you come on through? I'll pour us both a glass of cool iced tea on this hot day. How's that for civ'lized?'

Lionel pushed himself off the wall he'd been leaning against. The greasy plasterwork had left pale yellow smears on his jacket, and he rubbed at them ineffectually as he followed Ike through the dark cool corridors of the house and into the kitchen. The noise of the chickens was louder here, and they clucked with alarm as the men approached. Like the temple room on the floor above, the walls here were also lined with shelves, each stacked with mason jars, recycled pickle jars, corked bottles, plastic tubs and tin cans, all neatly labeled in Ike's spidery handwriting: 'saffron', 'goofer dust', 'Cayenne pepper'. There was an assortment of dried, dead animals: pine snakes and racers mainly, but the odd rattler and a cottonmouth, frozen in death; embalmed scorpions and lizards; cat skulls and rabbit feet. A padlocked green fridge hummed loudly in the corner. Lionel had seen its contents before and had no desire to look inside again. He took a seat at the table in the corner, as far away from it as possible and opened his bowling bag: Georgine's packets of herbs and spices were wrapped in wax-paper and tied with twine, and he laid them out carefully on the butcher's block while Ike poured the drinks and cast his eye over the goods.

'How much you want for all this?' he asked, inhaling the scent of a bundle of gnarly licorice root.

'Five hunnerd and twenty bucks. That includes my cut. Some of this shit is hard to *lo*cate,' Lionel replied, trying to sound confident. 'This 'specially,' he added, drawing Georgine's tiny envelope from his pocket and laying it carefully on the table.

'Ah, The Devil's Breath,' Ike smiled. He picked it up, rolled it across his knuckles like a quarter and with a flourish, showed the old man his empty palm. 'Jus' a parlor trick,' he mumbled to himself with a grin. From the top shelf, he took a jar labeled 'Aunt Sally's Pecan Pepper Jelly' - it was stuffed with tight rolls of cash: the profits from years of conjure balls, curses and hoodoo spells, and the subsequent cures and cleanses he had performed. He peeled off five grubby one-hundred-dollar bills, another twenty, and handed them to Lionel.

'You bes' be careful with that now. A man with yo' gifts shouldn't be foolin' with such stim'lants anyways. Y'all don't need it,' Lionel said, trying to flatter.

'Oh well, some of these folks jus' need a lil' push in the right direction, s'all. They needs a lil' *convincin'*.'

'The boy from the strip joint is going to take some convincin',' Lionel grumbled. 'A *gris-gris* ain't gonna cut it. Says he wants to meet you face to face.'

Ike took a long draft from his glass and wiped his

mouth with the back of his hand. 'Who do these people think I am?' he said and belched loudly, before adding 'Some back-alley snake-oil salesman?' The slight wasn't lost on Lionel.

'He ain't stupid, that's fo' sure,' he replied. 'The man has money troubles. Although could be so's that's 'bout to change. Drug money kind o' change. I tells you son, that place could be good fo' us. *Real* good.'

For all his posturing, Ike always listened to the old man when it came to business. 'Might need more than a lil' push, you think?'

'Uh-huh,' Lionel nodded. 'He don't want to part with cash for nothin'.'

'Is that what we're doin' here? *Nothin'*?' Ike asked, pointedly. 'Tell that to Miss Carmel.'

'What did you do to her anyways?' Lionel asked, unsure he really wanted to hear the answer.

Ike turned away and shrugged nonchalantly. 'I planted a seed, that's all.'

'Why din't you kill her like all the others? You could have… *taken* something,' Lionel suggested, choosing his words carefully.

'She wasn't one for the harvest – she had hate in her heart,' Ike sucked his teeth and peered at Lionel, 'Y'all could see that, right?'

Lionel shook his head sadly before blurting out, 'Can't you teach *me*, Ike? I don't want to kill no-ones. I just want to feel what it's like, what you got.'

Ike's pale eyes glittered in the dimness of the kitchen. 'What I got? The *pouvwa*?' he asked. '*Naw*. You had your chance, Lionel. You never believed before and look where you is now. Still shuckin' 'n' jivin'. Hell, that's all you *is* good fo'.'

'I could be the dog,' Lionel begged. 'Or the pig even? I could be lowly. I'd even get me my *own* mask. How 'bout it?'

'Can't just pass the power on to any old fool. Ain't for jus' anybody. Some of us is chosen. All you needs to do is focus on findin' us another avenue of... supplies. These stocks ain't gonna last forever,' he said, drumming his fingers against the side of the fridge.

'Can you help me out then? Give me a 'boost'? Seein' as I done *procured* all of them fine herbs and roots for yo' work.'

Ike slowly finished his tea without taking his eyes off Lionel's. 'Sure,' he replied, in his languorous way, 'Y'all knows the drill.'

Before Ike had the chance to change his mind, Lionel stood up and fumbled with his belt, dropped his trousers to his ankles and leaned back against the kitchen wall with his eyes closed. He could hear Ike shuffling around in front of him, preparing himself for the ritual, lighting candles and mumbling prayers. For his part, Ike was staring at Lionel's thin hairless legs, his swollen arthritic knees, and shinbones as sharp as wooden rulers. He wondered why anybody would take an interest in a washed-up old drunkard with no power, no *muti*. Even his body was failing him, stripping him of his own yearnings, and with that thought, the voodooist moved closer to Lionel, close enough to smell his Groom and Clean hair tonic and the sharp undertones of his nicotine breath. Ike Sugar cupped Lionel's withered genitalia in his hands and hummed to himself over and over again, '*Mwen pase, mwen pase, li mande san, ba li tèt kòk la....*'

Lionel braced himself for the inevitable pain and as Ike's chanting reached a crescendo, it came, almost worse for the anticipation, burning like white hot metal against his skin. He cried out and fell to the dirty kitchen floor, whimpering in shame as tears rolled down his gaunt cheeks. But already he could feel blood pumping through his veins, his heart beating steadily and purposefully as a metronome. Tentatively, he opened his eyes. Ike Sugar stood over him, and Lionel cowered at the sight. He had become used to the masks over the years: the slack jaw and sagging folds of graying pig skin, the glassy eyes and yellowed fangs of the dog, and now Ike's face was covered with a shell of hardened black wax, molded crudely around his nose into the shape of a sharp hooked beak. White feathers formed a crest around his pale eyes and nine real cockscombs and wattles had been roughly stitched together with black twine to add the finishing touches.

'You're the Rooster,' Lionel whispered reverently, as though he were witnessing a miracle.

'Yes,' Ike Sugar answered with pride, 'but I's becoming a god.'

five

So much can change in a few years, Brad thought ruefully, as he cruised uptown behind a Disaster Tour Bus. The Lower Ninth Ward looked like a film set: an apocalyptic ghost town with broken husks of houses and vast expanses of wasteland. On the Gentilly shoreline, historic buildings had been razed to the ground and replaced with chain-link fences and promises of development. Brad had wanted to get a sense of his hometown again, but instead he felt unsettled as he headed back south, into the areas he had known so well as a patrol officer in his early days on the force. Here, the layout of the streets had changed, derelict buildings stood out like rotten teeth, and dead ends – those mainstays of crime – were no longer dead ends. It felt like wading through another man's distorted memories of New Orleans.

In search of something to anchor himself to the place where he had grown up, Brad turned into the network of streets around Central City and parked his SUV, packed with his thrift store purchases, in a vacant lot on Clio Street. The skyscrapers of the Business District loomed in the east, just across the Expressway, which seemed like the border between two worlds. Behind him, in the doorway of an apartment block, three kids were passing round a crack pipe. Brad grabbed a beer from his emergency stash under the passenger seat, unlocked his glove box and took out his gun – a chunky snub-nose Smith and Wesson – which he rested on his lap in plain sight. Then he turned up the radio, drank and waited.

Six minutes later, two of the crackheads appeared in his rear-view mirror, moving warily, like hyenas approaching a carcass, as they walked towards the car. The first wore a baseball cap low under a hood, leaving only a pale chin in view. The second – stocky with a crew-cut – was definitely carrying: Brad could tell by his awkward gait that there was a gun stuffed in the waistband of his track-pants. Placing his hand deliberately on his own gun, Brad lowered the window.

'Hey,' he said.

'What're you doin' here?' Crew-cut asked evenly.

'Just taking a moment,' Brad answered.

'Yeah? Nice gat. You lookin' to shoot somebody?'

'No,' Brad answered, 'just protecting myself.'

'You a cop? You sound like a cop,' he asked with a sneer.

'No, I *used* to be a cop,' Brad said. 'Now I'm just a regular person, like you.'

At that, Baseball Cap stepped forward suddenly, shoving Crew-cut out of the way and leaning into the open window of the SUV to get a better look at Brad's face.

'Yeah, I thought I knew you all right. D'y'all remember me?' Baseball Cap croaked, pulling back her hood to reveal she was, in fact, a woman in her early forties, or possibly her thirties. She didn't look in great shape, Brad thought, but her face was familiar.

'You used to work with us,' Brad said, taking a punt.

'I used to snitch for you,' the girl laughed mirthlessly, 'Is that the same thing?'

Brad smiled, 'I didn't recognize you - how you doing?'

By now, Crew-cut had realized he was surplus to requirements and wandered back to his doorway.

'Doin' pretty good actually,' she sniffed, kicking at a lump of greenery bursting through the concrete, 'I won six-hundred dollars on a scratch card last year – *well, five hundred and seventy dollars* - so I got straight for a spell. That's most probably how come you didn't knows me straight off. I look a lot better than I used to.'

'That'll be it,' Brad said, taking in her broken skin, sunken cheeks and glassy eyes, the pupils still dilated from her last hit. 'Are you still in the game?' he asked. The 'game' was drug-dealing, petty theft and a sideline in prostitution. Back in the day, Brad would have busted her for some minor misdemeanor - soliciting or possession - then cut her loose whenever she gave up a name, a time and place, or even just a rumor. In her line of work, in the tangle of downtown alleys where she used to ply her trade, she invariably had something to offer.

'I quit for a couple years,' she said, picking at a scab on her neck, 'I even got a real job, handing out flyers in Midtown.'

'Why'd you start again?'

'It's the only game I know,' she laughed, pulling a glass pipe from one pocket and a lighter from the other 'and anyways, I do like getting high.' She took a long hit and held it in, sucking in gulps of air and dragging the smoke deeper into her lungs. 'So, you lookin' for business?' she asked, with a new, hard edge to her voice.

'Not as such.'

'What do you want then?'

'Hey, we're just talking here, right?' Brad said coolly. 'Ain't that enough?'

'Time is money,' she fired back.

Brad thumbed the furniture and boxes in the trunk and back seat. 'You're looking at my life right there,' he said, judging the lie wasn't too far from the truth.

'You're looking at mine,' she answered, turning out

the empty pockets of her hoodie.

'Okay, okay,' Brad relented, taking a five-dollar bill from his wallet and holding it up, '... and I'll throw in a cold one,' he said, cracking a can from the six-pack next to him.

'Ha! Throw me somethin' mister! Sure, what you wanna know?' she asked him.

'Voodoo,' Brad said simply. 'Who? Where? What?'

The snitch wrapped her lips around the tin and took a long draft while she thought.

'This is the voodoo capital of the country. Be more *pacific.*'

'Voodoo plus murder. That better?' Brad said.

'It's the murder capital too, last time I watched Fox News. There's some lunatic waving a flag for everything these days. Voodoo ain't no different. Try the St Louis Cemetery. Plenty of contenders down there.'

'Anybody you know?'

'Nah, I used to know a guy over in Metairie – Jimmy Gallo was his name – he had a bunch of voodoo shit in his house. Skulls and dolls and shit, but he got busted for selling Special K to kids. That was two years back. Any good?'

'I doubt it,' Brad said, licking the nib of his pencil, 'but you never know. What else?'

'Um. I know a few people who carry a *gris-gris*. You know? Like a lucky charm? There's a mechanic called Jon Shawger – Johnny Shotgun everybody calls him. He carries a rabbit foot. Tony Espadrilles – works at the pawnshop on Toledano Street – he's got a mojo bag too. I seen it one time under his shirt....'

Brad jotted down the names while she spoke, but nothing significant jumped out. Superstition and folklore was rife in Louisiana, and if a kid chose to carry a rabbit's foot for good luck when everyone around him was carrying nine millimeters and butterfly knives, well that didn't make him a Voodoo Killer.

'... Then there's the Mexicans – they're worse than all the rest.'

'How come?' Brad asked.

'Man, they got it stickin' in both ears. All that ancient Aztec, sun-worship bullshit *and* the Catholic guilt. Every one of them has red threads tied round theys wrists to ward off *el Diablo*, and crucifixes hanging round theys necks. I tell you, Mexicans is scared of *every* fucking thing. 'Cept guns and drugs.'

'I heard the Latin Kings were collecting teeth from other crews. You know anything 'bout that?'

'Nah man. Mos' of mine fell out all by theyselves. I *heard* about the Kings, but I never saw it myself. It was just one of them things that caught on, I reckon. Eye for an eye, tooth for a tooth - you know, like in the Good Book.'

'Sure. Anybody take it any further?' Brad asked.

'Not that I knows,' she shrugged, downing the last of her Abita and tossing the crushed can into the long grass. 'Anyways... five dollars. I'd say we're 'bout done.' The crack was beginning to wear off and she flashed Brad an aggressive smile.

'Wait - one more thing - where would somebody go for a first class 'read your future' tarot cards, crystal ball kind of deal?'

'How the fuck would I know?' she laughed. 'Try Jackson Square.'

'Jackson Square is for chumps and tourists. Come on...'

'You think I need somebody to read my palm to tell me where my life is headed?' she sighed and shook her head. 'Look, my auntie used to be into all that shit before she got hit by a streetcar. I guess nobody saw that one coming. Anyways, she used to swear by a Haitian reader up in Chalmette. She said that this woman had a *gift*. Don't ask me for a name, 'cause I don't know. She kept a place near some fabric store - that's hows my auntie found her. That's 'bout all I can remember.'

Brad found another five-dollar bill in his trouser pocket and handed it over with a second beer and his Florida business card.

'Here, don't spend it all on candy.'

The woman grinned and Brad continued, 'You hear anything that might interest me - voodoo, body parts, anything like that - you give me a call on my cell, okay?'

'Sure Bradley Durand, Private Investigator,' she replied, reading the card before pocketing it. She took a step away from the window, hesitated and then turned back, as if to share one final nugget of information.

'Hey Bradley Durand,' she whispered conspiratorially, 'in spite all o' this,' she said, gesturing back to the apartment block doorway and Crew-cut, 'and in spite o' the shit I still do, I mean, you can tell I have a good heart, right? I mean, you can tell I'm a good person?'

'Sure,' Brad nodded. 'I can see that. Y'all take it easy now.'

*

It was hard to concentrate, so rather than sit in the back office and stare at bank statements and angry letters from the loan companies, Odeo drove home to Metairie, took a shower and changed. He chose his light blue suit and lucky dice cufflinks in case the Mexicans decided to return that night.

On the way back to the club, he realized he hadn't

eaten anything in days, so he pulled into the Sonic Drive-In and ordered a chili-cheese coney and a cherry limeade. He pulled over, took one bite of the hot-dog and immediately felt seismic rumblings in his gut. He made it to a grass verge in the outdoor seating area just in time to vomit at the base of a palm-tree. At a nearby table, a mother and her two children watched him in disgust.

'I'm ok!' Odeo said, waving. 'I didn't get any on me!'

He peeled out of the parking lot and took another bump of cocaine while he idled on the 1-10 behind people staring at a road traffic accident. The cherry limeade settled his stomach. He lit a cigar. Everything felt better.

Drop top down, radio blasting, he caught every green light on his drive downtown. The Mexicans were coming! The Candy Cane Cavalry. Purveyors of the pearly Paradise White. Yes, yes, yes. Odeo drummed the steering wheel. Whilst the thought of drug-dealers frequenting his establishment cast a faint shadow, he knew that with a seal of approval from the criminal underworld, Cheaters' moment had finally arrived. His baby was growing up. It almost brought tears to his eyes.

He shot his cuffs and with a squeal of brakes, spun across the wet asphalt into Clinton Street singing 'Zip a dee doo dah' as the world turned around him.

*

'Priestess Lovelie Coulombe - Voudou Practitioner - Bone Readings, Cleansings, Blessings, Removal of Curses, Baptisms and Weddings - 2337 Lloyds Avenue, Chalmette, LA - (504) 459-9234'

'Who dat! Fuck you internet!' Brad mumbled to

himself, as he circled the ad in the Yellow Pages.

It had taken over an hour to scour all the listings, but Lovelie was the only clairvoyant he had found in Chalmette. He checked his watch - nearly six - and decided his visit would have to wait until tomorrow. It had been a long day and Brad flopped back into his new pride and joy: a huge forest green La-Z-Boy recliner he had picked up from the thrift store. Even with a broken handle and some dubious stains, at forty dollars it had still been a steal and definitely worth the fifteen back-breaking minutes it had taken him to shift it from the back of the SUV, up the stoop and through the front door. He sat in the center of his otherwise empty lounge, wishing he had also picked up a TV or a stereo, but consoling himself with his thirty-dollar mini-fridge which was fully stocked and well within reaching distance.

His cellphone buzzed in his pocket.

'Hey Zam. I tried calling you earlier but couldn't get you. What's the latest?'

'We're getting somewhere, Brad. The CSI guys found something in Eve Carmel's apartment which doesn't sit right. Seems she received a bracelet in the mail just before she croaked - I haven't seen it yet, but you know what I'm thinking.'

'I know what you're thinking,' Brad answered, 'but don't jump to conclusions, Detective. Hoodoo mightn't be the answer. We don't know if her death and our cases are even connected.'

'Well, Dale Kastelein might be able to answer that. He's being questioned at the station as we speak.'

'So where are you?' Brad asked.

'At the Coroner's Office. Walt Forager pushed hard for a full forensic report. 'One of our own' were his words. I'm trying to get the scoop from my girl on the inside.'

'Did they find any prints on the bracelet?'

'Uh-uh, nothing like that. But given the circumstances - you know, strange parcel, unexplained death - somebody got spooked and mentioned 'anthrax.' Then all hell broke loose. The place has been locked down.'

'So, it's anthrax-poisoning?'

'You *wish* it were that simple. Not anthrax, no,' Zam replied. 'They ruled that out half an hour ago.'

'What is it then?'

'They don't know yet. They're talking about some kind of cutaneous toxin - something taken in through the skin - but it doesn't fit with anything they have on record. You know what these people are like when they can't figure something out. They won't give you diddly squat.'

'Can you get me a photo of it?' Brad asked.

'The bracelet? I should be able to get a copy of the prelim crime report. Can I email it to you?'

'Only if you don't want me to see it,' Brad answered drily.

'Ok - I'll work something out. What's the rush anyway?'

'I'm hoping to meet up with a...' Brad searched for the right word, '... *voodooist* tomorrow.'

'Oh, he'll be fun,' Zam quipped.

'It's a 'she' actually - a *priestess* in fact - so yeah, whatever. I thought somebody knowledgeable could throw some light on our case. And it might be worthwhile running the photo past her. What do you think?'

'Sure, but remember - go easy on the details. I don't want to see this on the evening news.'

'No problem....' Brad said. There was a moment's awkward silence which he pushed through, 'Maybe if you're not doing anything later, we could catch up...?'

'I can't - sorry - I have Zumba tonight. And *nobody* sees me after that.'

'What's *Zumba*?' Brad asked.

'I doubt it's your thing, big guy. So, no, what are you up to?'

Brad leaned over to the mini-fridge and pulled out the first of many beers. 'Me? Oh, I might head out, grab a bite, listen to some music...' he twisted the cap off the bottle and took a long pull.

'*Dios Mio*, you're settling back in already....'

*

The augurs of the black chicken blood - usually so clear and bountiful - were perplexing. Ike Sugar searched for meaning in the images he had seen - the cautious alligator, the laughing skull, the dying bride - but found none. He had been poring over the books that Lionel had salvaged from the boxes in his mother's attic, but never bothered to read himself: *The West African Spirit Guide, Kaffir Folk-lore of the Bantu*, and his favorite, *At The Back of the Black Man's Mind*. These were his sacred texts, many containing passages written before the first white man came to the Dark Continent, and filled with rituals, spells and incantations passed down from generation to generation of black slaves. These were words which not only conjured up images of the birth of voodoo in the mangrove swamps and jungles of Africa, in the right hands - *his* hands - they actually summoned the spirits and invoked the magic itself.

When Lionel had first taken him in, he became aware of a heightened sense of the hidden touch in Ike: he could focus his attention to move sewing needles or to spoil fruit. He could kill sparrows in the backyard by snapping his fingers. One day he killed thirteen. After that, Lionel taught him to read with those same books - the only books he'd had - and Ike had studied them fastidiously ever since.

He placed his well-thumbed copy of *Songs of the Creole Slaves* back on the shelf in his temple room and tried to bring together his scattered thoughts. The Delgado woman had appeared in the blood again, alive still and searching for the path to him, but just as before, the faceless man stood behind her like a ghost. Ike closed his eyes and saw him again in the afterglow of the candle's flame: this shadow man, this man without *muti*.

There was also the sacrifice, and Ike thanked the spirits for choosing him for the task. He gave them praise, blessed himself with incense and blew out the candles.

*

The bottle in Brad's hand slipped from his grasp and fell, rolling loudly and gently spilling its contents across the floorboards of the empty room. It was nearly ten: Brad guessed that he had fallen asleep around seven, sometime between his fourth and fifth beer, whilst reading the sleeve notes of the albums he couldn't leave behind in the thrift store record boxes. The La-Z-Boy had proved to be much more comfortable than his camping cot and Brad could have happily stayed there all night, but he had woken with a raging hunger – he hadn't eaten since Betsy's and hadn't had the forethought to buy any food that day. With a yen for something he couldn't get back in Panama Beach, he grabbed his jacket and headed out the door into the night and the sounds of cicadas, sirens and other peoples' TV sets.

Within half an hour, Brad found himself wide awake and working his way through a plate of spicy chicken with a side of red beans and rice. Jazz was pouring out of the bars and clubs along Frenchmen – the locals' Bourbon Street – and frat boys from Tulane stood on the sidewalk laughing and flirting with a bunch of girls in pink tutus, all of them sucking on blue snowballs. The air was filled with the aromas of night jasmine, hot tabasco, roasted garlic, crawfish, chocolate sauce, perfume, reefer and cigars, and it all somehow blended together with the laughter and the music like a blissful psychedelic dream and not just any Monday night in the city. There was always a reason to celebrate here - a festival, a ball, a party, a carnival - always an excuse to get dressed up and get drunk. and for the first time since he got back, Brad felt something of the love he had lost for his hometown. He had seen a lot of the country over the years: felt the heat in Miami, the madness of Los Angeles and the pulse of New York, but to find that New Orleans, in spite of all her suffering, was still defiantly blowsy and decadent and still ready to welcome him back like an old lover - it almost broke his heart.

Brad smiled to himself and wished that Elaine were there to share the evening with him. In the early days, before real life set in, they had spent many a night together on these same streets, listening to the jazz in dirty dive bars and kissing until sunrise. *Is it too late to call?* he wondered. *Would* she *still have me back?*

He pulled out his cell and speed-dialed before he had time to regret his decision. It rang out and just when he was about to give up, his son picked up.

'Hey Kyle. It's your Dad.'

'I *know*, Dad,' Kyle replied, his voice dripping with teen ennui. 'Mom's not here.'

'Oh, that's okay,' Brad said, biting back his disappointment. 'I just thought I'd give you guys a call. Where y'at?'

'I'm okay.'

'How's school?'

'It's okay.'

'Yeah? What are your new teachers like?'

'They're okay.'

'Okay.' Brad changed tack. 'So, guess where I am…'

'I give up.'

'Back in New Orleans.'

'Jeez, Dad, why?'

'I'm working.'

'For the police?'

'Yeah, kind of,' Brad said. 'You should see the old house – it looks great.'

'M.I.A. says New Orleans is dead in the water.'

'It *is* not,' Brad retorted, springing to her defense a little too readily. 'Who's M.I.A. anyway?'

Kyle groaned.

'So… how is your mom?' Brad asked.

'She went to the movies with Evan.'

'That's not what I asked,' Brad replied sourly, pushing the image of Evan and Elaine necking on the back row from his mind.

'Hey, d'you know, Evan said that when I get my learner's permit, he'll hook me up with a Chevy. Is that cool or what?' Kyle exclaimed.

'Wow. That's… wow. What a guy,' Brad replied flatly. 'But you know, that's a way off yet, sport. And Evan might not be around for long,' he added, hoping to burst his son's bubble.

'Yeah whatever, I gotta go Dad. 'Family Guy' is starting…'

'Say hi to your mama for me,' Brad said.

'Sure. Bye Dad.'

'Bye Kyle. I love you, son.' The line was already dead.

'Nice chat,' Brad grumbled to himself. *'Hey Dad, Evan's groping your wife in the Cinemax. Hey Dad, Evan's gonna buy me a Chevy.* Muscling in on my kid now. I'm on to you, you motherfucker.'

'Excuse me?' said the waiter.

'Oh, sorry, guy. Not you. I'll take another one of these,' Brad waved the empty Abita bottle. As he shoved the cellphone back into his jacket pocket, his hand brushed against his notebook. Alcohol had clouded his judgment and when he remembered the real reason for his return to the city, the realization rolled over him like a wave of nausea: he had to push away his plate of unfinished food.

Brad cast a sour glance at the reveler's outside The Spotted Cat and wondered if one of them could be the next victim: another life cut short in its prime, another murder framed as a freak accident. Disconsolately he flicked through the pages of his notebook - lists of potential leads, random thoughts and theories, names and dates, the places where the bodies had been found…

'Six Flags Amusement Park,' Brad read aloud. 'Jazzland'

Eleven thirty in the city and the night was far from over. It was as good a time as any to take a drive.

*

In any other city, the New Orleans public transport system would have been considered a disgrace. The aging streetcars were always overcrowded, the buses smelt of piss and never ran on time, and the potholes on the main downtown thoroughfares were deep enough to swallow a wheel. Still, while most people in the Big Easy accepted its failings with a shrug, Ike loved it and looked forward to a bus-ride like a kid from the backwoods. Although his vocation was a solitary one, he wanted more than anything to be around people, observing their interactions with each other, with the city. He liked to eavesdrop on their banal cell-phone conversations and to watch them eating, reading, even sleeping sometimes. He marveled at the myriad ways they presented themselves: their seersucker suits, their body odor, the slogans on their T-shirts, their jewelry, the cut of their jeans, their dyed hair, short skirts, tattoos and piercings. He noted their affectations and peccadillos. He watched them watching one another. He saw through them.

Ike also liked to touch them *accidentally*, holding the rail in rush hour and rubbing up against the women particularly in the crammed, sweaty spaces. When the rides were quieter and the opportunity presented itself, he would often take a pair of nail scissors from his pocket and snip a little of their hair away without them feeling a thing. Just as he had snipped Eve Carmel's hair one evening as she rode the number twenty-eight home to her apartment; and the kid from the chicken farm – Ike had cut a lock from his hairline while he lost time in the back of his truck. He cut anybody who wandered into his world. He kept them all in a Love Hearts tin in the temple room, each one labeled with a tiny paper tab and tied with cotton: 'redhead scool girl wit red shoes mid-city', 'pregnunt woman gentily', 'fat soldyah boy 55 bus eleeshun feelds'

Ike slipped a hand inside the pocket of his coat. Sure enough, his little silver nail scissors were right there. The tool bag at his side contained everything else he needed for his work. The number 94 Broad service rounded the corner, its headlights glowing through the light mist and Ike straightened his hat and climbed aboard with a frisson of excitement.

*

Out of the city, Lake Forest Boulevard was poorly lit, and Brad's car rumbled over the cracks in the asphalt. He slowed to a halt as his headlights illuminated a thick, black tail slipping into the undergrowth at the side of the road; Brad had heard stories back in Florida of so-called 'urban' alligators roaming around town in search of food, but he'd never seen one in the flesh. He guessed this guy was a good five-footer. It didn't surprise him – the Boulevard crossed the Lake Michoud and Lake Marseille waterways, and the bayou itself was only a couple of miles up the Interstate. The hazy light of the cityscape picked up the clouds of methane out over the swamps and turned the sky the color of rust. He thought twice about his plan, wondering how many hungry gators might be out there, but pressed on regardless.

About a mile from the entrance, Brad pulled off the road and parked up. In one pocket he carried his gun; in the other, the NOPD badge he had never quite gotten around to surrendering. His footsteps and the occasional whine of a mosquito were the only sounds as he made his way toward the amusement park through the mist.

The sign on Michoud Avenue read 'CLOS D FO STORM', and Brad climbed over the concrete Jersey barriers blocking the entrance. 'Jazzland,' he snorted. There was more jazz in the municipal courts than there had ever been in Jazzland. Built in 2000, sold in 2002 and abandoned in 2005 as a lost cause, it had never been the success the Six Flags corporation had expected: too far from the rest of the tourists traps, too close to the poverty and crime of the Ninth District. Kyle had celebrated a birthday there once – his seventh or eighth. Brad had been working on a spate of armed robberies in Metairie at the time.

He cast an eye into an empty ticket booth and pushed his way through a broken turnstile. In the half-light of a yellow crescent moon, Brad got his first glimpse of the apocalypse. From Main Street Square to Goodtime Gardens, every accessible façade of the imitation Creole townhouses was covered in graffiti. All the windows had been smashed. The giant planters - too heavy for the average vandal to lift – bore the words 'NOLA RISING' in gold spray-paint, and held only the charred remains of their trees. A light breeze blew plastic forks, tin cans, toilet paper and dead leaves across the wide avenues built to accommodate the summer crowds, now empty.

Mardi Gras Land and Cajun Country had fared no better. Clearly, the investors had taken one look at the hurricane damage and stripped everything they could salvage from the wreckage, leaving behind a child's worst nightmare made real. Against the backdrop of the enormous rusting skeletons of broken rollercoaster rails, the ruins of the fairground were like nothing Brad had ever seen: stained and tattered tarpaulins; burnt-out bumper cars; and the once glorious carousel, listing like a ship in a storm and threatening to keel over at any moment. There were faces everywhere: a jester's head – the size of leering, vandalized a man - its stucco nose shattered, another missing an eye, a headless mermaid, a man falling through clouds, his face frozen in fear, and a huge, bejeweled voodoo skull presiding over it all and laughing. Brad caught a movement in the corner of his eye and turned quickly to see his own distorted reflection staring back a thousand times from a wall of smashed carnival mirrors.

Brushing the debris from the ripped vinyl seat on a broken chair-swing, he sat down, wishing more than anything that he had a drink with him and wondering what answers he had hoped to find amongst the rubble. He pulled out his notebook instead and tried to read the details of the killing that had taken place here - but it was too dark. He remembered Zam saying that the victim had been an 'urban explorer' - young and male of course, because no woman Brad knew would be stupid enough to wander around derelict factories and warehouses in the middle of the night. 'Burnt to a crisp and no hands,' Zam had said - he wouldn't forget that so easily. Still at least the kid died doing something he loved, Brad thought, because as cool places for geeks go, an abandoned amusement park had to be way up there.

He stood up to leave, already lamenting his decision to park the car so far away, when he saw something move in his peripheral vision and knew immediately that it wasn't a tarp snapping in the wind or the gates to a ride swinging open. Brad wasn't alone.

He crouched low, straining his vision in the darkness, a splinter of fear pricking his self-control. It had been a long time since he'd found himself in this kind of situation - balancing on a trashcan in a back alley, waiting for a Kodak moment of some guy cheating on his wife didn't quite cut it - but his years of training kept his 'fight or flight' instinct in check. Probably just another dickhead *urban explorer*, he told himself, but still finding reassurance in the grip and weight of his revolver. The seconds stretched out - he began to doubt what he was sure he had seen when a tall spectral figure crept across the avenue, moving like a shadow in the milky moonlight, not fifty yards from where Brad watched.

He needed to take a closer look, if only to satisfy his curiosity. Moving quickly and quietly for a man of his size, Brad stole along the broken balustrade at the edge of the derelict Orpheus Theater, trying to get a better viewpoint. He caught his breath as the specter reappeared, not twenty yards away now, picking his way with long, exaggerated steps through the tall weeds growing through the asphalt. Straight up and down and slender as a pine sapling, he was dressed in a long overcoat and silk stovepipe hat, which reflected the moonlight. He raised his hands to the night sky and then bent low, inspecting something on the ground at his feet.

And then Brad saw the girl – from a distance he hadn't noticed her body lying amongst the garbage in the middle of the avenue – and the impulse to save a life flooded him. Everything happened quickly and slowly, as Brad lunged forwards, ready to fire, clattering heavily across the wooden boardwalk. He should have shouted then - warned them who he was and that he was coming - but the words didn't apply anymore and they stuck in his throat as he ran.

Through the distortion of his adrenaline rush, he saw the specter turn slowly – his face hideously gaunt, painted bone white, his eyes like tiny pinpricks of light in sunken sockets.

'Get away from her! Get *back!*' Brad yelled, finally finding his voice and hearing it echo in the emptiness of the fairground.

The girl at his feet sat up sluggishly, sweeping a bridal veil from her face and looking to Brad, not for help, but with an expression of confusion and fear.

Brad opened his mouth to shout again, and then the halogen spotlight hit him, blinding him instantly and he had to stop dead in his tracks, his gun still pointed into obscurity. He didn't hear the footsteps behind him until it was too late, didn't even feel the blow to the nape of his neck. He was only dimly aware of the dirty ground flying up to meet him as he fell.

six

'Last stop! End of the line!' the driver shouted. 'All change please. Have a good night now. Thank you, have a good night, y'all.'

One by one, the few remaining passengers alighted the bus at the corner of Michoud Boulevard and Expedition Drive. Mani Lionne had been playing an early set at Sweet Lorraine's, but he left at midnight. It was a school night after all. He struggled up the aisle with his case and stepped off. Ike Sugar followed him slowly, pausing to touch the driver's neck and whisper something in his ear.

The easternmost part of the city: a clutch of streets with dynamic names and tidy bungalows scattered across the last stretch of civilization before the Bayou Sauvage. Mani stopped to light a cigarette, watching the rest of the passengers heading across Michoud towards their homes. He hadn't noticed Ike standing in the shadows behind him.

'What you got in the box, sonny?' he asked. 'Mus'cal instrument, I guess, but what kind?'

'Trombone,' Mani said, patting the case protectively, 'She's my baby.'

'Trombone, trombone,' Ike repeated. 'Ain't that the one that *slides* an' such?'

'That's the one,' Mani answered, bemused.

'Forgive me son, I never had much o' an education. I can't tell my ass from my elbow,' he chuckled softly to himself. 'Oh well, oh well. How 'bout a tune anyways?'

Mani laughed, 'I don't think so, dude.'

'Come on, I can pays you,' Ike pulled out a crumpled

twenty-dollar bill – the same amount that Mani had made from his share of the set earlier in the evening. 'How 'bout it?'

'Man, I'll wake up half the neighborhood,' he replied, warming to the idea.

'Best make it a good one then,' the voodooist grinned, revealing his perfect white teeth.

'You serious? Jeez, this is crazy. Sure, why not?' Mani said, before taking a final drag on his cigarette and flicking it into the street. It flashed in the darkness. He set his case down flat on the grass, opened it up and began fitting his instrument together. 'What should I play?' he asked.

'Oh, I don't know. Something sad,' Ike said, handing over the money. It was covered in a fine white dust which clung to Mani's fingertips. 'It's kinda a sad night, ain't it? Now play the tune, boy.'

The stranger's words seemed to have taken on a deeper meaning. They echoed in Mani's head, and without thinking, he raised the trombone to his lips and started softly playing 'My Melancholy Baby.' Without the backing of his band on trumpet and piano, his music drifted forlornly across eastern New Orleans, over Jazzland and the Lake, and out towards the bayou. He played it slow and heavy, slurring and smearing the notes, serenading the people of Expedition Drive, Adventure Avenue and Intrepid Street, slumped in front of their TV or in bed. There wasn't a soul around.

Ike knew nothing about music and didn't recognize the song, but he did enjoy listening to the boy play. Mani reached for a high note and closed his eyes as he hit it, too immersed in the moment to notice what was happening. Ike breathed deeply, lamenting both his actions and the inexorable passage of time. He pulled out the rooster mask from his tool bag and slipped it over his head, adjusting it so his eyes peered out through the feathered slits. His wax beak shone in the moonlight.

Ike felt the *pouvwa* of the ancient spirits coursing through him, stronger than the pig's ever was, or the dog's, and as Mani rolled into the final crescendo, he reached out, letting his mind flow to the very tips of his fingers, until his consciousness nestled in the empty spaces of the boy's young body. Ike felt for the chambers of Mani's heart, pulsing energetically, and then he unstrung them, pinching the tendons and pulling them apart methodically like he was teasing out the stitches of a pin cushion. The note died and Mani fell to the ground, fighting for breath like a fish out of water.

Ike watched impassively as the boy's heart gave out, right there on the side of the road. He dragged over his tool bag and knelt down beside the dying boy.

'*Mwen te fouye twou a, Mwen te fouye twou a...*' *I have dug the hole, I have dug the hole,* he chanted softly. From his bag, he pulled out his billhook - a ten-inch curved steel blade for cutting back shrubs and branches - two plastic bags for the gifts he was to receive, a single black feather and a small red candle - which he lit and placed on the sidewalk where its flame guttered in the cool night air.

'*.... ki mouri yo vle yon gwo foul...*' *Even the dead want a crowd at their tomb...*

Quickly and cleanly, he cut off Mani's thumbs, rolling the thickened nose of the blade down through the bones, like he was chopping through carrots. Mani's eyes bulged in pain and fear but his airless lungs could produce no sound.

'*Ban m 'pouvwa ou, Ban m 'pouvwa ou,*' *Give me your power, Give me your power...*

Ike placed them carefully in a bag. He artfully hooked the blade deep inside the waist of the boy's jeans, turned the blade and pulled back hard, popping the buttons on his fly and slicing through his underwear in one. He leaned forward over Mani's chest, pushed the curved tip of the knife up under his chin and stared hard through his eyes of his nightmarish rooster mask.

'Now,' Ike whispered, 'scream for me.'

*

'Jeez, what did you hit me with anyways?' Brad said, gingerly rubbing the back of his neck.

'This,' said Alan the cameraman sheepishly, handing it over.

Brad assessed its weight, 'Yup, that'll do the trick.' He didn't know which was more humiliating: getting knocked out by a one-hundred-and-forty-pound guy with a heavy-duty flashlight or trying to shoot the star of 'Zombie Honeymoon', a low-budget horror with a budget of six thousand dollars on location at Jazzland, of all places.

'It's like *totally* the right place for the *ambience* we're trying to reproduce,' enthused Derek - writer, director, producer, sound engineer and actor - once Brad had come round and his initial anger had subsided. 'It's got the whole dystopian, post- Armageddon, 'end of days' feel, you *know*? Plus, it's an amusement park, which is like…'

'… way cool?' Brad suggested taking a sip from a bottle of water.

Derek nodded emphatically, thrilled that Brad shared his vision.

The cast and crew - four in total, including Chloe and Keith, the zombie bride and groom - had hefted Brad into their motorhome once they discovered his police badge, and left him in the recovery position while they finished shooting for the night.

'You know you're trespassing though?' Brad asked. 'Somebody owns this place. It's not safe either. And I don't just mean structurally unsound – though I'm sure it is. There was a murder here last year.'

'A murder? So, it's official? Yes! We knew there was an *accident*,' Derek said excitedly, 'but the internet was, like, *rife* with rumors. Some said it was a terrorist plot gone wrong, others said it was a spontaneous combustion deal. I've even read that it was some kind of voodoo ritual.'

'I can't give you any details,' Brad replied, hoping Derek would fill in a few of the blanks himself. 'You guys don't really believe any of that old voodoo crap, do you?' he asked.

'I do,' Chloe, the zombie bride-to-be, piped up eagerly, before looking to the others for support. 'We all do, right?'

'Oh yes. If there *was* a *voodoo* murder here', Derek said knowingly, '… then - sure - we're taking a risk. And I know it *sounds* mercenary, but if I'm honest, that's all part of the appeal for filming Z-H right here. We're capitalizing on that *mythology*.'

'You see, 'Zombie Honeymoon' isn't just a job for us,' Alan said, his voice somber. 'It's part of our heritage. It's something we believe in. There's a dark side to this city. And voodoo is *central* to that. It's not all jazz and jambalaya, right? We're pulling back the curtain here.'

Derek looked emotional all of a sudden.

'Don't you believe in voodoo, Detective?' Keith asked, twirling his top hat in his hands as though he were about to pull a rabbit from it.

'Seeing is believing,' Brad replied sourly, taking

another sip of water and wishing it were something stronger, 'but sure, I'm willing to be convinced.'

'You should get yourself one of these,' Alan said, fishing a chain from under his shirt collar. At its end, a dark blue eye glared out from a golden palm.

'Isn't that... the Hand of Fatima?' Brad asked.

'Al, that's *muslamic*, you moron,' Keith laughed, 'What's *that* got to do with voodoo? Seriously, Detective, there's this tiny store on the corner of Bourbon and Dumaine called The Rainbow Serpent. Ask for Phillipe....'

Brad continued to feign a polite interest while forcing his groggy brain to commit to memory the names and places.

'.... he hooked me and Derek up with these,' Keith said, pulling a tiny, red felt bag from the pocket of his tailcoat. Derek gave him a high-five across the cramped motorhome lounge and dug out his own, tied around his neck with a leather thong.

'And that's a *gris-gris*...' Brad had never seen one up close before, and even though this one looked like something mass-produced in Taiwan and sold wholesale, he still held his breath as he reached for it.

'No way man,' Keith replied, snatching it away. 'You can't rub another man's rhubarb.'

'What's in it?' Brad asked innocently.

'I never looked in mine,' Derek said, rolling his softly, almost reverently between his fingers. 'There's something hard in there. Feels like a pebble. Or a *bone* maybe.'

Brad was considering his options for lifting Keith's bag, when under the glare of the fluorescent strip lighting in Derek's 'trailer,' Chloe quietly reached into her purse and placed a chicken-foot in the center of the fold-down table. Everybody stared at it in silence: four scaled claws, irregular in length, curled in death, stained the color of sickness, and preserved in wax. It was tied with bailing twine and a frayed scrap of red silk ribbon and trimmed with a single jet-black feather. Compared to the other trinkets, it was shocking in its authenticity: pure voodoo.

For a moment, Brad thought he could hear jazz floating in the night air.

'I was having some problems a while back,' Chloe began. 'Depression kinda runs deep in my family and I'd always known it would get me too, eventually. So, I guess I found myself in a downward spiral. I hit rock bottom in a motel room with a quart of vodka and a bottle of Tylenol. It wasn't exactly a suicide attempt, but it wasn't just a cry for help either.' She turned the foot over absent-mindedly as she spoke. 'Anyways, I kinda pinballed around the mental-health system for a bit before I started looking at alternative therapies: yoga, tai chi, that kinda thing. I even done six weeks of hypnosis. I was still getting nowhere when this *guy* found *me*. I was sitting at The Fly one morning, just - you know - reading the paper and eating a muffin and he just sat down next to me on the grass, this old black dude, and started talking. Real persuasive he was, like a salesman or somethin'. We were shootin' the shit, talking 'bout the weather and the good old days, where we was when the storm hit - that kinda thing - and then he just handed me this. Says if I give him all the money I have on me - all of it mind, and not one red cent less - then this *fetish* - that's what you call this, a fetish - then it would fix all my troubles.'

'And did it?' Brad whispered.

'I woke up the next day like a new person. It was like I'd had this weight on my chest all the time, pressing down, making it hard to breathe, and then it had just been lifted off me. I can't really explain it,' she giggled. 'I knew that there was nothing to worry about no more. Nothing in the world. I paid thirty-seven dollars and sixteen cents for that feeling. And I went out that morning, and I saw an ad for this role, and I met up with these *fine gentlemen*, and everything kinda fell into place. Just like that!' And she picked up the chicken foot and rubbed it affectionately down her cheek and across her lips.

*

Of all the trappings of professional success – the driver, the invitations to city events, tickets for the Saints games, not to mention the salary and the annual leave – nothing was quite as notable, nothing quite said Auden Tillery had *arrived* as his private bathroom. Any old dumbass could get an office these days. Even the janitor of the Eighth District Police Precinct had his own little room in the basement with a desk, a telephone and his name right there on the door. But a private bathroom - with marble-topped units and mahogany paneling - said so much more. It said that he was so important, he shouldn't have to share the intimate moments of his toilette with rank-and-file officers. It said that his time was so precious he should never have to wait for a stall or queue for the hand dryers. It said, quite frankly, that he had risen so far above the rest, that Auden Tillery should never have to smell anybody else's shit.

'Damn right,' Tillery said to his reflection as he ran his electric razor over his chin for the second time that morning. It was nearly eight o' clock. He sharpened up the edges of his mustache before carefully disassembling the shaver, brushing its head clean and placing it back in its case. Everything in its place.

There was a light knock at the door. 'Sir, I'm sorry to interrupt you, sir, but you asked me to let you know when they're ready for you. And they are. Ready, sir.'

'Thank you, Nicole,' Auden answered. Slowly, deliberately, refusing to be rushed, he poured a capful of mouthwash and continued with his ablutions. Let him sweat, he thought.

A full fifteen minutes later, he emerged pristine in his dress uniform, festooned in gilt, and swept through the corridors and down the stairs like the angel of death.

Brad Durand lifted his weary head from the table in Interrogation Room 3 and looked Tillery square in the eye as he walked in. 'What a surprise,' he said sourly.

'Bradley Durand,' Tillery said, 'I thought I told you I didn't want to see you again.'

'Yeah well, the feeling is mutual. And newsflash, dickhead, it's a free country. Wanna tell me why I'm here? Your bulldogs wouldn't give the time of day when they damn near kicked my door in an hour ago. So, what's the charge *Commander*? Sleeping under the influence? Possession of a reclining chair?'

Auden pursed his lips, knowing straight away that Brad Durand wasn't his man. Nobody facing down a potential murder rap was this cocky. 'There was an... *incident* last night, out in the east end of town.'

'Isn't that a little out of your jurisdiction?' Brad asked.

Tillery ignored him and continued, 'Where were you last night?'

'Drinking on Frenchman Street, then I went home.'

'That's interesting, since a vehicle with Florida plates, matching the description of *your* automobile, currently parked outside *your* house, was spotted by a patrol not far from the scene of a crime…'

Shit, Brad thought, *I've got to watch myself here.*

'... so, try again, Durand. What were you doing on Michoud Avenue last night?'

'I was at Jazzland,' Brad answered coolly.

'Jazzland?' Tillery blinked. 'The amusement park?'

'That's right. The *amusement* park,' Brad parroted, leaning back in his chair and folding his arms as though he had nothing more to say.

'Really? You expect me to believe *that*?' Tillery asked, feeling his temper rising. Brad Durand had always known how to punch his buttons. 'The Six Flags Park has been closed since the storm. Care to elaborate?'

Brad picked at something under his fingernail. 'I was doing a bit of *urban exploring* actually. I think that's what they call it. So - what? - are you gonna hit me with a trespassing rap now?'

'I could, but no,' Tillery gave him a thin smile, 'I'll play along for the moment. Who were you with?'

'A film crew. 'Zombie Honeymoon'. Seriously. It's gonna be *huge*. Swear to God. Coming soon to a cinema near you.'

Tillery shook his head. His control was crumbling. 'What time was this?'

'From midnight to about two am, I guess. *Then* I drove home. Next thing I know, The Keystone Cops are banging on the door.'

'There's blood in your hair.'

Brad instinctively felt the lump at the back of his head. 'I guess your goons cracked it pushing me into the patrol car. I don't remember,' he lied.

'And I assume...' the Commander's eyes narrowed perceptibly as the penny dropped. 'Wait... Six Flags... there was an accident there last year: a young man set himself on fire. And now this...'

'Now what? Brad asked, his interest piqued.

Tillery's voice was ice cold. 'What are you into here,

Durand? What are you stirring up in my district? I see you and Delgado are thick as thieves all of a sudden.'

'Why don't you leave her out of this...' Brad replied.

'Do you think you can come back to *my* town after all these years and actually *solve* something? And then what? Restore your shattered reputation? You must be insane.'

'What happened on Michoud last night, Tillery? Another kid get chopped up? What did he take this time?'

'Don't get smart with me,' Tillery barked, struggling to keep it together. 'Let's get something straight - *we* do the investigating 'round here. The N.O.P.D. Not some petty, washed-up, has-been dick from the *fucking orange juice state*!'

'Calm down, Auden. You're almost perspiring.'

'You always were a bullshit detective, Durand,' Tillery hissed. 'You got lucky. That's all. And this thing with Delgado...? Good luck with that,' he snorted. You're pissing in the wind.'

It was probably the worst thing a man in Auden Tillery's position could have said to a man as bull-headed as Bradley Durand. In that moment, Brad decided - quite simply - that he would solve the case, even if it took him a lifetime, as much to prove Tillery wrong as to prove to himself that he still could. Brad stood up and straightened his jacket. He was a good six inches taller than the Commander and his size was intimidating. Without warning, he flashed out a fist and grabbed Tillery roughly by the collar, rucking up his immaculate shirt and jacket.

'If you want to investigate this, be my guest. Otherwise, let a *real* detective do your job,' he said, gently shaking Tillery to emphasize his point. 'You've got a serial killer on your hands and when you're not wasting time kissing ass at City Hall, you're scoring points with me. So, are we done here or are you going to charge me?'

Tillery seemed panicked at the sight of his ruffled shirt and wayward tie, more so than Brad's threatening demeanor. He shook his head.

'No. I didn't think so. Now, get out of my way, you prick.'

Brad stormed along the corridors he had once haunted and out into the early morning sunshine. He bought himself a coffee and a croissant from the bakery across the street and wandered home, still dressed in yesterday's clothes, against the flow of people heading into work. There was a time when he would have recognized some of the faces, but not anymore. Now, they were all strangers, and walking among them was a sophisticated killer. Brad was determined to find him.

*

Although he couldn't remember making it home after the spirits had left him, Ike's eyes snapped open and he woke naked on the floor of his hallway, pumped up and full of blood. He pulled on his old dungarees, tied back his thick dreadlocks and set out barefoot to take in the morning air. It was early, the air was crisp under his scant clothing, and he felt reborn, as he often did on the first day of a new month. A bundle of nervous energy, fizzing with zeal: he fought the urge to sprint along the street, but when a group of six schoolgirls in pleated tartan skirts and tube socks passed by on the corner of Josephine and Prytania, giggling and gossiping with one another, Ike was so overcome with desire at the sight of their young nubility, he had to watch them from behind a low wall. He spilt his seed there in the thick grass, grunting like a wild pig and grimacing in ecstasy when two of them happened to look in his direction. They screamed and ran away.

Ike rolled back on the sparse lawn and felt so very *alive*, watching the majestic, pink-tinted clouds roll above him, listening to the birdsong, connected to the air, connected to the tree roots, connected to the world.

He sprung up, wiped his hands on his pants and made for a convenience store down the block. People were buying breakfast pastries and stocking up on cigarettes for the working day. Ike helped himself to a liter of orange juice, two of full-cream milk, a muffuletta loaf and a packet of beef jerky. These, he slipped into the body of his dungarees, cold against his bare skin, cupping his groceries like a pregnant belly and smiling benignly at anybody who cast a glance his way. He brought to bear all his concentration, deflecting attention from himself. Those that did notice him stared back dumbly, lost in his blue eyes, forgetting what they were doing and where they were momentarily. Even the Korean owner – a man who did push-ups on the sidewalk when business was quiet – waved as Ike strode out without paying, tearing off a chunk of 'Spicy Cajun Roadkill' and chewing it like a cowboy.

On the corner of the street, Ike popped the cap on the milk and gulped down nearly a liter, leaning back, one foot against a streetlight, the sun on his face, the heat of the jerky, the cool of the milk – he breathed in the moment, savored it. The boy's midnight trombone serenade and the prizes he had taken came flooding back. He thought about the rewards he had yet to reap. The possibilities, the possibilities.

Above his head, in the angle between the street-sign and the lamp itself, a spider had weaved a tiny intricate web which glistened with dew in the morning air. Ike could just make out its creator, striped and fat, sitting proud in the center. *Where does she end, and where does her web begin?* he wondered as he watched her waiting for a fly. Ike stretched out his arms, flexed his fingers and listened to the sound of his own heart beating in his chest. He was the pig, the dog, the rooster. He was the spider too, pulsing in the center of his own enormous web, his consciousness spreading out beyond his body to the people passing by: the suited office workers, the joggers, the tramp pushing the shopping cart, the drunk stumbling home. *Where do I end, and where do they begin?*

seven

Brad's head throbbed - part hangover, part lack of sleep, part being clubbed with a flashlight - and though all he wanted was to take a shower and fall onto the La-Z-Boy, he forced his brain into gear and came up with a plan of action. He pushed open his front door and stumbled inside to find an envelope from Zam waiting for him: a copy of the preliminary crime scene report on Eve Carmel's death.

'Good girl. That'll do for starters.'

Knowing that once he sat down, he might have trouble getting up again, Brad leaned against the wall instead and flicked through the pages. As well as a number of close-ups of the bracelet, there was a forensic breakdown of everything the technicians had discovered. Zam had highlighted 'Hair belonging to the victim' which had been used to bind the 'feathers: *(Gallus: gallus domesticus)* Ameraucana/ Black,' but there was no further information on the strange leathery diamonds, other than *'Organic material – (papillae to be confirmed).'*

Brad tried her cell - no answer - but managed to reach Lovelie Coulombe, the voodoo priestess, instead. Although she sounded perfectly balanced and professional over the phone and not at all detached from reality as Brad had expected, he couldn't help wondering if he was just spinning his wheels when he could be working through the snitch's list of low life acquaintances or paying a visit to The Rainbow Serpent. Something told him it was still worth it, and he arranged to meet her at eleven o' clock. Then he took his well-earned shower, shaved, changed and gathered up his files before heading out to start the day over.

He was cruising down Claiborne - past the Cities of the Dead: the St Louis Cemeteries - skipping through the local news stations for any word of a murder on Michoud, when he stumbled upon Rockin' Oldies Radio playing 'Turn Around, Look At Me' by The Lettermen.

In spite of his best efforts, Brad had been unable to persuade Chloe to part with her chicken claw. He had even offered to give her all the money he had in his pockets: eighty-seven dollars and some chump change, but she wouldn't budge.

All he managed to coax from her was a flimsy description of her salesman: black, old, gray-haired, pork-pie hat, cheap sunglasses. Brad had to admit, he didn't sound like a serial killer, but his instincts told him there was a connection. He was willing to bet that the chicken feather on her fetish was the same as those found on Eve's bracelet...

His cellphone chirped and he turned down the radio. 'It's me,' Zam said flatly when he answered, one hand on the wheel.

'Where y'at, Zam?'

'I've been reassigned.'

'No! What the fuck?!' Brad said, stunned.

'The order came from on high. I'm off Homicide. I've been busted down to Narcotics, effective immediately. You know who did this?'

'Oh, I know. I got pulled in this morning. Auden wanted a little tete-a-tete.'

'I heard. A couple of the older guys recognized you down at the station. Jeez, Brad, I was *this close*, and they pulled it out from under me...'

'I'm really sorry,' he said, feeling guilty for having forced Tillery's hand. 'Look, it's not necessarily a demotion. It's a fun time to be in narco. Lots of action. You could still make it up that way.'

'Don't give me that bullshit, Bradley. I'll be busting crackheads in the Ninth for the next five years. I may as well kiss any chance of promotion goodbye.'

Brad cradled his cell against his shoulder as he turned the corner under the St Bernard Flyover. 'Well, before you kiss it, what have you heard about Michoud Ave, last night?'

'That's why I'm calling - it's our man all right. The victim was a white kid - Manfred Lionne, seventeen years of age. Cause of death was cardiac arrest, but he managed to lose his thumbs, heart and dick in the process.'

Brad gave a low whistle. 'Was he a virgin?'

'Well, he was in a band, and - you know - chicks dig musicians, but he played the trombone, *not* lead guitar, so it's hard to say,' Zam said. 'But the thing is, they can't ignore it anymore. Tillery must know it. If the press gets wind of it - and they will because someone in this place will spill for sure - then it won't take a genius to connect this one to Shay Favreau. Did you get my report by the way?'

'Yeah. I'm heading over to the voodoo woman's place now.'

'Good - there's been an update though. The lab rats found traces of some trippy drug on the bracelet. Hang on... I've got the name in my notes here... 'scopolamine.''

'Scopolamine? *Burundanga*. That's *very* interesting,' Brad remarked casually.

'Run that by me again?' Zam said.

'Scopolamine. They cook it up in Colombia. Because - you know - sometimes cocaine just isn't criminal enough. They call it *burundanga* down there. Nasty stuff. And you're narcotics now - I don't think 'some trippy drug' will cut it.'

'Is there anything you don't know, smart-ass?' Zam asked tartly.

'Hey, I'm a big Discovery Channel fan,' Brad replied with a smirk. 'It still doesn't explain how our girl died though.'

'What? It's Miss Scarlet, in the bedroom, with the poison. Scopolamine. It's a done deal.'

'Back up rookie. Raw scopolamine can kill in high doses, but so can bourbon. It has some medical uses, but this *burundanga* is basically like… a kind of chemical hypnosis. Men use it to rape women; women use it to rob men. In Bogota, I mean. The CIA tried it as a truth serum back in the sixties, but it was too…'

'Trippy?'

'Well, it *was* the sixties,' Brad replied.

'And now it's here,' Zam said. 'Narco's not looking too bad after all.'

'It's no joke. I saw it on the TV.'

'Then it *must* be true,' she quipped.

'It leaves people *totally* suggestible,' Brad continued. 'You can give a guy just a whiff of *burundanga* and tell him to hand over his wallet or his car keys, and he'll do it, no questions asked. It strips your free will. But, as far as we know, Eve Carmel died alone, so…'

'… who told her to swallow her tongue?' Zam finished.

'Exactly.'

'Well, it wasn't Dale Kastelein. He's out of the picture. We'll keep an eye on him, but he has a watertight alibi from the moment Carmel left his office. We even checked his phone records. And he cried like a baby when he found out she was dead. You've never seen anything like it. We might be able to get him on obstruction of justice, but basically the guy signed off some invoices for goods he never received. Falsifying documents? Tax evasion possibly, but hardly a felony. Although, falsifying documents is a felony, but ok. Anyway, he was just trying to keep her happy.'

'I assume she wasn't a virgin then?' Brad said.

'You assume right. Forensics confirmed it. So, she doesn't fit our profile...'

'No, but if she was *misappropriating* body parts, it's unlikely she was mixing in the best circles. I don't know. It's just one dead end after another.'

'With that in mind, I've got to go and meet my new team,' Zam sighed. 'Keep me in the loop, yeah? I want to know what the black magic woman has to say. You're on your own for the moment, but I can't let this go. We'll get together later this week when the heat has died down.'

'Cool. Work this scopolamine angle: check the records for Colombian connections and dealers who specialize in unusual drugs - N-bombs, Meow-Meow, spice, peyote, even mushrooms - somebody's getting this stuff in somehow. And go back over the case files for the murders: see what toxicology came back with, if they even bothered to publish a report. Call me back when you got something.'

Brad cruised slowly down Lloyds Avenue, peering through the windscreen and checking the house numbers. Katrina had swamped and very nearly destroyed Chalmette completely; the storm surge had knocked over a huge oil tank at the nearby Murphy refinery and a slick added to the devastation caused by the fourteen-foot-high floodwaters. In spite of it all, the area was now a picture of quaint suburbia, with large, whitewashed clapboard houses, picket fences and porch-swings.

Brad pulled over and double-checked the address he

had scrawled on the palm of his hand. *2337 Lloyds*. There was a big, shiny blue truck parked outside, and neat rows of pansies in the flower beds. He wasn't sure what he expected to find, but it was hard to imagine a voodoo priestess living here. Unconvinced, he strode up the path and rang the bell.

Brad had imagined a toga, maybe a headdress, *boo-coo* jewelry at the very least, but the woman who answered the door was wearing jeans and a plain navy T. She wore her dark hair swept up in a loose chignon. She offered her hand to Brad.

'*M'sieur* Durand - pleasure to meet you,' she purred, in a voice rich with the lilt of the French Caribbean. 'Won't you come inside?'

'Thank you for seeing me, Miss Coulombe,' Brad said, as he stepped across the threshold.

'*Madame* Coulombe, please. Or just '*Mambo*', if you prefer. I didn't realize that you're a police officer,' she said, and Brad detected a slight admonishment in her tone.

'How can you tell?'

Lovelie Coulombe looked at him squarely, 'It is my *job* to tell.'

Brad gave an awkward laugh, 'Actually, I'm not a policeman - anymore. I do mostly private work now.'

'Ah *oui*,' she said, as though something had fallen into place. 'You're not here for a reading.' It was a statement rather than a question.

'Um... no. I was hoping you might be able to help with a case I'm working on.'

'That sounds.... intriguing,' she said, with a smile that didn't quite reach her eyes. 'Come through.'

Lovelie Coulombe led the way through her large, open plan house. It smelt of cinnamon and sandalwood. 'I usually perform my readings in there...'

she said, gesturing nonchalantly to a candle-lit room off the lounge. Brad stole a glance at the deck of tarot cards stacked on a small, round table. '... but since you're here on police business, perhaps we should talk in the kitchen. There's more light in there. *Voulez-vous quelque chose à boire?*'

'*Cafe? S'il vous plait,*' Brad said, batting back her French.

'Actually, I don't have coffee. You shouldn't drink anything which upsets your natural balance, *M'sieur* Durand. Let me make you something to restore your equilibrium.'

'I was working late,' he offered, wondering if she was already reading his mind or if his hangover was that obvious.

While she busied herself peeling ginger and crushing aniseed, Brad admired the framed black and white photographs which covered an entire wall of the kitchen. They showed wooden boats moored on windswept beaches, the wizened faces of elderly relatives, a man playing a homemade guitar, a boy proudly holding a haul of snapper.

'Haiti?'

'Yes.'

'What's it like?' Brad asked, just to have something to say, and immediately regretted it.

'Not what it once was, since the earthquake,' she gave a tight, thin smile, a signal that it was a subject she didn't want to discuss. 'You understand?'

Brad nodded, sure that she was referring to Katrina and his own experience of the devastation. Or was it more of a personal allusion? He couldn't tell.

'Do you have family here?' Brad asked.

'On my father's side. He was born here. My mother was from Port-au-Prince. We lived there when I was younger. But this is my home now. I couldn't go back to Haiti even if I wanted to. Here, drink this. It will help.'

Brad remembered the *burundanga* and hesitated. 'What's in it?' he asked, trying to sound blasé.

'It is just a tisane, *M'sieur* Durand. Why would I want to poison you?'

'OK, I think we may have gotten off on the wrong foot, Madame Coulombe,' Brad said, setting the cup down. 'Have I offended you in some way?'

Lovelie had been waiting for the moment and her eyes flashed fire as she spoke. 'Let me explain something, *Détective*. Every now and again, there's a murder in this part of the world that people find hard to explain. It's not the usual domestic affair or a gang-shooting. It's something vaguely out of the ordinary. And do you know what happens?'

'I have a feeling you're about to tell me...' Brad replied.

'The police and the press come around, pointing their fingers and sticking their noses into our community. They flash their badges and ask questions they have no right to ask. Voodoo is a religion like any other - older, more primitive, *oui* - but a religion, nonetheless. I wonder will you also be knocking at the doors of the St Louis Cathedral or the Touro Synagogue to investigate your murder...'

'Well, I've got a dozen murders actually. Maybe more,' Brad interrupted. 'It's hard to tell. The killer is very smart, very subtle.' At the back of his head, he could hear Zam warning him not to say too much, but he figured the story would be splashed over the front pages later and besides, he was on a roll. 'He - the killer - is taking *pieces* of his victims - fingers, thumbs, whole hands, eyes, ears - you name it. Personally, I don't think they're trophies but rather some kind of ritual sacrifice. I think he might even be selling them.'

'*Muti*?' Lovelie asked, aghast.

'*Muti*. That's right,' Brad answered, 'but there's more. Our main lead in the case was killed over the weekend. With what appears to be a very *un*lucky charm. That's our perp's M.O. you see? He covers his tracks with freak natural accidents. I've got heart attacks, brain hemorrhages, blood clots. I've got hypothermia in the middle of summer, and literally a bolt from the blue. Now if you don't want to help me…'

'*The loa*,' she whispered to herself and touched her fingertips to her forehead.

'… I'll just try somebody else in the Yellow Pages. Trust me, there's plenty of you lunatics in there…'

'*M'sieur* Durand, please!' the priestess exclaimed, struggling to compose herself. 'Drink your tea. You need a clear head. We have much to discuss…'

*

Jon Rubino was standing alone outside the station when Zam emerged, squinting in the sunlight, with a polystyrene cup of coffee. He offered her a cigarette.

'Rubino, you know I don't smoke,' she said, witheringly.

'I thought you might like to start,' Rubino replied. 'Seems like as good a time as any.'

It hadn't been the easiest of mornings. Having handed over her ongoing cases to Rubino and debriefed the rest of the homicide division, Zam had stepped outside for a breath of fresh air before heading to her new department. She threw the dregs of her coffee in the gutter and sighed dejectedly.

Rubino took a long drag. 'Look, maybe it's not as bad as you think. Narco is big business these days. Junk is big at the moment. Coke is huge. We're closer to Colombia than we are to Canada. The shit is coming up from Mexico *every day* and then it's transported to the north and west via Houston. We're on that route,' he said with a shrug.

'How come you know so much about it?'

'I was assigned to narco when I first came up. Two years. I guess some of it stuck.'

'Sure. I knew that,' Zam said.

Rubino dropped his cigarette and crushed it underfoot.

'New Orleans is perfectly placed for trafficking into the US.' He counted off on his fingers, 'One, you got drugs coming up the river in bulk on fishing boats, cruise ships, on helicopters from the Gulf oil rigs. Two, you got nationally affiliated street gangs - the Crips *and* the Bloods - all distributing coke and marijuana from here to Shreveport. Three, you got the motorcycle gangs - what do they call themselves? Um... the Sons of Silence, The Bandidos - they're dishing out the meth. And four, you got all the local crews dealing uppers, downers and all-rounders, 24-7. That's all spilling over into homicide. I'm telling you. It's an enjoyable time to be in narco.'

'Yeah, so everyone tells me. Well, I guess it's time to find out. Thanks for the pep talk, Jon. See y'around.'

Zam stepped inside, gave the sergeant on the front desk a mock salute and Janice the receptionist a wink. 'Wish me luck,' Zam said, retrieving the cardboard box of her personal possessions from under the front counter: framed photographs and certificates of commendation, crappy souvenirs from holidays across the border, her favorite mug. The ignominy of carrying it through the corridors for all to see was almost worse than the demotion itself. She was the player who hadn't made the cut. On the staircase, Commander Tillery marched past her like a storm-trooper.

'It's nothing personal, Delgado,' he managed, without looking her in the eye.

He didn't stop to hear her reply, which was probably best for all concerned. The entire building knew he was a control freak and Zam was sure the truth about her transfer would come out eventually, but still, for the moment, it stung like a slapped cheek.

She pushed open the door to the narcotics department. The tired, third-floor office with its nicotine-stained ceiling, filthy windows and faded rat-colored carpet tiles was the place where the careers of once-hardworking detectives came to die. At some point over the years, Zam had worked with all five of them, each one her senior. They had been beaten down by the work and the lifestyle and by time itself: a world-weary bunch now, content to sit behind a desk from nine to five, waiting for retirement. Out on the streets, meanwhile, the dealers were always dealing, and the city's drug trade was relentless. It didn't help that New Orleans ignored vice in general: decadence and debauchery was its lifeblood.

'We rely on two factors,' Detective Roland Lash said, after the initial pleasantries were out of the way; he was leaning out of the window to take a hit of his cigarette, 'neighborhood watch, and luck. Sometimes, handlers set up shop on a street-corner and the local neighborhood watch takes offense. Other than that, it's mainly down to luck.'

'So how many cases do you make these days?' Zam asked.

'Well, the foot-soldiers do most of the work. They average around fifteen-hundred stop-and-searches a month. That equates to, oh, a hundred convictions maybe.'

'Anything major?'

A couple of the men behind her snickered.

'We work closely with the DEA and the Feds. They tend to handle the high-end cases.'

'So where does that leave us?' Zam asked, beginning to see the extent of her demotion.

'Here,' Lash replied, and leaned out of the window again, indicating the conversation was over.

'So, you're telling me...' Zam began.

'What I'm telling you,' Lash said, dropping his cigarette and watching it fall to the street below, 'is that you may as well stick your thumb up your butt instead of your finger in the dam. But, hey, knock yourself out.'

Zam felt light-headed at the thought of ending her career *here*. 'Come on guys, there's got to be *something*,' she almost pleaded. 'There's got to be *somewhere* for me to start. Guys?'

The room fell silent. Roland Lash just shook his head as though she hadn't listened to a word. He picked up the newspaper.

One of the team piped up, 'If you want to start somewhere, try the strip-clubs. We haven't hit them in a while.'

'Uh-huh. Strippers do love junk,' Lash added.

*

'There was a revolution in Haiti at the start of the nineteenth century. Many American plantation owners were forced to flee back home. They brought their slaves with them of course. Their African roots had all but withered then,' Lovelie Coulombe said, 'but life was easier here in America, and New Orleans soon felt the beat of the *manman* drum.'

Over an early lunch - and something called a 'yerba mate tisane' which had alleviated Brad's headache - the priestess had filled the blanks in his understanding of voodoo. Fascinating, but he was no closer to finding his man.

'So Haitian voodoo is purer than Louisianan?' he asked.

'I wouldn't say 'purer' - that's a... *loaded* word, don't you think? But certainly, it's closer to the origin. Voodoo in Louisiana is a *mélange* of different religions and folklore, but in Haiti, we still worship the *loa*.'

'Is *loa* God?' Brad asked.

'There is only one God, Mr Durand. In my religion, he is called *Bondye*. But the *loa*... the *loa* are many and they are all around us,' Lovelie said airily, looking out of the window at the garden as though she could see them. 'They are the spirits of the trees and flowing waters, and animals, and the harvest and death. When we perform any kind of ritual - a marriage or a funeral, a reading, a sacrificial ceremony - we stand on the spiritual crossroads with *Li Grand Zombi* and invoke the *loa*.'

'Do you mind if I write some of this down?' Brad asked.

'Not at all, but you should understand that my interpretation of the faith will be different to another practitioner's. There isn't a bible of voodoo. You might find some old spell-books out there, but its central tenets have been passed down through generations of storytelling, over thousands of years.' She spread her hands by way of apology, 'I can't tell which chapter and verse will help you find your killer – *je suis désolée*.'

'But you see something here?' Brad insisted, pointing to the notes and pictures he had chosen to share with her. 'You see a pattern that I'm missing, right?'

Lovelie sighed and shuffled the papers.

'*Petèt.* Maybe. In Haiti, there are men of great spiritual power called *bokors*, chosen at birth, to serve the *loa* 'with both hands'.

'What does that mean?'

'With light and dark magic. They practice healing and medicine, but they can curse a man just as easily. Some say that Doctor John was a *bokor*. You've heard of Doctor John, I imagine?'

'Yeah - I read he was the first *commercial* voodooist.'

Lovelie nodded. 'That's a good description. Before Marie Laveau ascended to the throne in this city, Doctor John made a living from cursing people, and then lifting those curses for a fee. He used to collect with both hands. A *bokor*? Possibly. A very shrewd man certainly. *There* was a man who understood people.

'But a powerful *bokor* can invoke powerful *loa*. When I was a girl, my mother used to tell me stories of one who could pull lightning from the sky, rain rocks down upon houses, stop a man's heart and bring him back to life. I've seen zombies...'

'So have I,' Brad answered, painfully recalling the previous evening's escapade.

'No, not your Hollywood monsters, Mr Durand, I'm talking about real men and women, working endlessly in the sugar plantations. They're villagers with no souls, drunk on the Devil's Breath, at the will of their *bokor*...'

'*Drunk on the Devil's Breath*?'

'The Devil's Breath - it's a drug they make from Haitian moonflowers. Angel's trumpets, you call them here. *Don't fall asleep under the moonflower tree or the Devil will steal your soul*,' she gave a mirthless laugh. 'That's what we tell children in Haiti. But in truth, *bokors* use the drug to create zombies.'

'Do you mean *burundanga*? Scopolamine?'

'I'm not sure. I don't know the scientific name, I'm afraid.'

Brad pulled out the photograph of the bracelet from his file and pushed it across the table. Lovelie took a sharp intake of breath.

'This was delivered to one of the victims,' Brad explained. 'The forensic team found traces of a hypnotic drug called scopolamine in these feathers.'

'Whoever did this wanted to make sure your victim wouldn't talk,' she whispered.

'Well, he certainly managed that,' Brad said.

'No, you don't understand. There's a message here. She choked, didn't she?' Lovelie asked.

'Yes - how can you tell?'

'Here,' the priestess said solemnly, pointing at the mysterious strip of leather in the photograph.

'We haven't identified that yet,' Brad answered.

'It's a tongue, Mr Durand. It's a cat's tongue.'

eight

'Odeo! Odeo! Wake up, son! Wake up!'

It was mid-afternoon, and with nothing to stimulate his senses Odeo had retreated to the back office for a siesta after the lunchtime rush. If anybody could call it a rush. He'd been dreaming about Claudette again. 'What do you want, Lionel? What is it?'

'It's the Mexicans, Odeo! The Mexicans are here!'

'*Jezi-Kris!* The goddamn Mexicans are here?! Now?!' Odeo sprang out of his chair like a cat with its tail on fire. He pulled on his jacket, straightened his tie and started throwing papers off the desktop, searching frantically through the drawers. 'Where's my goddamn lucky goddamn cufflinks at?'

'Never mind that now, Odeo. You looks fine. Jus' be cool,' Lionel said, trying to placate him. 'Treyvon's makin' sure they's comfortable out there. Y'all be cool. You wan' a drink? Ain't you got nothing to boost yo' confidence, none?' he touched a finger to his own nose and raised an eyebrow.

'Nah man - *shit, shit, shit* - I'm all out!'

'Well, here then. I always keep a lil' on me - *laisser les bons temps rouler* - you knows what I'm sayin?' Lionel winked as he handed over a tight little wrap of silver foil.

'You wily ol' goat!' Odeo grinned and wagged a finger playfully at the janitor. 'I din't know you liked to party. You's a bonafide lifesaver!'

Odeo tipped the contents of the foil packet onto the back of his hand - 'I ain't sure this is gon' do it,' - he said, snorting it anyway.

He expected a hit that never came: there was no immediate rush of blood to the head, no quickening of his pulse, no sharper focus. Instead, the world seemed to slow down and slip into grayscale.

'What *is* this, Lionel? What did you give me?' he asked, but the words came tumbling off his tongue like he was spitting out a mouthful of spaghetti and meatballs. 'Cantfeelmydamnlips...'

Lionel stood, watching and waiting, his eyes tiny pinpricks of light in the darkness.

'Now why don't you sit yourself down, son. We gots to have us a *talk*...'

Ten minutes later, Odeo emerged from his office and joined the party. He walked like a man trying to prove he was fit to drive. His tie was askew. The Mexicans - one big, one small - were enjoying free cocktails and some personal attention from a couple of Cheaters' better-looking girls in a booth in the VIP lounge, which was separated from the regular lounge by only a length of purple velvet rope. The sour tang of stale beer and vomit still hung in the air in the otherwise empty club.

Treyvon appeared, shooed away the women and made the introductions. He eyed Odeo warily; there was something off about him. More drinks arrived. Cigars were lit. The small Mexican was speaking now, and Odeo swung his heavy head up to pay attention, but everything felt like a movie. Nuno Cherin was laying down his family's plans to buy out Cheaters - above market value - most through a simple bank transfer, the rest in cash. Odeo nodded like a dashboard toy. He thought he could hear the ocean.

'We have looked into your finances and frankly, Señor Boucher, you are in trouble. At this rate, you won't make it past Mardi Gras. Then what? It would be a shame if a guy with such grand ambitions ended up sticking a *pistola* in his own mouth. So, we will cover all your outstanding debts. We can write them off today. This should take some pressure off.' Nuno pulled two neat stacks of money from the inside pocket of his silver suit and laid them on the table. The yellow labels each read ten thousand dollars.

'Consider this a... how do you say? A show of faith. You can keep the club in your name, *claro*, and as far as you are concerned the day-to-day business operations won't change but - let's be clear here - if we make a deal, you'll be working for my family. And you are a *silent* partner, *entiendes*? For this, we will pay you a good salary. More than you are making now, that's for sure.'

Some part of this message seemed to shine through the fog of Odeo's subconscious. He gripped the edge of the table and sighed heavily. It was not gratitude - he neither liked nor trusted the shiny, little man laying down the terms - but it was relief. The stress had been eating him up for months. Cheaters was a sinking ship - he didn't care who was handing out the lifejackets.

Nuno reached into his jacket again and pulled out a final gift: a pound block of pure cocaine. He opened a clasp knife and took his time slicing carefully through the cellophane, scooping out a taster on the blade, and cutting a thin line on the tabletop. Odeo watched dumbly as Nuno eased a hundred-dollar bill from a stack and handed it over.

'This product comes from our homeland. Chiapas, in the south. High in the Andes.'

Odeo stared at the bill in his hand but had forgotten what came next.

'We don't sell Peru. We don't sell Colombia. We don't sell Bolivia,' Nuno continued. 'This product is one hundred percent Mexico. Totalmente *au-ten-ti-co*. This is how we do our business. My brother - Lauturo Francisco Remedios Cherin - does not put his name to an inferior product. We will supply this product to you, your dancers and customers at a reduced rate. It is good for business.'

Odeo slumped in his chair, a half-smile playing on his lips, his heart slowly thumping in his chest.

'So, do we have a deal?'

This was his moment and that was his cue. The words formed in his mouth unconsciously.

'No deal,' he said, without looking up. It was the only thing he could think of saying.

Nuno laughed and looked at his big partner, who followed suit. Odeo stared back with a deadpan expression until the laughter died out.

'This is a joke? You are joking, no?'

'No deal,' Odeo repeated against his will. It felt as though he was coughing up a fish bone.

The little Mexican blinked and gave a tight, pained smile. 'You are hoping for a better offer then? Name your price.' Irritation had sharpened his accent.

'No deal.' Odeo couldn't stop himself.

'You are a hard man to please, Señor Boucher.'

'No...' he tried to hold it back but couldn't. 'deal.'

At this point, the big Mexican stood up and started shouting in Spanish, jabbing his finger in Odeo's face. *'Pinche cabrón. Estas pero si bien pendejo...'*

'No deal. No deal!' Odeo exclaimed, wide-eyed, feeling like he was choking on the words themselves. Treyvon had arrived and was already breaking up the meeting, moving Odeo out of harm's way.

Nuno Cherin stood, picked up his cash and drugs and straightened his silver suit jacket. 'Very well. I will talk to my brother. He insists on hearing unwelcome news immediately. Perhaps we will meet again soon, Señor

Boucher.'

Odeo flopped back on the plush velvet sofa, unable to process what had just happened. 'No deal,' he sighed.

*

The scientists would work it out eventually, but Brad decided to give them the heads up anyway. Unable to reach Zam, he left a terse message with Rubino, her gofer, explaining that the bracelet sent to Eve Carmel was intended to keep her quiet.

'Listen Rubino, you don't have to believe it, just pass it up the chain. That thing was *made* with Carmel's hair: it was *made for* her specifically.' '*Like a key for a lock,*' the priestess said, and the words had sent a chill through Brad's bones. He snapped his cellphone shut and stepped back inside. 'Just filling in my partner on the information you've provided. You've really been extremely helpful.'

'You sound surprised, *Détective*. Didn't you think I would be able to help?'

'Honestly, Madame Coulombe, I didn't know what to expect...' he replied with a smile.

'Don't you believe in voodoo?'

'You know, that's the second time I've been asked that question in the last...' Brad checked his watch, '... twelve hours.'

'What did you say the first time?'

'Seeing is believing.'

'You have to have faith. What *do* you believe in?'

'Not much,' Brad settled back in his seat, contemplating how much of himself he really wanted to divulge to somebody he had only just met. The silence stretched out between them, but Lovelie only sipped her tisane and waited for him to continue.

'I suppose I used to believe in this,' he answered finally, pulling his old police badge from his pocket and handling it fondly, 'I don't anymore. And I used to believe in this,' he held up his left hand, so Lovelie could see his wedding ring, 'I don't anymore.'

'Anything else?' she asked, sensing he had more to say.

'Well, I used to believe in myself,' Brad said, glibly. 'And I'm still trying. Here I am, right? Still doing it. I'm trying real hard, but sometimes, I don't know what I've got left. So, you ask me if I believe in voodoo? In God? In religion? And I say, I'm sorry, join the back of the line. Cheers.' He raised his mug.

'You're a very hard man to read,' Lovelie began.

'So, my wife tells me. *Used to* tell me,' Brad corrected himself.

'The soul is anchored in the spirit world by all its desires and all its fears - those things that cannot be touched. Everything that we keep hidden from others. When I perform a reading, I look for those intangibles. But you're...' she tilted her head, sizing him up and searching for the right words, '... your soul is like a ship which has slipped its moorings.'

'That sounds like a euphemism for crazy,' Brad said and quickly changed the subject. 'There's something I've always wanted to ask... somebody like you.'

'Go on...'

'Why do people want to know their future?'

'Well, in some cases, a fixed point in the future can help a person progress through life. Think of it as a marker post along the way, rather than a destination. Many people do not know *who* they really are, and they look to me - to voodoo - for reassurance that they are on the right path. Are you on the right path?'

Brad frowned. He didn't like the way the priestess kept flipping the conversation back to him, forcing him to look inside. He had never been good with emotions - his own or anybody else's. It was one of the many criticisms that Elaine had leveled at him towards the end. 'Detached' she would call him in her lighter moments; 'dead inside,' when she wanted to hurt him. She believed he was unable to cope with the emotional heavy lifting expected of a man whose wife was facing down terminal illness, but it was Brad's only way of compartmentalizing the difficult aspects of his life.

He noticed a light rain had begun to fall.

'I guess... when you're a kid, growing up, you have this vision of who you're going to be. I don't mean... where you're going to live or what you're going to do necessarily... it's more of a feeling about the person you're going to become.'

'But then one day, you wake up and you realize that you're not that person - not that I'm saying anything changes dramatically - it's just like your compass wasn't quite pointing due north and after all this time, you've arrived somewhere else, way off course. Tiny choices have a major effect, I suppose. Anyway, I guess that's where I am right now,' he said quietly.

'You could still change though? Fix your compass? Find the path you lost?'

'You think I could still make it as a Saints player? Or a lumberjack?' Brad laughed, resting a hand on his sizeable gut. Lovelie smiled, but said nothing, waiting for him to fill the silence. 'Sometimes you catch a glimpse of that person, though. Not the football-playing lumberjack so much, but - I don't know - something you do, or a thought that crosses your mind, you know? It's like the sun shining through the clouds.'

'I know,' Lovelie gave him another understanding

smile, as though she was proud of the breakthrough he had made.

'Anyway, I'm sure you have... other... um... readings to... read,' Brad stuttered, suddenly ashamed of having laid himself bare.

'No, I have a very small, very loyal clientele,' Lovelie replied. 'If I wanted to make easy money, I could set up a table in Jackson Square and sell half-truths to tourists.'

'Still, I should be going.'

'One moment, *Détective*,' Lovelie murmured, 'I have something which might help you with your case.' She disappeared from the kitchen briefly and Brad could hear her riffling through cupboards and opening drawers.

'I've picked up a lot of trinkets and baubles over the years,' she said as she returned, 'but these have never really worked for me.' She handed Brad an ornate little wooden box, carved with Chinese symbols. He opened it cautiously, half-expecting to find a cat's tongue or something equally grisly. Inside were two identical silver balls, the size of tangerines.

'Oh... balls,' Brad managed. 'Thank you.'

'They're *Baoding* balls. Taoists use them to meditate. Think of them as giant worry beads: something to occupy the body while the mind finds its center.'

'That is good,' Brad said, without looking up.

Lovelie gave a tiny huff of exasperation. '*M'sieur* Durand, I'm not suggesting you need to seek inner peace. They will help you to delve into your subconscious. There is knowledge to be found within...'

'Ah,' Brad uttered, turning the box over, expecting to find instructions printed on the back.

'Simply hold them - one in each hand - while you wait

for sleep. Focus on your case. Ask yourself questions. *Li Grand Zombi* will bring you answers.'

'And - just remind me - who is LGZ again?'

'*Li Grand Zombi,*' she said, rolling the long Creole vowels around in her mouth like she was sucking on a jawbreaker, 'is the snake *loa*: an immensely powerful spirit. In my country we call him *Papa Legba*, but he has many names. He is the messenger between the worlds of flesh and spirit, and life and death. That's why our rituals often include a snake dance - to celebrate the link to his sacred and ancient knowledge. If you're lucky, you will catch him between the land of wakefulness and the waters of sleep.'

'Oh! I get it! Brad exclaimed, finally understanding and grinning widely.

'They're solid enough, so you won't break them. They jangle too. And they make less mess than beer bottles,' she smiled knowingly.

'That's very kind. I'll try them,' Brad said, tucking the wooden box into his jacket pocket as she led him out. '*Merci beaucoup* for your time, Madame - it's been very... enlightening.'

At the threshold, she touched his forehead lightly with her fingertips - a simple voodoo blessing - and Brad noticed the slightest frown momentarily clouded her expression.

'What do you see?' Brad asked, only half-joking.

'A struggle,' she said with a hint of sadness. 'Take care, *M'sieur* Durand.'

*

The story broke around four o' clock. WWOZ picked it up first, running with the jazz angle of Mani's murder, but it was actually WWNO – the university radio station -

which first made the connection with Shay Favreau's killing, five years earlier. By the time the evening news was broadcast, the words 'Voodoo Killer' were ubiquitous.

From the comfort of Georgine Rieux's soft bed, Lionel watched in horror, his eyes frozen on the TV screen. They had dug out a Michoud local, resplendent in a floral housecoat and curlers, who claimed to have heard Mani's final rendition of 'My Melancholy Baby.'

'I used to love that tune,' she was saying to the interviewer. 'Not no more. That Voodoo Killer done *spoilt* it.'

Lionel knew it was only a matter of time before Ike went a step too far, but slaying two boys in the same way was beyond reckless, even for him. '*Jezi-Kris* – that boy is a God damn *liability*,' he said aloud, angrier with Ike than fearful of the ramifications for himself.

'Who's that, *mon cher*?' Georgine asked, as she sashayed naked into the bedroom, carrying a large tray of homemade delights: egg salad, mushroom pinwheels, tiny crawfish pies, walnut scones and a pot of vanilla tea.

'Nobody,' Lionel answered brusquely, pulling himself up the bed to make space.

'"Voodoo Killer",' Georgine huffed. 'Hasn't this city suffered enough?' She picked up the remote and turned down the volume. 'Now, let me make you up a plate.'

'Nah darlin', I ain't feelin' too good.'

'Hush up now, hot-dog. You need to keep your strength up. Fo' me,' Georgine pursed her lips and gave him an impish grin as she popped a pinwheel into his mouth.

'I don' know where my mind's at,' he said apologetically, picking the flecks of puff-pastry from his lips.

While he was painfully aware that he had the 'liability' to thank for his current situation - his new-found vigor and the woman by his side - Lionel was beginning to think it was time to cut ties with his ward.

'Detective Delgado,' he muttered under his breath, as if just saying her name was enough to keep the evil spirits at bay. He didn't want to linger on the thoughts of betrayal for too long or too deeply. If Ike saw through his intentions, Lionel knew he might find himself on the butcher's block. 'I think I done los' m'appetite,' he said.

'What's the matter, *cher*? You can tell me.'

Lionel turned to face his lover and took her hand in his, while he searched for the right words. 'This thing we got, it's... *delicate*, Georgie-girl. Can't say fo' sure how long it's gonna last.'

'I knows that,' she answered, surprised by the turn the conversation had taken. 'We *old*,' she chuckled. 'We gots to make the mos' of our time.'

'No, it ain't that,' Lionel swallowed hard. 'If I had to go away, someplace else, would y'all come with me?'

'Why is you talkin' like this, baby?' Georgine placed her hand on the side of his face and looked hard into his yellowed eyes. 'Is you in trouble?'

'Maybes.'

The atmosphere in the room changed abruptly. Georgine's smile faded and she shrank away from him, wide-eyed. 'Am *I* in trouble?'

Lionel rocked his head from side to side, 'I needs to know I can protect you. From him.'

'From who?'

Lionel extended a bony finger and pointed ominously at the television screen. '*Him*.'

nine

Zam hadn't realized she was humming 'Love and Marriage' until Nathan Flowers told her to stop it.

'I can't help it,' she said. 'Narcotics and homicide. *They go together like a horse and carriage*.'

She was flicking through the files of ongoing cases. Most of them were cold or had been handed over to the Drug Enforcement Administration as part of bigger operations, just as Roland Lash had explained. In nearly all, however, there were footnotes linking the seizure of cocaine or heroin to the murders of young men, mostly, shot or stabbed to death while trying to score or sell. It was a dangerous game on both sides.

'What can you tell me about this guy?' Zam asked, recognizing a name from one of Rubino's cases.

Nathan bent his head to read it written at the bottom of the page, 'Francisco Pasamontes. Um... Patrol found him floating in the river, down by Woldenberg Park. 'First of August" he read from the notes. 'Couple o' gunshot wounds, but he was still carrying seventeen baggies of primo coke and a lot of cash...'

'Whoever killed him didn't need either,' Zam interjected.

'Correct. We been seeing signs of another Latino crew for over a year. Same top quality,' he said, referring to the cocaine, 'but all over town. So, we're thinking maybe these guys are pirates - no fixed turf - just quietly hustling across the whole city. If we're right, and this Pasamontes *was* a pirate - then he probably yo-hoed the wrong ho.'

'Was he in one piece when they pulled him out?'

Nathan gave her an odd look, 'Far as I know. Apart from the holes.'

'Any theories?'

'About who killed him? Sorry, not our job,' Nathan replied, with a lopsided smile. 'If I were to guess though, given the location, the way he was killed, *and* the fact that they didn't rob him first, I'd say it was the Italians.'

'The same Italians who run the strip-clubs?' Zam asked.

Nathan nodded.

'How many are there?'

'Clubs? Downtown, 'bout sixteen. And they own most of them. *Family* businesses. Mickey Lanza owns three. Frankie Tufaro owns four, plus a few dive bars and restaurants.'

'Yeah, I read that somewhere,' Zam said, flipping open another file.

'In terms of drugs, we don't tend to see a lot of street-corner action. You must remember that from your own days on the beat. Most of the scores go down at dives like Tufaro's. He'll have a guy working for him - like this fella,' Nathan pointed to a mugshot on the wall, 'That's Fat Alphonse Petto. He's a *real* piece of work - theft, larceny, extortion, assault, not to mention drug trafficking and distribution.'

'His mother must be very proud.'

'Hmm. You'll find Alphonse in The Toulouse most nights. He don't drink much, but he's takin' calls, textin', runnin' between the restroom and the street *all night*. And most of his customers are Tufaro's strippers. So, it's a nice little circle, you see?'

Zam nodded. 'Tufaro owns the club, pays the strippers, and encourages them to spend their wages in *his* bar and on *his* drugs. Sweet.'

'Plus, strippers do *boo-coo* drugs. That's an overgeneralization, I know, but there it is. Blame the losers groping them all night, or their 'daddy didn't love me' complexes, or the stigma of having to do what they do. Whatever. They make a ton of money too - not as much as they used to, but they don't go short, believe me - then they're plugged in to the drugs scene as soon as they start working for the mob. They're an easy target for us, but - here's the kicker - we can't touch the likes of Tufaro or Lanza. The FBI want those guys all to themselves. They're big fish,' Nathan looked slightly embarrassed. 'Too big for us anyways.'

'So, we go for the low hanging fruit?' Zam asked.

'Lower, sure. There're still a few joints which *aren't* family owned. We stake 'em out every once in a while, hustle the doormen, the customers, the strippers. Try to bust it up a bit, you know? It's pretty much all we *can* do.'

'Sounds good. When do we start?'

'You can start whenever you like,' Nathan said, easing himself out of his chair and grabbing his jacket.

'You're not coming?' Zam asked, surprised.

'What can I say? My wife doesn't really like me hanging out at strip-clubs. Have fun though. I'll see you tomorrow.'

*

Brad didn't notice the smell at first, not until later in the afternoon when he opened the kitchen window and it came seeping in like a poisonous gas, bringing with it so many memories from his former life: bodies folded in two and swollen tight in the trunks of abandoned cars, or putrefying in the dregs of dumpsters, corpses left to rot in the crack-dens and whorehouses that masqueraded as downtown hotels.

It wasn't necessarily a human body this time - more likely a cat or a dog, possibly a raccoon or even an armadillo trapped between the floors of a house or inside an air-conditioning unit. But Brad knew one thing: that smell wouldn't quit until the rotting flesh was buried in the ground.

'This office is now closed. Our opening hours are nine to five, Monday to Friday. If it is an emergency...' Brad hung up. Forced to choose between waiting till morning for the City Sanitation Department and dealing with the problem himself, he grabbed a garbage bag, found a pair of old gloves in the back of the SUV and went looking for the source.

The air outside was thick with the stench, but Brad followed his nose along the street, just beyond the old police jail and patrol station to a house fifty yards down. Its doors and windows had been boarded over for five years. A faded red 'X' spray-painted on the porch told Brad that the Urban Search and Rescue team had visited on the sixth of September - a week after the storm - and found '1': a dead body in the house. He had noticed the same markings on the broken houses all over town: an almost biblical indication of those which were spared from the flood and those which weren't. Brad tried to remember the owner - his neighbor - but neither a name nor a face came to mind.

He climbed around the back, through the cat's claw vines threatening to rip down the trusses. The back door was hanging open and the smell was stronger here. Stepping inside, Brad tried the lights - nothing - so picked his way cautiously through the darkness as his eyes adjusted. The wallpaper, black with mold, sagged under its own weight. Flies buzzed around, drunk on the foul air. Brad heard the familiar scuttle of rodents.

His cellphone chirped in his pocket, but he let it ring out, not wanting to drag out the moment any longer than was absolutely necessary.

He eventually found the body curled around the downstairs toilet – a big, black dog had crawled in to die on the cool of the bathroom tiles. Every one of its bones was visible. The smell was almost tangible now - a thick soup of dead fish and cloying rotten fruit. Brad snuffed down his nose to clear his head and stamped his feet to chase away the fat rats which were already feeding on the dog's guts, in a sick parody of puppies suckling at the teat.

The garbage bag was no good for the job - too small and flimsy. Instead, Brad found a filthy blanket piled in the corner of the lounge and laid it out in the hallway. He stepped into the bathroom, took the dog by a back leg, and slid it out from around the toilet and into the center of the blanket, taking care not to rip through the soft flesh. He felt his gorge rising at the sight of the swarming wasps and green bottles feasting around its ear and sunken eye. Hastily folding the blanket around the body, Brad pulled together the four corners into a thick rope with enough slack to heft the makeshift sack back through the house and out into the sunlight and fresher air.

Stooped over and gasping, he headed through the undergrowth of the backyard, across the wasteland in the vague direction of the outfall canal. Brad's thoughts returned to the case, and he remembered Nadia Romero whose body had been discovered uptown in the same waterway. He shook off the memory as he opened the blanket and rolled the body down the embankment into the water. It floated in the shallows and a cloud of flies and wasps rose up like a plague, but the sickening smell dissipated on the breeze; the twinge in Brad's lower lumbar the only legacy of the dog's passing. He trudged home, stinking, feeling the weight of a long, exhausting day and too little sleep with grand plans of a takeaway pizza and a six pack of Abita.

*

Nothing was going to dampen his mood. Ike had spent the afternoon dealing with the everyday practicalities of life, which brought joy in their simplicity: tending to his dogs and chickens, shucking corn and sharpening his billhook. With a little kerosene and a whetstone, he had honed its blade with long smooth strokes until it sang. He took his time, contemplating the marvelous visions he had seen in the chicken blood earlier that morning. Although Delgado had faded away, her companion had now moved to the foreground. Ike had seen him clearly for the first time - a big brute of a man, lumbering out of the shadows of his own conscience, like a black bear coming out of hibernation in springtime. Ike had plans for the bear. He would be ready when the time came.

Right now, his mind was elsewhere for it was the fire which had excited him most. There, in the congealing swirls, Ike had seen the flames, burning like a beacon and drawing him in. So brilliant was the vision, he could feel the warmth of the blaze touching his erotic core. When his ardor finally abated, Ike woke from his reverie drenched in sweat and utterly consumed. Just the thought of it caused Johnny Conqueror to twitch eagerly.

Sitting in the rose-glow of the setting sun, on a warped leather armchair which he had dragged outside, Ike cleaned his nails with the quill of a chicken feather and watched Lionel Root shambling up the stoop to knock on the broken door.

'Well, lookie-here,' Ike drawled, enjoying the sudden jolt of fear on Lionel's wizened face. 'I was jus' wonderin' to mysel' when you'd come 'round. And here you is.'

'Yeah, here I is,' Lionel said with a thin smile, regaining his composure. 'You seen the news?'

Ike shrugged. 'Am I on it?'

Lionel spat on the floor and nodded. He checked there was nobody walking by before whispering, 'You *is* it. They callin' you 'Voodoo Killer' now... Oh! You think that's funny, huh?'

Ike sighed. 'Oh well, oh well,'

'You jus' had to take that boy's twig, din't you?'

Ike sprang out of his chair and stretched. 'I does what the spirits tell me, old man. Can't argue with the spirits.' He clapped Lionel on the back. 'Come inside now. Tell me all your troubles.'

Ike kicked the swollen door closed behind them. The darkness swallowed Lionel whole. 'The *police* can't let it go now,' he said, filling the silence, only vaguely aware of Ike moving past him in the hallway. 'They's gon' be on us both like red beans on rice.'

A fluorescent strip-light flickered into life in the kitchen and Lionel shuffled toward it gratefully. His heart fluttered. Ike unlocked the green fridge and turned to show Lionel the small cigar-shaped package in his hand. It was wrapped in a muslin cloth and tied off neatly at both ends with twine.

'You bes' find a buyer for this then,' Ike said. 'That's your job, after all.'

Lionel felt his vision swimming. 'How much you think I can get for that lil ol' thing?'

Ike set the package down carefully on the table-top and circled his arms around it protectively. 'This here is the *real deal*, Monsieur Root. Virgin blood. And - *my, my* - did that boy scream,' Ike gave a low whistle. '*Muti* through and through. This ain't no scrap from the slab.'

'Them there *scraps* is what's kept us going all this time. You can't keep choppin' up virgins all over town. Not now you done put so much heat on us - that's for sure.'

'I do whatever the spirits tells...'

'You and your goddamn spirits!' Lionel yelled, surprising himself with the depth of his fury. He dropped his eyes and let the silence ride for a few beats, before whispering. 'I'm sorry, Ike. I jus' don't... want to do this no more.'

Lionel pictured himself at his own spiritual crossroads, the regrets of his life - his failure as a son and as a father of sorts, the years lost to drink and drugs - behind him now; a fragile love with Georgine stretching ahead. He watched as a skinny black cat hobbled awkwardly across the worktops towards the sink. It was missing its front paws. It tried to drink from the dripping tap. Lionel pulled out a rickety chair and eased himself into it. 'I'm tired, son,' he said. 'Ain't you *tired*?'

'*Tired*?' Ike scoffed. 'I's in my *prime*.' Ike moved around the table - 'And you ain't gon' *quit* me now,' - until he was standing behind Lionel. 'Not now, not never.'

'I'm done, Ike.' Lionel shook his head emphatically, as if trying to prove to them both that he meant what he was saying.

Ike saw his thoughts. He didn't need to read Lionel's mind: his intentions were plain as the wiry gray hair on his head and the liver spots on his hands. Ike wasn't surprised.

'What *am* I gon' do with you, old man?' he said, picking up the parcel on the table and testing its weight, 'Oh well, if you ain't gon' do this, I guess I gots another job fo' you. What you say? One last lil' ol' job fo' me?' He cooed like a lover.

When Lionel shook his head again, Ike slapped him - hard - knocking him out of his chair, onto the filthy linoleum. Lionel tasted his own blood, metallic and bitter on his tongue.

The words tumbled out of him like a curse. 'I *hates* you, Ike Sugar. Look at what you become. The rooster? The dog? The pig? Yeah, you an animal a'ight. Ain't a shred o' *humanity* in your body.'

Ike stood over him, pointing his finger like a pistol. 'One last job, Lionel, or I'll stop your heart.' A smile and a thousand-yard stare. 'And then I'll kill your whore. You hear?'

He knew it was hopeless: Ike could be very persuasive. The tears rolled like olive oil down Lionel's cheeks, and he nodded.

*

Brad tossed the last crust back into the empty box and downed the rest of his beer. He had tried a few times to return Elaine's missed call but kept getting her voicemail. He listened to her message again just to hear her voice. Communication was always on her terms. Brad saw it as a subtle power struggle: one she was winning. He toyed with the idea of calling Kyle's cell, but knew it was wrong to use the boy as a go-between. Better to wait. Better she won.

Earlier that evening, while he'd been waiting for the pizza delivery boy to arrive, Brad had pinned up a tourist booth map of the city on the pristine magnolia wall of his lounge. On the simplistic street plan, he had marked the dozen crime scenes and added a post-it note profile of each victim - name, age, cause of death and posthumous mutilation - in the hope of teasing out a pattern from the seeming randomness. There was nothing. As Brad stared at it now, digesting his meal, he felt his eyelids grow heavy, until he awoke with a jolt when his head lolled forward.

He forced himself to stand up, then stripped, brushed his teeth, and settled back in the darkness on his recliner with thoughts of voodoo in his head and Madame Coulombe's wooden box clutched in his hands. He opened it slowly and the silver balls reflected slivers of streetlight, gleaming like a pair of unseeing eyes. With one in each hand, Brad draped his arms over the rests of his chair, realizing with chagrin that he probably looked less like an enlightened Taoist monk and more like a fat Buddha.

With an effort of will, he pushed all thoughts of Auden Tillery's smug face, Zam Delgado's slim legs, Kyle, Elaine and the Chevy dealer from his mind and focused entirely on the case. The balls were cool and smooth in his hands. 'Ask yourself questions,' the Priestess had told him - '*Li Grand Zombi* will bring you answers.' But there were so many questions, and the few answers which had seemed improbable only days earlier when he shared his thoughts with Zam had now hardened into fact. The *whens* and *wheres* of the case had given way to the *hows* and *whys*: how was the killer choosing his victims? Why was he collecting body parts? Why was Eve Carmel murdered? How was the old man connected? Why the candles and the feathers? Why the cat's tongue? The pigskin cells and dog hairs? Chicken claws, cat feathers and pigs' tongues…

Madame Coulombe was right - they did jangle when

they hit the floor.

*

Temptations, Déjà Vu, Stilettos, Barely Legal... Zam trawled along the 'strip' of Bourbon Street. It was only ten o' clock but the party was already in full swing. Groups of baying men gathered outside the clubs, counting their sweaty dollar bills and drinking. The dancers occasionally appeared, whipping up a frenzy as they paraded through the crowds in sparkling bustiers and G-strings, hot-pants and cowboy boots, feather boas and fishnet stockings. From a distance, they were visions of brazen sexuality - like fallen angels - but up close, Zam saw through the façade. These girls were tired: dead-eyed, with dry, dyed hair and too much make-up. Hooked, without a doubt.

These joints were all off limits to Zam - even if she could afford the entrance fee and the drinks, there was nothing to be gained by ruffling FBI feathers. All the same, she turned down Toulouse Street to see if she could spot Fat Alphonse and sure enough, there he was, just as Nathan had described: sitting at the bar, sucking on a soda and jabbing at his cellphone with a boudin-sized index finger.

Zam circled back down Royal, past a five-piece jazz band playing ragtime, and tic-tacked through the streets towards a couple of clubs on her list. She was optimistic about 'The Artist Café' which Roland Lash had described as 'a hallway with a bar for strippers at one end'. 'Aim low, start small,' she told herself, already making plans for bringing down the drug rackets in the entire French Quarter.

Claudette Tremblay knew how to spot a cop and saw her coming a mile away. Odeo had always told her to be polite to the law, but her parents had engendered within her a deep mistrust of authority and Claudette couldn't help herself. She dropped her eyes as Zam approached.

'Cheaters,' Zam said, reading the word emblazoned in pink sequins across Claudette's chest. 'Was it that? A club?'

Claudette nodded, eyeing Zam's flat shoes suspiciously.

'Down there?' Zam asked, peering into the gloom of Clinton Street. It came as no surprise that this place wasn't on Nathan's list. 'Are you a dancer?' The girl didn't look like one: she was too sweet, too unspoilt.

'Nope. Mr Boucher pays me to *induce* customers.'

Zam smiled. 'What's your name?'

Claudette shifted her weight and stared off into space. 'Cherry,' she lied.

'Just Cherry?'

'Uh-huh,' Claudette shrugged.

'What's your full name, Cherry?'

'*Cherry Pie*! How 'bout *that*?' she huffed, staring back defiantly from under tinted eyebrows. 'Listen cop, why all the questions? Am I under arrest or what?'

"course not,' Zam said coolly. 'You seem a little young to be working this late, 's all.'

'Yeah well, I'm twenty-one *actually*. I jus' looks young for my age, *'s all*.'

Zam nodded. 'It's ok. I'm not looking to cause you any trouble.' *Let patrol handle it*, she thought to herself. 'So, you like working at Cheaters?'

Claudette's expression softened visibly, 'I guess.'

'You think I should give it a try?' Zam asked.

Claudette looked at her sideways, 'Is you into that?'

'If you mean, 'am I a lesbian?' - no. I'm just doing my job, Cherry. Just like you.'

'Well, at Cheaters, everybody always gets a free champagne cocktail,' she said robotically, handing Zam a pink coupon. 'So, here.' Champagne was spelt 'Champange.'

'Thanks Cherry,' Zam said. 'You're real pretty by the way, and I love your shoes.' Claudette cracked a smile in spite of herself and her face shone. 'Take care out here, ok?'

Zam strolled down Clinton. The darkened buildings seemed to lean over her. The doorman turned at the sound of her footsteps on the sidewalk and Zam saw his face illuminated in the blue neon glow. It was Treyvon Plummer - a rapist she'd sent down six years earlier. She cast a glance back to Cherry on the corner, turned up the collar of her jacket and kept walking. As she passed by the club entrance, Zam fondly recalled kicking Treyvon square in the balls while she read him his rights back in 2004, and wondered if he remembered it too. She had no intention of tangling with him now, certainly not without the back-up she'd had then. Perhaps she could convince Nathan's wife to let him come out to play.

All the same: quiet, secluded and with a known felon working the door, Cheaters Gentlemen's Club had certainly piqued Zamora Delgado's interest.

ten

The city was overrun with stray dogs. They roamed the streets in packs, hid in the tall grass of blighted plots, scavenged and bred. They spread disease and occasionally attacked kids and old people. They died in Brad's neighbor's abandoned house.

Brad had cross-referenced his street-map and matrix of murder victims with his notes from the pathology reports. Sure enough, there was the answer: Kimberly Kelly, 15 y/o female. canine hairs found on her clothes and face.

The wild chicken population had also boomed since the storm and twice Brad had been woken at dawn by the sound of their crowing. There were around a dozen poultry farms in the Greater New Orleans area, but during the recession many homesteaders had begun raising their own hens for eggs and meat.

He skimmed through the pages of his notebook, looking for confirmation: the Amercauna tail feather pinned under Erica Huffman's corpse. Another piece of the puzzle.

But, according to the autopsy, Stephanie Dee West had been processed as an assault victim, and as such, Walt Forager's lab technicians had clipped and swabbed her fingernails for evidence. All they found were 'pig skin cells' - and Brad couldn't think of a reason for it. The woman worked in a library, not a butcher shop and as far as he knew, nobody kept pigs in the city limits. Over a second cup of coffee, a theory - the germ of a theory - began to form. He decided to speak to an expert and found one in the Yellow Pages.

'That's right. Hautum Hams is the sole supplier of pork meat within the city limits. There are some abattoirs and slaughterhouses upstate, but we provide ninety-two-point-four percent of pork and ham products across the city. If you're eating bacon, belly, loin, side, shoulder, spare ribs... the chances are, it was produced here. We also specialize in Grand Reserve cured ham, bone-in ham, semi boneless ham, flat ranch ham, ham steak, ham shank, hot green onion sausage, rope smoke sausage, chorizo sausage, Italian sausage and wieners,' Dennis Hautum cleaned his spectacles with the end of his tie and managed to sound both proud of his business and bored stiff at the same time.

'That's what the butcher told me,' Brad said. 'More or less.'

Just as Madame Coulombe had predicted, *Li Grand Zombi* had revealed a secret, hidden at the crossroads of the *in-between*. Brad had been so blinded by the mysteries surrounding all the murders that he had neglected the obvious clues, most notably the pig skin cells under Stephanie Dee West's nails, left behind when she had scratched at her attacker's face.

The offices of Hautum Hams occupied a squat, gray two-story off Jefferson Highway, but Brad had to admit the boardroom had a splendid view of the river.

On a clear day, Dennis Hautum liked to stand in the boardroom and watch the boats heading north towards the bend. Dennis had never intended to be a successful businessman. He's been quite happy treading water after college, getting high and road tripping to Mexico, when his father's sudden death catapulted him to the top echelons of meat-processing in the state. Twenty years later, he realized that he hated the stress of accounting spreadsheets, marketing plans, social media, staff attendance, payroll, suppliers.

On top of it all, his wife had recently turned vegetarian, having watched a documentary about the sex lives of vegan celebrities, and she was forcing her opinions down the throats of anybody who would listen, including their three children: Dennis Junior, Jayden and little Caleb. Presented with zucchini fritters and five bean casserole where once had been roast pork po' boys and mixed grills, his sons were shedding pounds like jockeys before race season.

That morning had started out like any other, until his secretary nervously told him that a police detective was waiting in reception. Once the initial shock had subsided, Dennis welcomed the break from the tedium.

'We're just making some enquiries,' Brad began, flicking open his notepad and searching in his jacket pocket for a pen, 'just routine, nothing to worry about...'

'Is this about the attack? It's been so long. I didn't think the police were interested.'

Brad didn't miss a beat. 'The attack. Of course. I've read the report, but since I'm new to the case, could you fill me in on the details?'

'Sure. Let's see. It was July 2007, mid-morning. Friday the thirteenth actually. I had just finished a meeting with the sales team and I was standing right here, right in this spot. Back then, we used to give away the off-cuts every Friday morning.'

'Off-cuts of meat?'

'I'm not sure you could call it meat, but... yes. That's the packing plant down there.' He pointed across the industrial estate and shuddered imperceptibly. If the pressures of management weren't hard enough, he detested the factory and its frigid air, the feel of raw meat and cold steel, the look and smell of recycled sea-salt, yellow with old blood. Inside, unskilled workers would be chopping up pigs, trimming fat, removing the bone around each ham's hip joint with a set of industrial bolt-cutters. It made for a neater, more customer-friendly product when the meat tightened and shrank during the year-long curing process. The thought alone was enough to make Dennis's gorge rise.

'Bone shards, offal, snouts, ears, skin, trotters. We used to crate it up and give it all away every Friday morning. It was a publicity stunt at first. We were on the news. Groups of hunters would come before the weekend and queue up in the parking lot. Scraps for the dogs or bait for traps - I don't know. Anyway, word started to get around and lots of... um... poor folk started turning up.' Dennis paused briefly.

'Mr. Hautum?'

He was embarrassed. 'All those shopping carts and empty plastic bags. It wasn't an image we wanted for the company....'

'I see,' Brad nodded, hiding his distaste. The poor get poorer, he thought. 'Tell me about the attack.'

'Yes. Well, I was standing here that morning, looking out at the queue and wondering if I could squeeze in nine holes at Audubon Park,' he chuckled nervously, 'when I noticed this one guy - he didn't seem to fit in. You could pick out the hunters easily enough - you know - camouflage pants and checked shirts. This guy looked poor, but...' Dennis shook his head at the memory. Brad let him find the words. '... he looked so *proud* to be there. Like there was nowhere else he would rather be. I couldn't understand it. He was standing like this,' Dennis Hautum sucked in his gut and threw his shoulders back, 'like a statue. Like a *model*.'

'Can you describe him?' Brad asked.

Dennis snorted, 'Damn, if I close my eyes, I can still

see him. Barefoot. Denim overalls, covered in dark paint. Dreadlocks down to here. He stared right up at me. These windows are tinted,' Dennis tapped on the pane, 'but I knew he was watching me, watching him.

'I thought to myself, 'No way,' and I waved down at him. Like this. He just stared right back, right in my damn eyes. I was alone in here and I said to myself - to him - 'Can you see me?' and I swear to God, no sooner had I said the words, the freak grinned and nodded. You probably think I'm crazy but I'm telling you, *it happened*. He must have been a hundred meters away. More.'

Dennis Hautum was flushed and sweaty; his hands were shaking slightly as poured himself a scotch. He tipped the decanter in Brad's direction. Brad said nothing but held up his finger and thumb - half an inch apart - and winked.

'What happened next?' he asked.

'So, the guy moves to the front of the line. He starts… um… picking through the crates and whatever, putting the odd scrap in a bag and not paying me any attention, so I thought I'd imagined the whole thing.' He took a drink to settle his nerves.

'I couldn't see his hands. He had his back to me,' Hautum's voice was quaking now. He put a hand over his eyes. 'Then he turns around and I can see he's got a whole pig's face over his own, like a mask.'

Brad's blood turned to dust.

'I… froze. He pointed up at me and that's when I felt the pain in my shoulder. I thought I was dying. Which I was, I guess. My secretary heard me collapse. She called for the ambulance.'

'Heart attack?' Brad asked.

Dennis nodded and downed the rest of his scotch.

'First time?'

He nodded again.

'Had you been in good health before... the attack?'

'Yes,' Hautum said, without elaborating.

'So, you stopped giving the off-cuts away after that?'

'When I came back to work, yes. We reprocess all the odds and ends now. Pet food, economy sausages, recession-busting burgers, that kind of thing. Pigs' cheek and trotters became very popular again thanks to that TV chef, the British guy.'

"The Leftover Gourmet' - I like that guy,' Brad added.

'Me too. He probably paid for my Mercedes last year,' Hautum smiled, hoping to change the subject, but Brad wasn't finished.

'You never saw your attacker again?'

'No.'

'It's a long shot, but I have to ask - you got any security footage of that morning?'

'We did at the time, but the images were useless. Too fuzzy. We've upgraded to a hard-drive system now. High-def resolution, twenty-four hours a day. It covers, well, everything.'

'Sounds like a good idea,' Brad replied, hiding his disappointment. Another dead-end, he thought to himself.

Dennis had recovered his self-control. 'The officers I spoke to at the time - they clearly thought I was crazy,' he laughed nervously. 'After a while, I began to think that maybe they were right, that it was just a symptom of a heart attack. A rush of blood to the head or something. But you're different. You know I'm not making this up, don't you? He's still out there, isn't he?'

Brad finished his drink and stood up to leave. 'Thanks for your time, Mr. Hautum. Here's my card. If you remember any more details, if you happen to see the man again, even if The Leftover Gourmet comes by looking for pigs' cheeks, give me a call.'

'We had a guy here about a month ago,' Hautum interjected. 'Some old timer. My secretary dealt with him. Get this - he wanted to make a trade: a pig's face for a lucky mojo bag. He said it would bring the company 'great *poo-wah*', whatever that is. This city…' Dennis shook his head with a wry smile.

Brad sat down again.

*

'You seem more positive today,' Nathan Flowers said, peering over his newspaper. 'Did you get anywhere last night?'

'I did actually,' Zam replied breezily, without taking her eyes from her computer screen. 'I found a new place.'

'Yeah? A new strip-joint? Whereabouts?'

'Downtown,' Zam answered, tapping away at her keyboard.

'Any action?' Nathan shared a glance with Roland Lash.

'Perhaps. I don't like the smell of it, that's for sure. The whole vibe is off. The doorman is an ex-con, and there's an underage girl handing out flyers outside. I didn't manage to get in, but I'll be heading back as soon as I can score some surveillance equipment. Who do we normally go through?'

'Um… to be honest, the DEA tends to manage surveillance.'

'We don't run any ourselves?' she asked. Blank faces stared back. 'I thought we were supposed to… investigate stuff?'

Somebody coughed to break the awkward silence. Zam raised an eyebrow but said nothing. Nathan wheeled himself across the office on his swivel chair and pulled up beside her.

'Listen Zam,' he whispered, 'this is - what? - your third day? And you're coming on like gangbusters here. Not that we don't appreciate what you're trying to do. You know, it's good to have new blood, right? But take it easy, ok? These guys... they're just doing their jobs.'

'No, Nathan. *You* are *not* doing *your* jobs,' Zam hissed. 'You're sitting up here like it's the fucking chess and checkers club. Well, I'm not playing.'

'If you keep up the attitude, you're not going to make many friends.'

'I'm a big girl,' she scoffed.

Nathan clicked his fingers, 'Hey, I got an idea: why don't you give *Detective* Durand a call?' There was a flinty tone to his voice. Zam had wondered how long it would take for the gossip to trickle down. 'He was always such a reliable cop,' he continued. 'Faithful to the end. Right, Roly? Oh, apart from that time when he went AWOL for a month, I suppose.'

'I bet he's got some top 'surveillance equipment' too, now that he's working for Miami Vice,' Roland snickered.

'Shut your fat face, Lash,' Zam snapped, finally looking up from her work. She turned to Nathan. 'And you - you're their spokesperson? You're a pussy-whipped idiot. Do you think any of these guys has any respect for you, Flowers? They don't. And since I have your attention for the first time in three days, let me tell *all o' y'all* something else, just so's we're clear - none of you will ever be half the detective that Brad Durand is.'

*

The radio blasted but the sound was turned all the way down on the television in Tacos and Beer on St Charles.

All the same, Brad eyed the screen while he worked through his Big A$$ Burrito. Some heartless news team had hunted down Remy Favreau, Shay's father, to get his take on the Voodoo Killer. The former professor of linguistics at Tulane was whacking weeds in somebody else's uptown garden. He had nothing to say to the reporter and raised his hand to push the camera lens out of his face, but his 'drinker's nose' and glazed expression spoke volumes of his loss. Unable to bear the weight of her own grief, Mrs Favreau had left her husband and moved to Houston – the ultimate betrayal for any Louisianan. Brad looked at his fellow diners, chowing down on nachos and hot wings, and wondered if they could see something of Remy Favreau in his eyes too. Wiping his greasy fingers on a napkin, he typed a hurried text message to Elaine: 'I can change. x.'

But he couldn't bring himself to press 'Send.'

Brad had suspected the killer wasn't working alone: somebody who could call forth spirits from the next world wouldn't concern themselves selling chicken feet to suicidal adolescents. And certainly, no serial killer worth his salt would put his neck on the line for thirty-seven dollars. Dennis Hautum had promised to call as soon as the security firm found the images of the old mojo man in the memory banks, but he couldn't be sure of the date and there was a window of two or three days to examine. Until he did, Brad was at a loose end. Having ticked Jazzland off his list, he had intended to visit the rest of the crime scenes on his map of the city, just to get a feel for the killer's hunting ground, but it seemed like a fool's errand now. There was no pattern here. The snitch had suggested he visit the St Louis Cemetery, the final resting place of Marie Laveau, the nineteenth century Voodoo Queen of New Orleans herself. Her grave was desecrated with hundreds of 'X's scored into the stone - testament to the undying belief in her power. There was never a shortage of acolytes paying their respects and making offerings at her tomb in the hope of blessings in return, but somehow, he knew he wouldn't find any clues amongst the walking tours of the famous crypts and mausoleums. At least not in the light of the trombonist's murder: St Louis Cemetery wasn't the killer's style - too conventional, too obvious, Brad thought. His man was off center; not the pantomime villain portrayed on the news but something altogether more sinister and unpredictable, hiding in the gray areas between life and death, surfacing like a hungry Mississippi catfish, barbed and poisonous.

Tired of thinking, Brad caught the waiter's eye and ordered another beer and a Sazerac chaser. He was almost satisfied with himself. He intended to get very drunk.

*

The bell rang at eight thirty, but Claudette kept walking straight by the school as the kids streamed inside from the schoolyard. She didn't know where her feet were leading her. It seemed something had changed after all. Maybe she was overreacting, and her sense of hopelessness and desolation was nothing more than a lack of sleep after so many late nights at the club. Maybe it was because she just got her period. But she couldn't stop thinking about the policewoman and her headstrong, no-nonsense, can-do attitude, with her flat shoes and faux leather jacket. Even Claudette could see the cop had reached her peak and had nowhere left to go. But still she kept pushing, like a wasp beating against a windowpane.

The thought left her cold and empty. She had nothing to do. The club was closed at that hour. Shopping had no appeal, and she wasn't hungry. Even the idea of sleeping with Treyvon seemed repulsive now. What had she been thinking? She spat on the sidewalk.

Claudette's life dragged at her like an undertow, and she thought briefly about ending it. She felt like an actress, walking through the scenes of a gritty made-for-TV drama about the life of a sixteen-year-old girl in the Deep South. It would take something or somebody extraordinary to pluck her from this humdrum existence.

*

'Brad, I need you.'

'Elaine?'

'No,' she said, swallowing her embarrassment. 'It's me. Zam.'

'Jesus, Zam. What time is it?'

'Nearly ten. Rough night?'

'Rough enough,' Brad rolled forward in his recliner, sat up straight and rubbed his face. He couldn't remember when or how he got home. There was an empty quart of vodka on the floor. He couldn't remember that either. 'What's up? Did you catch a break?'

'Maybe. Did you?'

'I think so.' Brad forced his brain into gear and explained the details of his meeting with Daniel Hautum: the attack, the pig face, and the old mojo man.

'You think this guy is involved?'

'Well, I was beginning to think the killer wasn't working alone. Pork Pie doesn't exactly fit the profile.

Let's just put him in the 'person of interest' column for the time being.'

'Listen Brad, if you bring this in, it has to be my collar, ok?'

'It's yours, cub scouts honor. But that's not why you called...'

'Another favor'

'I'm still working on the first one,' he replied.

'What are you doing tonight?'

'What day is it?' Brad asked blearily.

'Friday. Want to come out on the town with me? I'm staking out a strip-club.'

'Wow - there's an offer. Sure, it's a date.'

'Okay. Hair of the dog,' Zam said.

'Say what?'

'Hair of the dog that bit you, Bradley. It's the only cure for a hangover. I'll call you later.'

Brad slumped in his chair, closed his eyes and tried to go back to sleep, but Zam's parting shot had broken his dream and he recalled it in vivid detail: the scratching at the doors, the howling in the street and the rotten and glazed eyes of the dead dog - the same one he'd dropped into the outfall canal - staring at him through his windows while he slept.

*

Unable to concentrate on anything else, Ike dedicated his day to the fire. It burned beyond the augurs now, flickering in the darkest corners of his mind, its flames licking constantly at his conscience. He would have lost the whole morning bathed in its sensual glow had he not dragged himself from his pit to prepare himself for its arrival. There was much to be done.

Mumbling Bantu prayers of penitence and humility,

he tended first to his attire. In an old wooden trunk in the attic, Ike had discovered a dark woolen suit - a uniform - plastic-wrapped and packed with mothballs. The jacket was large across his slender frame and the trousers needed taking in around the waist, but once the alterations had been made, the effect was fine. His reflection in the dark windows of the kitchen cabinets was one of a man transported from the forties, dressed in a zoot suit and ready for work. His teeth shone when he smiled.

Ike undressed and set it to soak in the rusting enamel bathtub upstairs with liberal amounts of baking soda to disguise the musty smell of mothballs. Next, he made shoes, carefully molding strips of bark-tanned pig-leather over his bare feet, taking his time with the stitches, and meticulously picking out the eyelets with a sharp bradawl, before mounting the molds on soles cut from tire rubber.

Everything hung on the line above the yard by mid-morning, drying in the weak sun while the chickens pecked at grubs in the messy corn rows below. Ike saw the fire in the sky.

'One day he rode around the farm, flies so numerous that they did swarm...'

He washed himself then, in the candlelight, kneeling upright in the tub, and singing while he scooped up bucketfuls of lukewarm tea-colored water and tipped them back over his head and back. *'... one chanced to bite him on the thigh, the devil take the blue-tail fly...'*

This was luxury compared to his previous life in the bayou and he felt like an African prince as the filth of sweat and caked blood streamed off his sleek arms and chest. With his billhook, he shaved, the way he had taught himself, the only way he had ever known, drawing the long straight edge of the blade down to his Adam's apple in smooth, careful strokes. He allowed himself a thin mustache and something of a gypsy twist at the tip of his chin. He soaked his clean dreadlocks in olive oil and rubbed the excess into his skin, drip-drying naked with his member standing proud and defiant as he sang to the fire.

A hearty meal of fried chicken, eggs, black eyed beans, okra and two cobs of hot buttered corn. Ike piled up the shucked husks and picked his teeth with a bone. The green refrigerator shuddered in the corner of the room.

Basking in the glow of the flames, he lost time again, high on home-grown Acapulco Gold, allowing his mind to wander through the abstract symbols of the evening augurs: the bear; the garden; the purse. It was the coming together of various threads. The universe was revealing itself to him, like a lotus flower blooming. Outside the sun was setting. Ike could barely contain himself as he dressed in his new suit and leather shoes, strapped on the sheath for his billhook, and headed out into the night.

*

On the corner of Clinton Street and Bienville, Zamora Delgado flashed her badge at the guy in the Caddy parked in front of a fire hydrant and told him to move along. She wanted his space: it had a perfect view of Cheaters' entrance. Tipping her seat back a couple of notches, she opened a bumper bag of Cheezums and waited for Brad to arrive and for the show to start.

It was a long shot, she knew, but there was a chance a Fat Alphonse equivalent might appear. She was playing the odds. In her experience, criminals - especially those of vice persuasion - liked to think they were above the law, not crawling somewhere beneath it. The paedos and serial rapists gave the cops some credit and had the sense to hide. But after a long week of extortion when they should play safe, stay home and count the cash with the curtains closed, the big dogs thought they could kick back just like everybody else. They couldn't resist the lure of a Friday night on the town.

Zam jumped as Brad slapped the window and slipped heavily into the little Honda. His size was even more pronounced in the cramped space.

'Hey,' he said. 'Where y'at?'

'Hey,' she said and passed him the sack of Cheezums. Brad took a handful and offered them up to his mouth like he was feeding an apple to a horse.

'You're disgusting,' Zam laughed. 'Nice costume though.'

Brad looked down at his tracksuit top and good jeans. 'These… are my real clothes…' he muttered through a mouthful of orange dust.

'Oh, sorry,' Zam said.

'So, what's the score?' he asked, 'Cheaters, eh? Looks like a salubrious establishment. The bouncer is…?'

'Treyvon Plummer. Former resident of The Farm,' she said, referring to the Louisiana State Pen.

'And you put him there?'

'No, Bradley, he put *himself* there,' Zam replied sweetly.

Brad chuckled. 'Ok, here,' he handed her his camera. 'I thought this might be useful. You never know. It's digital so take as many shots as you like. I've set it to night-mode. No flash. The zoom is probably better than your binoculars.'

'Thanks. I'll take good care of it.' She pointed it at Treyvon and snapped.

'You want me inside?' Brad asked.

'Yeah, if you're cool with that. This place is kinda

under the radar, so it'll go one way or the other. If anybody *is* dealing, maybe you'll recognize a face.'

'Maybe,' Brad shrugged.

'The owner is a guy called Odeo Boucher. No rap sheet. That's his car over there, so I assume he's inside.'

'Great,' Brad said, zipping up his top. 'It's go time.'

'What's the rush?' Zam said. 'That's the first customer I've seen in thirty minutes.' She nodded towards the hobo staring at the neon sign above the entrance.

'Still early, I guess.'

'Listen Brad, there's something else I want to say...' Zam paused and chose her words. 'I just hope you know how much it means to me, you helping me out like this. I know how hard it must be for you to be back here, after everything... with your job and... Elaine. But we really pushed the case forward this last week. For what it's worth. And anyway, now you're here, helping me out again...' She leaned over and kissed him on the cheek, 'You're one of the good guys.'

'Yeah,' Brad answered awkwardly. 'Thanks for that.' Her hand was still resting on his leg and he desperately wanted to hold it. *For what it's worth.*

'Whatever happens tonight, we should definitely catch up this weekend. Have a few cocktails or snowballs...'

'Or both. We could call them 'cockballs'.'

Zam snorted and hit him playfully.

'It's good to see you laughing,' Brad said. 'So, yeah, sounds good. I'd like that. Why don't you come over tomorrow night? We'll have a few drinks and swap notes. I'll see if I can find another chair, so we can both sit down.'

'Ok,' Zam smiled. 'It's a date. Now go, be lucky.'

*

Tired of sweating over the bills and bank statements, Odeo had stepped out of his cramped office to enjoy a cigar in the lounge. Tiffany was writhing on the stage, naked but for a tiny 'stars and stripes' G-string. Under the lights it was hard to make out her mass of freckles and her auburn hair looked purple. An old guy on pervert's row threw a dollar bill in her direction.

Odeo puffed on his Cohiba and cast an eye around the room: there were around twenty men half-heartedly watching the show and nursing their drinks. In the corner, a couple of kids were haggling over a lap-dance from Shaniqwa. When Odeo turned back to Tiffany, he was surprised to find a stranger staring right into his eyes.

'Oh! Bonsoir monsieur,' Odeo said, startled. 'I didn't see you there.'

The man leaned forward so he didn't have to shout over the music and as he did, the sharp odor of mothballs stung Odeo's eyes.

'You're Monsieur Boucher,' Ike drawled.

'I am,' Odeo answered loudly, extending a hand, 'Welcome to Cheaters Gentlemen's Club. I don't think we've seen you here before. I know most of our... clientele.'

'Lionel sent me,' Ike answered simply, by way of introduction.

Despite his best efforts to keep his cool, Odeo's smile faded, and his proffered hand dropped as he took in Ike's ill-fitting suit, the black and white chicken feathers crudely sewn into its epaulets and lapels, his misshapen shoes, the smell. 'You're the voodoo man.'

'I am,' Ike replied, holding Odeo's gaze. The silence between the two men drew out awkwardly until Ike broke it. 'Say, why don't we all have *ourselves a parlez* in your office? I can't hear mysel' think out here.'

Odeo nodded dumbly and led the way, so Ike followed, marveling at the wonder of *Li Grand Zombi* and his power to reveal the mysteries of the universe. Like a cloud of fireflies floating above the bayou, the shimmering curtain of light in the sky had brought him to Lionel's stripper bar and with a flourish he had deftly slipped past the dumbfounded doorman, through the lobby with its pink velveteen walls and into the seedy club, with its lowly men and diseased women, expecting at any moment to see the source of his fire. They said the King of the Jews was born in a stable after all, he mused. There was something here certainly: his heightened senses registered it in the atmosphere immediately, as though the temperature of the room had fetched up a degree, or the pressure had changed. Lionel would have called it '*p*otential' or one of his other fancy-ass white words.

At a corner table, Brad stuck a finger in one ear and pressed his cell phone against the other. 'No, nothing yet,' he shouted over the music. 'You're sitting outside for Chrissakes - we're not going to miss anything. There's a bunch of creeps in here, I'll tell you that much. Nobody with 'drug dealer' tattooed on their foreheads... I said, 'nobody with 'drug dealer'...' never mind. What? Yeah, it goes with the territory. The owner? Yeah, he just put in an appearance with some loony tune. Uh huh. Ok. Sit tight, I'll call you if anything changes, but don't get your hopes up. It's a waiting game.'

Odeo made space in his poky office, stacking boxes of toilet paper and cola syrup in the corner and shoving piles of paperwork under his desk. Ike took a seat and watched as the CCTV monitor on the wall flicked between a fish-eye view of the lounge, one of the bar, the restroom corridor, the entrance…

'So,' Odeo began, finding his voice, 'how can I help you Monsieur….?'

'Sugar.'

'Say again?' Odeo asked.

'Y'all can call me Sugar. That's my name. And I do believe *I* is here to help *you*, Monsieur Boucher.' He sat back in his chair, his pale eyes fixed on Odeo at all times as he searched his mind for answers.

Odeo cleared his throat. 'Well, ain't that a kick in the head. I was only thinking to mysel' this morning how things is starting to look up fo' me. No more hoodoo balls and such. The curse is lifted, I dare say.' He nearly added 'Praise the Lord!' but thought better of it. 'I'm meeting with some new business associates… um, soon, I hope,' he checked his watch involuntarily, 'and the club will be taking a new direction. So, that being the case and such…'

'You don't *believe*, do you Monsieur?' Ike interrupted.

Odeo made a face like he was trying to hold in a fart and laughed nervously. 'It ain't that I don't believe in… in…'

'Voodoo,' Ike offered. 'S'alright. It's jus' a word, now. Ain't gon bite.' His words each had a subtle barb. He spoke like a school bully, playing to his acolytes.

'That's it,' Odeo answered. 'Well, it's not like I don't believe in… *that*. It's just that I no longer need your services. As such.'

'You should believe,' Ike said, ignoring what Odeo had said. He pulled a small red felt purse from his inside jacket pocket and placed it on the desk. It was tied off with a long loop of bailing twine and covered in greasy fingerprints. 'Am gon' make you a true believer.'

Odeo laughed nervously. 'What you got there?'

'Now, this here is gon' bring you prosperity, Mister

Boucher. Yes sir.'

'It's a lucky charm. What did Lionel call it? A 'gree-gree', right?'

'This here ain' nothin' to do with luck, sonny. Ain't jus' no *gris-gris* neither,' Ike said, tapping the package with a long fingernail.

'What in the hell is it, then?' Odeo asked, confused.

'You wouldn't understand.'

Odeo raised a 'try me' eyebrow but said nothing.

Ike snorted with derision. 'How's that work?' he said tersely, pointing at the computer. 'How's that work?' - the cellphone. He picked up the stapler and shook it, 'Hell, how's this work? Jus' 'cuz you don't understand the workings of a thing, sonny, don't mean it don't have no use.'

The situation was trying Ike's patience. He sat back in his chair, hot and flustered in his heavy suit, wondering why the *loa* had led him there at all, if not to reveal the source of his fire. Once again, he evaluated the waters of Odeo's thoughts and found nothing but money worries and drug-addled paranoia. This man had nothing to offer: fat and useless, stinking of cigar smoke, no direction, his *muti* all but dried up. Ike could have found a weak spot deep in his brain, a cocaine blood-clot ready to be pushed into the wrong artery, but he felt the weight of the steel billhook pressed against his flank and more than anything he wanted to pull it out there and then and slit Boucher's throat, if only to see the blood spatter. For a moment, he wished Lionel were there. Lionel would have smoothed things over. He had a way of putting customers at ease and turning conversations around, without seeming too pushy...

Ike closed his eyes, took a deep breath and decided to give Boucher a stay of execution. 'There's *potential* in this place,' he began, channeling the old salesman's words. 'I likes what you got here. 'Cheaters' - I likes that. It's... ironical, right? I *gets* it. See, I likes what you're trying to do. I even likes you, Monsieur Boucher,' Ike said, smiling. His voice had dropped to a whisper, like the rustling of palm fronds in the autumn breeze, and in spite of his nerves, Odeo fell silent, staring into the twin pools of Ike Sugar's eyes.

'You think the drug dealers is coming, huh Odeo? The Mexicans? You think they're gon' save you? I tell you straight, sonny: *they ain't*.' Odeo looked on, a look of disbelief and confusion frozen on his graying face. 'Even if they was, they only gon' bring you mo' troubles.'

Ike took another breath and let the *loa* speak through him.

'But not me. No sir. I wants to help. You and me, men with *potential*, we needs to be raised up, not pushed down.'

Odeo listened. In that moment, there was nobody else in the room, nobody in the world, just the man in the black suit.

'Yup, yup, money. I hears you. Uh-huh. Money's easy. Money, *success*, fame, fortune, all that. Would you like that, Odeo?' His voice echoed along a vast tunnel, his every word detonating in Odeo's mind.

'I'd like that, Mr. Sugar,' Odeo slurred.

'Well then, this here,' Ike said, resting the tips of his fingers on the purse, 'is the key. This little thing will turn your club around. So how 'bout this? I'm gon' make you a deal.' Ike lipped his lips. 'You give me every cent you got in your pockets, right now, and you get my - what d'you call it? - my 'lucky charm' here.' Ike smiled again, feeling the *pouvwa* flowing through him.

Odeo nodded slowly and rose to his feet. He stuck his

hands deep into his trouser pockets and laid a wad of dollar bills and a handful of loose change on the desk between them.

Ike counted it slowly in the silence. Two hundred and thirty-eight dollars and a few coins - not much for the trombone player's favorite toy, but for once, Ike was looking at a bigger picture. An investment for the future: Lionel would have been proud. He had been right about this place. Ike pictured all the fresh, young blood in the strippers' lounge. All the *muti*. All that *pouvwa*.

'You gots to keep it safe, mind. Keep it close. In your pocket or 'round your neck. It likes to be close to flesh. But don't y'all go lettin' nobody else touch it, y'hear? Other people will steal its power. And feed it - van van oil - buy a bottle.' Ike tossed back a five-dollar bill. 'Them's the rules.'

His words hung in the air until he clapped his hands and broke the spell. Odeo cried out like a man lost in a nightmare, and delighted with the turn of events, Ike cackled loudly and reeled back in his chair like a child who had performed a spectacular practical joke.

'Oh well, oh well,' he smiled, 'I guess I bes' be leavin'.' He wrapped his knuckles on the edge of the table and stood, drawing himself up to his full height as he straightened his jacket on his shoulders and smoothed his dusty feathers back into place. 'Well now, Monsieur Boucher, it has been a *true* pleasure. You gon' be seeing a lot more of me arou…'

The words died on his lips. A warmth had blossomed in the tiny room, a lilac glow infused the dim light of the office, and as he turned his attention to the CCTV monitor on the wall, Ike saw her enter the frame, standing in the club doorway, in a tiny dress, a fur bolero jacket and high heels.

In his eyes, Claudette Tremblay was burning like a forest fire.

*

A four-beer fog had begun to cloud Brad's head, so he wandered over to the bar to order a cranberry juice. The woman on the stage was too old to be dressed in a skimpy school uniform and pigtails, but he liked the way she sucked on her lollipop. He twirled the straw around his glass while he watched, thought about Elaine and the last time they had made love, and absent-mindedly cast a glance at the clientele reflected in the mirrors behind the bar. His attention was waning; in the pink lights, he noticed a small, red 'x' on his forehead, but couldn't feel it with his fingertips. He looked at the crowd again, but only had eyes for drug dealers, so a moment later, when Ike slipped out modestly and picked his way across the lounge, past the bar, past Brad, close enough to touch, he went unnoticed.

Outside, the evening air was sharp, but Ike didn't feel its bite. He rolled down the center of the street, reeling like a drunk, tripping on cobblestones, his arms swinging heavily by his sides as he was drawn to the fire. It was difficult to breathe. There she was! He hiccoughed, laughed involuntarily, euphoric that he had finally found her.

All year round, the city streets were filled with characters - fancy-dressed revelers, drag queens and *carnivaleros* - so when Claudette turned and saw him, stumbling towards her in his baggy black suit with its feathers catching in the breeze, she stared back, a laugh bubbling up from within her, and Ike saw the flames dancing in her eyes. She lit up this dark street corner and he marveled at her *pouvwa*. It was a pure, pulsating energy, and he staggered forward, ready to be consumed by it.

Something about his expression spoke to her: it was one of unfettered joy. There were tears in his eyes when he took her hands in his and kissed them as though he had been searching for her across an ocean of time. 'I had a dream 'bout you,' he muttered, unsure of himself in her presence.

'Yeah?' she smiled. 'What was it about?'

'Well,' he coughed, 'we was walking through a garden, you and me. Everything was alive. Fruit was burstin' out an' fallin' cuz it was summer an' all. And we was listenin' to the insects crawling through the grass and the birds whistlin' in the trees, singin' like.'

Claudette's eyes sparkled: men didn't typically try lines like this on her. 'Then what happened?'

'You and me, well, we kinda lay down there in the wildflowers. And the sun and moon passed over us, and the stars was shining all bright and the universe done held its breath.'

Claudette bit her bottom lip. 'Did we... make love?' she asked coyly, her pulse quickening.

'No, uh, I mean, yeah, but it weren't no *love* 'tween us, see? You an' me,' Ike lowered his voice and leaned to whisper in her ear, 'we was *rutting* like wild animals,' he grinned widely. 'We was fuckin' under the stars. Like... *beasts*. Like a pair of jungle cats. Can you 'magine that?'

Claudette was taken aback by his bold words. She felt blood rushing to her head, an irresistible sense of urgency washing over her. With a slight shudder, she realized she was already wet with desire. 'I can 'magine that,' she nodded.

'I can show you. I got *so much* to show you,' Ike whispered softly. 'Let me take you to the garden. I can teach you. We can... know it all, fo' sure.'

Claudette felt she was tipping forward over a precipice, the ground beneath her feet falling away. Ike wrapped his arms around her, and she dropped her pink champagne cocktail coupons and they scattered across the sidewalk.

eleven

In spite of the media furore over the Voodoo Killer, the NOPD had refused to make a statement. An impetuous reporter dared to grab at Auden Tillery's arm and demand a comment as he left Police Headquarters on South Broad Street, but only felt the sting of the Commander's sharp tongue. The news channels had been showing the scene on loop, interspersed with footage of people leaving flowers and teddy bears at the bus stop where Mani Lionne had met his fate. Meanwhile, the police phone lines were flooded with calls from well-meaning citizens who had seen neighbors they had never liked behaving strangely, or teenagers performing black magic on street corners. A man dressed as the Devil on the St Charles streetcar was mobbed and beaten up. A Dixie carriage horse keeled over on Decatur and died, frothing at the mouth, in the middle of the day.

'Strange times,' said Janice.

'You can say that again,' Zam replied. 'They pulled you in on a Saturday for this?'

'Hey, if they want to pay me, I'll do the hours. I'd strip *nekkid* for extra money at the moment.'

Zam rubbed the back of her neck. Five hours hunched in the Honda watching the previous evening's comings and goings at Cheaters had left her stiff and aching. Brad emerged woozily around two. He had leaned into her open window, stinking of stale beer and cigarettes, and breathed, 'Like I told you, *s'waitin* game. Don't forget, t'morrow night, at my place. Pass a good time.' She had expected to hear his voice when her cell rang again on Saturday afternoon, but it was Janice D'Souza, the 13th District receptionist.

'So, what's up, hon? What have you got for me?' Zam asked.

'We've taken over a thousand calls since Thursday.'

'It's not even an official investigation yet,' Zam sighed. Nobody's admitting there's any connection between any of the killings.'

'That's as may be, but folks is still calling. We're still working through the backlog and looking for anything which might be useful. There's not a lot, but this one landed on my desk, and - I don't know - it kinda struck me as weird.'

Zam sat up. 'Yeah?'

'Well, the guy mentioned your name for a start.'

'Read it out to me.'

'Anonymous male. It says: 'This is a message for Detective Delgado. I know the Voodoo Killer. If you wants to talk about the cat's tongue, call me. My number is 284 9102. Three o' clock any day of the week.'

'Eve Carmel,' Zam whispered down the line. Her blood ran cold. 'We never released any details about the tongue. Janice, run the number for me.'

'I already did. It's a payphone on the corner of Baronne and Union.'

Zam said nothing. She checked her watch. It was seventeen minutes after two.

'I'm going.'

'You need back-up?'

'No way. Listen Janice - we never had this conversation. If Auden Tillery finds out I'm working this, he'll bust me down to traffic duty. Tell *no one*, ok?'

'Whatever you say, Detective. Take it easy.'

Zam sensed a tone of motherly concern in Janice's

voice. 'Don't worry. I won't do anything stupid.'

*

The bruise was fading - gray against Lionel Root's brown skin - but it was still visible. In addition, he had chosen to leave his teeth at home. Without them, his face took on a lumpen, fallen look which aged him considerably.

He stood under a restaurant awning, waiting for the payphone to ring and sheltering from the falling rain. It was bouncing off the sidewalk and soaking the cuffs of his pants.

Parked twenty yards down the road, Zam tried Brad's cell for the fourth time before giving up. Whatever he was doing, he wasn't answering. She dialed another number on her cell, her eyes on the old guy. She had been waiting there for fifteen minutes: the rain drumming against the roof of her Honda, the steady beat of the windscreen wipers. Now, she watched him move the moment he noticed the phone ringing. He willed his tired muscles to life, picking his way around the puddles before it rang off.

She rang off.

Lionel swore loudly and looked around: his feet soaking, water dripping from the brim of his hat, unsure of what move to make next. He picked up the receiver and dialed star sixty-nine in vain. Just as he was about to call the operator, Zam approached him from behind and tapped him on the shoulder. She flashed her badge, 'You looking for me, Mr...?'

'Oh, pardon me, I din't see you there,' Lionel's face folded on itself as he attempted a smile. 'I'm Mr. Laroute. But everybody calls me Root. On account of my work, y'see? Rootwork, that is. I'm a root worker.

Least I used to be.' He paused and took a deep breath. 'I'm talking too much, ain't I?' he said nervously. 'Y'all can call me Lionel,' he said bluntly and offered a handshake.

'You have some information for me, Lionel?' Zam asked, leaning closer to him so he could hear her voice.

'Can't we talk about it someplace else? Don't y'all want to get out o' this rain?'

'Sure. We could talk down at the station if you prefer...'

Lionel looked horrified. 'I don't think so Miss, thank y'all the same. I don't want to go down no police station. I'm just an old man, I'm trying to do my civic duty here. I'm putting my neck on the line...'

'Okay, Lionel,' Zam said, trying to placate him, 'It's fine, it's fine. Let's go get a coffee and have a tete-a-tete. Does that sound better?'

Lionel nodded and shrugged his collar up around his neck, 'I know a café a block over.'

'What's wrong with this place right here?' Zam asked.

'I saw the chef picking his nose here in 1993. Haven't been back since.'

*

Lionel stirred his coffee for a full minute before he spoke. He and Zam were sitting across from each other at a small table in Dee's Café. The rain had driven plenty of customers inside and the servers were struggling to cope with the rush.

'Your killer's name is Ike Sugar,' he said simply. It seemed to Zam that he was unburdening himself of a heavy cross. 'That's the name I done give him. It don't mean nothin'. He used to drink sugar-water. I liked the name 'Ike'. That's that,' Lionel shrugged.

'He's your son?' Zam asked, not entirely surprised.

'Not by birth. I don't know who committed *that* sin. Don't know his mother neither.' Lionel sighed deeply. 'How'm ah goin to tell you all this?' he said, staring down at his creased hands.

'Start at the beginning, Lionel.'

'All right. Let's see then. I can't say how old he is for sure now. Maybe twenty-five, maybe thirty. I reckon he was around seven or eight when he came to live with me. He always was a tall boy. It was 1994 and I was living alone above the drugstore. I used to run a drugstore over on Gravier Street. I sold potions and the like. Some might say I pedaled hoodoo: rootwork items, conjuration. Powders to help a man fall for a woman, potions to make a woman stay with a man, to curse your enemies, protect your home, anything you could think of. Oh s'alright - I never believed in any of that shit.'

'Neither did I until recently,' Zam said. 'Please, go on...'

'Well Miss Delgado, let me tells you, I had enough customers who *did* believe. It was my mother's business before it was mine, and when she passed, I kept it ticking over. Weren't nothing special, but it kept me in cheese and crackers. Anyways, one day, a lady friend of mine brought me this boy. No, it wasn't nothin' like that. She said this kid had the dark gift. That's what she said. '*The dark gift*'. You know what that is?'

'I can guess,' Zam replied.

'I din't believe her at the time, but I didn't argue neither. She found him living on the edge of the bayou, scavenging for food in the trashcans around her neighborhood late at night. She was thinking I could help him, I guess. Or maybe she thought *he* could help *me*. You know, like a pet? Momma understood the dark gift, so maybes this here neighbor thought I did too. Damned if I knows. Anyways, he was skinny as a whippet and didn't speak much. A wild kid. Half and half, like coffee with cream. He mus' been left in the swamp, cause of his color I reckon. Somehow, he survived.'

'So, you took him in?' Zam asked.

'Takin' him in makes it sound like I played a part in it. He stayed, that's all I knowed at the time. I was a drunkard then. We kind of looked after each other for a while. When he got older and he started to find words, he talked about the swamp.' Lionel shook his head at the memory. 'His stories sounded like dreams at first and I din't pay them no mind. Crazy stories about the spirits of the trees and the mangroves, 'bout how he talked with gators and wild dogs. I knew he wasn't right in the head, but when he... growed up like, came of age and such, that's when he really changed.'

'What happened?'

'He called it his 'wakening'. I'd gotten mysel' sober by then and I was working again. I came home one day and he was sitting at the table - I swear I thought I was losing my mind. I can see him now clear as I can see that there salt-shaker.'

'What did you see?' Zam whispered.

Lionel's eyes shifted about the room. 'As God is my witness, Miss Delgado - that boy was covered head to toe in 'roaches. They was crawling all over his body. All over his face. All over.'

Zam swallowed hard.

'You ever *tried* to catch a *cockerroach* one time? They's fast, *n'est ce pas*? They don't like us humans. And there he was, covered in them, laughing like it was something funny. They was ticklin' him, he said. I can still see them crawling through his hair. He said he been talking to them. We din't even have that many bugs in the apartment. He done *summoned* them. I never wanted a drink so bad in all my life.

'That was the first time. After that he got slicker. He'd kill things - birds and animals - jus' by thinking 'bout them. He killed a hornets' nest once, in the attic. Just waved his hand over it and they came fallin' out, all shriveled up like dried peas. Sometimes he'd bring things back, but mostly he liked killin' them. His *pouvwa* - that's what he called it - it did have its uses. He'd start fires, make little things move with his mind. Rooms felt cooler when he was in 'em. Time went slower. And you couldn't *never* beat him at cards. But it was all a game to him back then. Parlor tricks, he called them. You think I'm making this up? I ain't. It's the God's honest truth.'

'I'm trying to believe you,' Zam said reluctantly. 'But there's usually a rational explanation for these things. I mean, what are we talking about here exactly? Magic? Psychic powers?'

'Can't really put a name on these things,' Lionel shrugged.

'He's a hypnotist then? Can he read minds?'

'Not as such. Ike can notice the things what you fear, the things what you want most, but he can't read you like a book. His instincts is stronger, is all.'

'So, when did he start killing for real?'

Lionel leaned forward in his seat. 'When he was fifteen. I got him started. A widow in the neighborhood was dying. Old woman, riddled with cancer. She stunk of it, but you know, her body wouldn't let her go. Flesh is stubborn like that sometimes. Anyways, her family asked me to do what the doctors wouldn't. So, I took Ike along. He laid his hands on her, said some words and she passed. Just like that.'

'So, he did a good thing,' Zam said.

'I guess so. It cut him up though. Killing sparrows is one thing, but touching God's children? That's something different. It changed him when he crossed that line. After that day, there was always a shadow behind his eyes.' Lionel's lip quivered slightly.

'What is it?' Zam asked.

'I don't knows,' he sniffed. 'Look at me: *stoopid* ol' coot. I guess part of me feels responsible s'all. *Maybes*,' he shrugged. 'Maybe he woulda gone bad anyways.' He rubbed his hands over his face and blew out his breath, then looked around to check nobody was watching. He stirred his coffee again and slurped a mouthful as he composed himself.

'Same time, business was good. I wasn't complaining. Between the two of us, we started making mojo bags, *gris-gris*, amulets, fetishes. They worked too. Better than any of the bullshit I used to hawk. Word gets 'round, you see. We was making lots of money, all over town. We sold *hunnerds* of quality items. It got so good we couldn't keep up with demand.'

'I didn't realize there was such an interest in voodoo...?' Zam said.

'Oh yeah. Whatever you want to call it - juju, mojo, karma, chi - there's a balance in this world Miss Delgado, you see? It's all give and take. Like a teeter-totter,' he gestured with his arm. 'When someone's rising, someone else is fallin'. That's just the way of it. Ike would take the power out o' one and transfer it to 'nother. But after a time, the animals weren't strong enough. Not enough *pouvwa* in 'em. Can't take a battery out of your TV remote and 'spect it to start your automobile, can y' now?'

'I guess not,' Zam answered, searching for the flaw in

his logic.

'Rabbit paws and chickens feet is all you needs to fix some problems,' he continued, 'but if a fella wants to get rich, or a woman wants to have a baby when nature says she can't, or you want to kill a man and leave no trace, that kind of deal costs. So, we done *diversified*.'

'You started stealing body parts.'

'Not stealing, no. We *paid* for them. I did deals with porters, janitors, nurses at the hospitals and the morgue, anyone who could hook us up. Then Ike would bless the parts, make up the goods with my oils and herbs, and I'd sell them. That was my job.'

'Eve Carmel? Was she one of your contacts?'

'Uh-huh. Until she wanted out and Ike fixed her. Different like: he didn't need her *pouvwa* as such. He jus' wanted her dead.'

'The hypno-drug, right? How did he do it?' Zam asked.

'Ah, you ain't gon' get it. May as well try to explain... television to a dog. No offense.'

'Try me.'

'Okays...' Lionel shook his head and searched for the words. 'You ever make anything for yo' momma when you was a little kid? A macaroni necklace, a pin-cushion, somethin' like that?'

Zam nodded, 'Sure. I made a ragdoll one time.'

'Well, I bets a good girl like you tried real hard with that ragdoll. Poured all your effort into it. And yo' momma was so happy and so proud. She could *feel* how much you wanted her to love it.'

Zam pictured her work - scraps of felt and dusty wool - still sitting after all these years on her mother's dressing table. 'Yes. She could. What's your point?'

'Ike poured his *pouvwa* into his trinket - his cruelty, his will to kill - and forced it into that girl's mind. Made her *believe*. He's clever like that.' He sipped his tea. 'Shame. I liked Miss Carmel. She was interestin'. For a white girl.'

'OK, so you've got quite the slick little operation going up until then. A regular supply chain. Tell me about the demand. Who were you selling them to?' Zam asked.

'Oh, businessmen mainly. Some women. Rich university kids. Store owners, company men, judges, doctors, politicians, crim'nals, police officers, you name it. I ain't givin' you no names. What you gon' slap them with anyways? Handling stolen goods?' Lionel blew through his lips.

Zam wasn't sure, but she wasn't about to back down. 'It's a crime to possess human body parts unlawfully. Your... *clients* represent part of an ongoing homicide investigation. How's that grab you?'

'I still ain't sayin'. Ain't I givin' you enough here, lemon-drop?'

Zam changed tack. 'So, you're telling me that some bigshot is walking 'round town with Manfred Lionne's prick in his pocket, and he's ok with that?'

'That's between him and his God. I ain't no priest and these people ain't fools. They knows what we's sellin'.'

'Anybody I would know?'

Lionel turned an imaginary key in front of his lips and looked into the distance.

The rain hammered against the windows. A harried waiter pushed past Zam's chair as she waited in vain for Lionel to give her a name.

'Well, Lionel, let *me* tell *you*, if you think the NOPD is ok with that, you're wrong. But fine, let's put a pin in that for the time being,' Zam said, determined to have the last word. 'When did Ike start killing for true?'

'After the storm. He knew that storm was coming

months before. He could feel it in his blood, so he said. He went back to the bayou when they was evacuating the city. Said the spirits were calling him back to his roots and they would show him the path. He was gone a year. I thought he was dead. I kinda hoped he was, truth be told. But there it is...

'When he came back, he was stronger. Like liquor, distilled. He said he'd had a vision of the future. Talked about harvesting true *pouvwa*, insisted we keep up business with the morgue - you can imagine we got a lot of custom in the years after the storm - so I done resumed that, but when the spirits spoke to him, he would take a life.'

'How many has he killed?'

'I los' count. How many do you make it?'

'That's classified information.'

'How many?' Lionel asked again.

'Eleven,' Zam said reluctantly.

Lionel wagged his finger like he was scolding a child. 'Y'all can triple that figure, I reckon. He's smart at hiding his killings. But you already knows that, I guess. Your people gon' have trouble making any of this shit stick. Thing is, it ain't about business no more.' He lowered his voice in spite of the noise in the cafe, 'Ike thinks he's becoming a god. He's doing this because he thinks he is *divine*. He's changing into the *loa*.'

Zam had heard enough. 'Where can I find him?'

Lionel seemed taken aback. 'Why would you wants to do *that*?'

It was Zam's turn to be confused. 'What do you think I'm here for, Lionel? We're not just chewing the fat.'

'You're damn right 'bout that. Ain't you listened to anything I told you?' Lionel asked sharply. 'I ain't telling you this so y'all can catch him. This here is a warning. Ike Sugar's got a bead on you, Miss Delgado. He's ready to take your warm heart to the cold. If you got any sense in your pretty head, you bes' be thinking 'bout leaving this place. I reckon it's time fo' a career change.'

'Are you threatening an officer of the law?' Zam asked, hoping to hide the fear in her voice.

'It ain't a threat, *cher*. Least not from me. It's reality.' Lionel stood up slowly and picked up his hat from the back of his chair.

'Sit down, we're not finished,' Zam said, angry now.

'Oh, we's finished,' Lionel ignored her. He dropped a five-dollar bill on the table. 'Can't you *feel* him? In your *head*, Miss Delgado? Ike Sugar's right there, right in front of y'all, right behind. He's everywhere.'

*

Covered with old sheets, strips of tattered fabric, stolen overcoats and a threadbare rug, four wooden pallets and a thin mattress made up the bed where Claudette Tremblay fervidly cast off her virginity in the early hours. In the gray light, she listened to the rain dripping through the roof and thought about her transition from a bud to a blossom. Any fears stirred up by the swaggering, bawdy gossip overheard in the school bathrooms were unfounded. There was pain at first, as she had expected, but nothing that could ever outweigh the pleasure which followed. Claudette had never seen the ocean in real life - only in movies - and yet at the height of their passion, she felt like a golden shoreline and Ike Sugar the wild surf, beating against her tirelessly. All night, he brought her to the edge of herself repeatedly, wrapping his mind around her every erotic whim, until she believed her body was made for his. Just as his dream had predicted, they had not made love, but rather come together like two animals driven by a force of nature.

It was already dawn when they finally gave in to sleep, and when she woke, Ike was gone and the old house was silent. She curled like a cat in the warmth of the bed and dozed for another hour or so, pleasurably tender, at once both satisfied and still wanting more. Her lips were swollen and her thighs ached.

Hunger eventually drove her out. It was late afternoon and Ike was back - the sounds of footsteps and bottles downstairs. Wrapped in an old fur coat, she wandered through the empty rooms, treading lightly on the dusty wooden floorboards, until she followed the sharp smell of reefer and incense and found him behind one of the few unlocked doors, basking in the glow of nine candles, his eyes red and his pupils dilated. He was buck naked apart from his rooster mask, pushed back on his head.

'Come on in, come in, *cher*,' he whispered huskily, 'I wants you to see.'

'What are y'all doing, sugar?' she asked, taking in the holy statuettes, the jars of herbs, the bottle of dark rum, the soft layer of chicken feathers under her bare feet.

Ike leaned forward into the candlelight. He was stitching a tress of Zam Delgado's dark hair onto the head of a corn dolly.

'Daddy's working baby.'

*

By early evening, the rain clouds had blown over and the city was bathed in the glow of a beautiful sunset. Brad stood on his stoop and breathed in the smell of earth kicked up by the downpour. A little girl in rubber boots was stomping in the puddles while her dad looked on, and Brad reminisced about the days when Kyle used to play in front of the house, perfecting his skateboard skills or playing catch - just father and son - while Elaine watched. The neighborhood was different back then: neighbors knew one another, community spirit actually meant something. There were crawfish boils, cook-outs and street parties. Everybody used to leave their doors open all day long in the summer.

Brad knew it was useless, living in the past. He could never go back, and shouldn't ever try to, but more than anything he wanted to relive those days. Being back in the city had awakened something in him: a desire to live again. For so long, he had been floating like a boat which had slipped its moorings, just as Madame Coulombe had said. He had settled into a routine, where nothing really upset him, but nothing really excited him either. And now Elaine had moved on.

'Perhaps I should do the same,' he muttered, as his thoughts turned to Zamora Delgado. There was something between them, something more than professional camaraderie. More than friendship - possibly. There was attraction too, on his part, but Zam was thirteen years younger than him. It didn't even seem legal. Still, he found himself quietly excited by the prospect of seeing her again, not least to share the details of his day. Brad rolled her name around in his head, along with everything else he had discovered on his rounds. He waved to the girl in the rubber boots and stepped inside, leaving the door wide open as a nod to his nostalgia.

As a married man, Brad had never embraced the idea of cooking, even less so after his wife had left him. Back in Florida, he survived on take-out and TV dinners, but in an attempt to impress Zam, he had bought a bottle of wine, some crudités and a Cajun hot crab dip. He was struggling to peel a carrot when he heard somebody on the porch.

'Zam? Is that you?' he hollered. 'Come on through, I'm in the kitchen.'

Her footsteps were slow and heavy, but Brad didn't sense anything untoward until she appeared, silhouetted in the kitchen doorway. It didn't take a detective to see that something was seriously wrong. Zamora Delgado, normally so neat, so well put-together, looked like she had just pulled herself from a car crash. Torn clothes, wild hair, and make-up smeared across her grinning face.

'Hey.... *sonny*,' she slurred, in a voice not her own. She reeked of alcohol.

'Jesus Christ, Zam!' he said, rushing to help as she tried to steady herself, 'What the fuck happened?'

She stared back at him with frightened eyes, but the crazed smile never once left her lips. With sharp, jerky movements, like those of a string puppet, she pushed him away and hoisted herself up onto the counter, where she spread her legs to reveal her lack of underwear. A mascara-stained tear spilled down her cheek. Coquettishly, she stuck her finger in her mouth, but bit down hard on the chipped nail and ripped it away from its bed, without even flinching.

'Oh well, oh well,' she mumbled, before spitting it out.

Brad tasted bile. 'I think... we need to... call somebody,' he said absently, fumbling for his cellphone.

'Not yet, m'sieur, let me get one last good look at y'all,' Zam drawled, piercing Brad with her gaze. 'Ahh, there you *issss*.'

She swept her hands across the worktop, knocking over the wine, the carrot sticks and plates. The bowl shattered on the floor, spattering yellow crab dip over the immaculate kitchen cupboards. Her fingers found the kitchen knife and as Brad turned, she pounced on him, with a strength which belied her size, and buried the blade up to the handle in his stomach. It sounded like a kiss.

Part Two

twelve

It's not about voodoo, Odeo told himself. It's about money. Spanish moss grew thick on the City's oaks, but US dollars didn't. In New Orleans, just like anywhere else, everything came down to hard cash.

Granted, his little red purse had helped. Relieved of his crushing financial fears, his mind no longer dulled by low quality coke, the ideas began coming to Odeo in his dreams. Brimming with confidence and purpose, he convinced the Fidelity bank manager to extend his loan repayments and with the last of the company's money, Odeo made better choices and smarter investments than he had in a long time. Within days, Cheaters was transformed: its hard edges all smoothed off. He pulled on his cigar and watched one of the bow-tied mixologists behind the bar pouring a round of gin rickeys for a cigarette girl server. On the stage, rolling in a carpet of customers' cash, one of the new burlesque dancers was gently flossing herself with a feather boa while the jazz quartet in the corner played mellow variations on classics. The pink décor remained, but the strobe lights had gone, black and white stills from old movies and prohibition era posters had replaced the neon Playboy bunnies and photos of women in latex bondage gear, which he sold as a job-lot on eBay. Outside, men - and a handful of women - were queuing all the way down Clinton Street to the spot where Claudette used to stand. Inside, above the crowds, in the Champagne Lounge, the jilted Mexicans in sunglasses and Cuban heels were wondering what had changed.

Cheaters' newfound success thrilled and scared Odeo in equal measure. The money was wonderful of course: with each loan repaid, his burden eased a little more. But still he was preoccupied. It wasn't the drug-induced paranoia which gnawed constantly at the edges of his mind - he had grown accustomed to its chatter over the years. It wasn't the police either: with more customers and more cash changing hands he had expected more heat, but that was under control too. Every time a local patrolman passed by on the beat, Treyvon made sure they got a soda or an alcohol-free beer with a twenty-dollar bill wrapped around the can.

Odeo's unease boiled down to his dislike of Ike Sugar. The way he loitered in the corridors, smoking his home-grown weed and selling the last of Lionel's fetishes and mojo bags to the musicians and waitresses; his habit of lurking in the backrooms like a malevolent spirit, eyeing the dancers as they undressed. He regularly hid himself away in Odeo's office for hours at a time, meditating. Once, Odeo had walked in unannounced and found him cutting lines into his forearms with an edge of a foot long blade. The voodooist's chanting stopped abruptly, and he stared hard at Odeo in the uncomfortable silence. There was always something unsettling about his pale eyes and at times, Odeo believed he could feel the physical pressure of his gaze, but he was willing to admit that the substantial amounts of cheap, Mexican cocaine he was consuming night after night might also have played a part.

What's Sugar's plan? Is he pushing me out? Planning to bump me off? These questions permeated his every thought. He felt like an old racehorse being fed sugar cubes, while the owner contemplated his future. Odeo knew he was being watched and he didn't like it.

Lionel had disappeared. Probably dead. Claudette wasn't answering her cell phone. His only ally now was Treyvon. He was standing near the doorway, with half an eye on the crowd, rolling a toothpick between his teeth. His mind was elsewhere. Odeo sensed that he too felt threatened by the turn of events and though neither of them wanted to be the first to broach the subject, there was a shared understanding of the gravity of the situation: Ike Sugar was a powerful, dangerous man and now he had a foot in the door...

Odeo remembered his grandmother Odile, who in her later years used to sit on the porch of her Baton Rouge duplex, chewing coffee beans and shouting a bizarre mix of biblical verses and obscenities at her neighbors and the people passing by. 'The eyes of the Lord are in every damn place, watching the good and the evil!' 'God damn you if you do not have faith!' and - most pointedly - 'Don't invite the Devil into your goddamn house and be surprised when he makes himself at home!'

*

In all of her young life, Claudette had never imagined that anything could feel so good. Flushed and lightheaded, she wrapped a wet towel tightly around her neck and moaned in breathless, overwhelming bliss as Ike, kneeling at the edge of the bed, lapped at her. She liked the way the feathers of his rooster mask brushed against her thighs, the pressure of its hard waxed beak: she liked his tongue below. He heard all these thoughts, watching through the rough slits of his mask, as her naked body writhed before him on the makeshift bed. Ike pushed her legs further apart and Claudette - starved of oxygen and drunk on a cocktail of Devil's Breath tea, Rougaroux Dark Rum and marijuana - watched the swirling colors and pinprick lights flashing across the bedroom ceiling and could no longer hold back the tidal wave of her ecstasy.

Afterwards he left, as he always did, day or night, and Claudette was alone in the empty house, trapped by her own desires, her cup slowly refilling until he returned. It was difficult to focus - she hadn't been truly sober in weeks - but she knew the house held dark secrets. There were rooms which Ike insisted were off-limits, padlocked chests, private things. There were sounds in the night - not least the comings and goings of her lover or the noises of the animals downstairs - but the echoes of her own nightmares: muffled cries and moans, the baby-like mewling of fighting tom cats, the painful crack of bones breaking.

When she slept, her dreams were often filled with shadows and demons chasing her along the backstreets. *What was the name of the place where she worked?* When she woke, she felt hollowed out, sick with worry, as though she had forgotten something crucial, or spoilt some beautiful thing.

In her more lucid moments, she convinced herself she was happy to sit and watch him in his temple room, rendering tallow from chicken fat and dyeing the candles red with blood, reading the augurs. Like a keen young boy, he showed her his collections of herbs and spices, his boxes of bones and jars of dead animals preserved in honey and rubbing alcohol. Sometimes, he read to her from his books, defiantly persevering in spite of his stilted rhythm. She never laughed at him. She knew better than that.

For his part, Ike welcomed this role of teacher. Nobody had ever paid him any attention - Lionel had barely noticed him until he became a source of income, then only nurtured him until he became a threat. Odeo Boucher saw him as a means to protect his business interests, and a spiritual guide of sorts, but the way she stared at him, hung on his words, revered him like a god - Claudette was unlike anybody else. She believed in him completely, just as Ike believed completely in his religion. And she was his *Erzulie* goddess of passion, both his strength and his weakness, seducing him, raising him up and leaving him to weep at his own failings. When he should have been working, he found himself stealing offerings for her: cheap perfume, cigarettes, gaudy bangles and earrings, an entire Doberge cake, anything he thought might please her.

Before the Halloween killings, Ike bound his *muti* to hers by branding her initials nine times on his flesh, and insisted she did the same. He held her tight while she shook and screamed as the red-hot knife seared her flawless skin.

But when her fire continued to burn too fiercely, Ike mixed a teaspoon of her moon blood into a bowl of his oatmeal, in an attempt to take back control of his life. It had the opposite effect. For a solid week, her voice whispered to him through sleepless nights and wrenched him from his daily routines: scratching at him, urging him home. Dog-tired, he resorted to the Devil's Breath to dull her senses. Only the drug brought any real respite, and when she succumbed to its effects, Ike was able to think clearly again: think about the spirits, think about Odeo and the club, think about the future. It was tedious work without Lionel's help - working the flesh, preparing the fragile bones and stitching the bags - but *Li Grand Zombi* was his master and his spirits had willed it.

He sat at his table by candlelight and tested the weight of Lionel's tiny envelope - it felt exceptionally light. He'd already ground down the crystals into a fine powder but there was hardly any left. His thoughts turned to the witch on Dumaine Street. He was suddenly tempted to lick his finger and dip...

'Sugar daaaddy...' Claudette purred from the doorway. Her lips were cracked and her eyes sunken. 'When you gon' come to bed?' Her cup was overflowing again.

Ike smiled. He moved slowly, methodically, locking the last of the Devil's Breath in the desk drawer and closing the door behind him. Up close, Claudette smelled sharp and sour, but Ike liked it. 'You my lil' grapefruit,' he cooed before he scooped her up like a honeymoon bride and carried her upstairs.

*

Newly promoted Detective Jon Rubino sat in his department-issue Taurus in the Quicky's parking lot and listened to the local news. '... *town, will bring the magic and spirit of the holiday season alive for visitors of all ages with a special lighting ceremony...*'. The traffic was heavy on South Broad Avenue and when Jon saw him shuffling slowly across the intersection, he half expected him to be plowed down by a bus at any moment. Rubino leaned over and pushed open the passenger door and Brad Durand slumped heavily into the seat, his breath ragged.

'Morning. You're running late,' Rubino grumbled.

Brad nodded but said nothing. He swallowed hard, rocked forward and grimaced.

'Please don't fucking puke in my car, sir.'

'I'm not going to - just give me a minute here,' Brad croaked, leaning back and resting his head, eyes closed. Rubino noticed the yellow hue of his skin, the patches of missed stubble.

'Seriously, Detective Durand - you look like shit. What's going on with you?'

'Infection of the gut, doctor says.' Brad fished a bottle of pills from his jacket pocket, popped the cap and shook two straight down his throat. 'Calm down - it's not contagious. Got it from the knife.' Brad took a deep breath and turned in his seat. 'So, what have you heard?' he asked.

Rubino snuffed down his nose, exasperated. 'Listen sir, I've told you already: if I hear anything you'll be the first to know. We've issued a BOLO and I personally filed the missing person report with Commander Tillery. Believe me, nobody wants to find Za... Detective Delgado more than we do.'

'She was a pain in Tillery's backside,' Brad answered. 'I doubt he's losing any sleep. Homicide don't need another case and narcotics didn't care about her. And look at this...' he pulled a grubby newspaper article from his inside pocket and unfolded it. 'Five Gruesome Halloween Murders,' read the headline.

'Come on man, you know shit always goes down during Halloween...' Rubino sighed, 'And they're not even confirmed homicides yet. They could still be natural causes.' He didn't sound convinced.

'Bullshit. It's the same pattern as before and you know it. All the victims were under twenty-five and all five bodies were missing something: fingers, thumbs, an ear. One clown had his nose sliced off for Chrissakes. Not a clown nose. The guy's *real* nose. A goddamn journalist managed to piece this together and the NOPD is doing nothing. Why is that? You know this is related, *don't* you? Why is Tillery dragging his heels on this? It's already been a week and you haven't arrested *anybody*.'

'Who are we supposed to arrest?!' Rubino shook his head and spread his hands apologetically. 'We're... investigating... all possible leads,' he managed finally, reverting to the police department's favorite cliche. 'The night-club - Cheaters? I know they've sent patrols every week. Nothing is going down there. Nothing out of the ordinary anyway.'

'Because the club *means* nothing. How many times do I have to tell you? It's just some titty bar. I've been down there myself a dozen times. And Zam was following up a lead from narcotics. She didn't even go inside! This -' Brad shook the newspaper article, '- this is what her disappearance is about. There's something bigger going on here. The killings, the body parts, that Coroner's Office woman who swallowed her tongue - it's all connected and, I'm telling you this, Rubino, it stretches all the way back to that kid.'

'Shay Favreau,' Rubino answered quietly.

'Yup,' Brad nodded.

The two men sat in silence for a minute, watching the cars speeding through the puddles and spraying water across the sidewalk. Suddenly, Rubino felt completely out of his depth, as though he'd been running a game on the entire NOPD and the real policemen, having been taken for fools, would be coming for his gun and his badge.

The truth was it would take a detective of Zamora Delgado's caliber to solve Zamora Delgado's disappearance. Not him. The 'incident' - that's what they were calling it around the station - had cast a pall over the entire police force in the Crescent City. Here was a woman, who after years of chasing an elusive promotion, only to have it pulled out from under her, had simply *broken down*. The stakeout she staged at the strip-club - a move which Tillery and the narcotics team had effectively forced her to make - must have been the final straw before she flipped out, went *loco* and stabbed Durand.

'Women,' Rubino said aloud.

Of course, the Florida private eye was selling his own brand of crazy now, covering his ass and claiming that voodoo spirits had possessed Delgado when she attacked him. Convinced of his involvement in her disappearance, Tillery had personally conducted two interviews at the side of Durand's hospital bed. The word at the watercooler was the second had lasted nearly three hours, and only ended when two orderlies had to forcibly remove the Commander from the ward, on the authority of the doctor in charge.

Whatever went down in that house, whatever reason she had for stabbing Durand, Rubino reasoned that he would probably never find out. Zamora Delgado had been missing for six weeks. Chances were she had already taken the truth to her grave. He missed her.

'This is the safest corner in the entire city,' Rubino said.

'Yeah? How do you figure that?' Brad replied, almost happy to change the subject.

'Well, that's the Sheriff's Department over there and the Police Department. There's the Crimestoppers Center and the Criminal Court is just down the way.'

'Uh huh,' Brad grunted. 'Maybe I should move here.'

Rubino leaned over and opened the glovebox on Brad's knees. He pulled out a large blank envelope. 'Here, I asked around - nobody in the department knows your man. The Feds have facial recognition software, but I can't go down that route: Tillery would tear me a new asshole if he found out. I had the tech guys sharpen up your photo - it's the best I could do. Sorry Mr Durand.'

Brad pulled out a grainy photo of the 'old timer'

who'd been caught on the security camera pushing mojo-bags at Hautum Hams. It was a good shot - he was staring straight at the camera, pork-pie hat tipped back on his head, his mouth puckered in distaste. 'I'll see what I can do with this. Thanks.'

Brad's eyes widened momentarily; Rubino followed his gaze.

'What is it?'

'Do you see that dog right there?' Brad asked, a slight tremor in his voice.

Rubino peered out through the windshield. 'Where?'

'Over there. Big, black dog. Right *there*,' Brad insisted.

'Uh... no. I don't see no dog, sir.'

'It's gone now,' Brad whispered, almost to himself.

Rubino started the engine. 'Look, I gotta get going. I can't meet you again, Mr Durand. You're on your own now.'

Brad nodded.

'Will you be ok?' Rubino asked.

Brad ignored the question as he gingerly eased himself out of the car, the stitches in his stomach pulling tight as he stood straight.

'Listen, Rubino, do your job and find Zam. Leave the killer to me.'

Six weeks earlier, Zamora Delgado had stuck a kitchen knife deep into his gut, slicing through Brad's intestinal wall. He nearly bled out on his own kitchen floor waiting for the EMTs to arrive, but it was the subsequent infection which nearly killed him. Still, he had wasted too much time slowly recuperating in a hospital bed, sitting in waiting rooms, visiting doctors. His disdain for those in the medical profession - all of them, from the bitter, long-serving receptionists to the smug consultants - had done nothing to improve his worsening health. He emerged from his involuntary hiatus with post-traumatic hallucinations, stitches in his abdomen and a fire in his belly: the Voodoo Killer was still at large, slaughtering his victims and chopping them up with gay abandon in the shadow of the Halloween festivities. Mardi Gras was less than four months away, and Brad was expecting a bloodbath.

In the meantime, driving was out of the question - he couldn't sit for any period of time without the pain in his gut becoming unbearable - so Brad caught a bus out to Jefferson, past the housing estates and furniture warehouses on Tulane. He stood all the way and watched the world go by, reminiscing about old apartments, old cars, old cases, thinking about Elaine and Kyle, and wishing he could lay his demons to rest.

He saw the black dog squatting to piss in the rubble of a derelict plot and again, two miles later, watching him impassively from a motel parking lot as the bus rolled by.

The weight had fallen off him, but still he stepped down heavily onto the sidewalk, a stone's throw from the Hautum Hams plant. Zaddie's Tavern was calling to him from down the block, and it seemed as good a place as any to start. He'd spent enough years working the beat to know there was no better way to dig up information than by looking people in the eye and asking them straight. The plan was to start at one end of town and work his way to the other, stopping at every seedy dive bar - Ms. Mae's, Aunt Tiki's, The Saint, and The Saturn Bar - that he happened upon.

It was harder than he had expected. By three o' clock, Brad had been walking for miles, doggedly - painfully - working the streets around Jefferson, down through the park to Magazine before limping through Milan, the Garden District and Central City. Over a dozen sodas, Brad must have flashed the photo of the old boy in the pork pie hat to two hundred people: fat, suspicious bartenders, dead-eyed waitresses, hardened drinkers, dried-up hookers and drag-queens hiding from the daylight. They stared more at Brad himself than the picture - his bloodshot eyes and sweaty, sallow complexion, his crumpled, baggy suit - and took him for one of their own: another washed-up alcoholic, clinging on to some semblance of a life. Some took pity on him and offered him a drink, and though he wanted nothing more than to sit down at the bar, chew on peanuts and get hammered, the doctors had warned him plainly that the cocktail of drugs keeping him alive wouldn't mix well with alcohol. He wiped his face and got his bearings: only a couple of blocks from Martin Luther King Boulevard and the Coroner's Office. Rather than admit defeat and stop for the day, he decided to pay Walt Forager a visit. In the twists and turns of the last few weeks, the Chief Medical Examiner had fallen off the radar, but Brad thought it worthwhile to turn over the details of the Halloween killings with somebody who might have a different perspective on things. Though never friends as such, he and Walt had always had a professional respect for one another.

Brad rang the doorbell and was buzzed in immediately. A surly receptionist with very red hair eyed him suspiciously but before she spoke, Forager himself shuffled in and took the words out of her mouth.

'Well, look what the cat dragged in,' he exclaimed, good-naturedly. 'If it isn't Detective Durand. How're you doing, young man?'

Brad extended a hand and the doctor shook it, frowning slightly as he did.

'How are you, doc? It's good to see you again.'

Walt nodded. 'I heard you were back in town. And I

also heard about what happened. Come on through, we can talk in my office. Daphne, could you hold my calls and whatnot for a few minutes?'

Using his sleeve to wipe the sweat from his forehead, Brad followed Forager along the corridor to his cramped little cubbyhole.

'Take a seat, Bradley.'

'I'd rather stand if that's ok. No offense. The stitches...'

'Sure, sure. Terrible thing, what happened. Just terrible. You were in the Times again. Any news on Miss Delgado? Do they have any leads?'

Brad shook his head. 'If there were, I'd be the last to know. Tillery's men play their cards pretty close to their chests.'

'What does your gut tell you? Oh, sorry, poor choice of words.'

Brad managed a smile. 'Well, Zam Delgado's alive. Somewhere. I *think*. I don't know,' he said, defeatedly. 'The whole thing is a... *fucking headfuck*. Pardon my French.' Brad leaned back against the tower of box files and pushed the heels of his palms against his eyes.

Walt coughed to fill the awkward silence. 'She certainly was - *is* - a determined young lady. I can't say I approve of her methods. She's a terrier. Just like you were - *are*.'

'No doc, you were right first time. My dog days are over. I've just got to finish this.'

'Is that wise? In your current condition?' Walt asked.

Brad shrugged. 'I'm getting closer. As soon as we started poking this voodoo business, the whole thing blew up in our faces. We were on to something, fo' sure.'

Forager cocked his head to one side. 'Voodoo, eh? Do you still believe that? The voodoo angle. Isn't that a little too... *intangible* for a man like you?'

Brad recognized the veiled reference to Elaine's illness: Walt Forager - a man of medicine - had been one of the first he had turned to for answers when his wife's fibromyalgia had been diagnosed. He looked hard into the doctor's eyes before answering.

'Voodoo is alive and kicking in this city. Has been for three hundred years. Tell me I'm wrong, doc. Sure, it's all dressed-up and Mardi-Gras-ed to shit for the tourists, but some people still take it *deadly* serious. So much so, there's some freakshow running around town in a pig mask, killing virgins in the name of religion and selling those same body-parts that Kastelein bought from your late pathologist. Of that,' Brad wheezed, 'I'm one hundred percent certain.'

Forager steepled his fingers and leaned back in his chair. 'One thing I've learned in my line of work, is that it's wrong to speak ill of the dead. Not because it shows a lack of respect, but rather, more often than not, one's comments will...' he spread his hands, looking for the words.

'Bite you on the ass?' Brad offered.

'Exactly.'

'I'm not a cop anymore, doc. Nobody's even paying me to do this. I'm only trying to find this one guy and then I'm done.'

Forager nodded sagely. He chose his words before he spoke.

'This is just between you and me, now. Off the record and all.' Walt nodded before collecting his thoughts. 'Well now, Eve Carmel had her secrets. I think it's safe to say she engaged in something... nefarious. What, I don't know. I'm not sure I'll ever understand the game she was playing with Kastelein, or what became of those body parts she... *procured*. She certainly stirred up a hornets' nest around here, I'll tell you that much.

My team is working *flat out* to update the computer systems. *Flat out.*'

A lab technician sauntered by the office, picking his teeth with a pen lid.

'Unexplained deaths do occur but given the circumstances, hers raises a number of questions.'

'I saw your report,' Brad said.

'You shouldn't have. They're not public documents,' Walt pursed his lips, in a show of frustration.

'Do you have any theories?'

'And here I was thinking this was just a social call, Detective... well, since you ask, she most probably suffered some kind of febrile convulsion and choked on her own tongue.' Forager looked Brad in the eye and they both knew he was lying. 'Hot baths and showers can trigger epileptic fits. In children at least. It's possible that...' his words trailed off.

'What about the scopolamine?'

'What about it? That's your department,' Forager answered, testily.

'Take it easy, doc. We're just talking hypothetically. Do you have any theories about those kids murdered on Halloween?'

'Two heart attacks, and a brain aneurysm. One kid who choked on his own vomit. Murders? You're reaching, Bradley.' Walt Forager opened the bottom drawer of his desk and pulled out a bottle of single malt. 'Kids these days are injecting bath salts, snorting plant fertilizer and chasing it all with six packs of high-caffeine energy drinks. If you think we have the resources to pinpoint what killed them, you're mistaken. I miss the good old days of liquor and heroin.' He poured out a small measure into two plastic cups and handed one to Brad.

'I'm not supposed to,' Brad demurred.

'Drink it. It'll do you good.'

'If you insist.' Brad raised his cup and knocked the drink back in one, but the alcohol caught the back of his throat, and he erupted in a coughing fit which bent him double. He grunted through the pain as he tried to catch his breath.

Forager handed him a paper napkin. 'How are *you* doing? Physically, I mean. What have they got you on?'

'I rattle when I walk,' Brad answered as he pulled the bottles from his jacket pockets. Forager picked one up and looked over his spectacles at the label.

'Hell's bells. This is strong stuff. When were you released from the hospital?'

'A week ago.'

He picked up another bottle. 'Hell's bells' he muttered, 'these could kill a horse. Listen, Brad, would you mind if I took a look at you?'

Brad gave a crooked smile. 'If it'll make you happy doc, then sure, why not?' He pulled his shirt out of his trousers.

'No, Bradley. I think you'd better come with me.'

They maneuvered their way awkwardly out of the office and Forager led the way along a dark corridor to a dimly lit examination room where the autopsies were performed.

'Woah, doc. This is starting to get a bit weird,' Brad said.

Forager ignored him, snapped on a pair of plastic gloves and told him to sit down. He began a cursory examination, taking Brad's temperature, checking the dilation of his pupils, feeling his lymph nodes.

'I fell into this profession,' he mumbled, partly to Brad, partly to himself. 'Good grades, you see. So, when the draft started, they said I'd make a good medic. Safer, better pay. Suits me, I said.' He rolled a fresh sheet of hygienic paper over the steel table. 'I was a US Army Captain Medic when I finished my final tour. That was sixty-seven. I thought I'd seen enough death in Vietnam, but I guess not. OK, take your clothes off and hop up. Leave them on the chair. Yes, pants too. There's a good fellow.'

Brad did as he was told and gingerly hoisted himself up onto the table. In spite of the frigid air in the room and the feel of cold metal against his skin, the moment he lay back and closed his eyes, he could have fallen asleep. Walt had found an old stethoscope and was checking it still worked.

'We don't get much call for these,' he muttered as he pressed the bell against Brad's chest and listened to his heartbeat. He nodded to himself and moved his fingers lightly down to Brad's abdomen.

'Have you lost any weight since the incident?'

'I'd say,' Brad snorted. "Bout forty pounds.'

'Gee whizz. That's gotta be good for your game.'

'I don't have 'game' anymore, doc.'

The three-inch scar was still a livid purple smile against the pale skin of Brad's stomach, puckered like a seam in leather. Forager pressed the area around it and Brad winced. 'Might be able to do something with the scar tissue at the right time. Lift your left leg please. And the right. Any pain? Any trouble urinating? Passing stools?' Brad answered all the doctor's questions. 'OK, you can get dressed.'

Brad struggled back into his clothes. 'So, how long have I got, doc?' he joked, as he stuffed his shirt tails into his pants.

The chief Medical Examiner said nothing at first. He perched on a stool, took off his spectacles and rubbed his eyes.

'You know what a placebo is, I assume?'

'Sure. What? You gonna give me some sugar pills?' Brad smiled.

'Sugar pills - that's right,' Forager placed his glasses back on and continued. 'It's a Latin word, 'placebo.' Know what it means, Bradley? It means 'I will please.' *Please* a patient with some sugar pills - like you say. Convince him that they work, then effectively, their faith in medicine does the job. And back then - in Ancient Rome - that's all medicine really was, faith. That's where the term 'faith-healing' comes from. By forcing faith, so-called physicians used the *will to heal*. Nowadays, it's different of course, medicine has come a long way, but we still use placebos. Clinical testing and whatnot.' He turned on the faucet and washed his hands.

'Here's the funny thing though: these days, whether a doctor gives a patient a placebo or a real drug for their symptoms, the medic is obliged to explain the health warnings and side effects of the *real meds*.'

'To keep up the pretense. I get you,' Brad said.

'Exactly. But what science *can't* explain is why some placebo patients actually *do* suffer from those side effects. It happens all the time. Not just subjective symptoms either - headaches and nausea and the like -' he waved a hand in Brad's direction, 'but skin rashes, low blood pressure, enzyme levels. Real, quantifiable data. Don't take my word for it: read the American Journal of Medicine. And you call that the 'nocebo' effect.'

'"I *won't* please'?' Brad quipped.

'Close. 'I will *harm*'. The nocebo effect isn't just limited to pills. The mere suggestion can be enough to cause harm. Priming someone to *think* they are ill can produce the actual symptoms of a disease.'

'I wondered when we were going to get back to Eve Carmel,' Brad said.

'I'm not talking about Eve Carmel. I'm talking about you, Brad.'

Brad laughed. 'Thanks doc, but I don't think I'm that gullible.'

'It's not a question of gullibility. Eve wasn't a gullible woman. She was sharp as a tack. And you, you're a fine detective - I imagine it takes a lot to pull the wool over your eyes. But...'

'But what?' Brad snapped. 'Jesus, doc. I was stabbed. I lost four pints of blood. I've got a perforated intestine. I'm thirsty all the time but drinking anything makes me want to puke. I can't piss, shit, eat or sleep properly. And you expect me to believe it's all in my head?'

'It is,' Forager replied bluntly. 'Your scar has healed nicely. There's no sign of infection. Your vital signs are good. Your heart sounds like a metronome. You've lost weight, so much so in fact that your BMI is almost textbook for a man of your size. You're taking enough antibiotics to cure TB, MRSA and HIV. And what? In spite of all this, you're dying.'

Brad opened his mouth to say something but was lost for words.

'Yes, Bradley, you - are - dying. You can imagine how many corpses I've seen in my time and frankly, many of them lying on that bench were in a better state than you are now. You look like the walking dead.'

If anything, Brad was pissed off. 'So, what's your advice?'

Walt Forager sighed heavily again. 'What can I tell you? 'When you're going through hell, keep going.' Winston Churchill said that. Take on board what I've told you and believe that you're going to get through this. Take courage. Have *faith*. Have a goal. Find something you love dearly and hold on to it. Your life depends on it.'

Brad nodded. 'Are we done here?'

Forager rounded on him like a father scolding a son. 'I'm serious, Bradley. Beware of the scaremongers. Because if you're determined to see this through to the end, you'll have to kill them before they kill you.'

thirteen

Anticipation. If Ike Sugar had known the meaning of the word, that's what he would have labeled the feeling he had come to associate with a 'becoming.' He felt it in his bones and blood: a not-unpleasant tightening in his chest, a quickening of his pulse. It manifested itself in the intensity of colors of the leaves, in the waxing of the November moon, and the sense that nature itself was rushing headlong towards its inevitable winter death. It came as no surprise to Ike.

'You reap what you sow,' he told himself, knowing that the sheer number of sacrifices he had made to *Li Grand Zombi* in recent weeks had presaged the change.

From pig to dog, from dog to rooster, the becomings had always been preceded by a period of increased effort on his part. The spirits were pleased, and Ike allowed himself a moment to bask in his pride, having cut down so many young lives and offered so much back to the loa. The club had been instrumental in his success, and he prided himself on his restraint with Boucher in allowing him to live and the business to thrive. There were scores of virgins to choose from: men mainly, willingly dragged along for a first time in a strip-club or celebrating bachelor parties with older friends and relatives. And women too, on occasion, curious and experimental with their own sexuality who had come to see what Cheaters - safer and more secluded than the other downtown bars - had to offer.

Ike picked his way through the midnight crowds, snipping at locks of youthful hair in unguarded moments and adding them to his collection, occasionally brushing a little Devil's Breath on their bare skin, just in case. Sometimes he waited outside in the shadows of Clinton Street and watched for the straggler, the lightweight, the teetotaler, the girl who had to get home, the boy heading in the other direction from the group. And then he followed, whispering his voodoo prayers and choosing his moment in the quieter streets of the Crescent City, where he would flood lungs with blood, crush hearts or pinch closed vital vessels. The pickings were rich: fingers and thumbs and ears and eyes for the taking. He cut the foreskin from a cruise ship sailor and tipped his paralyzed body into the Mississippi. He blocked the windpipe of a waitress closing up for the night in Bywater and sliced off her luscious, cherry-red lips. Halloween fell on a Sunday; people had been drinking all day. Overwhelmed by the costumes and decorations, the music, the noise, Ike took five, strutting audaciously through the crowds around Jackson square in his feathered suit, his face painted in the blood of his victims.

Even the media was working to his advantage. In a perverted twist of human nature, rather than dissuade people from visiting New Orleans, the news reports of the murders had driven tourists to the city to sample its myriad delights: the chance of being slaughtered, voodoo-style, adding a certain piquancy to the gumbo. The streets were thronged day and night with customers: old, sunburnt and ripe for Ike's genuine hand-stitched *gris-gris*, guaranteed to bring luck, increase wealth, boost potency. He reeked of authentic Creole and the out-of-towners from the north of the country lapped up his patois and readily handed over their crisp dollar bills from their fanny-packs, nodding reverently when he warned them *never* to open their mojo bag.

'Y'all don't wanna ruin yo' hoodoo, do you?' he'd say, with a wide grin.

Meanwhile, beyond the relative safety of the French Quarter, Mid-City and the Garden District, Auden Tillery's initial theory about the source of the killings began to play itself out. Once news spread of the rash of dead bodies and their missing parts, the Young Melph Mafia, 110ers and 3NG naturally followed suit, cutting off souvenirs and mementos of their gangland killings to prove themselves to one another. For his part, Tillery arrogantly chalked all this up to good old-fashioned police work and turned a political blind eye to the gangs reducing their own numbers, as long as no law-abiding citizens were caught in the crossfire. There was no conjecture in the newspaper or on TV about how young men with multiple stab or gunshot wounds had died here, but it all helped to muddy the waters as Ike happily went about his work.

Behind a graffitied transport container on a vacant Louisa Street lot, he looked up at the stars whirling above him and anticipated the change. Then he bent over the body of a seventeen-year-old girl, dead drunk on peach snowballs, and leaned his full weight against the handle of his billhook until he heard her breastbone snap.

'*Mwen te fouye twou a…*' he sang quietly.

*

Driven from the comfort of his recliner by the pain in his gut, Brad took a circuitous route through the downtown crowds around the French Market, hoping to tire himself out. Even at nearly two in the morning, Café du Monde was still full, serving café au lait and beignets to tables packed with tourists. The management liked to make a big deal of deliveries, and hessian sacks of roasted coffee beans and five kilo bags of icing sugar were unloaded right there in front of the customers, who lapped up the spectacle. As he watched, a bag of sugar slipped off the cart and exploded on the sidewalk to the general delight of the crowd, who were briefly engulfed in a cloud of sweet dust. Brad licked his lips and tasted it in the air. A surly waiter picked up the broken bag and dumped the lot in a trashcan, ruining the moment for everyone. Brad couldn't resist as he walked by the garbage can, he licked his index finger and stuck it deep in the broken sack and licked again, like it was a giant Fun Dip. Brad winked at a watching kid.

In the weeks since her disappearance, Cheaters had become something of a shrine to Zam Delgado, at least for Brad, and he had been making his own personal pilgrimage to Clinton Street as often as his legs would carry him. His visits were driven primarily by guilt, but he also couldn't help feeling that there - of all places - he might stumble upon a clue to her disappearance. The bar seemed to have a gravitational pull. She had been right of course: it was plain to see that there were drugs - coke and molly, Brad guessed - no surprise given the club's star appeared to be in the ascendant.

He didn't go inside but lingered on the sidewalk instead, checking his watch and pretending he was waiting for somebody as he watched the customers come and go. A bunch of college students stumbled out of the velveteen lobby: boys playing grown-ups with daddy's money at a strip-club. They were certainly drunk and probably high, Brad knew, but he wasn't a cop anymore, so he didn't stop them, not even the last kid in the pack, who tripped off the curb and bumped into him, burning a cigarette hole in his jacket as he did so. Brad grabbed him, stood him up straight, told him to be more careful and sent him on his way: all this while the door attendant looked on impassively. He seemed to clock that although Brad was police - or something like it - he wasn't looking for trouble. *Maybe he thinks I'm waiting for one of the dancers*, Brad smiled to himself.

Without warning, the bouncer squared his shoulders and cocked his head like a boxer coming out of his corner and strode across the cobbles toward Brad.

Fuck, thought Brad.

'Hey,' said Treyvon.

'Hey,' Brad replied, trying to be nonchalant.

'You want one of these?' Treyvon asked, offering Brad the can of soda wrapped in a twenty-dollar bill, that he'd been hiding in the pocket of his overcoat. It was grape flavored Big Shot.

'Can I take the twenty and you keep the soda? How's that sound? I'm up to here with soda,' Brad joked.

'We got alcohol-free beer,' Treyvon pulled a second can from his other pocket. 'You want alcohol-free beer?'

'Sure. Why not?' Brad said. 'Seriously though, you can keep the money.'

'You're police, right?'

'I'm a private detective. Does that count?'

Treyvon grunted in the affirmative but peeled off the money anyway. Brad popped the tab and took a slurp. It wasn't bad. 'You know,' he mused, 'I don't think I've ever tasted alcohol-free beer my entire life. All this time.' He chugged again. 'You wouldn't know it wasn't the real deal.'

'First time for everything,' Treyvon answered. 'So, what are you doin' for?'

'Oh, I'm just looking for somebody. Not like that. I was

a friend of the police lady who went missing a while back. D'you read about it in the papers?'

Treyvon shook his head.

'Well, she disappeared. And she was here the night before, I know that. I guess I'm just looking for answers.'

That seemed to satisfy Treyvon for the moment and the two men settled into a comfortable silence, which Brad promptly shattered.

'So, you did a spell in Angola for raping a kid, right?'

The muscles in Treyvon's jaw clenched involuntarily, but he said nothing.

'It's ok, dude. You did your time. Now you're here, doing your job, and we're just two guys, drinking a beer - kinda - well, I am - and that's that. We all make mistakes.'

'Mistakes?!' Treyvon spat, his face now inches from Brad's. 'That *bitch* told me she was *twenny* one, and I was stupid 'nough to believe her! Mistakes?!' he scoffed. 'You knows how it is with girls these days. They's all pushed out in the right places and... glamorized and shit. Then my hot-shit lawyer comes along, tells me to take the plea deal and straight up fucks me again. Another goddamn mistake! So don't talk to me 'bout no mistakes!'

'I hear you,' Brad said, cool as whipped cream. 'Women. Yup, they'll fuck you over. Lawyers too. Was your lawyer a woman?'

Treyvon screwed up his face sourly and nodded.

'There you see: that's the 'double fuck,' right there.'

Brad's words of wisdom helped to ease the tension and Treyvon exhaled and collected himself. He shook his head sadly.

'Sorry 'bout that. I still gets all worked up thinkin' 'bout it.'

'No need to apologize, dude. I thought we'd clear the

air, s'all. Police know everything that goes on. We're worse than dogs barking. Anyway, now we both know where we stand.' Brad drained his can. 'You like working here?'

'It's ok, I guess. The money's gettin' better,' he shrugged.

'Yeah, I see a lot more customers these days. What's with that?' the detective asked.

Treyvon was about to answer when he stopped himself - his moment's hesitation not lost on Brad.

'Say, police know everythin'? You ever hear anything 'bout a girl called Claudette Tremblay?'

'Another girl?' Brad asked. 'Is she twenty-one, too?'

Treyvon grinned, 'I do likes me a fresh peach, but this un's too fresh even fo' me. Nah man, she used to work here, and then one day, she just din't show no' more. I thought maybes you might know somethin'.'

'Claudette Tremblay? I don't recognize the name,' Brad said. 'When did you last see her?'

'Couple months. End o' the summer, I guess.'

The same time Zam disappeared, Brad thought to himself, his interest piqued. 'How old is Claudette? Really?'

'Sixteen if a day. And so fine. Like an African princess.'

'Sweet sixteen and never been kissed? Now be honest with me, young gun, did you ever tap that fine African princess ass? Tell me straight now…' Brad said.

'I swear on my mother's eyes, I din't never. I confess, I did think 'bout it more than once, but I never done the deed,' Treyvon replied, as innocent as an alabaster cherub.

'You sure now? A big, healthy boy like you - money in his pocket - you couldn't turn that girl's head?'

'Maybe I coulda, but honest truth, I kinda gots the feelin' that she was still waitin' for that someone special to pop her cherry, you catch my drift...'

Brad did. 'Here, take my card, son. That's my cell number, right there. I'll see what I can find out 'bout Miss Tremblay - I still have... well, I still know people on the force. If you remember anything else about that police lady, give me a call. Or if you want to talk about the club here, or whatever....'

The two men locked eyes and shared something unspoken. Treyvon took the card and shook Brad's hand. 'See y'around.'

*

Drinking starts early in New Orleans, and the good times roll until the wee small hours. By ten, an hour after Brad hit the streets again the following morning, his legs were already aching, and he was sweating like a teenager in confession. The plan was to work from the east side towards downtown, but the pickings were slim: and only the hardened drinkers paid him any heed. He ordered a club soda and lime and slumped in a corner of the Cat's Meow balcony, looking down on Bourbon Street - and the black dog staring back at him - and listening to the blood thrumming in his ears.

He couldn't shake the dream he'd had. Zam Delgado was painfully pulling thick strands of hair from her mouth, gagging on them as they came up, like a sickening parody of a magician pulling out colored scarves. Finally, when it seemed she might actually choke to death, she coughed up a big ball of red wax, threaded through with the hair and said, with such relief, 'It's jus' a parlor trick, sonny!'

Brad shook his head to try to clear it.

The server must have been something in her day, but her dyed auburn hair, beads and tattooed arms were more suited to a younger woman. She leaned forward to wipe down a table next to Brad's and he nearly choked when he saw the fetish swing out from her low-cut shirt. It was smaller than the zombie bride's, but otherwise the same: a chicken foot, red silk ribbon and a black feather, tied off with bailing twine.

'Take a picture - it'll last longer,' she said, half-joking, when she noticed Brad staring at her chest.

'Hey - sorry - I didn't mean to... I was actually looking at your... your *charm* there,' Brad said, feigning embarrassment.

'It's ok. I was just pullin' your chain,' she said with a wink.

'It's a fetish, right? That's what you call it?' Brad asked, eager to keep the conversation going.

'Sure is.'

'I'd like to get one of those for my wife,' Brad replied, carefully feeding out his line, and took a sip of his soda. His first bite in two days: he didn't want to scare her off.

'There's a voodoo store just down the block. You can get a nice one there, f'sure.'

'Oh yeah - I guess - but I want a *genuine* one. You can tell yours is the real deal, right?'

'Yeah, this one's special,' she replied as she gently rubbed the curled chicken claw and tucked it back inside her collar. Her eyes were kind but when she smiled, Brad wondered whether it was just pity. She turned away to wipe more empty tables.

'Where'd you get it?' Brad pressed her, struggling to keep the edge from his voice, worried he was losing the moment. 'My wife sure would love one like that.' The ice cubes rattled in his glass.

'Well, an old boy sold it to me. He used to come by here, but I guess I haven't seen him around in a while.'

Brad didn't let his disappointment show. He fingered the photo in his jacket pocket and wondered about coming clean. One more play.

'Never mind,' he said breezily, 'Brad,' he said, extending a friendly handshake.

'Karen,' she answered instinctively.

'Nice to meet you. I used to come here all the time with my wife,' Brad said, nonchalantly looking down over the balcony at the tourists below. 'We live out of town now.' It wasn't strictly a lie. 'You worked here long?'

"Bout seven years. I'm from Chicago originally.'

'Well, the weather's certainly better down here,' Brad quipped.

'I'd say 'different'. I'm getting used to the hurricanes, I s'pose,' she said, brushing her bangs out of her eyes. 'Can I get you another drink, Brad?'

'Um… sure. Is it too early for a Sazerac?'

'It's never too early here, is it?' Karen laughed.

Brad stood, trying not to wince from the pain. 'I'll just go splash a little water on my face. I've been away so long I can't take this humidity any more….'

Under the harsh fluorescent lights of the bathroom, Brad's pallor was reptilian. He could just make out the faint 'x' on his forehead, but when he rubbed at it, it didn't shift. The tap water had a strange metallic taste, but when Brad spat it into the sink, he realized his gums were bleeding again. He splashed cold water on his face and let it drip on his shirtfront before heading back. As he eased himself gently into his seat, Karen appeared with his drink. 'You ok hun? You don't look so good.'

'I'm fine. Just getting over surgery,' he replied stiffly, handing over a twenty.

'Well, take it easy,' she smiled. 'That should help numb the pain. I'll get your change.'

There was nothing else for it. Brad knew he had to lay

his cards on the table, show Karen the photo and confess that he was police - or something along those lines - looking for the Voodoo Killer and - *yes, Karen* - that sweet old guy knows something about the recent spate of murders. *And no, I don't really want a fucking chicken claw for my wife. She left me for a used-car salesman.* He downed his cocktail and braced himself to broach the subject as the waitress sauntered back across the room.

'There you go,' Karen said, handing him his change. 'I was thinking, the voodoo guy told me to buy some special oil for it from some lady in Treme. I wrote the address down for you.'

*

'2066 Dumaine K x'

Brad didn't think grown women should dot their 'i's with little hearts, but he felt elated at finally having a lead. His pavement-pounding had paid off and when he stepped out of the Cat's Meow, a mile or so from the address on the napkin, not even the sight of the black dog with its jutting ribs and hollow eye could foul his mood. It sat on the other side of the street, next to an old beggar who was shouting 'Betcha I can tell ya where ya got dem shoes!' to every passerby.

'Face your fears,' Doc Forager had told him.

So, Brad buttoned up his baggy suit jacket and crossed through the crowds, staring down the canine like it had just chewed up the couch. The dog barked once, rolled its head and trotted away in the direction of the Cathedral. Brad picked up the pace and followed, watching as it weaved through the tourists.

The absinthe and cognac stung his empty stomach and when he belched, he tasted acid. The cool of the early morning had given way to humidity and sweat beaded on his forehead. He stumbled off the curb as the dog turned down St Ann where the local artists hung their gaudy cityscapes on the Jackson Square railings. The myriad colors hurt his eyes and he squinted against the glare, trying to focus on the dog as it slipped away through the crowd. Brad knocked into a couple taking a photo of themselves and mumbled an apology. The dog barked behind him now and he spun around, conscious that people were looking at him, pointing and staring at the tramp, the bum, dressed in a dirty suit and drunk before eleven in the morning.

'Beware the scaremongers,' Doc Forager said.

Brad caught a glimpse of the dog again and gave chase, but his legs felt like they weren't his own and as he rounded the corner at Chartres, his ankle buckled and he crashed spectacularly into a fortune-teller's stall, scattering a pack of tarot cards and smashing a crystal ball.

'What the *fuck* man!' the clairvoyant screamed, before she saw Brad's face.

'*Jezi-Kris*! Get *away* from me!' she shouted, the fear evident in her voice as she recoiled, 'Don't touch me!'

People turned and Brad caught the terrified expressions of every hokey psychic and would-be prophet on the stretch. The tourists stared open-mouthed at him like he had the plague and for a second everybody stopped and there was silence in the square. Breathing heavily, Brad sat up and turned back to the clairvoyant - her eyes were wide behind her thick spectacles.

'What?' he shouted, panicked, touching his face. 'What is it?'

'Man, don't you know?' she said. 'You done been

hoodooed!'

Barking wildly, its rotten, purple lips curled back in rabid fury, the dog came flying out of the crowd, snapping viciously at Brad's feet as he scrambled backwards across the sidewalk, screaming in fear. It yelped in pain as he managed to kick it once in the muzzle, but it came again, more determined now, clawing at his stomach and chest. Brad rolled frantically and covered his face with his arms like a boxer caught against the ropes, but the dog seized his wrist in its wet jaws and clamped down so hard Brad felt its yellow canines pierce his flesh and heard the bone break before he passed out.

*

Claudette wandered around the empty house, testing locked doors and trying fruitlessly to pull open nailed-shut sash windows. For the first time in weeks, she had woken from a nightmare with a memory of her brother and a longing to hold him and be hugged by him. Recently, she felt she had been building up a resistance to Ike's cocktails and night-caps - those which had previously left her feeling as though she had been wrapped in a heavy, warm woolen blanket.

She pulled away the cardboard and tape covering a filthy windowpane on the second floor of the house. The morning light spilled into the room, illuminating stacks of boxes filled with mildewed paperwork and obsolete computer keyboards and telephones. Claudette stared out and let her eyes adjust to the bright sunlight. In the yard below, she saw for the first time the abandoned corn rows where a pair of scrawny dogs were sniffing at each other. A woman walked by on the street beyond the yard and instinctively

Claudette banged on the glass and tried to call out, but her throat was dry and her voice thick. She couldn't remember the last time she had spoken to anybody.

'I can't remember,' she whispered, shaking her head. 'I can't remember.'

The city skyline sparkled in the sunlight, but she couldn't get her bearings. Uptown somewhere. Lafitte maybe. When was the last time she had been outside? The seasons had changed. *It will be cold outside the club tonight.* 'Cheaters.' She closed her eyes and pictured Treyvon's face and a sob caught in her throat. Treyvon and *Mr Boucher*. That was his name. Mr Boucher would help. Tears spilled down her gaunt cheeks. If she could just find Mr Boucher, he would surely help her.

'He'll help me. He'll help me.'

'I'm Claudette Louise Tremblay,' she said aloud.

fourteen

Brad woke up swaying gently on the porch swing of a little shotgun house, but he couldn't fathom how he'd gotten there. As his mind slowly turned over the memories of a smashed crystal ball, a terrified clairvoyant and finally the ferocious black dog, a bolt of pain shot through his wrist; he rolled up his shirt sleeve to investigate the extent of the wound and was both relieved and sickened to see nothing there at all. He pressed his fingertips into the points where he *knew* the dog's teeth had punctured his flesh, but... *nothing*. He remembered the Sazerac then, and the waitress. As her note and its message burst up through his memories like a bubble from a tarpit, he reached into his pocket and read it again, '2066 Dumaine'. Brad craned his neck and saw the same figures nailed vertically on the porch post. It was when he returned his gaze to the house that he noticed the face, scowling at him suspiciously from behind some net curtains.

'They brought you here,' she said.

'Who? The scaremongers?' Brad croaked.

'Men. I told them I didn't want nothing to do with no hoodooed man. But they done brought you anyways.'

Gingerly planting his feet on the porch, Brad rubbed his fingers through his hair. 'How...' he began.

'You collapsed in Jackson Square. Some kinda fit, they said. Oh, you was yammerin' 'bout this place, sayin' you needed to get here and such. They was gon' call an ambulance, but some kind soul put you in the back of his automobile and brought you here instead, given how close y'already was. I guess kind souls do still exist after all. I told them to leave you out there though. I don't want no *hoodooed* man inside my house.'

Brad nodded slowly, still refusing to believe he had been cursed, but beginning to accept that others thought he was. *Maybe I'm losing it*, he wondered, trying to pull apart the logic. *But how would I even know?*

'You're *police*, I guess,' the woman continued. She still hadn't plucked up the courage to open the door. 'Lionel said you'd come. Eventually. Have you found him?'

'Who? Lionel is... the mojo man? In the pork pie hat? This guy...' Brad fumbled in his pocket for the photograph.

'That's him,' she said, before she even saw the picture. 'Have you found him?'

'Found him?' Brad shook his head, confused. 'No. That's why I'm here. Is he missing?'

'Been gone six weeks now. Hey mister, you gon' puke on my flowers?'

'You his wife?' Brad pulled himself up, ignoring her question. 'Any chance we could continue this conversation inside?'

'Oh, you can't come in,' the woman told him, pointing a finger down to signal the thin line of red brick dust trailed across the threshold.

'I'm not going to puke... oh *that*... no, I don't believe in that shi... stuff,' Brad said, but as he approached the door, a wave of nausea rolled through his gut, and he had to scrunch his eyes shut until it passed.

'Told ya. That there keeps bad spirits away, and son, you is *riddled*,' she said, wrinkling her nose. She opened the door, but remained inside, content at least that he posed no threat to her home. Georgine Rieux wore a long-flowered dress, Mardi-gras beads and her gray hair loose over her shoulders. Brad thought she looked like an aging black hippy, but where there should have been lightness and spirit in her eyes, he saw only sadness. She saw that same sadness - an overwhelming misery - reflected back at her and her heart softened a little.

'I'm Georgine,' she said curtly. 'You don't look so good, son. Why don'chall sit down a while and I'll bring you a glass o' lemonade. You hungry?'

Brad did as he was told.

She emerged five minutes later with a tray - a bowl of white beans and shrimp, a cornbread muffin and a thin slice of pecan pie, plus a tall glass of sugared lemonade - which she handed over to Brad, careful not to let her fingers touch his. Lighting a Marlboro, Georgine leaned back against the porch railing and blew a long stream of blue smoke into the air.

'It's getting so you can't smoke anywheres these days, huh? Not even in your own home,' she grumbled, as Brad shoveled food into himself. He tongued a molar which felt loose in its socket. 'Folks is sayin' they gon' prohibit it in bars next. Where's the sense in that? This ain't New York. This ain't Los Angeles. This here... is a party town,' she said, sounding like anything but a party girl.

'You were telling me about Lionel,' Brad uttered through a mouthful of bread and beans.

'Was I? There's not much to tell. Something - some*one* - scared that *son of a bitch* and he ran away, I reckon. Right after that woman *police* went missing.'

'Did he have anything to do with that, do you think?'

'My Lionel?' She tutted loudly. 'He wa'n't no saint, but I swear that man wouldn't hurt a fly.'

'You two a couple?' Brad asked.

'Nah. Well, kinda. I guess. Lionel Laroute and me goes

back a long way,' she smiled sadly.

Brad kept eating and said nothing else while Georgine talked: Lionel's drugstore, her herbalism, his addictions, the years of lost contact, his newfound zest for life and their resulting love affair, 'if you could call it that,' she said, stubbing out her cigarette angrily. 'I warned him,' she said, shaking her head. 'I told him to be careful. You play with fire, you always get burned.'

'You mean selling *gris-gris*?'

'Hell no. Ain't no harm in that. In itself. Only that it tends to attract a certain class o' people. And them people tends to attract another class o' people. Y'know?'

'So, you think he was involved with The Voodoo Killer?'

'He's a stupid old coot. Always getting mixed up in all kinds of *non*sense. He dealt with a whole stew of people over the years - good and bad alike. I can't say fo' sure if he was *dealin'* with this Voodoo Killer, but I knows this much, he sure was scared of that cat.'

'Did he ever talk about him?'

Georgine lit another cigarette. 'One time, we was watchin' the news on the TV, and he got real scared. He said something 'bout needin' to protect me from him.' She fanned her hands through the smoke. 'For a man of his age, he talked a lot of garbage and let me tell y'all, I done managed a *long* time, wi 'out no man to protect me.'

'Let's say they *were* doing business. What would Lionel be dealin', exactly?' Brad asked, knowing he was treading on ice.

Georgine gave him a sideways glance.

'Listen, Ms. Rieux, I ain't police, and I don't care what you're growing in your glasshouse back there,' Brad said. 'That's not why I'm here. I'm just trying to get a bead on this murderer, and if Lionel's relationship with him gets me one step closer, then I'm one step closer, s'all.'

The old woman sucked her teeth and weighed his words, before giving the slightest nod of her head.

'Good. So - apart from the mojo bags - what was he pushin'? Pot? Mushrooms? Laudanum?'

Georgine took a drag on her cigarette and reached up to pluck a large pink angel's trumpet blossom from the bushes growing over the porch. 'You ever heard of *burundanga*?' she asked. 'On the street, they call it 'The Devil's Breath'.'

*

'This here is weak,' the herbalist explained, gesturing to the blossoms above their heads. Brad sighed contentedly, his stomach filled with Georgine's home-cooked cuisine, while she continued to fill the gaps in his knowledge of *burundanga*: how to make it, mix it, use it. 'The good stuff comes from way down south: past Mexico. Colombia, Venezuela way. Well, everything's hotter and wetter down there, I guess, it makes for a stronger brew. Down there, the whores spread it on theys bosoms. Did you know that? Uh huh.' Georgine sucked her teeth like a disapproving mother. 'I s'pose those girls must build up some kind of 'munity to it. Anyways, along comes a John de Cockeroo, all full o' blood and the like and when he gets a face full of them titties, well…. he's about as done as a lobster in a pot.'

'Not the worst way to go,' Brad murmured.

Georgine scoffed. 'Now Mister Bradley, don't you be foolin'. The Devil's Breath'll steal a man's memories, steal his soul, kill him stone dead. Where them titties gon' get you then?' She was serious, but Brad liked the way her eyes twinkled for the first time since they had met.

'How much?' Brad asked.

'How much what?'

'How much would it take to steal a man's soul?' He remembered Zam ripping her fingernail from its bed. 'Or a woman's soul?'

'*Burundanga* ain't like cocaine or pot. You can't buy it on the street. It's not like that because there ain't no pleasure to be had in it. The only value it has is causing pain. A gram costs two hundred dollars, give or take. That's all I gave to Lionel - just a lil' ol' packet - and that was three months back. How many people you figure your Voodoo Killer spiked?'

'Definitely two, but there's been so many strange murders recently - five on Halloween alone - I wouldn't be surprised if there were more.'

'So, you think his supply will be runnin' low?'

Brad stared out at the sun hanging low over the city. 'That's what I'm hoping.'

*

There was no turning back. The rooms with the windows were all locked, As soon as she had broken one lock, Claudette figured she may as well break them all. She found a sturdy knife in the kitchen, but only managed to snap the blade trying to lever open the door. The tools she found in the workshop downstairs were better, although it took all her strength to wield the hammer: her wrists were weak and after just a few blows she was sweating, exhausted, and sank to her knees in the empty house. At least her mind was sharper now and she focused her attention on escape.

'Escape,' she tasted the word on her dry lips.

The front door was boarded up with panels of thin wood, held in place with haphazard nails to keep people out, rather than in. Claudette sat and wedged the claw of the hammer behind the board nearest to her and levered it upwards. It didn't budge. She stood, panting, and chose a panel at waist level. Again, she positioned the claw in the recess behind the panel, in the gap between two rusty nails, but this time she bent her knees and locked her wrists, fingers tight around the grip. As she stood upright, groaning through the pain between clenched teeth, she felt the panel bend and she pulled harder, forcing it away from the doorframe. The nails screeched as they were prised free, but not before the plywood splintered and snapped, sending a thin strip of wood the width of the hammerhead skittering across the floorboards. The rest of the panel remained in place, but in that instant, Claudette realized two things.

One: the world was out there, still breathing, still alive. She could see through the gap, push her fingers through it. She could prize the rest of the panel off. Or smash it now. She could wait for somebody to pass by. She could call for help. She could escape.

Two: she only had one chance, and if she didn't get out clean, Ike would know.

*

In 1867, yellow fever had spread like wildfire through the city, claiming the lives of more than 40,000 citizens: mostly unacclimated, lower class Europeans and northerners. The minister of a tiny parish prayed to the patron saint of good health - Saint Roch - for salvation. Miraculously, not one member of his church fell ill and in time, the Chapel of Saint Roch became a shrine where the locals who had survived illness and injury came to give thanks for their recovery.

More than a century on, the chapel had evolved into a bizarre museum, full of vintage medical votive offerings to the Saint: polio braces, rusting crutches, dental plates, glass eyes and prosthetic limbs. They were nailed to the wall, from the marble bricks of the floor - each one inscribed with the word 'merci' - to the Virgin Mary pale blue ceiling. One pink plaster-cast human heart bore a water mark, a garish testament to how high the floodwaters had risen after Katrina. The candle stand was covered with silk flowers, handwritten notes, and photographs of loved ones; a sole flame guttered in the darkness.

Georgine Rieux didn't like to venture out after dark. The city had its fair share of trouble - the news these days seemed to be filled with muggings and stabbings - so rather than walk, she had chosen to take the bus from the corner of Claiborne. The driver, whom she knew from around the way, had tried to engage her in conversation, but Georgine only nodded politely, uttered some truism and shuffled to a seat, where she turned the rings on her fingers and worried about what she was about to do.

Even at this hour, though the cemetery was long closed, there were tourists posing for photographs and young men in hoods and heavy leather jackets loitering under the statues at the locked gates, while the dead lay sleeping just beyond. Clutching her purse, Georgine turned down North Daubigny - passed the house-like tombs and the honeycomb graves built into the whitewashed exterior walls - and then left into Music Street, to the Campo Santo gate. It swung open.

A breeze blew through the willows. Here she stopped

for a moment and listened to check she hadn't been followed and also to allow the peace of the cemetery to envelop her. Many of her old friends and family were buried here in the 'campo santo,' the holy ground, but Georgine Rieux would take her recollections of one particular procession to her own grave. She recalled the solemn ride in the limousine and the mournful march of the accompanying jazz band. The overpowering smell of lilies. As they lowered her Michel's casket, she had said, 'That's all I can give you now, cher,' and with that she turned around in her high heels and black dress, throwing her head back and dancing her way out of that graveyard.

'That's how we do death in New Orleans,' Georgine whispered to herself.

The chapel door was open. Behind the altar, in the flickering light of the votive candle, a pair of yellow eyes watched.

'If y'all is in here,' Georgine called, as she pulled the scarf from her head and shook out her hair, 'now'd be the time to come on out.'

She saw a movement in the gloom and in spite of herself, caught her breath and felt her heartbeat quicken as he slowly emerged.

'Hello Lionel Laroute,' she said.

*

'Where you been at?' Georgine asked. 'Y'all look like you been sleepin' at the Salvation Army center.'

Sure enough, Lionel Root was even more disheveled than usual. His clothes were thin - inappropriate for a man of his age at this time of the year. There was a mustard stain on the lapel of his jacket and the seam of one of his loafers had come loose. He had a hungry, haunted look, like an old fox caught in the headlights.

'Oh... I've been around,' Lionel replied sheepishly. 'Jus keepin' my head down an' such.'

'You been hidin' is what you been doin', you ol' fool. Why would you wan' go and get involved with that voodoo man, now?'

'Yes, why would you?' Brad asked, stepping heavily under the arched entrance into the chapel. He held the Smith and Wesson high enough to be seen. 'Pork pie,' he gave himself a self-satisfied smile. 'Evenin', Miss Rieux'.

'Well, shit!' she cursed sourly.

'Woman, I *told* you to be careful!' Lionel snapped.

'Well, I din't think he had it in him!' Georgine replied. 'Look at the man! Shit, he was at death's door when he showed up by my house this mornin'!'

'He still is,' Lionel said, stepping closer to get a better look. The short walk following Georgine around the cemetery walls had left Brad out of breath. 'Looks like he got to you, huh?'

'Oh, he's hoodooed alright,' Georgine added.

'Whatever,' Brad wheezed. He kept the gun pointed at Lionel but stepped closer to the lady.

'What's in the purse?' he asked.

'None of your goddamn business,' she snapped.

'That's enough,' Brad said, 'Hand it over, Miss Rieux,' he said, before briefly turning the pistol on her. 'Please.'

She acquiesced, and Brad hitched his leg up against the side of the altar to hold the bag open on one knee. Inside, there was a mix of Tupperwares and aluminum foil packages, and his immediate thought was he had hit paydirt and she was working as Lionel's drug mule. But then the scent of lemons, warm bread and smoked sausage wafted up out of the bag and assailed Brad's senses. 'What the hell is this?' he asked.

'Shrimp Louie, chicken gumbo, red beans and rice..., um, muffuletta, okra Creole... Lionel, I brought you two clean shirts also. They's wrapped in plastic in the bottom there, so as they don't get no cooking aromas...'

'Georgie girl, you is an angel. Truly,' Lionel beamed, his anger immediately forgotten.

'And what's this?' Brad asked, holding up a tiny cardboard envelope, homemade and bound tightly in scotch tape. He had frisked enough people over the years to spot a hidden pocket.

Nobody spoke for a beat, but everybody knew what was going down. Lionel finally whispered, 'That ain't no wrap o' cocaine you got there.'

'Is this what I think it is...?' Brad asked, holding the envelope up in the light, like a magician revealing the trick card. 'So, you *are* a mule, after all. Is this authentic or did you make it yourself in your glasshouse, Miss Rieux?' With a penknife, Brad slit the envelope and pinched it open. The fine white powder within glinted like sugar crystals.

'That there's the good stuff,' she answered dejectedly and sucked her teeth. 'Now son, you gots to be careful with that little thing now, y'hear?'

'Burundanga,' Lionel whispered, with something akin to reverence.

'The Devil's Breath,' Brad said, and he folded the envelope tightly closed and slipped it into his inside jacket pocket. 'Did you get that, Rubino?' he said loudly, touching his ear. 'Good. Send in the cavalry. OK,' he said, focusing on the old couple, 'you're both coming with me. Let's go.'

Georgine opened her mouth to protest, and at that same moment, the blue lights of a squad car flashed through the small window of the chapel.

*

Rubino placed a hand on Lionel's head and eased him gently into the back of the cruiser, next to a foul-tempered Georgine. But the old man stared back out of the window with a look of - what? - Brad thought he saw relief in his tired eyes. Then his focus shifted, and he caught his own reflection, sallow as wax, his own eyes sunken and the cross in the middle of his forehead as black and bold as a fresh tattoo. Rubino leaned in through the front window.

'Take them downtown and hold them for now,' he told the officer. 'I'll follow behind.' He rapped his knuckles on the roof and the car moved off, past a gathering crowd of rubbernecking locals.

Rubino turned and extended a handshake to Durand. 'We'll take it from here. Seriously though, Detective, thanks for all your help.'

'If I could just...' Brad began.

'Really, you've done more than enough. God knows, we needed a break in this case. Tillery has been riding our asses for months, so I can't thank you enough.'

'I think... you know... if I could just get *five* minutes in the interrogation room...' Brad continued.

'You know that's not going to happen,' Rubino said apologetically. 'The Commander....'

Brad threw his hands up, 'Yeah, yeah. I know. What the commander wants...'

Rubino nodded.

'Do me a favor?' Brad said, 'Don't tell him I had anything to do with this? I want to savor that moment for myself. You'll get the collar, don't worry. Just leave me out of the picture for now.'

'Sure. No problem.' Rubino smiled knowingly. There

was a moment's uncomfortable silence between the two men. Brad kicked a pebble across the asphalt. 'Oh, the… um … burundanga?'

'Nearly forgot,' Brad fished the packet out of his inside pocket and handed it over. 'Be careful with that now.'

'Thanks. So, you think he's the guy?' Rubino asked, tilting his head in the direction the squad car had taken.

Brad looked down the street. The crowd had already dispersed. 'Maybe, maybe not,' he answered absently. 'He knows something. That's fo' sure.'

'So, what now?'

Brad fixed his eyes on the young detective, but Rubino recoiled from his thousand-yard stare.

'Now? Keep moving forward,' he said. But in the glow of the streetlights, Brad Durand looked like a dead man, ready to take his eternal rest in the cemetery behind him.

*

Odeo knew he was a fool, but not a complete fool. For the first time in months, Cheaters was debt free, and that felt good, incredibly good, even if the freedom had come at a high price. It was true that one or two of the Voodoo Killer's victims had been last seen at his nightclub, but he cooperated with the police when they came to investigate, even though he never quite managed to say anything incriminating about Ike, choosing instead to question his own motives when he sidestepped their enquiries. Was it loyalty that stopped his tongue? Fear? Either way, the thought of losing Cheaters after so many months struggling to make ends meet was too much. The idea of Ike Sugar cutting his throat was worse still. Odeo also knew that by incriminating Sugar, he would only be laying the blame at his own doorstep. Anyway, he hadn't lied. Not as such, anyway. He'd just convinced himself that the police - in their ineptitude - hadn't asked the pertinent question. Yes officer, there's always plenty of unsavory characters hanging 'round the strip bar. Any strip bar surely? No officer, nothing out of the ordinary. Really officer, I can't be expected to know every man's business. Odeo even ushered the detectives into his tiny office and showed them his CCTV footage of the lounge, the bar, the restroom corridor, the Clinton Street entrance. In the end, only his own sanity was questionable: the security cameras hadn't managed to catch even a single shot of Ike Sugar. He was a shadow. A ghost.

The following evening, determined to know his own mind, Odeo steeled himself for the inevitable confrontation. In the relative safety of his office, he finished a large shot of bourbon and a line of coke before stepping out into the corridor where he found Ike sitting on an empty beer barrel in a dark corner, rolling a joint and humming to himself. He was wearing his homemade shoes, and at first glance seemed to have nothing under his bird-shit splattered rain-slicker.

'How can I help you, Monsieur Boucher?' Ike asked, with none of the respect his words implied, as he peered up at Odeo from under the brim of his hat.

'Jezi, Sugar,' Odeo began. 'Can't you at least smarten yourself up a bit when you is... on the premises. Y'all look like a damn *hobo*.'

Ike's eyes never left Odeo's, but a smile played over his lips as he licked his cigarette paper.

'Is that it?' he said softly.

'Is what it?' Odeo snapped, trying to exert an authority he didn't have.

'That what you came out to say? That it?'

Odeo snuffed down his nose. 'As a matter of fact - no - it ain't. *Ike*. The police was here yesterday. I had another conversation with them. The *police*, that is. Another murder, they says. Somebody who was here earlier on the night of... the night of the murder. The night in question....' Odeo trailed off. 'Upshot o' all this is they're looking at *us*. The police is looking at my club, Sugar.'

'*My* club.'

'How's that now?' Odeo asked.

'It's *my* club, sonny,' Ike answered, drawing himself up to his full height and tipping his hat back on his head so he could now look down on Odeo.

'Now you listen to...' Odeo began, but Ike cut him dead.

'No sir, *you* listen. If you was so worried 'bout the situation at *your* club - all these here slaughterings and hullabaloo - why din't y'all say something, Odeo? Damn, them police coulda had you in *protective* custody by nows. Ain't that what they calls it? *Protective* custody?' Ike's eyes glittered, like it was all a grand joke. 'Why din't you lay the finger on me, sonny?'

'I... I... ' Odeo stammered.

'You wanna know why? *I* knows why. You wanna know why?'

Odeo stared open-mouthed, unable to nod his head nor shake it.

Ike chuckled, "Cause you and me both knows... that if you laid this on me, Odeo... if you pointed the finger at me...' he drew his billhook out from a slit in the side of his rain-slicker and held it up for Odeo to appreciate, 'I'd take this here blade and cut you a new mouth.' Ike licked his lips. 'I'd cut you a new fucking mouth, Odeo. All the way from here... to here,' he said, grazing the knife lightly across Odeo's throat as he moved it slowly from one of Odeo's ears to the other. 'How 'bout that?'

They locked eyes for a moment, before Odeo croaked, 'You're a goddamn psychopath, Sugar. Get out. Get the fuck out of my club!'

'Psycho-path?' he snorted, 'Oh well, oh well. Buddy boy, I am *becoming*,' Ike added - or at least Odeo heard: it seemed the words were spoken *through* him and perhaps Ike's lips hadn't even moved. The men stared at one another for a few more seconds before Ike pushed his foot off a beer barrel and stalked off down the corridor, leaving a cloud of pungent smoke in his wake. As Odeo watched him go, he had the distinct impression that something *else* was moving under the folds of Ike's rain slicker.

*

'I said *no* mayo! *No* mayo!'

The server - Craig - apologized, moved the sandwich to the side and started afresh, slicing a twelve-inch Hearty Italian sub, and dealing out pre-cut circles of ham, salami and pepperoni. He added the lettuce, sliced tomato, triangles of cheese and everything else from the original order, trying to concentrate this time around, keeping one eye on his work and the other on the dude sitting in the booth, sucking on a coke.

Granted, it wasn't the most salubrious sandwich emporium in the city and this guy looked like a hobo, dressed in nothing but a filthy raincoat and weird shoes, but he held himself ramrod straight, not slumped against the wall, drunk or asleep, like most of the homeless guys who managed to panhandle enough change to come in for a cookie. This guy exuded - what? - self-confidence and self-esteem in spite of his appearance. He had been sitting there for around thirty minutes since he ordered, just drinking, and talking to himself.

Ike chewed on his straw, stressing about the turn of events. He mulled over the conversation with Boucher, turning over the words, the threats, the fear in Boucher's eyes. His paranoia had led them to this point.

'I ain't to blame,' Ike muttered angrily.

But if he could only have been more like Lionel. Reasoned, persuasive and cajoling, rather than aggressive and violent. He felt trapped by circumstances: Odeo Boucher and his den of iniquity had become a liability, and now the police were involved there was only one option, even if it caused more shit further down the line. Insignificant people and their problems had a habit of biting you on the ass. 'Oh well, oh well.'

There was still a snag however, and Ike saw it. Odeo Boucher was protected, covered by Ike's own voodoo. As long as he was wearing that *gris-gris* 'round his neck, he was virtually untouchable. But Lionel had said Odeo was his own worst enemy. He had other vices.

'Can't protect a man from himself,' Ike said aloud. He just had to be pushed in the right direction.

Aside from the reefer, Ike was a reasonably clean-living kind of guy: he didn't drink, got plenty of fresh air, stayed away from red meat and always ate his vegetables. A regular boy scout. But if there was one thing he enjoyed about living in the city, it was a goddamn, Big Gulp classic Coca-Cola. He slapped the table, content that he'd worked through a thorny issue and come to a satisfying conclusion. Outside, the heavens opened, and he sucked his giant paper cup dry, watching tourists and locals alike, scrambling to take cover in doorways and under shop awnings.

But Ike Sugar loved the rain. He got himself another

Big Refill, pulled up the hood of his slicker and headed out. Passing the counter he caught Craig's eye, winked, and watched him drive a tomato knife into the palm of his hand.

fifteen

'Mister Boucher! Mister Boucher! Get yo 'self under this umbrella, sir. *Shit*, it's *really* coming down now. Mister Boucher! *Man*, you is soaked *through*!'

The storm had blown in out of nowhere, it seemed, tearing through the fall remains of the sweet potato vines and petunias hanging from the balconies of the French Quarter and driving litter up Clinton Street like tumbleweed. Treyvon had ushered the few customers into the club and positioned himself under the old entrance to Ely's Gift Emporium, where he could shelter most of his physical bulk from the driving rain. He was peering out from under his umbrella when he noticed his boss standing alone by the dumpsters on the other side of the street. Boucher's suit hung off him like a cutter's sails, and his hair was plastered to his forehead.

'Mister Boucher! Sir! Is ev'rythin' ok?' Treyvon shouted over the wind.

'Hey there, *sonny*,' Odeo stammered, saliva dripping from his lip. He was shaking, grimacing with pain, and as he tipped back his head into the glow of a streetlight, Treyvon saw the wet dusting of cocaine caked around his nose and mouth, thick as icing sugar on a beignet. Coke was smeared around his eyes.

'*Jezi-Kris*, Mister Boucher,' Treyvon whispered, incredulous, 'look what you done did...'

Treyvon put an arm around Odeo's chest and took his weight, fishing in his own coat pocket for his cell phone. The man was burning up - steam was coming off his body in the chill air.

'We gots to get you some help, Mister Boucher. Come on inside now.' As Treyvon struggled to heft Odeo's body towards the club, he seemed to gather himself, blinked his deadened eyes and focused on his doorman.

'You're a... good boy, Trey,' he growled through gritted teeth. 'A good boy,' he said, reaching up to pat him paternally on the cheek. 'Here, I want you to have these things. Stand me up now. Quick now, quick...'

From his sodden pockets, he drew a lump of wet dollar bills and a few coins and thrust them into Treyvon's hands. When he clumsily slipped his watch off his wrist he dropped it in a puddle in the process, and gave a weak sob, as though it were lost forever. Treyvon picked it off the sidewalk - it was silver, heavy and expensive. 'I can't take your watch. Mister Boucher.' Treyvon realized with a heavy heart that his boss - the man who'd taken a chance on an ex-con - was dying in his arms.

'You... keep it,' replied Odeo, fixing the doorman with a deathly stare. 'And this,' he reached inside his wet shirt and with a grimace, snapped the twine holding the *gris-gris* around his neck. 'Here - take it. *Quickly*,' he said, his breath ragged.

Treyvon stared at the greasy, little red bag in the half-light as the raindrops rolled off its surface. 'I... don't...' *want it,* he tried to say, but Odeo cut him off.

'Take it. It's too late now. I don't want any of it. You keep it *all*. It's.... evidence. You hear me, boy? *Evidence.*'

*

Ike stomped in the puddles like Gene Kelly, kicking sheets of it out of the gutter as he walked home. It reminded him of his time in the bayou, and he closed his eyes and remembered the sound of drops beating on the leaves of the cypress trees above. The rain cleansed. The rain purified, and no doubt the *Li Grand Zombi* wanted everything just so before his becoming. Ike called to mind the passages from his treasured books: *'Li Grand Zombi tells us to lay down among the leaves and roots and let the snakes come and crawl over us. He tells us to become. Fill yourself with rainwater, until you yourself swell and become a serpent. Then you will know.*

Rounding the corner, the house loomed out of the darkness, black against the dark green sky. Home. No, Ike thought. Just a building on a street. Just a street in a city. Just a city….

As he rattled the long key in the lock, he noticed the missing panel. The door swung open, heavy on its old hinges. From the other side the damage was worse. Ike moved slowly, cautiously. A vision of the shadow man - the man without *muti* - clouded his mind momentarily. Ike struck a match and lit a candle. In the half-light, he saw Claudette's body slumped on the floor. It was a wonder he hadn't fallen over her. She was semi-naked, unconscious, her arms tossed above her head, the carefree way a baby might sleep. Ike felt a frisson of desire stir in his groin. Her fire smoldered now, not quite the conflagration it had been when he first laid eyes on her, but now somehow deeper, more dangerous. He remembered seeing a bolt of lightning hit a tree once, deep in the bayou. It seemed to weather the blow at first - a grand black swamp tupelo, shaking off leaves but standing tall. Days later, however, the fire burst out of it, red and radiating from within, like a disease, like its heartwood had been set alight and it could no longer contain the heat. Ike saw that same passion radiating in Claudette. And if he was honest, it frightened him. He didn't like that.

At her side was the hammer. That's what she used, he thought, poking his fingers into the quarter sized holes in the door. His anger flared, but he kept it in check long enough to search the house for something to fix the damage. Taking the hammer, he smashed apart an old bookcase in one of the rooms upstairs and returned with splintered shelves and supports and a jar of bent nails, which he hammered straight against the floor and placed in his mouth for safe keeping. It was a hot night, the beginning of storm season, and by the time Ike had finished hammering the first planks into place, there was sweat running down his back. He wiped his brow and turned his attention to his 'sour little grapefruit,' awakened by the sound of his work.

Claudette watched him closely, weak with exhaustion and dehydration though she was. When had she passed out? She couldn't remember, but she sat for what seemed like hours, her hand poking through the gap she had made in the door, waving, waiting for anybody to walk by. There was nobody. It was a thoroughfare for cars in an otherwise quiet neighborhood. When hope faded, she attacked the door, swinging and smashing, gouging with the hammer's claw. Screaming until her voice was hoarse. The exertion must have proven too much.

And now the opportunity was lost.

She had played her hand.

Here he was again, shifting in the candlelight, always graceful even when performing a task as physical and effortful as mending a broken door. He muttered, 'Oh well, oh well' to himself, said nothing directly to her but cast dark, malevolent stares in her direction, as he pulled the nails out from between his teeth and knocked them into place with precision and ease. To watch him, one would think he was a practiced carpenter, or depending on the task in hand, a butcher chopping through a rack of ribs, a candle maker drawing out lengths of wax, a tailor meticulously double stitching a seam. True, his finished work was far from perfect, but Ike had a certain physicality, and the way he moved was mesmeric. He was sleek and lithe, and watching his muscles and sinews ripple beneath his dark skin still made her mouth water.

He finished his work and turned, focusing his gaze upon her. His yellow eyes flitted from her bare feet to her breasts, to her thighs, to her grazed knuckles, to her face. Like he was sizing her up.

'I was downtown jus' the other day,' he began, moving slowly towards her on all fours. 'You know them stores downtown - voodoo stores - for stupid white folks? Tourist stores.' He stopped and gathered his thoughts, licking his lips.

'I was thinkin', this ain't *real*. What they sell. It ain't *real*. Not like this. Not like what you and me got.' He moved again, slowly, carefully, always watching. 'They sell all kinds of shit, dressed up like the real thing. Little bottles of potions. Love potions. Potions to hurt people. Potions for a lucky break. Ain't nothing but cheap *Has No Hanna*,' he spat referring to the perfumed oil peddled by hustlers on Dumaine and Decatur. He stopped and smelled the air, remembering the aroma of night-blooming jasmine in the bottles.

'They got jars - jus' like my jars - but they's nothing but plain ol' dirt and sand. They got skulls made outta gypsum, all polished up. Fake. Fake. All of it. I tells you, Claudette, it makes me fuckin' *sick*.' He was close now, close enough to touch and he placed his hands on her legs and leaned forward to smell her crotch, pressing against her. Her eyes followed his as he stared up at her. Claudette felt unable to move, pinned both under his weight and his gaze.

'See, what they sells is the *idea* of voodoo. It ain't the real thing. Mumbo jumbo. That's what you could calls it.' He took her hands gently in his and spread them out at her sides, palms up. 'Like see, they sell these little dolls, made o' scraps of sackcloth and buttons an' such. Full o' sawdust, I guess.' Ike pushed her feet apart with his own, so her body was open and displayed. His face swayed above hers. 'And what you do is, you take this here lil' dolly and you gives it a name - somebody who done wronged you - and then you stick pins in it. Hat pins. To hurt that same somebody who wronged you. How 'bout that? Can you believe that?'

Ike's eyes were only inches from Claudette's now, and he grinned broadly and there clamped between his teeth, were maybe a dozen rusting, three-inch nails.

'Jus' a parlor trick, s'all.'

He pulled one out, between his finger and thumb, held it up to the light and asked, 'Did you wrong me, Claudette?' She didn't - couldn't - answer. Ike had stopped her tongue and closed her vocal cords. Her body was frozen tight. With a sigh, he forced the nail through the palm of her left hand until he felt it touch the floorboards beneath. Ike released the hold he had over her and Claudette bellowed. More war-cry than scream. She sucked in huge lungfuls of air and yelled again, right in his face. Like she'd been holding it inside for months. He only laughed back.

'There you is! There's your *muti*!'

He pulled another nail from his mouth. This one he pushed deeply into the flesh of her shoulder, grimacing himself as he did so. Her skin succumbed to it with an audible *pop*.

'Did you *wrong* me, Claudette?' he asked quietly over her wracked sobs. 'Did you wrong me, cher?'

Another nail, then another, then another. He pierced her thighs, left then right. Ike punctured her right hand, grazing the nerve at the base of her knuckles and bringing fresh levels of agony. He touched the tip of a nail against her eyeball and asked again if she had wronged him. He pushed a nail in between her breasts, struck bone, and left it sticking out, quivering there as she breathed.

'Like a hat pin!' he exclaimed proudly.

Then Ike Sugar grew tired of her crying and spat the rest of the nails in her face and left her lying in her blood and urine. He had work to do.

*

There was a time - maybe twenty years earlier - when the sound of a woman screaming in a neighborhood house would have brought Brad running. Not anymore. It was somebody else's problem now. He had stopped to vomit in a trashcan outside the Prince Hall Masonic Temple. There were leering faces in doorways. The rain had stopped by the time he made it home.

Home. The word felt like a kick in the stomach. Florida, Louisiana, Georgia... goddamn Alaska, Brad thought, it didn't matter anymore: nowhere felt like home. 'There's no place like home, there's no place like home,' he muttered absent-mindedly, channeling his inner-Dorothy as he fumbled in his pocket for keys. Gone were the nights when he would arrive home after a long day on the job, home to his wife and son, to kiss them both, to join them on the sofa to watch TV or play Sega. Kyle in his pajamas, allowed to wait up for his dad; the smell of a home-cooked meal; a real conversation with his wife, a couple of beers on the porch, a warm bed; a house filled with love.

An animal skittered across the road behind him: a big rat, or a skinny wild chicken. Brad slipped his key into the lock, and as the door opened, something rolled away across the wooden floor. He trod heavily and felt something crack underfoot like a hard-boiled egg. Fear and confusion shot through him and when he flicked on the light, his mind listed like a boat on a heavy sea. There were crosses, 'x's like those on Marie Laveau's tombstone - dozens, hundreds of them, of all sizes - scratched into the new paintwork and the floorboards, scored into the windowpanes and cut in the leather of his recliner, and waxen conjure balls - black and red as malevolent blood-clots - scattered across the floor.

Brad shut his eyes tight to block out the vision, but the darkness behind his eyelids was so dense that the very idea of light now seemed inconceivable. A voice seemed to whisper through him, *'there is no one to help you and no way to escape'* and truly, though his mind tried in its desperation to reach for something good, something positive, Brad Durand was overwhelmed by the certainty of his never-ending suffering. He tried to combat his own confusion with logic, but it was futile. He was cursed. Hoodooed. He knew it. *Is this what losing your mind feels like?* he thought to himself. What had Madame Coulombe said she saw? A struggle. Yes, Brad Durand felt like he was struggling, like he was drowning, looking up hopelessly from the depths of a swamp, somewhere deep in the bayou, weak light flickered above him through the brackish water. Mangrove roots caressed his face but caught in his clothes and he struggled to free himself, aching for breath, desperately stretching for the surface, the light and the air. And the voice said again, *'there is no one to help you and no way to escape'* and Brad had to open his mouth and filthy swamp-water poured down his throat...

When he opened his eyes, he saw that his lounge was untouched, his new magnolia walls smooth once again, his shabby La-Z-Boy still intact and no nightmarish wax balls to be seen; only Madame Coulombe's set of silver Baoding balls, glistening brightly in their wooden case like a pair of knowing eyes. He picked them up and took comfort in their coolness, their permanence and their solidity.

His cellphone was chirping in his pocket. He flicked it open but said nothing.

'*Durand*?' said a hushed voice on the other end of the line. 'Detective Durand?'

'Who is this?'

'This is Treyvon Plummer. I'm the door attendant at Cheaters strip joint? I guess... well... I guess, there's been a murder.'

sixteen

The interrogation rooms in the South Broad Street Police Department had been recently repainted in soothing colors. The cover-all slate gray walls had given way to pastel shades in green and taupe. The harsh overhead lighting had been replaced too: now it was softer, more reminiscent of a health center or a nursing home. The thinking in steering groups far above Jon Rubino's pay grade was 'less coercion, more cooperation'. Training sessions with consultant organizational psychologists encouraged rapport-building, tension-avoidance and negotiation skills. There was no more 'good cop, bad cop' routine. The modern interrogation room was a safe space.

Rubino sighed with exasperation, because clearly, Lionel Root didn't get that memo. Having waived his right to a lawyer, he'd sulked petulantly throughout the interview, silently shrugging off questions he didn't like and muttering incoherently at those he deigned to answer. Given the media furore following the first arrest in the Voodoo Killer case, Detectives Rubino and Sokolow had decided to plow ahead with an initial interrogation rather than wait until the morning. But two hours in, it seemed like they'd wasted their time.

Jon Rubino checked his watch: nearly midnight. 'Mr. Laroute - *Lionel* - work with me here,' he almost pleaded. 'It's not looking good for you. Your partner, Mrs. Rieux filled us in on the -' he paused to check his notes - 'scopolamine. That same drug was found at Eve Carmel's apartment, shortly after she died in suspicious circumstances. We *know* you knew her. What's more, the lead investigator in that case - Detective Zamora Delgado - is a missing person. She visited Cheaters nightclub the night before she disappeared. The nightclub where *you work* as a janitor....'

Dave Sokolow leaned back in his chair and crossed his arms over his thick paunch while his partner continued.

'Then there's April Recer. Murdered on her way home from - yes - Cheaters. Don't get me wrong, that club is definitely on our radar. And this big ol' ball of string? We'll unravel it sooner than later. We know you're involved, Lionel. So, why not do the right thing? We can get this started now, get some details down on paper, and then call it a night. How 'bout it?'

Sokolow gave Jon an approving nod. Less coercion, more cooperation. The clock on the wall ticked a full minute. Eventually, Lionel raised his flat eyes to stare at both men. Then he sucked in his cheeks, took out his false teeth and laid them on the table.

Jon closed his eyes. 'I think we're done here.'

There was a knock at the door. 'Interview paused at 23:57,' Sokolow said and stopped the recorder. If Rubino's face showed any surprise when he opened the door, he managed to suppress it. Standing there, in full dress uniform, was Commander Tillery. He had descended from on high.

'May I have a word, Detective?'

'Of course, sir,' Rubino replied, almost standing to attention. 'Shall we…?' he gestured down the hall to his office.

'No, not you. I would like a moment... with the suspect,' Tillery smiled coldly.

'Oh, I… understand,' Jon Rubino managed to utter, clearly not understanding at all. He shot a glance at Sokolow, who scrambled to his feet and both men cleared out.

'Oh, Rubino?' Tillery called as he left, 'Turn the camera off.'

Jon Rubino knew better than to argue, so he just nodded stiffly and did as he was asked.

Tillery closed the door softly and stood motionless until the red light on the CCTV camera in the corner of the room stopped blinking. Then he undid the buttons of his blazer, took off his service cap and sat down. He smoothed the crease in his trousers and brushed his hand across the tabletop in front of him. He pointed at the dentures sitting wetly on the table and Lionel grudgingly slipped them back in.

'I don't think we've been officially introduced,' Tillery began. 'I am Police Commander Tillery. I *am* the police from Treme to the Irish Channel. And you're Monsieur Lionel Root, is that right?'

'Lionel *Laroute*, *o-fficially*, but Root'll do jus' as fine.'

Tillery opened the case file before him. There was a cover sheet of Lionel's previous arrests and incident reports. Tillery licked his finger and turned the page. Here were Lionel's fingerprints. Here was a photo of him as a younger man. And another: younger still. Tillery compared the faces on paper to the face before him. Less cocky, but harder, more bitter now.

'Not your first time in this position, Mr. *Laroute*....' Tillery continued to flick through the pages of the file, pausing here and there to check a detail.

'No, not my first,' Lionel replied with some pride.

'But most likely your last,' Tillery said without looking up.

'I'll take that as a ref'rence to my age, rather than a threat.'

'Take it any way you wish, Mr. Laroute.' Tillery finally closed the folder and pushed it to the side of the table.

He pocketed his spectacles and focused his full attention on Lionel. 'Can I get you anything? A coke? Something to eat? Would you like another cigarette?'

'I'm doin' fine,' Lionel replied. He seemed resigned to his fate. 'I been here two hours a'ready, so why don't y'all say what y'all came to say?'

Tillery chose his words carefully. 'Those detectives - Rubino and Sokolow - they're good men. Good policemen. I'm telling you because although this is a complicated case, they'll close it in time. Now that we've found you. Mark my words.' He nodded sagely as if to emphasize his point. 'Or maybe they won't.'

'But - here's the thing - as long as we put on a good show for the judge and jury, it won't really matter. The newspapers will eat you up. You and Mrs. Rieux of course. You two are a regular Bonnie and Clyde.'

Lionel sucked on his dentures.

Tillery steepled his fingers and continued. 'Of course, there's a good chance Mrs. Rieux will sell you out, I suppose. A woman of her age. She's bound to roll over once we make it clear that otherwise, well... she'll die in prison.' Tillery shrugged. 'Either way. Will it be swift justice? No. But the NOPD will take the win. *I* will take the win,' he smiled.

'That being said, I believe we could wrap this whole thing up right now - just you and I.' Tillery cast a glance at the camera, just to check. 'You see, Rubino and Sokolow don't know what I know.'

'And what's that?'

'That you're nothing more than a middleman, Mr. Laroute.'

If the truth of that statement stung Lionel, he didn't show it. Tillery continued, 'They might think they've caught a murderer, but they're young and hot-headed and they don't have the benefit of my experience. I have no doubt you're a resourceful man, Mr. Laroute - you strike me as a survivor - but let's be frank with one another: the so-called Voodoo Killer, you... are not.'

'Never said I was,' Lionel agreed.

'But you know who he is. And you know where he is,' Tillery pressed.

Lionel turned all this over in his mind, finally pleased to find the baby in the king cake. '*Humm*. Let's say I do. Why would I roll over? What's in it fo' me? Maybe I am a survivor, like you says. You thinks that there *Voodoo Killer* with all his smarts is gon' let *a middleman* like me jus' walk outta here knowing I've squealed to the *police*?'

'You're already *squealing*,' Tillery answered simply.

'What? This little tête-à-tête of ours? Ain't the same thing, boy.'

'Oh, sure it is,' Tillery was smiling now. 'How about we put your face on the front page of the Times tomorrow morning and tell the world you're helping us with our enquiries? How about we do that, then just cut you loose? See who comes sniffing at your bones.'

Lionel gave a hollow laugh. 'Brother, I'm a dead man whichever ways you slice it. Do you think anythin' you says is gon' give me pause now? It *ain't*. Same as them two ding-a-lings out there. This whole parade ain't nothin' but a waste of my precious time. If I had anythin' to say to y'all, I woulda said it already. The way I sees it, I gots me one route out of this, and it jus' sat down in front o' me.'

Auden Tillery blinked and sat a little straighter in his plastic seat. Lionel had called his bluff and both men knew it. The Commander soldiered on.

'We can protect you, of course. You *and* Mrs. Rieux. If you were to turn state's evidence, a lenient sentence for an elderly member of the community wouldn't be out of the question. Immunity from prosecution might even be a possibility. The D.A. is a personal friend...'

Lionel held up a finger to stop him mid-flow. 'You talks too much, *Tillery*. Din't your mother ever tell you that? See now, you the *big man* and all. *Commander* Tillery, sir. Medals and stars all on your shoulders and shit. Sure, you gots your file and you knows who I is, but don't forget,' with this, his eyes glittered, '*I knows who you is too.*'

Tillery said nothing, but his expression tightened.

'Oh you din't think I'd remember? An elderly member of the community like me. No, no. Oh I'm good with faces, Tillery. How long has it been? Must be near on fifteen years, I reckon.'

'Yes,' Tillery managed. 'Now you mention it, I do recall meeting you before. One of your previous arrests, I imagine...' he pulled the file toward him again.

'Oh, don't bother, you asshole,' Lionel sighed. 'It ain't like yo' face ain't on the TV all the damn time, anyways. I couldn't forget y'all even if I wanted to. But *dat* camera ain't runnin', so how 'bout we start over?' Lionel shook a cigarette from the pack on the table and lit it. He drew long and hard, savoring it like it was his last. Tillery stood up to leave, thought better of it and sat down again. The color had drained from his face.

Lionel cleared his throat. 'So, tell me now, how's everythin' worked out fo' you, *co-mmander*? Looks like life is treatin' you pretty good. That right?'

'I've been... lucky,' Tillery muttered.

'Luck got nothin' to do wi' it, son. I know how to pick a winner, s'all.'

'Is that what you do?' Tillery said, with a note of hope in his voice. 'Pick winners?'

'Not as such. But I ain't sellin' our goods to no hobos or dead-beats, am I? Where'd the point in that be? No, no. That'd be *foolishness*, plain and simple. It's like those two Jew boys said: *I'm just tryin' to keep my customers satisfied.*'

'Are you saying... I could have been a winner, in spite of your... goods?'

Lionel rolled his head from side to side, 'Maybes. Maybe not. Who knows fo' sure? We just pushed you in the right direction. You stay on this track, you'll be police chief in a few years. In't that what you've always wanted?'

'Yes,' Tillery answered greedily.

'That's *fine* then. A man needs an ambition. Intell'gence without ambition is like a bird without wings.'

Tillery raised an eyebrow.

'What?' Lionel retorted. 'You think a man like me ain't got no culture? I read that on a sugar packet. I forget who said it.' He took another long drag and flicked ash on the floor. 'So, you still feedin' it?' he asked.

'Yes,' Tillery replied quietly: an admission of guilt. 'Van van oil. Once a month. Like you told me.' He instinctively patted his chest.

'Good boy. Course, you's about due for a, a... what's the word them kids use nowadays? Another *upgrade*,' Lionel grinned. 'You should see our new stock.'

Tillery was suddenly repulsed by this gurning old man. He wanted to be anywhere else but sitting in this beige room, discussing his innermost secrets and desires.

'I know it's hard, Auden,' Lionel said, reading his mind. 'But truth is, you done made a deal with the Devil and this is the price you pay.' He drew once more on the butt of his cigarette then stubbed it out on the tabletop. 'Now, I'm gon' give you - ooh - fi'teen minutes - and you's gon' do your thing, sign your papers and such, and then me and my Georgine is gon' walk right out the front door. Jus' like Bonnie and Clyde.'

Auden Tillery nodded, but he wasn't really listening. At some point during Lionel's speech, he had slipped his hand inside his blazer, his fingers between the buttons of his shirt, to his own little mojo bag. It was years since Lionel had sold it to him on a cold night on Tupelo Street just up from the House of Dance and Feathers. Back when he was still little more than a beat-cop, looking to step up the ladder, looking for an edge. Once soft and red, now his *gris-gris* was a hard, tight knot of discolored leather, and Auden rubbed it gently, lovingly, between his finger and thumb. His mouth was watering.

He reached down to his holster and unclipped his duty weapon: a pristine Glock Model 22.

'Actually, Mr. Laroute, I don't think I'll be able to do that.'

*

Odeo Boucher died on the wet cobblestones, just a matter of yards from the entrance to his club, which he'd built on the back of hard work, his life's savings and voodoo magic. The police cordoned off both ends of Clinton Street, which wasn't necessary and only served to attract more people to the area, craning their necks to get a glimpse of the goings-on: more than Cheaters could have hoped for on an average night. The paramedics had arrived on the scene within a few minutes of Treyvon's 911 call, but by the time they took over the CPR, Odeo was already gone and he showed no sign of coming back. They said he'd had a heart attack - probably a big one - given the amount of cocaine he'd obviously taken, but it would be down to the Medical Examiner's office to determine the cause of death.

Treyvon wasn't buying it.

'I knew he liked blow, man. Everybody knew. But he wasn't a coke fiend, you know what I'm saying? There's a *difference*, dude. Between *that* and *that*.' Treyvon chopped his hand down on the tabletop twice to emphasize this point.

He and Brad were sitting at a long table at The Deja-Vu Bar and Grill on the corner of Dauphine and Conti, a five-minute stroll from Cheaters. It had been a red-light opium den at the turn of the last century and at four in the morning, surrounded by semi-comatose Friday night revelers, Brad imagined that not a lot had changed in the last hundred years. He was present at least, if not actively listening. Finally, after an hour of conversation, Treyvon seemed to be getting to the point of his initial phone call.

'There's a difference. That's all I'm saying.'

'Listen, Plummer, people OD on coke all the time. Like, *all* the time. I guarantee your boss won't be the only one tonight. I shit you not. So, what makes Boucher any different?'

'You din't see his face! Dude was fucking *covered* in blow. I seen some things, inside *an'* out, but I ain't *never* seen *nothin'* like that. Anyways, Odeo was a businessman. He knew what he was doing.'

'Bullshit,' Brad replied flatly. 'Next you'll be telling me he could have given up any time he wanted.' He was playing devil's advocate, but at the same time, his patience was wearing thin. 'Look man, you obviously liked the guy and I'm sorry for your loss and all that, but honestly, I've heard this song before.' He downed the last of his club soda. 'It's late,' he said and stood up to leave. Treyvon grabbed his wrist and told him to sit down.

'Plummer, what *aren't* you telling me?'

'This ain't the first time somebody who was at the club ended up dead, you know?' Treyvon said conspiratorially.

'Are you talking about Delgado? My friend, the policewoman?' Brad asked, before adding, 'She's not dead.'

'Neither is Claudette Tremblay. At least that's what I keep tellin' mysel'. But where's she at? Treyvon asked rhetorically. 'No, I'm talking 'bout April Recer. D'you hear 'bout her?'

Brad shook his head and Treyvon swelled up like a pufferfish, full of his own importance.

'April Recer was some chick. Like seventeen, I guess, lesbian looking. Got found in a parking lot near Giroud Street. The dude who found her, Mahir Ellwood - he's my second cousin's neighbor - anyways, Mahir swears she was still alive when he found her. *And* talking for *minutes* before the cops arrived, but there was a hole in her chest, size of a goddamn cantaloupe, where somebody had done chopped her heart out,' Treyvon was wide-eyed and whispering.

Brad flipped his notebook open and wrote down the name on his list of victims. 'Must have missed her,' he muttered to himself. 'R-e-c-e-r?'

'Yep. April Recer. When I saw her obit in the paper, I recognized her face. She was at the club the night she got killed. Fo' sure.'

'I'm gon' go ahead and say what you won't, Treyvon. We're talking about the Voodoo Killer, right?'

Treyvon nodded but didn't reply.

'And you're telling me that Cheaters is at the heart of this whole thing, and this Recer girl, and Zam Delgado, your Claudette, and now Boucher are all dead because of it?'

He nodded again.

'Level with me, Treyvon.'

'I… can't,' he said, ripping the cellophane off a fresh packet of cigarettes.

'I mightn't have a badge no more, but trust me, I can still take you downtown and let the cops lean on you for a spell. Maybe have a word with your parole officer.... How clean are you these days?'

'But you wouldn't do that,' Treyvon said coolly. 'No sir.'

'Oh, no? Why not?'

'Because, Detective Durand, you's one of the good guys.'

That caught Brad off-guard momentarily.

'Am I right?' Treyvon pushed.

Brad cleared his throat and changed tack, still playing the innocent.

'Listen, Boucher OD'ed, right? Claudette blew off a minimum wage job and never came back. She's a school kid. Maybe she's... knuckling down for college. Who knows? Recer gets stabbed in Giroud Street. That's got to be a mile away from here. And Zam Delgado? I was there with her that night. *Nothing* happened.'

'You don't know that for sure. Something coulda happened....'

'Jesus, tell me what you know!' Brad snapped, exasperated.

'Maybe somebody saw something they didn't like...' Treyvon continued.

'She didn't even go inside the club!' Brad shouted.

'You cops know it better than most: do you really believe in coincidence, Detective? Come on. Why am *I* the one doin' the convincin' 'round here?'

'So, convince me, son. Because you're giving me nothin' here.'

Treyvon sucked on his cigarette and turned his head to blow smoke away from Durand's yellow face. He seemed to be wrestling with a decision, before he shook his head and relented. He put his hand inside his black jacket and laid the mojo bag on the table between them. It lay there in the red light of the Deja-Vu like a spider, the twine wrapped around it like its own silk.

'*Gris-gris*?'

Treyvon nodded.

'But not yours?'

He shook his head.

'Boucher's? He gave it to you.'

'He said it was 'evidence'.'

'Where'd he get it? Lionel Root?'

'Lionel Root? The janitor? I doubt it. That dude wouldn't hurt a fly.'

'The cops arrested him earlier tonight. *That dude* was dealing psychoactive drugs inside the No 1 cemetery.'

'Oh... snap.'

'So where *did* he get it?' Brad pressed.

'Don't… make me tell you, Mr Durand. I can't. Please don't make me.'

Brad had seen fear before - he'd known his fair share - and he could see that Treyvon had reached his limit.

Brad poked the little red purse with his pen and flipped it over. 'Have you looked inside?'

'No, and I ain't gonna. I don't want to know. I'm done with all this shit.'

Brad unfolded a paper napkin from the stack in the center of the table, wrapped it over the *gris-gris* and pocketed the whole thing. 'Leave it with me.'

Then a curious thought struck him. Nothing more than

a notion. *Every red cent.* On a whim, he took out his wallet and counted the notes. He laid the twenty-seven dollars neatly on the table and while Treyvon looked on perplexed, Brad stood up to dig deep for every last cent of loose change in the pockets of his jeans. He dumped the coins on the table, not bothering to count it.

'Take all that.'

Treyvon opened his mouth to speak but Brad silenced him with a palm. 'Don't ask. Just take it.'

With a shrug, Treyvon scooped up the cash and offered him a cigarette in return, and Brad took one and lit it, savoring that first smack of nicotine. 'I tried to quit. So many times,' he said, blowing a plume of smoke straight up, 'but I reckon I'm dying anyway, so what the hell,' he laughed mirthlessly. His skin was yellow.

'Take the pack, man. I think I'm done.'

Brad slipped it into his jacket. 'Tell me one more thing, Trey. Just one thing. Because I know you know. If it ain't Lionel, then who is the Voodoo Killer?'

Treyvon shook his head slowly. 'No. I wish y'all the best o' luck an' everthin', Mr. Durand, but I can't tell you nothing else.' As he stood up to leave, Brad didn't stop him.

Brad Durand sat a little longer alone in the bar, surrounded by the noise of young people, and the smell of beer and the fug of smoke, and he thought about his own mortality and about life here in the bar, and outside, pressing down and crowding in on him. He thought about Elaine and Kyle, and Walt Forager, and his own father, and Zamora Delgado, and Auden Tillery and the snitch, and wondered where they all were and what they were doing and where he fitted into it all. He picked at a scab on the underside of his wrist, where another black cross, scored into his skin, had drawn blood. They were all over his body now. Some rubbed off like smut from a fire; others appeared like fresh wounds. In the bathroom, earlier in the evening, with his head tilted back under the fluorescent lights, Brad was sickened to see one at the back of his throat. *He's inside me now*, he thought. *Like cancer. How long have I got?*

Unwrapping the paper napkin, he tipped the mojo bag into the palm of his hand, turned it over and tested its weight.

'Well, I paid for it,' he said to himself.

Unraveling the twine, he slipped the *gris-gris* over his head, tucking the little purse under his collar so that it pressed against his flesh. He felt his heart beating under it.

seventeen

'... *Member of the Louisiana Hall of Fame and you'll remember he played Cajun and western swing bands for over sixty years. So that's comin' up later today. Right now, you're listening to Rockin' Oldies Radio and this is The Youngbloods...*'

Brad squinted against the low sunlight streaming in through the windshield. Overhead, seagulls were calling. He looked around and tried to get his bearings. In front of him, the fortified levee of the Pontchartrain Lake sloped up. He was north of the city, northeast maybe, out towards the I-10 and the bayou, but he didn't recognize this part of town and he couldn't remember driving here.

Brad was sure that Treyvon Plummer and their meeting at the Deja Vu had been real and not the idling of his addled mind. In his rearview mirror, he saw a car reverse out of a driveway and slowly turn away. It was still early. He turned the key in the ignition and checked the clock. 6:24. He breathed deeply and stretched; that's when he noticed it: the pain in his gut was gone.

The pain which had continually woken him in the night, acutely stabbed at him when he urinated, and left him short of breath on staircases, had disappeared. He consciously breathed again and gingerly touched his abdomen, waiting for the pain to come.

But it did not, and Brad tentatively stepped out of the car and stood in the early morning sun. He filled his lungs, assuring himself that it was only the chilly air blowing off the lake that had brought tears to his eyes.

For the first time in months, he felt alive again. His hands and wrists no longer showed any sign of the black crosses which only hours earlier had been etched on his skin. He grunted: a gruff, approving sound and all he would allow himself, which signified his deep satisfaction that this trial was over and that he could finally move on. Brad Durand looked towards the heavens and might have thanked God.

Then he lit a cigarette, tipping his figurative hat to Treyvon Plummer for the gift. 'I'm never giving this up,' he told himself proudly as he felt the hit of nicotine.

He popped the trunk of his car: there was an old windcheater under the usual debris, and he pulled it on and jammed his hands into the pockets before walking up towards the lake. It felt good to be out at this time of day and he strode with ease up the grass verge to the levee wall. At the top, the vast, glittering expanse of the Pontchartrain spread out in front of him, its gray waters lapping against the concrete steps of the shoreline. To the east was the bayou and the mysterious darkness of the wetlands; to the west, in the distance Brad could make out the control towers of the Lakefront Airport jutting into the water on its tiny peninsula from the city itself. He pulled a piece of paper from the pocket of the old windcheater and was delighted to discover it was a crumpled ten-dollar bill.

'This might be the best day of my life,' he told himself, only half joking.

It was only then that Brad remembered the mojo bag hanging around his neck and made the connection with the uptick in his good fortune.

'*Can't be...*' he whispered to himself, but Walt Forager's talk of placebos and nocebos niggled at the back of his mind. '*I will please,*' he said to the wind.

He was suddenly aware of the weight of the purse

hanging around his neck and could feel the leather against his skin. It felt like a living thing touching his chest, and Brad had to fight the urge to think too deeply about its contents. The temptation to fling it in the lake was almost too much. Almost.

'Not yet.'

Around the sweeping curve of the shoreline walkway, a jogger was steadily approaching. Generally, Brad didn't trust those people who indulged in physical activity for fun, especially not at this time of day, but there was nobody else around and he needed information, fast. The jogger pulled up when Brad effectively flagged him down like a cab, but he kept his engine running, hopping from left to right, left to right, in his electric blue spandex leggings. 'Hey, can I help you?' he said, pulling out his earphones. Brad heard the tinny whine of electronic dance music but managed to hide his distaste. He blew his cigarette smoke in the other direction.

'Yeah man, sorry to - like - disturb your... exercise. I know it's early and you're probably not even from around here... but do you know if there's anywhere nearby where I can get some breakfast?'

*

'This *is* the best day of my life,' Brad sighed happily, as the waitress placed the two plates before him. One was loaded with the Waffle House All Star Special: fried eggs, sausages, bacon, grits, toast and their signature 'scattered, smothered and covered' hash browns. The other had double waffles with pecans and maple syrup. The coffee was black and steaming and Brad had the entire place to himself. The radio was even playing his station. He picked up his knife and fork and went to work.

Twelve minutes later, Brad leaned back, belched, lit a cigarette and gestured to Bernadette for a refill to wash down his breakfast. It was 7.15 and he figured Rubino would be at his desk already. He fished out his cell and dialed.

'NOPD. Detective Rubino.'

'Jon. Brad Durand. Before you say anything…'

'Hey Brad…'

'… just hear me out. I had an interesting conversation with….'

'Brad, listen...'

'… Treyvon Plummer last night - he's the security down at Cheaters strip joint and there's something I need to share…'

'Brad…'

'…. with you. Like I said, I know you told me that you *couldn't* let me see Lionel Root, but if you possibly… well *could* do that for me - even for *five* minutes - I would…

'I can't.'

'Oh, now Jon, don't give me that *jurisdiction* bullshit.'

'I can't…'

'We both know that Root wouldn't even be there if it wasn't….

'Brad… '

'… for me. You'd still be walkin' 'round with your thumb up your…'

'Durand! Sweet Jesus, man! You can't see him because he's dead.'

'What? You're joking?'

'Lionel Root shot himself last night.'

'This better be a joke, Rubino, 'cause you're about to ruin a real solid day if it ain't.'

'Like I said, Lionel Root, in the interrogation room, with the revolver.'

'Wait, the interrogation room? He got hold of your weapon?'

Rubino measured his next words. 'Not. Mine.'

'Whose? Who was your secondary?'

'It wasn't like that. Look, I can't really talk at the moment. Internal Affairs are already here and besides, I don't know all the details…'

'Who?'

'I shouldn't….'

'Jon, who was it?'

'It was… Tillery.'

Brad was silent for a moment. Fortunately, Bernadette chose that second to refill his coffee mug, otherwise he might have flung it across the restaurant. He nodded his thanks. When he spoke again, his voice was tight, but at least his temper was in check.

'Listen, I'm in Little Woods, in a Waffle House on Bullard Avenue. You know the Holiday Inn? Just before it. Come up.'

'I… probably should stick around here….'

'I'll buy you breakfast. You can fill me in on the details.'

'You know, why not? I'm just kicking rocks here. I'll be there in about fifteen minutes.'

*

A man shouldn't eat alone, and Brad didn't want to appear rude, so he ordered another couple of waffles to work through while Rubino ate his cheese omelet and recounted the events of the previous evening, from the moment they left one another at the St Louis Cemetery, to the single gunshot which echoed through the corridors of the 8th Precinct.

'So, what's he sayin' now?' Brad asked.

'Tillery? Not much. I guess he's tripped up enough perps over the years to know that less is more. So he keeps spinning this line about Root taking him by surprise and jumping over the table to grab the gun. *'Moved so fast... caught me off guard....'* Like it was some freak thing. That's what I keep hearing, anyways,' Rubino pushed the last of his omelet around the plate.

'Freak thing?! You can say that again. Root must have been in his seventies. I saw him with my own eyes creeping out from behind that altar last night. The guy moved like a sun lounger.'

'Yeah well, Tillery was sure cut up about it all. Greg Darjean said he was crying in the bathroom.'

'What? His private one? Fuck Greg Darjean, whoever he is,' Brad answered sourly. Jon ignored him.

'Not crying over Root's death, but the impact on the case. He apologized to me personally.' The detective made it sound like he'd been awarded a medal.

'Yeah? He tell you why he turned the camera off?'

'Well, no, but I heard that they - Tillery and Root - knew each other from back in the day and the Commander was just trying to urge him to do the right thing and confess. He didn't want to foul up the interrogation but given that we were winding up for the night.... I don't know.' Rubino ran out of steam and took a sip from his coffee mug.

'If you ask me, it all sounds like some primo bull*shit*,' Brad replied.

'Maybe. But if he's lying - and I'm not saying he isn't - he's one cool cat. By the time I left the station, he already had IA eating out of his hand.'

'Goddamn shitweasel.'

Rubino laughed in spite of himself. 'Let it go, dude. It

ain't your fight anymore.'

'I can't. Zam...' Brad began but didn't know what more to say. They both watched as the waitress bustled past, coffee pot in hand. Jon broke the awkward silence.

'So, anyway, why'd you call? You said you had something you wanted to tell me about Cheaters and the doorman...?'

Brad felt the weight of the *gris-gris* once again and had to fight back the compulsion to take it from around his neck and confess his secret to Rubino. *Evidence* - that's what Odeo Boucher had called it, and he was right, but still. 'Oh... forget about it. Now that Root's dead, it's all kinda moot.' Another thought crossed his mind. 'Did you test the burundanga yet?'

'Nope,' Rubino said. 'Sent it to the lab. Should hear in a couple of days *if* we're lucky.'

Brad nodded. 'Well, that's something, I guess.' He had been sitting in the Waffle House for two hours. He was tired of talking and wanted nothing more than to digest - not only the large amount of carbohydrates he had just consumed - but also everything he had learnt about the latest turn of events. 'Listen, I'm going to split. I got some stuff to sort out....'

Rubino raised an eyebrow. 'Like I said, it ain't your fight anymore.'

Brad shrugged and looked out of the window at the people driving to work. He thought about the absence of pain in his gut and pushed aside any deeper contemplation of what he had actually overcome. Rubino had a point: Brad felt he had come close to the brink already – maybe it was time to call it quits and head back to Florida, bruised but alive at least. But still, Zam Delgado, his rookie cop with her bright eyes and apple cheeks, was out there somewhere. Dead or alive, he felt a sense of paternal responsibility to find her.

And then there was Tillery. How did *he* fit into this picture? Brad remembered their moment in the interrogation room the morning after his trip around the Six Flags theme park, when he'd decided - no matter what happened - he had to solve the case. But what was he trying to prove? That he was better than the great Auden Tillery? That he still *had* it?

'Maybe,' he said aloud, answering both Rubino's remark and his own question.

Just then, something sparked in the back of his mind - *the morning after Jazzland* - but Brad couldn't say for sure what it meant. *Tillery's interrogation*. Brad knew this feeling. It was an idea, a memory, a solution, and all of those things at once. Give it time, he told himself, it will come. He forced himself to focus on something else. Stand up, pay the check, thank the waitress, shake Rubino's hand, walk outside…

He picked a flier for a carwash from under his windscreen wiper and let it fall on the ground. *Littering*, he thought, *sue me, Nola*. In the comfortable, stale tobacco bubble of his SUV, muffled from the outside world, he turned on the radio: Rockin' Oldies Radio was playing 'Kind of a Drag', a song that he hadn't heard in maybe thirty years and which brought to mind another time, another car and another girl, and it was she who finally pulled him away from his unanswerable questions. Brad waited for Rubino to spin his car around in the parking lot and head out, before he followed.

The drive home in rush-hour traffic took twice as long as it should have. Uptown was quieter, Lafitte even more so, and his street was empty. He drove slowly through his neighborhood, taking in afresh Katrina's destruction, to which even he had become inured in recent months. The old police station on the corner of

St Philip Street - rotten and covered in blight - looked like a stiff breeze would raze it to the ground.

Brad half expected to see a burning cross on his front lawn, or some hideous incarnation of *Li Grand Zombi* standing in his hallway when he gingerly opened the front door, but with a sigh of relief he saw only his recliner, his TV, a few empty beer bottles and Madame Coulombe's wooden box. Its contents might offer some answers, but they would have to wait.

He showered and shaved, taking time to inspect his face and body in the mirror for any rogue black marks or crosses. There were none.

'Beware the scaremongers,' he said to his reflection, noting for the first time in weeks the extent of his weight loss.

He was a shadow of his former self and though he looked older, and certainly tired after a long night, he liked the new angles of his jawline and cheekbones and there was a healthy glow to his skin again. He nodded appreciatively. He looked deep into his own eyes and felt recharged. It was time to work. The Baoding balls had a magnetism of their own. Brad found a pair of fresh sweatpants and a clean T-shirt and went downstairs.

Outside, the clear morning had given way to a bruised sky, but Brad decided to close the blinds to block out the daylight as best he could. He sat back in his La-Z-Boy and instinctively reached over the armrest to grab a bottle and twist off the cap.

No, he thought, *stay focused*.

At least before midday. Instead, he bent to pick up the polished wooden box and opened the lid. The silver balls glinted knowingly in the half-light, and he spun them in one hand as he allowed the thoughts which he had repressed earlier to float to the surface of his consciousness once again. The morning after his visit to Jazzland began to play in his mind like a memory of a movie from another time, separate scenes coming together to form a whole: the beat officers banging on his door, the drive downtown, his first time in the *back* of a squad car. He recalled Tillery of course - when he finally appeared in the interrogation room - perfectly presented in his dress uniform and oozing superciliousness. He remembered feeling tired and hungover, slumped on the wrong side of the table, and living up to the Commander's low estimation of him. Snippets of their conversation came to mind and resolved themselves into an approximation of what had been said between the two men.

I was doing some urban exploring it's going to be huge there's blood in your hair a young man set himself on fire you think you can come back after all these years and solve something to restore your shattered reputation you must be insane a two-bit, washed-up, has-been from the fucking orange juice state you got lucky that's all you're pissing in the wind you got lucky that's all you think you can solve something...

You got lucky.

Even in his waking dream, Brad felt his anger flare at the insult that he was somehow less than Tillery: less of a detective, if not less of a man. He clenched his hand around one of the metal balls just as he recalled grabbing Tillery's shirt and jacket lapel. Brad's inner mind narrowed to that moment, and in his dream, he saw both himself and Tillery frozen in time. It gave him some tangible satisfaction to ruck up that pristine uniform, and to see the expression in Tillery's eyes: it was fear, but not the fear of Brad's cocked fist.

Why was he so scared? Brad's subconscious whispered to the Baoding balls.

And the answer came to him then, up from the depths of his mind, like a methane bubble bursting up from the bayou, at the same instant that Brad clearly remembered feeling through the fabric of Tillery's immaculately pressed and starched shirt, the hard tight knot of an old leather *gris-gris*.

Brad understood. Auden Tillery was terrified of being discovered.

*

In his temple room, Ike Sugar was preparing for the becoming. The rains presaged it. The augurs of the chicken blood foretold it, and he could feel now, more than just a spiritual sensation, rather a physical change in his bones. His pulse raced and were it not for his chain-smoking of homegrown pot, Ike felt he might pass out from the fervor. He was sweating in the fetid heat of dozens of homemade candles and the green fug of marijuana. The wooden floor was slick with chicken shit and greasy tallow. There was so much work to be done before nightfall. The fabric was hard to work with, so silky and diaphanous, even Ike's most delicate stitches tore through it. Instead, he realized that he could stick it directly against his skin with a thin coating of corn flour and water. And so, when Claudette emerged from her blood-stained mattress, she peaked through the crack of the door jamb and saw him slathering his sleek arm with an old paintbrush dipped in this thin, white glue. His torso and lower body was already covered, his face and neck spattered, and he looked like a ghost moving in the candlelight. Though she watched silently, Ike became aware of her presence - as he always did; he heard the strain in her pained breaths, and he stretched out his lithe limbs so she could appreciate the spectacle. Claudette wished she could walk away, but his yellow eyes held her gaze and the pair continued in this strange dance, neither speaking.

The pain of the previous evening's abuse had sobered her completely, and while she still harbored thoughts of escape, her mind now had turned to the notion of killing Ike Sugar. But how? She grew weaker every day. He turned suddenly, grinning - *had he heard her thoughts?* - and as he approached the door, she realized with horror that he was holding a tumescent erection.

'Cher,' he purred through the crack. 'Doncha wanna kiss it?' Claudette fled, partly from fear of her captor and tormentor, but partly from revulsion at her own desire.

Ike stood for a moment contemplating her dying embers. Her *muti* was all but extinguished now – Ike had consumed her flames in order to *become*. But even now, starved and filthy as she was, scabrous and diseased, he wanted to feel the heat of her fire again and his member throbbed at the thought of the swells and curves of her nubile young body. Yes, he understood, the spirits must be fed, but some still human part of him ached at the prospect and wished his life had rolled a different way. What would he cut from Claudette Tremblay as a final offering to *Li Grand Zombi*?

'Oh well, oh well,' he muttered to no-one as he returned to the task in hand.

*

The clouds continued to roll in from the lake throughout the day and by late afternoon, rain was falling heavily across the Crescent City. Nobody was saying the word 'hurricane,' but plenty of people were thinking it. Those born and raised in New Orleans knew better however: at worst, this was shaping up to be one of those 'one night stand' storms - hot and heavy while it lasted, but over by the morning and soon forgotten.

After a long day of interviews with the Internal Affairs officers, Auden stepped outside the police precinct like a man with the weight of the world on his shoulders. He took some comfort in the fresh air of the otherwise foul weather. He had been 'suspended pending investigation, effective immediately'. It hadn't come as a surprise: IA was only following protocol. Would there be repercussions? Unlikely. Auden knew that a man of his position and experience was hard to force out without a long, drawn-out inquiry - not to mention a serious severance package - and nobody in the Mayor's office wanted the PR fallout from that, especially in an election year. Just like the storm, this whole thing with Root would soon blow over.

It was early in the evening for the sky to be so dark. Briefcase in one hand, suit bag and umbrella in the other, Auden stepped through the police parking lot adjacent to the station, avoiding the puddles. He pressed his key fob and the lights of his Mercedes flashed in the gloom, but still he didn't notice his assailant crouched behind the car until it was too late. Brad had no qualms about attacking people from behind and he had waited a long time to kick Tillery's ass. Unprepared, the hard jab to his kidney knocked the wind out of Auden completely. He dropped his bags and would have sagged to his knees on the wet concrete, but in one deft move, Brad spun him around by the shoulders and dealt him a left-right combination which laid him out across the bonnet. Stunned but still clinging to consciousness, the Commander automatically reached for his service weapon only to find it wasn't there.

'Hey shooter,' Brad hissed. 'Where's your gun? I guess IA took it.'

Brad cocked an ear for anybody who might have heard the noise and decided to investigate. There were at least twenty police officers in the vicinity after all. Tillery groaned as Brad ripped open his shirt. A button bounced off the windscreen. Just as Brad had known, there was the *gris-gris*. The sight of it, something so malevolent, something which seemed so incongruous to his beliefs about a man like Auden Tillery - turned Brad's stomach. Under the halogen lights of the car park, the little bag looked like a cancerous growth on Tillery's chest.

'Keys,' Brad demanded and slapped him across the face for good measure. Tillery handed them over. His nose was bleeding.

'Get in,' Brad snapped. Tillery stumbled towards the driver's door. 'The other side, dickhead.'

They drove through downtown traffic, the windscreen wipers beating a steady rhythm in the otherwise stony silence. Brad headed north, away from the office blocks and high-rises and back to Pontchartrain, where the last of the fading daylight could be seen in the skies over the lake. Lightning flashed on the horizon.

Brad turned off the engine, pulled out his gun from the pocket of his windcheater and rested it on his lap in plain sight. 'Start talking…'

Tillery - having regained his senses, most notably his sense of indignation - scoffed. 'Are you planning on shooting me, Durand?'

'The thought had crossed my mind. We're going to have a chat, Auden, just like old times, but if I don't like what I hear,' - he pushed the muzzle of the snub against

Tillery's leg - 'then I'll put a bullet in your knee. Maybe I'll say you grabbed this off me and shot yourself. That's how police interrogation goes down these days, I hear.'

Tillery curled a lip in contempt. 'You don't know what I know. A man in *my* position...'

'Spare me the lecture, *Commander*. I'll keep it simple and you fill in the blanks, okay? Lionel Root sold you the *gris-gris*. When?' Tillery said nothing. 'When?' Brad insisted, pressing down on the gun.

'I bought the *gris-gris* from him in 1995, but we'd had dealings before then.'

'When?'

"Eighty or 'eighty-one. I don't recall exactly. My mother knew his mother. She knew their drugstore. My mother... God rest her soul... was a *believer*,' he scoffed at the word. She bought me a chicken foot fetish to keep me safe on my rounds, not long after we graduated. Lionel Root delivered it to me personally.'

'And you kept it?'

'First of all, I kept it to appease my mother.'

'Then what?'

'Then, after a time, I came to... well, not *believe* in it as such, but I didn't feel right if I didn't *touch* it before a shift. It was a lucky charm. Some of the men have rosary beads, or silver dollars, or they shine their shoes a certain way. I don't know. After a few years, I grew to depend on it. We... *I* was under a lot of pressure. I was already married. We had bills. We had plans. You wouldn't understand.'

Brad snuffed down his nose but ignored the condescension. 'So, apart from your troubles, you've got your lucky chicken foot and all's well in the world. Then Root shows up and what, offers you a leg up the career ladder, is that it?'

'Something like that,' Tillery nodded. 'I'd seen him

around on the beat over the years - he was a drunkard and a petty criminal: he peddled the same nonsense drugs and potions as his mother - but we didn't cross paths again until 1995 when I bought the *gris-gris*.'

'How much did you pay for it?' Brad asked.

'Twenty-two dollars, eighty-seven cents.'

'Did it work?'

Auden barked out a laugh. 'I'm *here,* aren't I?' he said, referring to his professional status, rather than sitting in a car with a gun pointed at his kneecap.

'You don't think…. you would have made it on your own steam?' Brad asked, thinking about the *gris-gris* hanging around his own neck.

Tillery spread his hands and shrugged. 'I remember, there was something *different* about him. Root had turned himself around. He was like a man who had found God. I guess I wanted to feel that…'

'Do you know what's in it?' Brad asked, gesturing to the mojo bag.

'I have my suspicions but… you're not supposed to look. Just feed it.'

Brad gave him a sideways look.

'You have to *feed* it oil - special oil - every month. Otherwise, it doesn't work.'

Another streak of lightning lit up the sky.

Tillery sighed and began to speak, and the more he talked, the more the words poured out of him. 'When the first killings began, I didn't think anything of it. I certainly didn't think it had anything to do with Root. We were used to high crime figures before the storm. Well, you remember. But Katrina changed everything. The people changed. You weren't here afterwards…' - Brad bristled at that, waiting for the usual value judgment, but it didn't come. Tillery continued, '… but I saw it. I saw the monsters that came out of the woodwork. The suicide rate went up *forty percent*. The economic fallout... killed countless more. So those particular deaths - the murders - were unconnected. Freak accidents. Unexplained events.'

'It was Delgado that started to put it all together. She was a hell of a detective. We were all still firefighting across all the departments, day in, day out, grinding through cases, even years after the storm, but Zamora was the first of us to start looking at the bigger picture again. A fresh pair of eyes, I suppose. But I was convinced it was gang-related. The city was an easy target: rich pickings for the gangs. The body part angle tied into all that. And I forced her down that line of investigation. But I guess, in doing so, I... see now that I pushed her towards you.'

'That's no bad thing,' Brad said, feeling a modicum of sympathy. 'We're closer to ending this now. When did Root come back into the picture?'

'Some of the stranger cases... brought something to mind. There was an element of human sacrifice. The girl in the canal - '

'Nadia Romero,' Brad interjected.

'Yes. She'd lost a hand. It reminded me of... a comic book of all things. From my childhood. A black magician and a mummified hand that could open any locked door. Just a stupid story for kids, but it got me thinking...'

Brad nodded grudgingly in agreement, remembering Kyle's football poster, 'Sometimes that's all it takes. Go on...'

'I didn't want to believe Root could have anything to do with it, so I had homicide look into the usual suspects in the local community. Nothing turned up. Then the Carmel woman died, Walt Forager's assistant and I began to suspect Root was involved. She was selling body parts. I'm not a fool - I know what's in these things,' he said, touching a finger to the *gris-gris* around his neck.

'Why didn't you raise the alarm? Put out a search warrant?'

'And implicate myself?' Tillery retorted. 'No. I tried to trace him on my own, but he's a hard man to find. No fixed abode. No family. Most of the ex-cons he shared a cell with over the years are already dead or still inside. So, I waited… '

'You let me find him,' Brad said sourly.

'I knew you would.'

'And then you killed him.'

'That's not what happened,' Tillery answered. There was a note of sorrow in his voice.

'Don't give me that - I'm not buying it.'

Auden shook his head. He opened his mouth to speak and then closed it again. Finally, he spoke. 'He wasn't your Voodoo Killer, Durand.'

'How do you know?'

'He told me. Before he shot himself.'

Brad never thought that he would ever see Auden Tillery break down, but here he was with tears rolling down his cheeks. *Jeez.* He pressed the heels of his hands against his eyes and tried to compose himself.

'Why don't you tell me what happened?'

Tillery let out a long, shuddering sigh. 'We were so young,' he began, 'so young.'

Brad assumed he was talking about their shared time together, back in the police academy in 'seventy-eight. 'We were,' he said gruffly, laying a hand on Tillery's shoulder in a feeble gesture of support.

'Not *us*, you moron!' Tillery snapped, brushing Brad's hand away. 'My wife and I. Isabel.'

'Oh, right.'

Tillery put his head in his hands. 'We had plans. Everything was going so well. We were going to get engaged.' He sobbed again, 'It was just a mistake. An *accident*.'

Where's he going with this? Brad thought but said nothing.

'My mother never approved of course. Prejudice cuts both ways, Durand. She never did like Isabel. There was no reason for it. Only plain racism, I suppose. Her parents were no better. They hated the idea of us even seeing one another. My mother has grown to accept her over the years, but... there's still no real warmth between them. I guess back then, she hoped I'd wake up one morning and realize the mistake I was making. Find myself a nice black girl from the neighborhood.' He turned away and looked out of the window while he continued.

'I've never told anyone this. *Anyone*, Durand,' Auden spat, suddenly angry, as though his confession was being forced. 'We found out Isabel was pregnant in the spring of seventy-nine. The idea of having a child out of wedlock was *anathema* to both of us. We couldn't get married - we had no money. We didn't even live together. I'd only just graduated from the academy. Even if a termination had been possible, there was no *Planned Parenthood* back then. Isabel was too far along for *traditional* methods.'

Brad felt a coldness swelling in his stomach.

'We didn't know where else to turn. We swore Marjorie Laroute to secrecy. She had ideas above her station anyway - some... *misguided* sense of doctor-patient confidentiality. It was laughable really, given the nonsense she 'prescribed', if you can even call it that. 'Devil's tisanes' she called them. They were nothing but.... Bella donna and raw eggs!' he scoffed. 'When that didn't work, she made Isabel take a bath in scalding water filled with turpentine and cayenne. She whispered *incantations* from these *ridiculous* books of African black magic. Nothing worked. The fetus... *endured.*'

'Time was running out. It was almost impossible to hide the pregnancy. We had Isabel's stomach wrapped tight in bandages. She was in terrible pain. We were desperate, Durand. Laroute - the mother - tried to invoke voodoo spirits, as a last resort, in a... black mass of sorts. Candles, rooster's blood, silver pins, the whole nine yards. Have you ever heard of *Li Grand Zombi*? The great Voodoo God or... well, whatever. Christ only knows what these heathens believe. He was supposed to take the child before he was born. Well,' Tillery gave a dry laugh, 'he didn't.'

'I don't want to hear...' Brad began, shaking his head, but Tillery was speaking to himself now, confessing his sins.

'The baby was born October ten. A boy,' he whispered. 'Fit and healthy. Marjorie helped with the delivery, and I cut the cord. His mother never held him. He was only a few hours old when I drove him to the bayou.' Auden sobbed again. 'We didn't even give him a name.'

Brad watched with something close to horror as Commander Tillery crumbled before him.

'I left him there. I was supposed to... kill him. But I couldn't. Couldn't bring myself to do it. I left him there, in the middle of the swamp, for the snakes and alligators.' He put his head in his hands and cried.

The two men sat in their own uncomfortable silence while the rain hammered against the roof of the car. There were lights out on the lake: a little fishing boat heading home. Brad watched it moving towards the docks for what seemed a lifetime. He finally spoke.

'Why are you telling me this? What does it have to do with Lionel Laroute? Did he know? Is that it? Was he trying to blackmail you?'

'No, nothing like that,' Tillery sighed. 'He *was* trying to use this *gris-gris* against me, that's true. It's hardly befitting a man of my position. But no, I don't think he even knew about the baby, or the part his mother played in the whole thing.'

'Then, what?'

'You've met Lionel Root - you know as well as I do that the man isn't a killer. He's a hustler, at best....' Brad nodded as Tillery continued, 'I asked him - straight up, in the interrogation room - 'Who is the Voodoo Killer?' and when he wouldn't say, I threatened to shoot him. I laid my piece on the table. It was an empty threat, but there it was. He laughed at me. He said, 'may's well kill me now, Auden, 'cause I's a'ready a dead man.' When I asked him to explain, he wouldn't. He held out and held out on me and I kept pushing him and pushing him. Eventually, he just looked at me, like he was looking for some kind of forgiveness and he said it. He said those words to me. And when he did, it felt like a... *fucking curse.*'

'What did he say?' Brad asked, torn between needing to know and wanting to bolt from the car and never look back.

Tillery's eyes were wild as he turned to face Brad. 'He said the Voodoo Killer... was *'the boy from the bayou.'*

In the warmth of the car, Brad's whole body felt cold. He swallowed hard and managed to say 'That doesn't mean... anything. It could be... anyone.' But his heart, pumping hard in his chest, knew the truth.

'He's come back for me,' Tillery said. 'Li Grand Zombi *spared his life and watched over him and now he's*

back. Now it's his turn.'

'Who is he?' Brad whispered in the darkness.

Tillery scoffed, 'I don't know. Root wouldn't tell me. He only said we'd never find him. We may as well stop trying because he's somewhere we'd never think to look. Then he grinned - this big, smug grin and said, *'Oh well, oh well, sonny.'* They were his *goddamn* last words. And then he picked up my weapon from the table and he blew his brains out.'

*

By the time Brad hit the main thoroughfares back into the city, the evening traffic had abated, but not the rain. Rockin' Oldies Radio was playing 'Magic Town' by The Vogues but neither man was really listening. It filled the silence. Tillery was turning over painful memories, some thirty years old, some from just the day before.

For his part, Brad was trying to process everything that had just been offered up. He felt like a man walking away from an explosion: his ears were still ringing from the blast-wave.

Auden Tillery, the most decorated police officer in the city of New Orleans had just confessed to... what? Child abandonment? Criminal neglect? That could mean a felony charge and time in the Alcatraz of the South. Brad tried to push that much out of his mind and focus his attention on the case. The details were incomplete at best. If Tillery had anything more to share, he wasn't talking now, at least not to Brad, but his lips moved over conversations he'd buried and regrets he should have voiced long ago.

From what little Brad could glean, Lionel Root hadn't said diddly squat that could lead them to their suspect. Apart from his age, they had no idea of his appearance, name, or where to find him. And, in spite of the years of bad blood, Brad wanted to believe that Auden was jumping to conclusions, and that the cops were still the good guys, the villains were still the villains and there was balance in the world. Yin and yang. But in his heart, Brad knew that the universe had a habit of getting the last laugh, and every move he made from that moment on would only serve to prove that Tillery was right: that his abandoned son had somehow survived and now there was a price to be paid.

You may as well stop trying to find him because he's somewhere you'd never think to look.

Brad kept turning that line over in his mind like a cryptic crossword clue. Where *wouldn't* Tillery think to look? *'Any place serving decent beer,'* Brad mused, wishing he were sitting at a bar right at that moment.

He swung Tillery's Mercedes into a parking space outside the Orleans Parish Sheriff's Office on Dupre and turned off the engine.

'Sweet ride,' Brad said, just to have something to say.

'Yes, it's… a lovely automobile,' Tillery replied, like a robot. 'So… what now?'

'What now?' Brad shook his heavy head. 'I don't know, Tillery. I think I need to sleep on it. So do you. You're… a good cop,' he managed, the words sticking in his craw like a fishbone. He wasn't sure what more he wanted to add. *'But you're such an asshole,'* came to mind.

'That's it?'

Brad shifted in his seat so they could face each other. 'But I was a good cop too. I *was,* Auden. You don't seem to understand that. I didn't run away from the storm, like everyone said. Like *you* said. I didn't run away from my *duty.* My wife, my son: *they* were my duty. Christ, I gave *enough.* And all this,' he gestured outside the car window at the whole universe, 'it's all a balancing act. You can't keep all the plates spinning forever. Ah shit, man, I don't know.' He ran out of steam and fumbled in his pockets for a cigarette to cover his embarrassment.

'What are you saying, Durand?'

'Just, sometimes you just have to stand up and admit your mistakes, as a human being. It doesn't mean you're a bad person. We've all got our demons. You've got to let them go, or they'll drag you to hell.'

'But you're not taking me in? You're just leaving me… here?'

Brad glanced around at the Sheriff's Department and the Police Department across the street, the Criminal Court up the way and he remembered Jon Rubino's words.

'This is the safest corner of the city, Tillery. Cops everywhere. If you want to hand yourself in, go right…'

Realization struck him like a thunderbolt.

'Auden, you need to get out. *Now!*'

eighteen

The car peeled down South Broad Street, bouncing heavily over the potholes in the asphalt, and straight over the intersection with Dumaine. A horn blared angrily behind him. Brad's mind was working harder than the engine. He'd left Auden Tillery standing dumbfounded in the rain outside the Sheriff's Office, spun the Merc hard into oncoming traffic and hit seventy before he found the switch for the lights and sirens. There was no room for tourists on the ride, and though some back-up might have helped, Brad didn't relish the thought of watching *this* particular father-son reunion.

Somewhere you'd never think to look.

It was a five-minute drive from downtown. Brad made it in three. He killed the Merc's lights and rolled to a stop on the corner of North Dorgenois and St Philip, not two hundred yards from his own front door. He got out and stood in the falling rain, watching and listening for signs of life. There were none, in any direction, and when Brad walked out into the middle of the road, he felt this was no longer just a quiet spot in a residential neighborhood of his hometown, but rather the spiritual crossroads of the world, the *in-between* that Madame Coulombe had spoken of. 'The cops would never think to look here,' he said to himself, 'on their own turf.'

Somebody had taken a few pot-shots with a BB gun at the metal sign which read 'Property of NOPD. KEEP OUT. Trespassers will be prosecuted.' The temporary fencing looked like it had been erected before Katrina and somehow weathered the storm: now it was rusted and sagging on its posts. It had been prised open and folded back upon itself in a couple of places. Nobody would have cared if they had even noticed. Brad ducked under and through the gap with ease. The cracked, yellow sign above the large doorway read, 'Police Jail and Patrol Station'. Brad knew he had been inside in the past, but he really couldn't recall when. The building had obviously been beautiful once: a two-storey Queen Anne house with tall eaves, sloping lead rooftops and an ostentatious bay window. In its heyday, it would have been the jewel of the Esplanade Ridge neighborhood, in spite of its role as an overflow for the central police station, for the drunks and pickpockets, the rapists and murderers. The two storeys loomed over him in the darkness, darker than the night itself, like a black hole, sucking in the surrounding light. He walked up to the stoop, where insidious blight had already taken hold in the brickwork and saw that somebody had set an old leather armchair on the porch to sit and watch the world go by. How many times had he driven past this place in the last few months? How many times had someone watched him? Most of the windows were broken and boarded up - from the inside, he noticed - with pallet wood. Those that remained intact were whitewashed or covered with cardboard boxes. Whatever was going on inside, he wasn't supposed to see.

Brad turned his back to the house and checked his gun in the dim glow of the streetlights. Six bullets. He thought about calling Rubino. Hell, he thought about calling 911 and running home but even so, there was something more: the notion that whoever was inside *knew* that Brad would be coming. The fact that they had somehow sent that message down the line - through Lionel Root and Auden Tillery - blew through

Brad like a chill wind. The whole deal felt like an invitation to a final performance: a one-man show, just for him. Once, as a younger man, he'd jumped out of an airplane at a charity event organized by the force. He remembered how some inner momentum had pushed him into signing up, then collecting sponsorship money over the next month, driving to the airfield in Texas on a gray Sunday morning, strapping a parachute to his back, stepping into the little plane and subsequently stepping out of it at 12,000 feet. At no point had he stopped to question his actions, to ask himself whether he actually *wanted* to skydive. But then, just as now, he was compelled by something, some inner momentum, to keep moving forward. And it was this thought, this impetus of being swept out of an airplane above a field in Texas, that came to him when he placed his hand on the door, found it unlocked, and gently pushed it open. It creaked like a cliché.

A single candle set on the floor of the entrance hall cast a cold, yellow glow about the room, highlighting the molding plaster, the rotting, broken spindles of the staircase and the entrance to the rooms beyond. *Somebody is expecting me*, Brad thought. He took a moment to get his bearings, remembering that in the past there had been a large booking office leading to the holding cells at the back. Upstairs he assumed that there were offices, storage rooms... he knew there had been a couple of dormitories where officers could catch a few hours' sleep in between shifts, but he'd never seen them, certainly never needed to use them, so with no better option he decided to head towards the back wing of the building.

Heel to toe, he quietly crept along the hallway. Sure enough, here were the remnants of the old booking desk. Its thick rosewood frame had stretched from floor to ceiling, with toughened glass panels to protect the duty officer behind the desk from the criminals on the other side. Somebody had smashed it to pieces with a fire extinguisher and completed the circle by burning the wood right there on the antique pressed-concrete tile floor. The light from a second candle in the room beyond ushered Brad onwards. The smell hit him then: neat ammonia at first, so strong it stung his eyes, followed by the odors of wet rot, chicken shit and general decay that the chemicals were trying to cover. He found himself in a large kitchen where the floor was sticky. The candle he'd seen from outside was placed in a dirty saucer in the middle of a big butcher's block: its light illuminating the myriad mason jars and bottles along rows of shelves. Though it was difficult to make out their contents, any doubts that Brad might have still held about the building's new inhabitant disappeared the moment he read the labels: 'blakk salt', 'mandrayk', 'ros buds'. The childish handwriting and spelling reminded Brad of what Tillery had said: 'the boy from the bayou.' Already, Brad was forming an image of a semi-illiterate savage, slavishly manipulating a pencil and laboring over every word. In another world, it would have been heart-breaking, but not this one.

A fifties style refrigerator in the corner of the room shuddered to life. Brad quietly circled around the table to take a closer look and noticed the rusting hasp and staple crudely screwed on to the door, but there was no padlock. Another invitation. He took a deep breath and yanked the handle. The candlelight cast the contents into shadow, but as the door swung open, they were slowly revealed. At first glance, it seemed like a haul of meat packed tightly into the shelves, some in Ziplock bags, some neatly wrapped in wax paper.

Then, Brad saw a finger. And then an eye. He didn't need to see any more. 'Forensics can pick through that,' he thought to himself, closing the door tight.

A current of cool air blew through the kitchen from the back rooms, where Brad could hear movement. The smell of decay was stronger here. He steeled himself and breathed deeply through his mouth, fighting the urge to retch. Flipping open his cell phone, he let the light of its screen shine around the four old holding cells. Graffiti covered the walls, but the scrawling of previous inmates had been scored over with a bunch of creepy symbols, odd letters and drawings, something akin to hieroglyphics which Brad was glad he couldn't decipher. He opened a cell door and leaned in for a closer look, careful to keep his center of gravity low. The light from his cellphone timed out - Brad pressed a button and in its dead glow, he thought he could make out blood stains on the floor.

Something moved in the second cell. He turned slowly, one hand on his gun, the other holding the phone out like a crucifix to ward off evil. An orange eye blinked against the glare. Brad nearly laughed aloud with relief. Sitting on wooden poles balanced across the adjacent bars of the jail cell, were a dozen or so plump chickens. Most were sleeping, only their coxcombs protruding from between their shoulders, but a few ruffled their feathers cartoonishly at the intrusion. 'Sorry, ladies,' Brad muttered.

Then it hit him - whatever it was - hard, in the stomach. Like a linebacker sacking the quarterback, it laid him out on the slick floor and drove the wind from his lungs. Brad's head smashed off the wrought iron bars behind him, but he had the sense to roll away before the next onslaught. It had been crouching in the recess between the cells, waiting for its moment to strike and now it howled - an inhuman sound - and came at him again, clawing at his face in the darkness. *It's the black dog*, Brad panicked - *it's come back to finish me off*. Under its weight, Brad's head was ground painfully against the filth on the floor. He tasted blood. With a supreme effort of will, he managed to get a knee up to his chest and tried to push the thing away from his body, but it was relentless, ferocious. Without thinking, he pointed the weapon in his hand aimlessly and squeezed off a couple of shots.

With the sudden flash of fire, the roar in the confined space and the acrid reek of gunpowder, Brad's breath came flooding back and he groaned loudly, scrambled back, kicking out in the darkness, pushing himself away from the cells, back towards the light and the relative safety of the kitchen. He rolled backwards, over himself and managed to stagger to his feet. Sobbing with fear, he clattered against the butcher's block, abruptly aware of the cacophony of the squawking chickens over his own labored breathing. Brad wiped the blood and chicken shit off his face with his sleeve, never once taking his eyes - or his gun - from the doorway to the cells, waiting for the black dog to emerge so he could put a bullet in its rotting head.

What came instead was a thousand times more terrifying. It took a moment for Brad to realize that the thing creeping through the door on two feet was the same creature which had just attacked him. Naked and bleeding, covered from head to toe in mud and filth, it staggered forward, unsure of its movements on its frail limbs, and moaning like a mute. Brad's mind reeled: was he looking at *the boy from the bayou*? Then he noticed the jutting hip bones and the emaciated breasts. Some flicker of human life in its sunken eyes reminded him of...

Zamora Delgado lunged forward, shrieking like a banshee and raking at the air with black fingernails. She never took her eyes from Brad's, as he stumbled back around the table away from her. Once he'd put a couple meters between them, he found himself on the far side of fear, where his adrenaline had begun to swing towards fight rather than flight.

'Jesus, what has he done to you, Zam?'

Shoot and assess. He positioned himself, aimed and pulled the trigger. The bullet went straight through her thigh, and she collapsed as her leg went out from under her. It was a textbook shot. No bone, through and through, just as he'd been taught to stop an unarmed man back in his academy days, but Delgado barely noticed. She struggled to her feet, grunting with animal exertion, and lurched forward again.

Neutralize the threat.

'Zam!' Brad shouted, locking his eyes on hers. 'Delgado! Come back to me, babe! Zamora Delgado!'

If there was any human part of her still there, Brad could not determine it and the thought of putting a bullet in her head and ending it there flashed through his mind.

'Zam!' he roared, more than aware that if he hadn't already, he had now alerted everybody in the building to his presence.

Neutralize the threat: that's what they'd drilled into him at the academy. Put your man down. Zam Delgado - or whatever she'd become - was not going to stop. He exhaled, summoned up his resolve and raised his revolver.

But he couldn't kill her.

With the pistol in his right still pointed at her head, Brad used his left hand to shove the table separating them with all his force, pinning Zam momentarily against the wall. She pushed back, struggling violently to free herself, but Brad planted his legs firmly and as she dropped to her knees to escape under the table, he shoved again, trapping her head, like a man in the stocks. Zam let out a strangled cry, baring her rotten teeth. In one fluid movement, he jumped up on the tabletop, with an agility he hadn't displayed in twenty years, spun the gun in the palm of his hand and cold-cocked her hard across the temple. She slumped then, unconscious, but still pinioned at the neck. He jumped down and pulled the table away, and her body fell to the ground. Kneeling to feel her pulse - still strong - Brad cast an eye about for something to tie her hands. He was unwilling to search too hard in the kitchen cupboards, for fear of what else he might find, 'like hepatitis,' he muttered bitterly. On the wall in the chicken cells, there was a length of bailing twine, thin but strong enough. He looped it twice around the water pipes that ran along the wall, working quickly, quietly, securing Zam's wrists and ankles, with half an eye always on the kitchen door, ready to rock and roll. It won't go down like this, he told himself, knowing that Zam was just a grim warm up, an undercard fight before the main event.

Brad found an old tablecloth and draped it over Zam's naked body, taking a moment to look at her gaunt and bloodied face; her eye, already blackened from the blow. Somehow, in spite of it all, she had regained a whisper of her former self in her slumber. He sat down on the tile floor next to her. He brushed the hair back from her forehead, remembering the phone call and their dinner in Valerio's, not six months ago when she'd first dragged him into all this. With a sigh, he thought about shrimp chalupas and cold beer. He shook his head in the gloom and lit a cigarette with a match from a box on the stove. He had a gnawing sense of unease that it might be his last.

'What a fucking mess, Zamora,' Brad said aloud to nobody, wondering if either of them would ever make it back to the land of the living. He tried to imagine how things might play out. He'd been in situations like this before, on police raids and drug busts, but never had it felt quite so visceral or surreal. Never without back-up. Never so unsure of what he was facing down. Brad was painfully aware of his lack of firepower: three bullets in an old handgun.

There was a killer hiding somewhere in the shadows of this old jailhouse and maybe they were destined to meet, but in that moment, Brad would rather have taken his chances against a coked-up 3NG homeboy swinging a sawn-off in a Central City crack house. He knew this guy favored a blade - a big one if the autopsies were to be believed, but what else was he holding? Instinctively, Brad touched the *gris-gris* around his neck, hoping it might offer some protection.

'I could be going up against the Devil himself,' he mused, taking a deep hit on his cigarette before stubbing it out on the floor. At times like these, life is measured in seconds and minutes, not years, he realized.

Still, when he stood up, Brad's bones felt like reinforced steel and his blood thrummed in his ears. He strode back through the booking hall, back to the vestibule and noticed immediately that the solitary candle had been moved: it was now positioned on the first step of the stairs, almost inviting him up. Brad leaned his back against the stair post and looked up into the darkness above him to the abyss beyond, feeling once again its undeniable pull. He thought he heard something move on the landing and a smile edged his lips.

The candle felt greasy between his fingers: clearly handmade and undoubtedly covered in beautiful textbook prints in the soft tallow for the boys and girls from forensics, but Brad wasn't going to risk walking blindly into a trap. Its light threw long, sweeping shadows of the broken balustrade as he edged upwards, weapon out, wall at his back, until he reached the small landing. Casting the light around, Brad saw that the layout of rooms was different from the floor below, with several doors immediately within reach.

Was there any reason to be quiet? He doubted it. He had felt the hidden presence from the moment he stepped into the house and was certain he was being watched. It all felt like a play, one he knew well, and he'd played his part so many times before on night raids - either as part of a team or solo - that it was second nature now. Desensitization was the name of that play. Or compassion fatigue. Or burnout. Brad stealthily slid to the far wall and positioned himself where he had an unobstructed view of the landing. He set the candle on the floor and wiped the grease on his pants. Beyond its arc, the darkness was absolute. A vision of the monster Zam had become flashed across his mind - her frantic, bloodshot eyes and blackened gums - and he shuddered involuntarily. How many nights would that face revisit him in his nightmares? He tried to push the thought away and focus on the moment. Around him, the contracting ductwork in the walls and ceilings ticked like a clock, urging him onwards. Time to act.

Brad blew the air out of his lungs instinctively, cocked his gun and reached for the brass handle of the first door. Locked. Undeterred, he moved diagonally across the landing to the next, systematically looking for the blind corners. This time the handle turned, and Brad let the door swing open on its hinges. Bracing his body against the jamb, he moved just his head, shoulders, arms and weapon into the room, sweeping it across the shapes in the gloom. Finger on the trigger, ready for any sign of movement. As his eyes adjusted, he could make out a makeshift pallet bed, sheets and little else. Could he smell the faintest trace of a woman? He took a step inside, angling his body so that he could keep one eye on the landing - he had no desire to be rushed from behind and overpowered. And then what? Captured? Tortured? Maybe worse. Killed and sacrificed to some heathen god? Chopped up for *gris-gris*? Brad felt his heart hammering in his chest and his thoughts spinning away: he breathed and centered himself, finding as he did, that he'd wrapped his fingers around his own mojo bag.

'You have to feed it,' Tillery had said, and he found himself nodding in agreement.

Part of him was disgusted by his new-found belief in the bag, but another part of him, a part he didn't like to acknowledge since it didn't fit with his old worldview, knew the bag was alive and did need to be fed, like any other living thing. A dark part of him wanted that chance, and as he stood alone in the shadows of Claudette's cell, he allowed himself a moment to imagine a future beyond the next hour of his existence.

Another step and Brad's foot knocked against something he hadn't noticed at first: a box. It rattled against the floorboards, like something was rolling around inside it. He knelt to investigate; it was a small wooden crate - like a miniature tea chest - upended, so that its aperture lay flat to the floor. Brad nudged it again with his foot, and again it rattled on the wooden floorboards before abruptly coming to rest. Something alive, Brad thought: some other creature hoping to escape from this fate. A rat, probably, or another chicken, Brad reckoned, and without another thought, he lifted the box gingerly with his boot, so whatever it was could scuttle out the other side.

But it didn't scuttle. It slithered.

With a sound like a knife slowly slicing through paper, it slid out of the room and across the landing. Brad thought he saw its form - possibly its bright patterned back - rippling in the candlelight, and his stomach lurched. The candle flickered then and seemed to burn brighter, and though a warmth had blossomed in the dank house, Brad felt the chill of another presence all around him.

'He is the messenger between the worlds of flesh and spirit, and life and death.'

In a fleeting moment of bliss, Brad believed dawn was breaking and the light suffusing the room was the sun rising over the city and penetrating the cracks in the boarded windows, but his relief was short-lived. The light was coming from a room at the other end of the corridor, pulsating in waves: a fire rhythmically sucking in air like a living thing. And with his gun hanging uselessly at his side, towards its glow Brad staggered along the corridor, hand on the door now, ready to be consumed. He was tipping forward again, over the precipice, the solid floor of the airplane beneath his feet left behind, falling into the sky.

nineteen

Ike gasped, in spite of himself, for the vision was so perfect, so reminiscent of his first glimpse of the brute, an age ago in the swirling chicken blood: the bear lumbering out of the shadows of its brumal cave, that he felt he already knew the man standing in the doorway. It was like seeing a movie star in his own humdrum world.

Brad also stared back, dumbfounded at the *tableau vivant* before him: something between a moment stolen from some dark avant-garde play and a snapshot of a vaudevillian carnival freakshow. His mind tried to wrap itself around what he was seeing; how many years had passed since the world had conjured up something so completely new for somebody like him, who thought he had seen it all? The moments which had punctuated his life played out again like a grainy Super 8 montage: shooting a gun, a school of dolphins in the Gulf, his first dead body, fireworks on the 4th of July in 1965, losing his virginity at the high school prom, stealing and crashing his father's motorcycle, Kyle's birth, his mother's funeral, Hilda, Camille, Katrina....

'Yes, this *is* your life,' Ike said, as if reading Brad's thoughts.

Brad snapped back to reality, to the intense shimmering light and heat of a hundred candles burning in a small room, the cloying stench of smoke and blood, lavender and sweat and a musky stink of rotten-eggs; he looked beyond it all to Claudette Tremblay, wearing just a T-shirt, cowering in the corner:

painfully thin, her face bruised and swollen, the letters 'IS' branded down her leg. He even managed to disassociate his thoughts from the scores of snakes covering the floor, writhing everywhere like something from a horror movie, trying to climb the walls, sliding among the books and candles and jars and trinkets on the shelves: harmless pine and comically striped milk snakes mainly, but Brad definitely recognized the triangular head of a fat, brown water moccasin - a 'cottonmouth' - curled heavily and staring malevolently with obsidian eyes. A rattlesnake reacted noisily to the change in the dynamic, but remained coiled under a wooden pallet, peeking out of the slats, tasting the air with its tongue. Brad remembered hearing on the Discovery Channel that the fear of snakes is innate in humans - a relic of our prehistoric ancestors - and that our fear of everything else - spiders, thunder and lightning, heights - is learned when we're just kids. Snakes have a hold over us: it's written in our DNA and there's no denying it. This knowledge gave him little consolation as he took in everything around him and shuddered involuntarily.

In spite of it all, his focus was drawn to the figure in the center of the room, maybe ten feet from the doorway. Ike Sugar was standing with his arms outstretched, like Christ the Redeemer. But his entire naked body was painted ghostly white with cornstarch and water, streaked over the contours of his sleek limbs, cracking in the spaces between his fingers and the lines around his eyes and mouth. And on top of this, thin, beige diamonds of sloughed snakeskin had been meticulously adhered across his chest and torso, cascading symmetrically down his abdomen and over his shaved genitalia like overlapping scales. Ike had been collecting live specimens for months, calling them to the yard, summoning them from the streets and sewers and the swampland beyond the city limits, *wearing* them under his rainslicker, about his person. Now he had fashioned himself as one of them, as their master.

His long dreadlocks, shaped and pinned at the nape of his neck, framed his head like a cobra's hood, and his face - similarly streaked in whitewash - was studded with dozens of tiny lines of snakes' teeth, radiating from his own painted lips, to which he had stitched a pair of inch-long rattler fangs. His own blood had congealed around them. His pale eyes glittered from within dark sockets, ringed with kohl and they held Brad.

'Do ya see me?' he asked, and when he spoke, in that low whisper, all the snakes appeared to stop and listen to the smooth cadence of his voice.

Brad took a beat to turn the question over before replying carefully, the way one might speak to a man with his finger on the pin of a grenade. 'I see you. But who are you?'

'I got lots o' names. Maybes y'all knows me as Ike Sugar, but that is *not* my name,' he spat. 'That name was given to me when I was jus' a boy. Y'all won't find that name on no social s'curity card or no birth certificate because *Ike Sugar* din't ever exist. See? Ike Sugar does not represent my *true self*.' He paused to control his rising temper, then smiled at Brad benignly. For a moment, Brad could see a flicker of Auden Tillery in Sugar's serene face. It was there, across his eyes, in his expression.

'Do you see, Bear, that I is both connected, *and* I *is* the *connection*. Do you see me here at these crossroads? Do you see how I has discovered mysel' and all my *pouvwa* - in me, in this place, in ev'rythin'. I can't goes back now. Now I has changed. I has *become*.'

'So, you are not Ike Sugar,' Brad confirmed, and he cast an eye in the direction of Claudette. Tears were rolling down her cheeks. 'What should I call you then?'

'Like I said, I gots a whole lotta names. I am the serpent, as you can see,' he said, gesturing to his costume. 'But I'm also the rainbow. I'm the earth *and* heaven. I stand at the crossroads. Do you see?' Each of his statements was accompanied by a complementary gesture - the voodooist had clearly been preparing this routine for some time.

'Are you... *Papa Legba*?' Brad asked, remembering Madame Coulombe's words and trying to appeal to Sugar's vanity.

'*Yeah!*' Ike replied proudly, like he was speaking to a child who had uttered something intelligent. He closed his eyes and puffed out his chest slightly, 'You *do* see me! But, sonny, you oughta know that I likes to call mysel' *Li Grand Zombi*,' and when he smiled widely, the rattlesnake fangs grazed his bottom lip.

There was a moment's silence. Both men stood, observing one another, assessing the situation and waiting for the other to speak or move. Brad had always enjoyed this little power struggle and he settled into the silence like it was his old green leather recliner, wrapping his fingers a bit tighter around his gun like it was his last bottle of beer. *How many bullets were left?* A snake wrapped itself around Ike's bare feet.

"Course, you are the bear,' Ike sneered, breaking the silence after growing tired of the pleasantries. 'Oh, I know - I been lowly animals too.' He sucked his teeth as though he were confessing to a sin. 'I was the dog once, and the pig. They was jus' *steps* though. I was becoming somethin' greater. But you's never gon' be nothin' but a *stoopit*, lumberin' bear.' And Ike laughed at that, shrill and mocking. He was savoring this moment.

Still Brad said nothing, allowing a few heartbeats to pass. Something changed in the atmosphere, like the temperature cooled just a degree and the snakes sensed it in their cold blood. They turned their heads to stare at Brad, and from beneath the pallet in the corner came an ominous rattling, like he was suddenly a threat. Claudette felt it too and drew her knees up to her chest and whimpered.

The billhook appeared as if by magic, conjured out of thin air into his right hand, both edges gleaming. Ike waved its curved tip in Brad's direction, like an admonishment.

'You's a strange one, alright,' he screwed up his eyes and cocked his head cartoonishly, as though he were trying to figure him out. 'What's your name, sonny? Naw, fo' get it. Am gon' call you 'Bear.' That's yo' name, fo' sure. *Bay-uh*.' He smiled coldly at that. 'Y'know, Bear, 'I saw you comin'. Long time ago. But when I saw you - first time - you had no *pouvwa*. Not a drop. You know 'bout *pouvwa*?'

'Sure, *pouvwa*. Power. *Muti*,' Brad answered, but his tongue felt slack and his throat dry.

Ike's eyes widened again. 'Right again, Bear! *Damn*, you's a regular know-it-all, huh? First time I saw you, you was like a shadow, a... *dead* man, only you din't know it yet. Stumblin' through yo' sad life. You done got yo' groove back now though. Yeah, you got yo' groove back...' His pupils seemed to dilate as he spoke, soothing Brad in his persuasive tone.

'I guess... you gave me... a reason to live, *Grand Zombi*,' Brad replied, hoping to play to Ike's vanity, although he knew his words had an element of truth. He shook his head to clear it.

'You right again, Bear. Yeah, I saw you comin'. Hell, I

made you come! I gave y'all life again! You got yo' groove back. Lord ha' mercy!' Ike grinned, moving his head back and forth, back and forth, in a lazy rhythm, his dreadlocks swaying,

'I got my groove back,' Brad answered, but he didn't recognize his own voice. It sounded like a vinyl recording, scratchy and distant, played on an old gramophone, like the one his mama used to play her Nat King Cole records on as she cleaned the house on Sunday afternoons.

Ike's eyes didn't leave Brad's for a moment; Brad realized that for his part he couldn't tear his gaze away, '... And now y'all gon' give it to me. All yo' sweet *pouvwa*. Mmm hmm. You *and* the lady. I's gon' show y'all... *eternity*.'

Ike's voice had taken on a different quality, reverberating in the small room. It was like he had a direct line to Brad's mind, to his soul, and as he spoke, Brad's limbs became flaccid, the weight of the gun in his hand suddenly became almost too much to bear, his eyesight shrouded in a cool, dense fog. His legs - so tired now - tingled with pins and needles and he dropped to his knees with an immense lethargy, just as the snakes came.

In his mind, Brad reached out for the thick exposed roots of a tupelo, where he could make out Claudette reaching for him from the safety of its hefty boughs - but he couldn't cry out. His heart was barely beating now and the heaviness in his arms couldn't match the pull of the mud, slowly drawing him down into the cool waters of the bayou. With a strangled sob, he closed his eyes and gave in. He was slowly being pulled down into Ike's childhood swamp.

The reptiles moved silently, inexorably at the voodooist's command, over Brad's legs and up his torso: their combined weight pulling him to the wooden floor of the temple room. He slowly tipped forward on to his front, until he was lying prone, and the snakes covered his back and head, writhed in his hair, coiled under his groin and arms, under his chin and around his neck and began to smother him.

'There is no one to help you and no way to escape....' Ike said methodically as he pushed a foot under Brad's chest. He bent his leg and with a grunt, rolled him onto his back, trapping a few indignant snakes which hissed angrily. Then he flicked back his dreadlocks as he knelt down beside Brad's head and sang gently, *'Mwen te fouye twou a, Mwen te fouye twou a....'*

Claudette knew the meaning of these words and she sobbed in desperation as Ike drew the billhook and placed the straight edge against Brad's neck.

'ki mouri yo vle yon gwo foul, ki mouri yo vle yon gwo foul...'

In the candlelight, the cottonmouth coiled itself languorously on Brad's chest and waited for its own moment to strike.

'Ban m 'pouvwa ou, give me your power...' Ike whispered, and put his body weight down on the blade. He paused momentarily, desperately wanting to savor the moment, but the desire grew too strong, and Ike pushed, willing the billhook to slice through the soft flesh of his victim's windpipe. He drew blood - just a scratch - but he couldn't cut deeper: he felt his arms were held back by some invisible force and in that instant, in that fleeting moment of his own bewilderment, the spell was broken. Brad reached from under the waters of the swamp and kicked away the roots encircling his feet and ankles. His eyes flicked open, and as he gulped down oxygen, he instinctively reached for the gun at his side and in less than a

second squeezed the trigger three times.

The first blew the blunt head off the cottonmouth: a million-to-one shot since he was only hoping to scare away the snakes - the bullet spattered strings of flesh and blood across both his face and Ike's before burying itself in the ceiling. At that range, the gunshot sounded like a bomb blast and Ike recoiled instantaneously, missing by only a fraction of an inch the full force of the second shot as Brad swung his hand free and wild and fired again. The bullet grazed Ike's ear: it creased his skull and punched a burning hole in his dreadlock hood. Brad overcorrected with the third shot, missed the voodooist completely and blasted the side panel off the shelf-stand next to Claudette, sending candles and books, ornaments and live snakes crashing to the floor. In the chaos, Ike spilled backwards, away from the pain and the noise and the harsh smell of burnt gunpowder in his nostrils, rolling off Brad, clutching his hands over his bleeding ear, screaming in agony and disbelief at the turn of events, at the insult, at the sacrilege, and every snake in the room reared up and moved to strike at Brad, baring their thin fangs and dipping their blunt heads aggressively.

Still gasping for breath, Brad spat out snake blood. 'Look at that, dickhead. I got my groove back.' He checked his gun, found it empty and tried to hide his deep dismay by snapping shut the barrel with a confident, seasoned flick of his wrist. It was no use: Ike saw through the bluff and in spite of his pain, he smiled knowingly. 'Empty again, huh? No power left in that lil' ol' thing neither...' He touched his ear gingerly and sucked the blood from his fingertips with gusto, as though he had just finished off a glazed doughnut.

Brad ignored him. 'I don't like what you did to the lady downstairs,' he said, pocketing the gun, 'and I don't like… whatever you're doing to that lady right there,' he nodded in Claudette's direction.

It was more bravado, and if Brad had any illusion he was now in control, he was wrong. Ike blew the air out of his lungs, closed his eyes and found his center again, willing the pain to disappear and the bleeding to stop. The whole right side of his face felt like it had been doused in kerosene and set alight, but he focused on his memories of submerging himself in the cool waters of Black Bayou and pushed the discomfort from his mind. He breathed deeply and concentrated the pain into the white heat of his fury, whilst all around his feet the snakes gathered, still swaying their heads and mock-striking at Brad.

Brad set his shoulders and raised his fists in a boxer's stance. 'Come if you're coming,' he growled at them all.

At this provocation, Ike seemed to physically swell with anger. Every candle flame flickered in his direction, like plants bending toward the light, and the room - the entire house - began to tremble, shaking the windows in their frames so much that they hummed. A statuette of St Peter spontaneously exploded, sending shards of ceramic across the room like shrapnel. Claudette screamed in the face of the oncoming storm as Ike clenched his fists, lowered his head and came again at the detective. The force of his will hit Brad like a category five hurricane, forcing the air from his lungs and knocking him back down to the floor. The voodooist's piercing eyes - his pupils thin as stab-wounds - found Brad's and when he held his gaze Brad groaned in agony: his lifeforce - his *muti* - was being squeezed from him. Ike reached out psychically, casting for Brad's heartbeat, feeling it racing with panic and waiting - like a python - for it to slow in death.

Brad opened his mouth to yell but found there was no

air in his crushed lungs. Ike Sugar was suddenly, simultaneously everywhere, all around him, restricting not only Brad's every physical movement, but relentlessly punishing his mind, bombarding him with dark visions of his victims' final horrific moments. Through Ike's eyes, through the thin slits in the pig mask, Brad saw the Favreau boy, screaming on the broken jetty in the midday sun, the knife slicing across his fingers as he tried to protect himself from the attack. He saw Nadia Romero, still alive, lying in the mud on the bank of the canal, her face frozen in a rictus of pain and fear, as Ike cheerfully hacked through her wrist bone. Nothing in the case files could prepare Brad for the raw terror in Adam Beaupre's paralyzed eyes, or the thick, choking sound Mani Lionne made as Ike pulled his heart to pieces.

At this thought, Ike seemed to relent involuntarily - he had remembered some previously forgotten memory and it gave him pause. He loosened his grip and again Brad fought for air like a man cut loose from the gallows. He rolled onto his knees and retched, coughing up blood, and as he did, the *gris-gris* strung around his neck slipped out from under his shirt and hung there, swinging beneath him.

Brad backed himself up against the wall and managed to sit, his hand now clasped around the mojo bag, for what it was worth. It felt like Ike Sugar had possessed him, ravaged his thoughts and shook-up everything Brad had buried over a lifetime deep down in his subconscious: every corpse, every lifeless face, every one of his own bleak thoughts, his failures, his dark desires and guilty secrets, stirred up like poisonous seeds and bitter leaves.

Ike looked down at him, again trying to figure out what was holding him back. He frowned and rubbed his chin: a parody of a man thinking. Brad couldn't even hold his gaze. He wiped the spit from his lips with his sleeve. Eventually, Ike shrugged and smiled: a thin, calculating smile.

'Oh well, oh well. I'll find a way, sonny,' he threatened.

Brad nodded in agreement. None of it mattered now. There was no fight left in him. There was some comfort in having found the Voodoo Killer - and *so nearly* put a bullet in his skull - but he resigned himself to the fact that he couldn't save Zamora, or Claudette, and in the absence of some kind of miracle, he wouldn't be saving himself either. How much protection could one mojo bag offer? *What am I insured against?* Brad wondered. *Third party, fire and theft? Snake bites? Demonic possession?* He watched impassively as Ike Sugar grabbed the girl by the ankle and dragged her into the center of the room and laid her flat on the floor, before taking a jar of red brick dust and pouring a rough circle around her body.

'You stays right there, cher.'

Brad thought about seeing his wife one more time and apologizing, promising to be a better man, asking for another chance. And Kyle: holding him again, in a way that he hadn't been able to since they had long grown apart, telling him that he loved him, and being his father again. But these notions seemed impossible dreams now: the distance from this present to that future too great.

'That's right, that's right,' Ike continued, 'The *loa* are with us, Bear! They's testin' me. They want you to watch. They want y'all to witness my *pouvwa*. That's it.'

Brad adjusted his goals: the only thing he wanted in the entire world at that very moment was a cigarette and - God damn - he blessed Treyvon Plummer for the pack he'd handed over in The Deja Vu. He'd wasted almost all of them in the Waffle House, over the delights of the All-Star breakfast, but there were still a couple of soldiers left standing. He patted his pockets, searching for his lighter, but found none. He was about to make a move for a nearby upturned candle, scorching the wooden floor, when he felt a book of matches in his inside pocket.

But when he pulled it out, Brad saw it wasn't a matchbook.

And then he laughed. It bubbled up like a belch.

And then he stopped himself

Because he saw a way out.

His thoughts cascaded, as he imagined a scientist: nobody he knew, no one he had ever met, just another lab coat, in a bio-med company contracted by the NOPD, working late perhaps, on Detective Jon Rubino's insistence, analyzing the chemical profile of an exotic, tropical, psychoactive drug, an amnesia-inducing, inhibition-stripping knock-out, derived from Colombian nightshade flowers and now - thanks to the city's latest nut-job - doing the rounds on the streets of New Orleans. Scopolamine hydrobromide no less.

Only it wasn't that drug.

Because when that lab technician shook her test-tube, or held the solution over her Bunsen burner, or dipped her litmus paper, or did whatever she had to do to test the properties of that drug, she would believe herself the victim of a practical joke, a prank perpetrated by her male coworkers, for she would have discovered immediately that it was not in fact scopolamine hydrobromide, or any such schedule 1 substance, but rather a chemical known as $C_{12}H_{22}O_{11}$. Or more generally sucrose. Or more commonly still, *icing sugar*. The kind you find in abundance in a box of six Cafe Du Monde beignets.

Brad turned over the little packet in the candlelight of the temple room and allowed himself a sigh and a smile, in spite of it all. Back on Thursday night, he just couldn't bring himself to hand it over to Rubino outside the St Louis Cemetery. At the time, he didn't know what he was going to do with the scopolamine, but earlier that same day, he sat at home and - over a box of those lovely doughnuts - he ruminated on how things might fall out when they shook down Lionel Root and Georgine Rieux, if it all went to plan. He remembered then and now what she had said to him in her garden - *"A gram costs two hundred dollars - just a lil' ol' packet"* - and he brought to mind the surly waiter outside Cafe Du Monde and the burst bag of icing sugar in the trash, and before he knew it, he had made himself a little envelope of cardboard torn from the box-lid and he was carefully tipping the remaining sugar into it. *The old switcheroo.* He handed Rubino the sugar for chemical analysis and kept the burundanga for himself. Some part of him then thought it might come in useful. As a truth serum, or a bargaining chip. Hell, he could even sell it if things got real bad.

And here it was.

Ike was distracted, laying out Claudette like a rack of ribs on a slab and mumbling his African prayers to the loa, so Brad seized the opportunity. Feigning illness, injury, or both, he slumped over to the side and carefully tore open the edges of his cardboard envelope, cupping the packet in the palm of his hand, so that for the most part the drug wasn't in contact with his skin. Georgine Rieux had been emphatic about its potency, and Brad wasn't about to assess its efficacy by inadvertently knocking himself unconscious. He pulled himself back up, grabbed a candle and lit the cigarette hanging from his lips. If he was going to go down, he wanted to go down in style. He took a couple of big drags and cleared his throat before coming out swinging.

'Hey! You fuckin' freak!' he began, startling even himself. Ike was similarly surprised, but not amused at the interruption. His costume was beginning to wilt in the heat, thin sheets of snakeskin had slid off his torso in the fracas, the white paint was cracked and fading.

'Are we done here? Yeah, you heard me right, you fuckin' freak.' Brad was warming up now. 'Wanna know a secret, motherfucker? 'Because I got a secret for you, gimp. *Listen - Bom, Bom, Bom - do you want to know a secret?*' he crooned, starting to enjoy himself. Ike turned away, refusing to pay him any attention.

'I'm talking to *you*, snake-hips! Why don't you leave that girl alone? Don't you *want* to know who left you in the swamp?'

Now he had Ike's attention. He fixed his cold eyes on Brad.

'Oh yeah. Now he's listening! Back when you was a baby. Hey, you wanna know when your birthday is? You wanna know how old you are? Yeah, freak, I've been talking to *your* daddy.'

Ike stepped toward him cautiously, sniffing out the trap, but his curiosity was too acute. As he inched closer, Brad tightened his right hand around the *gris-gris*. He wanted to keep it hidden. In his left, he held the packet of burundanga. His fingers were beginning to feel numb. Ike licked his lips.

'You been talkin' the ol' man?' Ike asked, searchingly.

'*Your* old man? Or Lionel Root? Which is it?' Brad asked.

'Root, I guess,' Ike replied. 'He been spillin' his guts 'gain?'

Brad laughed dryly. 'Not quite. But he *is* dead.' Brad

took a little bump of pleasure in Ike's expression. 'Din't you *feel* that, *Zombi*? Weren't you in his head at the end? Din't the *loa* pass that information along?'

'Watch yo' tongue, sonny,' Ike hissed, but Brad pressed his luck. 'Here's the kicker though,' he dropped his voice, 'here's a secret for you: your daddy - yo' *real* daddy, that is - he was in the same room when Lionel put a bullet through his brain. How 'bout that?'

'You *lie*,' Ike sneered.

'No, *Zombi*. F'true. *Your* daddy - the same one that left you fo' dead in that bayou when you was just a baby - he watched Lionel die. They say...' Brad paused for dramatic effect, '... he even shot himself with your daddy's gun.'

Claudette lay slumped in her circular prison, her breathing shallow and fitful. Ike had abandoned her and forgotten his 'becoming'. His eyes were wide as saucers. 'And y'all know him?'

'Oh yeah.'

'Tell me.'

'You wouldn't believe it if I did,' Brad slurred his words, and his vision swam briefly. The burundanga was taking effect.

Ike closed the gap between them in a flash, leaning down and grabbing a fistful of Brad's jacket. 'You gonna tell me, Bear, or I's gon'...'

'What, Ike?' Brad snapped. 'Gut me like a catfish? Don't bother, *sonny*. You can't hurt me no more. Know why?' he asked, raising his voice. 'I got another secret for y'all. You wanna know why you can't kill me?' he yelled in Ike's face. 'Here's why! You can't fight your own fuckin' magic!' And he screwed his eyes closed and held up the little mojo bag like a light in the darkness, like a talisman.

Some part of him hoped for a lunar eclipse, fire and

brimstone, or at least a bolt of lightning but where there had previously been screaming and gunshots, now there was only the quiet ringing in his ears. Brad opened his eyes, waiting for the thunder, but Ike Sugar only hawked and spat, cocked his head like a bird and watched Brad until the latter grew tired of holding out his arm and let it fall to his side and the *gris-gris* rest against his heavy heart.

'Ain't you jus' full of surprises? That's one o' mine, huh?' Ike said, gesturing with the blade. 'Well, you got taste, Bear. You knows what's in it? You know *who's* in it? I guess not. Oh well, oh well. Y'all is protected huh? Fo' now, Bear, for now. But don't y'all go lettin' nobody else touch it. Even me. Other people'll steal its power.' He winked and whirled away, and Brad knew he had missed his chance. He leaned his head back against the wall and closed his eyes. The scopolamine was slowly working through his bloodstream, dulling his senses and clouding his brain. Ike's words echoed in his mind like the toll of a church bell.

Then he felt the point of the blade, scratching across his chest, working its way under the leather cord of the *gris-gris* and when he looked, he saw Ike's face, not a foot away from his. He was kneeling in front of Brad, his narrowed eyes fixed on the mojo bag.

'I'll find a way,' Ike grinned, just like a snake, and the threat in his gravelly voice was palpable. He pulled the cord tight against the billhook, letting the blade do the work.

Spittle dripped from Brad's lips. He whispered something under his breath and Ike leaned forward to hear it, 'What you sayin', Bear?'

Brad whispered again, but still Ike couldn't hear. 'Say *whut* now?'

'*It's just a parlor trick,*' Brad said. *Now or never*, he

feinted with his right fist, twisting away from the weapon, and lunged forward with his left, just as Ike moved back and away, unwittingly into the direction of Brad's oncoming attack. His open palm came wheeling around in a wide arc - like a pizza chef slapping the dough into shape - and Ike took the full force of the smack in the face. The packet of Devil's Breath exploded against Ike's cheek, and with a final battle cry, Brad pushed himself forward, away from the wall, using everything he had left in his body and soul to smash the cardboard and its contents into Ike's eye.

Blinded, Ike cried out and swung wildly with the billhook; Brad rolled back on his heels but not quickly enough and the blade buried itself deep in his shoulder. In the moment, he felt nothing: his adrenaline carried him over and he ducked under a second blow and hit back with a crushing haymaker, instantly breaking Ike's nose with a satisfying crunch, but slicing open his own knuckles on the snakes' teeth sewn into Ike's skin. Sugar's head hit the floor, but still he kicked and struggled, raving like a madman and clawing at his face.

And then he stopped and lay still, all of a sudden, like a puppet with its strings cut, breathing heavily, his chest rising and falling from the exertion of the fight, but otherwise making no sound or movement. Brad struggled to his feet, suddenly aware of the blood soaking through the shoulder of his shirt. The pain would follow soon enough. He stood and looked down at Ike Sugar: his costume was in tatters, his entire body now a sweat-streaked, dirty white mess. He looked like he had been pulled from the rubble of an earthquake. There was blood around his nose and mouth and one of his eyes was already swollen shut, but the other, thickly caked around the eyelids with pasty burundanga, stared back at Brad, wide and fearful.

Brad's head throbbed. The scopolamine in his system had left him dry-mouthed and nauseous - even the low candlelight was hard to take. He wiped the palm of his hand on his pants, for what it was worth.

'Do you see me?' he asked. His voice seemed to come from a long way away.

Ike's neck twitched, like he was trying to speak, but his lips didn't move. A vein in his forehead pulsed angrily.

Brad didn't know what else to say. He thought absently about reading Ike his Miranda rights and making a citizen's arrest, but in his current state he wasn't sure he could remember the words, and besides, this wasn't exactly your average breaking and entering bust. For his own part, Ike remained silent.

There was movement behind him, and Brad spun around, half-expecting Bigfoot or Count Dracula, or a giant anaconda for sure. In the chaos, Brad had lost track of Claudette, but here she was, standing before him, like a tiny bird. She took his bleeding hand and placed it against her face and mouthed the words 'thank you' because she thought her voice would fail her. Fresh tears spilled down her cheeks.

Brad couldn't think straight anymore. He nodded and managed a 'No problem' but that was the extent of his conversation. She had found herself some kind of black silk robe - like a kimono - probably Ike's. It was covered with red phoenixes, rising from flames on the hemline. He watched silently as she picked up a jar from the floor and began carefully shaking out its contents in an outline around Ike's prone body. He followed her movements with his one good eye. Next, she set two lit candles close together on the floor and knelt before them, making sure that her tormentor could see everything. Then she reached over and picked up the billhook, taking the time to wipe off Brad's blood on the folds of her gown. She tested its weight, before holding the blade over the twin candle flames. The metal seemed to ripple as it changed from gray to black to red in the heat.

Softly, a little self-consciously at first, Claudette sang the lines like a lullaby.

'Mwen te fouye twou a, mwen te fouye twou a, I have dug the hole, I have dug the hole...'

But before she finished, she turned her angelic face up to Brad's - it seemed to glow for him - and right there and then he would have done anything she asked. When she spoke, her words came like a commandment from God, bursting in Brad's mind like Fourth of July fireworks.

'You should probably go and get that checked out,' she said, pointing at his shoulder.

'Right,' Brad replied, and he turned and made towards the door, no longer sure if he was in control of himself or under the sway of the drug. Either way, Brad Durand stumbled out of the temple room, clattered down the wooden staircase and spilled out into the front yard like a drunk, just before Ike managed to find his voice.

twenty

When Brad woke, the memories came back together like a jigsaw puzzle. He found himself in hospital, half asleep on a gurney in a corridor.

'Where 'y'at?' A nurse was standing over him. Her name badge read, 'Hello, my name is Simone.'

'Hello Simone,' Brad croaked.

'We let you sleep fo' a while, since it's quiet.' She had a gap between her front teeth, which Brad had always found endearing in adults.

'So, Bradley Durand...' she said, reading her notes. 'Lordy, what happened to you, young man?'

'I don't… rightly know.'

'Uh-huh. Well, we done stitched you back together, Mr. Durand and we pumped your stomach fo' good measure. Lord only knows what you been doin'. Nuthin' I ever saw before. We had to throw away some of your clothes, I'm afraid. But the good news is, we dug out a nice track suit for you in the lost and found.'

'Sounds fine, Simone.'

'Yeah, yeah. Now, your insides are gon' hurt like a bitch fo' a few days, so go steady on the gumbo. No drinkin' neither. If yo' hungry now, I reckon we can find you a nice bowl of rice pudding. Would you like that?'

'That would be very kind, Simone.'

'Huh!' She grunted but there was a twinkle in her eye. 'I'll says this fo' you, Mr. Durand. Even in the state you was in when you walked in here, you's about the most *obedient* patient I ever known!'

*

There was a bank of callboxes in the hospital lobby. Brad made two phone calls. First, he dialed 911 and told the operator to send a police unit and at least one ambulance to the old jailhouse on St. Philip Street. He gave the code for 'officer down' - 10-999 - but hung up when she asked for his name. He took a beat, pressing the receiver to his forehead and listening to the dial tone, wondering why he didn't want to be the hero of the hour. He closed his eyes and pictured what those poor bastard cops and paramedics were going to find when they got inside that house. Not least Zamora Delgado - if any part of Zamora was still alive in her body - starved and naked, shot, beaten and left for dead in a filthy kitchen, slumped against a fridge full of random body parts. And Claudette Tremblay: physically and sexually abused, drugged, burnt and tortured. And whatever was left of Ike Sugar, living or dead. What she had done to his inert body. He saw Ike's panicked eyes, staring out at him...

A floor buffer thrummed into life in the lobby.

Brad stuck a quarter in the slot and called police headquarters. He left a message with the staff sergeant for Jon Rubino. 'Yes officer, I realize what time it is. Please just have him call me back as soon as possible.' He gave both the number of the call box - just in case - and his own cell phone number before hanging up. Then he slumped in an orange plastic chair in a waiting room, watching the cleaner methodically polish the floors, until he fell asleep.

At around five in the morning, against Simone's advice, he checked himself out. There would be time for rest but now he needed to move. He pulled the plastic ID bracelet off his wrist and zipped up his new tracksuit top. The early morning air was crisp. He had no recollection of how he had covered the distance between the house of horrors on St Philip and the emergency medical center on Tulane; he made a cursory tour of the hospital parking lot, looking for Tillery's Mercedes and half hoping to see it scraped to shit and wearing a wheel clamp for good measure. Eventually, he wandered out into the dead streets of the Business District, and before he knew it, he was ambling back towards Gravier where he'd left his car the night before.

The clock on the dash read 5:47. He dropped his keys, fumbling with unsteady hands for the ignition, but as he groped for them in the footwell, Brad came upon a beautiful bag of Chili Doritos hidden under his seat. His cellphone chirped - Rubino - and Brad opened the bag, started the engine, and hit 'accept' as he swung out across four empty lanes of South Broad Street, running the red lights and heading towards the river.

'Hey Jon.'

'Hey Brad. Where y'at?'

'Shut up and listen….'

As Brad cruised down Tchoupitoulas, skirting the floodwalls, he laid it all out. Almost all of it: Ike Sugar, Lionel Root, and the refrigerator full of body parts in the old jailhouse on St Philip. He decided it best to keep Auden Tillery's name out of the picture. There was a lot of information to impart and an order of events that needed to be followed, but Brad had to remain selective in his recollection of certain details, partly for his own protection, partly for his sanity. He played down the more supernatural elements of the night, reasoning that a man like Jon Rubino would have trouble taking him seriously if he tried to describe the voodooist's command of the snakes, the mind control, the telekinesis…

Brad talked steadily, recounting the deductive reasoning which led him to the patrol station and the fight which left him lying in hospital. Again, he glossed over the true version of events - his interpretation of it at least - but had to smile when Rubino interjected to tell him they had cut loose Georgine Rieux, since the lab results had come back negative for scopolamine. 'It was icing sugar! What a fucking gip!'

He drove with nowhere in mind, until he realized he was gravitating again towards Clinton Street and Cheaters, so he turned north, escaping through the silence of Mid-City, where the only other signs of life were a couple of garbage trucks doing the early morning rounds.

Maybe he was wrong about Rubino. Maybe a man twenty years his junior would be more accepting of less traditional explanations. His generation wasn't so 'old skool' as Brad's: relics who had been around the block a few times and saw history repeating itself everywhere, over and over, from ten o' clock news stories about ructions in the Middle East to the cut of the reporters clothes and the length of their hair.

Up towards Metairie Cemetery, with its giant elaborate marble tombs glinting in the first blush of dawn, and out along the 17th Street Canal, where Katrina first topped the levees in 2005. He swung west to join the Causeway.

But Brad also knew what he'd encountered in that building fell beyond the realm of normal human experience, and he'd carry those dark memories - like so many others - to his grave. Years ago, he'd weighed that burden and reconciled it with his life as a cop. Dead or not, he could still feel Ike Sugar casting about inside his head and in his heart, and he wasn't ready to say those words aloud to anybody. Not yet.

'Something else: Zamora Delgado's there.'

'In the house? Fuck, I'm sorry, Brad - I know you two were close.'

'No, It's…. actually, worse than that, Jon. When I found her, when I left her…' he struggled to explain, 'she was still alive. Barely alive. She'd been tortured pretty badly. I don't know what you're going to find when you get there. There was nothing I could do. I couldn't get her out. Her or the Tremblay girl.'

'OK. I hear you. Jesus.'

'I called it in… an hour or so ago. I don't know what the situation is now. You'll need a whole team. The works. And if they haven't already, make sure you have some women officers with you when you get in there. What can I tell you, dude? It's a nightmare. I'm still trying to get my head around it.'

Lake Pontchartrain shimmered like a million pink diamonds in the sunrise. The bridge ahead disappeared into the morning mist in the distance. Brad couldn't see a single car in either direction.

'Listen, Brad, you're still one of us, you know? We look after our own.'

Brad nodded, but he couldn't trust his voice.

'It's not like it used to be,' Rubino continued. 'We have trained staff who can help now, you know? Psychological support. I can set it up if you want to come in….'

'Thanks… but no thanks,' Brad answered gruffly. 'Think of this all as an anonymous tip. I just had to get the wheels turning. It's all yours now.'

He slowed to a halt and pulled over in an emergency lay-by.

'What are you going to do?'

'Oh… I don't know. This and that,' he replied, stepping out of the car to take in the view. The Lake was so vast it felt like being back on the Gulf again. 'I'm going to take some time off, I guess. Try to forget about it all. Go back to Florida. Take the boat out. Go fishing.'

'We're going to need to ask you some questions further down the line,' Rubino said.

'You've got my number.'

'Thanks for sticking at it, Brad. Take care, ok.'

'You too, Jon. See you around.'

Brad hung up, walked over to the edge of the bridge and flung his cellphone into the water below. His arm ached. The other - festooned in a sling and sporting thirteen stitches in the meat of his shoulder - ached even more. Hell, his entire body ached, but still, for the first time in a long time, he felt alive. *You got your groove back.* Under his maroon velour tracksuit top - courtesy of nurse Simone - the *gris-gris* still pulsed against his chest. He pulled it over his head and held it out by its leather cord, letting it swing gently in the breeze. It had kept him alive. *Hadn't it?* He couldn't be sure. The sun was up now, and Brad realized that he could see his own elongated shadow, stretching out fifteen feet below him on the surface of the green water, holding out the shadow of the little bag.

The Causeway split the Lake in two. Behind him, just a couple of miles to the south, the Crescent City was already fading away like a dream. He could just make out the bulky towers of the Hancock Whitney Center and Place St Charles. To the north was Mississippi and Tupelo. North was Elaine and Kyle. Even with a long stop for an All-Star breakfast, he could be there by noon. And like that, the decision was made. He would miss his old green recliner and his Baoding balls. He wasn't going back. Maybe someday, he'd feel the pull of his hometown again. But not now, not yet.

Brad thought about what he'd told Rubino, and the

parts he'd omitted. He wasn't a superstitious man. He knew his own memories would fade over time, logic would prevail, and fact would replace fantasy. He looked at the *gris-gris*. He thought about letting it drop and watching the splash when it met its shadow. But he didn't, because in the meantime, he might need a little luck.

about the author

Peter Bouvier is a copywriter for the healthcare industry, writing for health organisations in the UK and Europe. He lives in Spain with his wife and two children and writes novels in his free time. His first novel, The Scioneer, a sci-fi thriller set in the near future, was completed in 2011. His second book, The Game Changer, published in 2013, delves into the world of international cyber attacks. Peter has also written two children's books on the fictional island of Tikulo and the adventures of its warring tribes, the Bora and the Concha. He joined Provoco in 2021, and Demons of New Orleans is Peter's debut novel for the publishing company. We are looking forward to his next one!

Printed in Great Britain
by Amazon